Praise for
The Malcontenta

"A wryly humorous style and a well-paced plot make Maitland's series a growing pleasure."
—*Portsmouth Herald*

"The second of Mr. Maitland's Kathy and Brock mysteries, *The Malcontenta* is as complex as his first, *The Marx Sisters*. He has two intelligent detectives and point[s] them in readable, entertaining directions."
—*The Dallas Morning News*

"The Malcontenta, an eighteenthth-century mansion near Rochester, Kent, forms the backdrop for another superior mystery from Creasy Award nominee Maitland. . . . This is only the second [Kathy and Brock mystery] to be published in the U.S. With any luck the rest of this literate series will soon become available here."
—*Publishers Weekly* (starred)

Filled with "depth, bite, and nuance."
—*Kirkus Reviews* (starred)

ABOUT THE AUTHOR

Barry Maitland, recipient of the Ned Kelly Prize for Crime Fiction (Australia's equivalent of the Edgar Award), was born in Scotland and raised in London. He now resides in Australia, where he recently retired from teaching architecture at the University of Newcastle. He is also the author of *The Marx Sisters*, which was shortlisted for the British Crime Writers Association's John Creasy Award for Best First Mystery.

THE
MALCONTENTA

A Kathy and Brock Mystery

BARRY MAITLAND

PENGUIN BOOKS

For Clare and Alex

*With my very special thanks to Margaret,
and to those people who have helped bring
Brock and Kathy to print, in particular
Kate Jones and Jill Hickson.*

PENGUIN BOOKS
Published by the Penguin Group
Penguin Putnam Inc., 375 Hudson Street,
New York, New York 10014, U.S.A.
Penguin Books Ltd, 27 Wrights Lane, London W8 5TZ, England
Penguin Books Australia Ltd, Ringwood, Victoria, Australia
Penguin Books Canada Ltd, 10 Alcorn Avenue,
Toronto, Ontario, Canada M4V 3B2
Penguin Books (N.Z.) Ltd, 182–190 Wairau Road,
Auckland 10, New Zealand

Penguin Books Ltd, Registered Offices:
Harmondsworth, Middlesex, England

First published in the United States of America by
Arcade Publishing, Inc., 2000
Published in Penguin Books 2001

10 9 8 7 6 5 4 3 2 1

THE LIBRARY OF CONGRESS HAS CATALOGED
THE HARDCOVER EDITION AS FOLLOWS:
Maitland, Barry.
The malcontenta : a Kathy and Brock mystery / by Barry Maitland
—1st U.S. ed.
p. cm.
ISBN 1-55970-527-2 (hc.)
ISBN 0 14 10.0144 5 (pbk.)
1. Police—England—London—Fiction. 2. London (England)—Fiction.
3. Health resorts—Fiction. 4. Policewomen—Fiction. I. Title.
PR9619.3.M2635 M35 2000
823'.914—dc21   00–35582

Printed in the United States of America
Set in Sabon

Part One

I

Kathy could feel the tension in Gordon Dowling at her side, and it irritated her unreasonably. They were only going to London, for God's sake. He had developed this frown as the landscape had changed from the rolling countryside of the green belt into the constipated clutter of the outer suburbs, and the frown had deepened and his nose developed a nervous twitch as they had worked their way further into south London. 'Do you get up to London much?' she had asked at one point, and he had answered in a tight monosyllable, 'Once.' It was unbelievable. He had spent his whole life in the southern counties, and he had only been to London *once*.

What really irritated her was that she was getting edgy too. She had probably made a mistake picking the B road across country to Westerham. She had done so because of the gleeful warnings on Radio 1 of jams on the M20, A21 and M25. Snow had begun falling during the night, just when everyone was beginning to feel that spring couldn't be that far away. At first it had seemed charming, turning the brown countryside pristine white and the villages into winter postcards. But then the fall had become heavier, the sky blacker. By the time they reached the outskirts of London a dark gloom had settled, and the Saturday morning traffic, headlights blazing, had become paralysed in a morass of slush and minor accidents. When they reached the south circular and found it locked solid, they had come less than forty miles in one and a half hours and felt as if they had entered an alien country.

In an attempt to get free of the jams, Kathy had then turned north off the main road in what had seemed to be the

3

right general direction. It had been a terrible mistake. They had quickly become entangled in a confusing system of residential culs-de-sac and streets cut in two by arrangements of tree-planting and bollards designed to block through-traffic, in what the planners like to call 'traffic-calming'. Brought to a stop for the fifth time, Kathy thumped the wheel in exasperation and admitted defeat.

'We'd better check the *A–Z*,' she sighed, then noticed that Dowling was staring over her shoulder towards the rear of the car. Half a dozen figures, the hoods of their parkas zipped against the snow, were closing in on them. Kathy heard the tightness in the young man's voice as he muttered, 'Do we look like coppers?'

She lowered the window and called to them. 'Any idea how we can get to Herne Hill station? Or North Dulwich?'

One of the figures approached and tugged open the fur around the opening of the hood to expose a few inches of black face. 'Yeah, you passed the turning into Croxted Road back there, didn't yer.' He pointed back the way they had come.

'Thanks.' She pushed the gear-stick into reverse and carefully did a three-point turn through the group, which parted and moved on.

Somewhere north of Dulwich they stopped by a small park. They had described a large circle and were lost again. Although it was now mid-morning, the pale-grey light penetrating the dark clouds above was no brighter than at dawn, and the snow had settled into a steady fall which was building up on the deserted footpaths and gradually overwhelming the slush on the roads. A sign was visible in the gloom saying 'Wildwood Common', but no such place existed in the *A–Z*. Kathy was thoroughly regretting the whole thing. What had seemed the previous week to be a brainwave now appeared pointless. Worse, it seemed dangerous. Their isolation suddenly brought home to her what she was risking, for both of them, if their superiors came to hear of it. The Deputy Chief Constable would go spare. And Tanner would love it, of course. Her stomach turned at the thought.

'That says Matcham High Street over there,' Dowling said suddenly, his nose still twitching fretfully. Kathy peered through the misted windscreen and finally spotted the sign pointing towards a gap in a row of terraces.

She nodded. 'One last try, then. At least we might find a coffee shop before we give up.'

After the stillness of the deserted common, the high street was chaotic with traffic and pedestrians fighting through the snow. They missed the turning into Warren Lane the first time and had to turn on the far side of the railway bridge and crawl slowly back. They saw why they had missed it when they almost did the same thing again, for the entrance to the lane was no more than an archway in a block of shops, and when they turned into it they found themselves in an empty yard dominated by a large and gloomy brick warehouse.

Kathy stopped the car in the middle of the space and stepped out, shivering suddenly as the cold hit her. The noise of the high street was muffled by the snow and by the wall of old brick buildings around her, all of which seemed to be deserted. A faded sign above the door to the tall warehouse baldly gave the information 'SMITH'S'. Nearby, the skeleton of a large horse-chestnut tree in the far corner of the courtyard showed black through the snow.

'This can't be right,' she sighed. 'Trust Brock to be difficult.'

She took a deep breath and walked towards the chestnut tree, feeling the irregular surface of cobble-stones under the snow beneath her feet. Beyond the tree she made out a narrow lane running out of the far corner of the courtyard. One side of it was lined by a hedge, and the other by an irregular terrace of brick cottages, two and three storeys in height. She walked to the first house, her feet crunching through the undisturbed snow which had drifted into mounds around the base of the buildings. Searching for a number, she cursed silently as her foot struck some obstruction under the snow, and when she kicked it away she saw an old iron boot-scraper set into the cobbles. She lifted her head and saw directly in front of her on the wall a brass plate, filmed with snow dust, upon which was inscribed the single word 'Brock'.

Dowling was glumly listening to a medley of Italian pop tunes which a sadistic Capital Radio disc jockey had put on to remind drivers stuck on the motorways of the hot Mediterranean summers they were not currently enjoying. He jumped as the car door was yanked open and Kathy put her head in. 'Come on,' she said. 'I've found him.'

Brock's large frame filled the small front door when he opened it, making him look even bigger than he was. He beamed as he ushered them in, and Kathy was immediately reassured, recognizing that his pleasure at seeing them was genuine.

They squeezed into the small hallway while Brock hung their coats on pegs on the wall, then followed him up the stairs, which rose steeply ahead. At the top they came to a landing, the walls of which were lined with bookshelves from floor to ceiling, so that the doors leading off appeared to be cut into the packed books. A short corridor, also book-lined, twisted away to the left, and by the time they reached another small hallway with the foot of another staircase visible ahead, Kathy and Dowling were becoming disoriented. Brock opened a panelled door and led them into a bright room, warm, with some music playing quietly as a background to whatever they had interrupted. Kathy was surprised to hear the voice of kd lang. She glanced quickly at a long bench down one wall, cluttered with papers, books and two PCs, one with its screen alive with a rotating pattern as it waited for further instructions, the other a laptop.

'Come in, come in,' Brock growled, waving them in. 'You'll be freezing. A terrible day to be out and about. I heard the reports of the pile-ups on the motorway and thought you might not make it.'

'We almost didn't,' she laughed, already feeling at home as he led them over towards the gas fire. 'This is DC Gordon Dowling, Brock, who I mentioned on the phone, the one I've been working with. Gordon, this is Detective Chief Inspector Brock.'

The two men shook hands, Dowling deferential and awkward, Brock expansive and amiable. He turned to Kathy again. 'And you, Kathy, how are you? You're looking well.'

That was only partly true, he felt. She had lost some weight, her face was thinner, and while this probably made her more attractive in a slightly haunted sort of way, she looked less healthy than when he had first met her a year ago. Less happy too, perhaps, although he hadn't really been in a position to judge that.

'The side?' He glanced at her right side where the worst wound had been.

'No, it's fine,' she smiled. 'No more twinges. And you, Brock, you're looking really well.'

Though she too had doubts. He had put on weight, just a little but enough to notice. He looked as if he hadn't been out of doors much lately, and she spotted the way his eyes narrowed with discomfort as he straightened his back, as if he'd been spending too long sitting in front of a keyboard. His bushy grey hair could definitely do with a cut, and his beard a trim.

'You'd probably like coffee?'

'Oh yes,' Kathy said. 'That would be wonderful.'

'And something to eat, I expect, Gordon?'

Dowling shrugged non-committally, not wanting to seem too forward with the great man, although now food had been mentioned he realized he was starving. Brock nodded and left the room.

Kathy was drawn past the leather armchairs clustered round the gas fire to the far wall, almost entirely filled by a range of windows through which pale, snow-filtered light illuminated the room. She discovered when she reached it that the last three feet of the room were in fact an enclosed balcony overhanging the lane, like an aerial conservatory. From here she could see why the lane was only built up on one side, for the hedge opposite had hidden a sharp drop into a railway cutting. The roofs of houses showed dimly on the far side.

There was a low window-seat around the balcony, and she sat there for a moment, suspended in a swirling cloud of snowflakes, as if in the gondola of a hot-air balloon.

She looked back into the room, snug, simply furnished, purposeful. It seemed both an office and a living room. The morning papers were scattered beside one of the armchairs, and there were several empty coffee mugs on the bench. There was only one picture on the plain white walls. She got up and went over to have a look. It was composed of odd scraps of paper stuck together. She made out an old bus ticket and a fragment of a German newspaper with Gothic script. At the bottom was a pencilled signature, 'K. Schwitters'.

Behind her she heard Dowling swear quietly. She turned and saw that he had touched the mouse on the PC with the active screen pattern, which had immediately come to life, scrolling down lines of data.

'Kathy!' he hissed in panic. 'How do you turn it off again? He'll be back in a minute.'

'You'll just have to wait. It'll turn itself off in a minute, I expect.'

She went over to have a look. The screen held a data sheet with details of a man – physical, biographical and case references. She hadn't heard of him, although apparently ten

8

years ago he had cut a Birmingham family to pieces with a Japanese ceremonial sword.

'Bloody hell, Kathy, I can hear him coming! What's he going to think?'

'That you're a detective, Gordon,' she smiled. 'Come and sit down by the fire and hope he doesn't notice.'

Brock bustled in with a large tray which he set down on a low table in the middle of the ring of armchairs. As well as the coffee things, he had brought a plate piled with slices of bread and crumpets, a dish of butter and a large jar of honey. He reached for a long steel fork which was hanging from a hook beside the fireplace, and offered it to Dowling.

'Gordon, would you take charge of this for us?'

Dowling looked lost.

'The toasting, Gordon. Haven't you done it before? I suppose you only have central heating with radiators. The main point of an old-fashioned gas fire is to toast things while you sit around it and talk. Didn't you know that?'

Dowling accepted the ribbing with a shy smile and took the handle of the fork while Brock speared a crumpet on to the long prongs.

'I haven't had a crumpet since I was little,' Kathy said, and caught Dowling's eye, nodding her head surreptitiously towards the bench on the other side of the room. He glanced over, and she saw the relief dawn on his face as he spotted the pattern slowly rotating again on the computer screen.

Brock was crouching, pouring the coffee into mugs and passing them round.

'You like kd lang, do you, Brock?' Kathy asked.

'Of course,' he smiled, easing himself back into his chair. 'And how is the country suiting you, Kathy? Are they teaching you anything?'

Kathy was about to come out with the opening she had prepared, then stopped. 'Good question. I suppose that's it, really. No, they're not.'

'Because of your murder?'

She nodded. She had said very little to him on the phone, just enough to get him interested, although he had told her often enough to keep in touch with him and let him know how her spell with the County force was going. It suddenly occurred to her that he may have made some inquiries of his own after she'd rung. She hoped not – not before she'd put him in the picture.

'But the whole point about your being down there is to broaden your experience – they know that. We've done these rotations with them before. There's no point to it if you're not learning anything. We might as well pull you back to the Met.'

'Yes,' Kathy said doubtfully. For her, the whole point was to get back, not just to another division in the Met, but to SO1, the Serious Crimes section at the Yard.

'Have you spoken to whoever's supposed to be supervising your assignments?'

'He's a DI, Ric Tanner. Yes, I have, and got nowhere. He made it plain that I'm being punished – not in so many words, but there is a . . . lack of confidence in my ability to perform at a higher level.'

Brock snorted. 'Bullshit! Who's his instructing officer?'

Kathy sighed. 'That's the problem. The programme comes under the Deputy Chief Constable's office. His name is Long.'

'Long?'

'Bernard Long. Both he and Tanner came from the Met originally. They knew each other there. And Long became involved in the murder case – personally involved.'

Brock frowned. 'You'd better tell me about this murder, Kathy.'

'Brock, before I do, I want to be clear about this. I'm not making a complaint. I just want the advice of someone whose judgement I trust. But I don't want to put you in the position where you feel you have to follow up. In fact you may very well want to be able to say later that you knew nothing about it.'

'Ah.' Brock gave a little smile into his coffee mug. 'But you've brought Detective Constable Dowling with you, Kathy.'

Kathy coloured. 'I brought Gordon because he's become tainted along with me. I was in charge of the investigation, and he was my main assistant. When things turned sour he stood by me. Now he's getting the same treatment I am. Only he won't be transferring out in another month or so, as I will. He's stuck. That's why I brought him, that and the fact he may be able to add to what I say. But if you'd rather he left, of course he'll go.'

Brock nodded non-committally, hearing the tightness in her voice. 'All right, but I'm not joining a conspiracy, Kathy. If I feel I have to act in a certain way after what I hear, I'll just have to do it. That could be awkward for Gordon, perhaps. What do you say, Gordon?'

The young man straightened from the fire. Two toasted crumpets lay on the plate in front of him, a third almost finished. He was twenty-five, just six years younger than Kathy, but, as he cleared his throat to speak, she realized how protective she had come to feel towards him. His slow and rather tentative physical movements seemed to have the effect of making hers quicker and more adept, and the same happened with his speech. As he hesitated, she had an almost overpowering desire to break in and answer for him. Yet when he did eventually speak, he did so with such a depth of concern in his voice that she felt ashamed of her impulse to patronize him.

'I believe . . .' he began, and for a moment it sounded as if he was about to recite the catechism, 'I believe that Kathy was right, all the way down the line, in the way she handled the Petrou investigation. They tried to make her look incompetent, but she wasn't. The way they treated her, they wouldn't have done the same if she'd been a man. At least' — he ducked his head — 'that's my opinion.'

He stared gloomily at the toasting fork in his hand while they waited to see if there was more. Finally Brock said, 'Yes, I see. But you look, well, uneasy, Gordon . . . about being here. Are you sure you want to be involved in this?'

Dowling raised his eyes to face Brock. 'Oh, yes, sir. If Kathy thinks you should know about it, then I agree and I want to be part of it. I was in her team, I trust her judgement.'

Chastened by his loyalty and anxiety, Kathy lowered her eyes and said nothing, waiting for Brock's decision.

He stared at Dowling for a moment, scratching his beard, then nodded. 'So do I lad,' he said. 'So do I.'

They followed his example and took a crumpet each, letting the butter melt before they spooned honey over it.

'Last October, you said,' Brock prompted, and she nodded, mouth full. 'Mmm, the end of October. There'd been quite a lot of rain, remember?'

2

Kathy had hung back as the others filed out at the end of the early Monday morning briefing. Detective Inspector Tanner threw the last file behind him on to the table he was half straddling, and made some comment to one of the sergeants as he passed. They both laughed, and the other man replied, saying something about snatching defeat from the jaws of victory. Kathy waited for them to finish, their easy banter making her feel even more uncomfortable.

'You watch the match on Saturday, Sergeant Kolla?' Tanner asked suddenly, looking back over his shoulder. The other sergeant smirked and looked at his feet.

'No,' she said. 'No, sir, I didn't.'

'No . . . well. You want me?'

'I'd like a word, if you've got a minute, sir.'

She was very careful with her words, with the tone of her voice, with the expression on her face as she answered him. He had never been overtly rude to her, always listened to what she had to say, always given a reasoned response. Yet from the very first time they had met, she had felt his hostility. At that stage she had had no opportunity to give offence, yet it was palpably there from that moment, and had continued, unprovoked and unacknowledged, ever since. It was a chilling undercurrent to the formality with which he treated her and lack of interest in what she had to say. There was something rather frightening about it – the unreasonableness, the pointlessness of it and, worst of all, the way in which it had gradually inspired in her an equally unjustified aversion. She resented being forced to protect herself by allowing this feeling to grow, of antagonism towards someone she hardly knew, of being drawn towards a confrontation that lacked any reason. He was an admirable officer in many ways – he worked longer hours than anyone else at Division and, like Kathy herself, he had driven himself up the ranks without the benefit of a higher education. He had made no attempt to modify his broad Tyneside accent, which he sometimes seemed to exaggerate as a point of pride. He was tough, experienced and proficient. And he made Kathy's skin crawl whenever she found herself in the same room with him.

The other sergeant left, closing the door behind him, and Tanner turned to face her. 'Speak.'

'I wondered if you would consider a change in my duties, sir.'

He stared at her for a while, his face expressionless, then lowered his eyes and picked at a thumb-nail. 'Why would I do that?'

She took in a deep breath, steadying her voice. 'Since I've been here, for the past six months, I've been working with Sergeant Elliot in Family and Juvenile Crime. I wondered whether I could have some time in other areas. Maybe with Sergeant McGregor in Serious Crime.'

'Don't you get on with Penny Elliot?' He brought his eyes back up to hers as he completed the sentence, looking for her reaction.

'We get on fine. It's not that. I've learned quite a bit from working with her. She's very good at it. But it's not really the kind of detective work that I'm interested in.'

'That you're interested in,' he repeated. 'Wouldn't you call domestic violence and child abuse serious crime?'

'Of course. But I'd hoped to get some experience in organized crime – some murder investigations perhaps – while I'm here.'

'Murder investigations,' he again repeated her words, managing, without any particular emphasis in his voice, to make them sound vaguely absurd and self-indulgent.

Kathy flushed. When she spoke again, her voice was harder. 'Under the terms of my transfer to County . . .'

'I'm quite familiar with the terms of your transfer, Sergeant,' he broke in, without raising his voice, 'according to which you go wherever, in my best judgement, I think you should.'

He paused, giving her more of the cold eye. 'What's so special about murder investigations? You think they're glamorous?'

She was about to tell him that she had already led one murder investigation while she'd been with ED Division at the Met, then remembered he knew that.

'You don't have some kind of unhealthy obsession with death, do you?' he went on. 'Some kind of fetish?' He gave her an unpleasant little smirk.

There was a knock on the door. Without turning, Tanner barked 'In', and the sergeant he'd been speaking to earlier put his head round. He handed Tanner a note. 'I'll take it if you like, Ric.' He was pulling a coat on over his jacket.

'No.' Tanner read the note, the sergeant waiting motionless with one arm in the coat. 'No, Bill. I want you to stay with the cars.'

'Shall I give it to Arnie?'

'No. Sergeant Kolla here is very interested in unnatural deaths. This should appeal to her.'

The sergeant glanced at him, then at Kathy, shrugged and left. Tanner handed her the note. It read: *0855 hrs, 29 October. Request for CID assistance. Suicide hanging at Stanhope House Clinic, Edenham. Patrol car at scene. Police Surgeon notified.*

'Looks like the angels were listening to you, Sergeant.' Tanner's smile was very tight. 'The angels of death, perhaps. It's all yours. Your very own investigation. Take that sleepy bugger Dowling with you.'

He turned, swept up his files and walked out of the room.

*

She had spoken to Penny Elliot about Tanner. Penny didn't particularly like him, thought him fairly unsympathetic on a personal level, but couldn't fault him in his dealings with her. Although he wasn't much interested in the areas of domestic crime that she was concerned with, he had made sure that she had received a fair – and in recent years a growing – share of resources. She had experienced none of the animosity Kathy felt.

'So it's not common-or-garden sexism; it must just be *me*,' Kathy had said, and Penny Elliot had smiled.

'Well, he does like to control things. Maybe he doesn't like the fact that you really belong to the Metropolitan Police and are only here for a year.'

Maybe. Kathy stared gloomily out at a wood of dark pines that flashed past the car window. Dowling was skirting the edge of Ashdown Forest on the way to Stanhope House. Making a report on a suicide wasn't exactly what she'd had in mind when she'd finally worked herself up to approach Tanner. She wondered why the uniformed branch couldn't have dealt with it themselves. 'What is this place we're going to, anyway? Any idea?'

She hadn't worked with Dowling before and asked the question as much to make conversation as anything, as he'd been very quiet since they got in the car. He chewed his lip for a moment, concentrating on a bend.

'Er . . . some kind of health farm, I believe, Sarge.'

'Call me Kathy. You're Gordon, aren't you?'

'Er . . . yeah, that's right, Sarge.'

Sleepy Dowling, Kathy said to herself. *Thanks a lot, Inspector Tanner.*

There were puddles by the road from the recent rain, and the woods looked sodden. Through Edenham, a small market town whose streets were still almost deserted this Monday morning; lights on in the two glass-fronted supermarkets which had pushed their way in among the old brick and half-timbered houses of the high street; the largest building in the street a pub, formerly a coaching inn, the Hart Revived, whose painted sign of a deer drinking from a pool was suspended over the pavement. Beyond the town, more belts of dark conifers; then high hedges closed in on either side. Sporadic patches of mist crossed the road and Dowling slowed, peering forward through the windscreen.

'Somewhere around here . . .' he muttered. Then, with satisfaction, 'There!'

A signpost marked STANHOPE indicated a narrow lane branching to the right. More hedges, then a cattle grid, beyond which the hedges stopped abruptly, opening up a rolling landscape of sheep-cropped grass dotted with small copses of oak and beech. They came to a river, maybe ten yards wide, which they followed until a bridge appeared, a single high arch of weathered grey stone decorated with elaborately carved balusters and urns.

'Wow,' Kathy said, and then repeated herself a moment later as Dowling carefully steered the car up to the crown of the arch, and a panorama of Stanhope House, half shrouded in a bank of silver mist, presented itself before them. A pale-grey cube made of the same stone as the bridge, in the same classical style and embellished with a tall pedimented portico, the Palladian villa's original simplicity and symmetry had been ruined by a later wing grafted on to the left side, like the single ungainly claw of a hermit crab thrust out of a perfect shell.

On the far side of the bridge the metalled road curved away to the right, and a gravel road branched off it towards the house. Beside the junction stood a dark-green sign with white lettering, STANHOPE NATUROPATHIC CLINIC, beneath a symbol based on the design of the front portico of the house. The winding gravel road took them around the edge of the meadow which lay in front of the house, and soon revealed a red-brick stable block among the trees further to the left. Perhaps thirty cars – Jaguars, BMWs and Mercedes accounting for more than half – stood in the area between the stables and the house.

'No sign of the patrol car,' Dowling said, and then spotted a uniformed officer standing under the trees. He slowly rolled forward and Kathy lowered her window, filling the car with cool morning air sharp with autumnal smells of damp and rotting leaves.

'You follow that path' – the man pointed to a gravelled way leading off through the trees between the stables and the house – 'past the staff cottages to a turning circle at the end. You'll see the patrol car there. The body's in another building in the grounds on the other side of the main house.' He sounded cheerful. 'Young male. One of the staff, apparently. My partner's round there waiting for you with the bloke that found him and the Director of this place. I'll stay here for the doc.'

Kathy nodded. 'Why did you call for CID?' she asked.

He hesitated a moment, then, 'Just to be on the safe side, Sarge.' He grinned and stepped back to let them continue.

Once through the trees, they passed four identical brick cottages set out like doll's houses along the curve of the drive, each fronted by a narrow bed filled with recently pruned rose bushes. Between the houses they caught glimpses of the high brick backdrop of a walled garden. Soon they saw the patrol car ahead of them, the driver's door open, a man in uniform sitting behind the wheel, looking up from his notepad. A dozen paces away stood two men, watching them approach, waiting.

Kathy got out and walked briskly to the patrol car as the officer got to his feet. She introduced herself, keeping her voice low. 'What's going on?'

'We answered a 999 call timed at 0832. Arrived here at 0845. The Director of the clinic, over there, Dr Stephen Beamish-hyphen-Newell' – the policeman spoke with a strong cockney accent and pronounced the name laboriously, raising one eyebrow, as if there were something dubious about it – 'met us at the front of the main building and brought us back here to a building they call the Temple of Apollo' – again the raised eyebrow – 'behind the trees over there.' He pointed with his chin towards a dense thicket of rhododendron, yew and laurel, through the upper part of which Kathy could just make out a stone parapet. In contrast to his partner's cheerfulness, this man's forehead was scored with worry. He referred back to the notes on his pad.

'The other bloke, name of Geoffrey Parsons, is the Estates Manager, looks after the grounds. One of his jobs is to open this temple each morning. Apparently, this morning he found a member of their staff, a Mr Alex Petrou, hanging in there. Stone cold, no chance of resuscitation. He ran back to the main house, found the Director. They both came back out here, then back to the house to ring for us.'

He tore the sheet of notes off the pad and handed it to Kathy, then closed the pad and looked at her uneasily.

'Why did you ask for CID?' she asked.

'I think you should have a look down there, Sergeant. Without those two, I might suggest.'

'OK.' She looked over at the two men. There didn't seem much doubt which was which. One was wearing an old tweed jacket over a thick sweater, and brown corduroy trousers tucked into green gumboots. He wore a tweed cap on his head, which was bowed as he slowly shifted his weight from foot to foot. The other man wore a black double-breasted suit, grey polo-neck sweater and black shoes. His thick black hair stood up from his scalp like a long crew-cut, and the neatly trimmed goatee beard on his chin had a silver streak. He stood motionless, staring intently at Kathy, with his hands clasped in front of him, black leather gloves adding to an effect both theatrical and funereal.

She walked over and he held out his gloved hand. His eyes

were very dark, unblinking and hypnotic. She thought what an asset they would be in an interrogation.

His handshake was firm, his voice soft and, surprisingly, almost as broadly cockney as the patrol officer's. She guessed he was in his forties.

'I'm Stephen Beamish-Newell, Director of Stanhope, and this is our Estates Manager, Geoffrey Parsons.'

'Detective Sergeant Kolla and Detective Constable Dowling from County CID, doctor. I understand you've both seen the victim and that he is known to you both?'

'Of course. Alex Petrou.'

'What can you tell me about him?'

'Age about thirty, I'd have to check his file to be precise. He came to us last spring, around April I'd say. I took him on as a general physiotherapy assistant. We're deeply shocked. I don't think either of us was aware of any problems that might have led him to this.'

He glanced at Parsons, who merely shook his head.

'I'll need to get some more details from you, sir, but it'll probably be more convenient in your office, with your records. I'd like to see the body first, and wait for the doctor. When I'm finished I'll come back to the house and see you there.'

Beamish-Newell hesitated a moment, as if about to suggest something else, then nodded and turned to go. Parsons made to follow him.

'I'd like you to stay with us if you would, Mr Parsons. To show us around.'

Parsons hesitated, nodded, lowered his head. Kathy looked more closely at him. Under the cap his face looked white. He was younger than she had first assumed, early thirties perhaps.

'Are you feeling all right, sir?'

'Yes.' His voice was weak and he cleared his throat. 'Got a bit of a shock. Just catching up with me, I think.'

'Of course. Do you want to sit in the car for a while?'

He shook his head, cleared his throat again. 'No, no. It'll help if I walk.'

He led them to a narrow gap in the wall of vegetation and into a tunnel of dripping rhododendron branches. It led out on to a lawn which stretched away to their right, down to the rear façade of Stanhope House. Ornamental pools and terraces were laid out on the axis of the house, and carefully clipped yew hedges and pergolas contained the gardens on the far side.

Parsons turned left, leading them towards a classical temple front, now visible on a knoll, facing the house. They climbed the stone steps of the plinth up to a row of four columns supporting the pediment. Tall glass-panelled doors formed an opening in the stone façade. Parsons pulled out a thick bunch of keys and, with some difficulty, unfastened the lock.

'I'd better hang on to that key, Mr Parsons,' Kathy said. 'Why don't you wait out here with my colleague while the constable shows me round? I'd like you to think over the sequence of exactly what you did before and after discovering the body, so we can take a statement from you.'

Parsons nodded and removed his cap to wipe his forehead with his sleeve. His hair was lank, sandy-coloured, thinning on top. It was plastered to his head with recent sweat.

The interior of the temple was lit by a dim green light. It smelled strongly of damp and mould, and the air was warmer than the outdoor chill. Rows of wooden chairs were set out on each side of a central aisle within the narrow chamber, whose walls were lined with columns and panels of marble – dark green and black and, in a few places, the startling blue of lapis lazuli. Overhead a plain vault ran the length of the building and was punctured towards the far end by a dome with a small lantern toplight in its centre.

Kathy and the patrol officer walked down the aisle until they stood beneath the dome. In front, a brass rail separated them from what in a church would have been the chancel. Here, however, Kathy was surprised to find that the floor was cut away, revealing a lower chamber. On the wall on the far side of the void hung a large oil painting, so faded that Kathy had to peer to make out the figure of a naked youth on an open hillside, gesturing towards a glowing cloud. Puzzled, she looked round, her eyes coming to rest on the series of heavy brass gratings set into the marble floor. With a shock she realized that the biggest one, on which she was standing, was cast in the pattern of a large swastika. A red nylon rope was looped round the centre of the broken cross.

'That's where he is,' the uniformed man murmured. 'Under your feet.'

'Oh.' Kathy's voice echoed up into the dome. 'How do we get down there?'

He took her to one side of the chamber, where a door opened into a narrow spiral staircase leading to the lower level.

'Aren't there any lights?' Her voice sounded muffled within the stone shaft.

'Apparently the wiring is dodgy – they've cut everything off except one small light at the organ console, and a heating circuit to keep the damp out of the organ chamber. Watch your step at the bottom here.' He flashed his torch at the stone floor at her feet. She was now standing in the lower chamber, below the oil painting.

'There's an organ?'

'Yeah. The main part of it – the pipes and so on – are in a pit below the floor of the hall upstairs. That's what the floor grates are for – to let the sound out. This area down here is where the choir or orchestra or whatever would be. The idea apparently was to fill the space upstairs with sound, without the audience being able to see where it was coming from.'

'Bit weird.'

'Yeah.'

He turned, and the beam of his light swept round the wall to a recess below the brass rail at the end of the upper floor. The body of a man was suspended there.

Kathy froze, staring at the figure, taking it in.

The space beneath the grating was almost as high as a normal room, and she could make out the stops and foot-pedals of an organ console behind him. The organist's stool was lying on its side below his feet, as if kicked away. Her eyes traced the taut red rope from the back of his head of thick, black, wavy hair, up the short distance to the underside of the grille, then diagonally down to a series of loops tied around part of the body of the console. He was dressed in a green tracksuit, with bright white Reeboks on his feet.

There was something odd about his posture, she thought, although she had never seen a hanging in the flesh before. He didn't look slack, like the photographs she had seen on detective courses, where the bodies looked like pathetic sacks of potatoes. He seemed hunched, his right arm half drawn up across his body, and his legs didn't reach to the same length.

'Was he handicapped, do you think?' She found she was speaking in a whisper.

'Maybe he was beaten.'

'Why do you say that?'

'Look.' He moved closer to the figure, pointing the torch at its head. Although the stark contrast of light and shadows from the flashlight obscured it at first, Kathy soon made out what he was talking about. The flesh looked puffy and distorted, its colouring blotchy, with a strong pattern of white and dark-purple areas.

'Could be bruising, do you think?' the officer asked.

'Mmm. The doctor will tell us. Anything else?'

'Down there, in the corner.'

He swung the beam away from the body and down into a narrow space at one end of the organ console. All Kathy could see was something black.

'I can't make it out,' she said. He handed her the torch without a word. She knelt down within a couple of feet of the thing – two things, she realized, both black, made of leather. One was a bunch of thongs, with a handle shaped like a phallus.

She straightened up. 'I see. What's the other thing, with the whip?'

He frowned, shrugged. 'I don't know. I didn't touch anything. I thought it might be a glove, or a hood. I'm assuming that the two who found him didn't spot them. Without a torch you wouldn't pick them out. They only had the organist's console light to see by. That's the only light in the whole building. Apparently it was on when Parsons came in this morning. He noticed the faint glow through the grating.'

'Who turned it off?'

'They did, when they left to phone us.'

It seemed an odd, parsimonious gesture.

'The switch is over near the foot of the stairs.' With his torch he showed her the white line of a new length of cable which was tacked to the wall and ran to a switch. She went over and turned it on. There was just enough light to illuminate the organ controls. Kathy could imagine Parsons' shock as he went down the stairs and saw the dangling figure silhouetted against the glow.

They heard the creak of the front doors opening, and the voice of the other uniformed constable echoed above them, 'Sergeant . . . Hello . . . You there?'

'We're down here,' Kathy called out.

'I've got the doctor.'

He was young, fresh-faced and almost completely bald. He shook hands with Kathy enthusiastically and followed her over to the body.

'Can we have more light?'

'I'm afraid not. At least, it may take half an hour or more for me to arrange it. We can get some more torches, though.'

'Yes, that might help.' He held the corpse's wrist for a moment, peering at its head.

'Long gone.'

'How long?'

The doctor shrugged. 'Twelve hours at least, I'd guess. But that's only a guess. I'd like to take his temperature, but . . .' He took the torch from the uniformed man and looked closely at the head and hands. Finally he stepped back and shook his head. 'I'm not going to touch this,' he said. 'You'd better see if Gareth Pugh is available. If he is, he'll want to see it undisturbed. If he isn't, then I'll do it.'

'Gareth Pugh?' Kathy asked.

'He's the County's Senior Forensic Pathologist. Professor Pugh. Haven't you come across him? I'm sure he'll want to do the post-mortem if he can. I'll try to call him from my car if you like. And I think you should get some lights fixed up for him.'

Kathy nodded. 'And some SOCOs?'

'Well, that's up to you, really, but I'd say so. Certainly a photographer. In fact, you'll probably need everything.'

'You think the circumstances are suspicious?'

He shrugged. 'Looks pretty odd to me.'

For the first time Kathy let the sense of anticipation that had been building in her since she first saw the body, come to the surface.

'Good. You go ahead and contact the pathologist, then, doctor. I'll get things organized down here.' She turned to the two uniformed men, telling one to remain there and touch nothing, and the other to return to the car park to direct people to the temple as they arrived.

'Several people have come over and asked me what's going on while I've been stood out there,' the cheerful one said.

'Don't tell them anything. And both of you, don't mention anything about the things in the corner – to anyone.' She saw him smirk. 'I mean that,' she glared at him. 'Not a soul.'

Dowling and Parsons were sitting talking on the steps at the front of the temple. They scrambled to their feet as they saw her come pacing down the aisle.

'Mr Parsons, would you take a seat inside, on one of those chairs? I won't be a moment.'

She drew Dowling away down the steps. 'Gordon, get on the car radio and send a scene-of-crime team out here. The photographer in particular – right away. Also a mobile generator – there's no light down there.' She looked around. 'It'll have to stand out here, so they'll need plenty of cable.'

He was startled by her energy. 'What's going on, Kathy?'

'Looks like we've got a suspicious death, Gordon.' She grinned at him. 'Something to brighten up your Monday morning, so get moving. Oh, and Gordon . . . try not to get Inspector Tanner when you radio through.'

He looked blank, then turned and scrambled off down the path.

Kathy went back into the temple. She was wearing her black woollen winter-coat, which almost reached her ankles, with the useful deep pockets. From one she drew out a small dictating machine and checked the tape. 'Mr Parsons –' she pulled a chair round to face him and showed him the machine in her hand – 'I'll use this if you don't mind. My shorthand's hopeless.' Big smile. He gave her a worried look, alerted, like Dowling, by the light in her eyes.

'How are you feeling now?'

A non-committal shrug. He still looked very pasty.

'I'd like you to describe for me exactly what you did this morning, leading up to discovering the body, and then afterwards.'

'I . . .' he cleared his throat. 'I got up as usual, around six-thirty, got dressed and then came out.' More throat-clearing. 'I was on my way to the stable block, but I came here first to open up the temple – Dr Beamish-Newell likes it to be open

26

during the day for patients to come in and sit if they want, and to try to air the place.'

'The doors were locked as usual?'

He nodded, 'Yes, I'd locked them myself last evening. It was just getting dark, about a quarter to five.'

'And what time was it when you came to open them this morning?'

'Oh . . . about eight. I'm not sure exactly.' A fit of throat-clearing. 'Sorry.' He wiped a hand through his hair.

'And there isn't another door into the building?'

'Yes, there is. Down in the lower chamber. There's a service door from a flight of outside steps at the back. That door is bolted from the inside.'

'All right, so you opened this glass door.'

'Yes. I don't normally spend any time here when I open up. This time I just noticed a couple of chairs that were out of line, so I came in and straightened them.'

'Which chairs?' Kathy interrupted.

He hesitated, 'Those two, over there, at the end of the first row. Anyway, then I thought I could see the organ light showing in the floor grille, there. I went over and saw the loop of rope. I didn't understand what it was. I couldn't really make it out through the grille, so I went downstairs. Then I saw him.'

'Did you recognize the rope?'

'The rope?' Parsons blinked with surprise.

'Yes, the type. Have you seen anything like it around here?'

'Er . . . I'm not sure.' He sounded confused. 'Can I think about that? Offhand . . . I don't think so.'

'All right. Did you recognize the man straight away?'

'Yes . . . well, no, not straight away. The light was behind him. I had to get fairly close.' Parsons was breathing heavily, his face stark white.

'You were sure that he was dead?'

27

'Oh yes. He was so cold!'

'So you touched him?'

Parsons nodded. 'His hand . . .' He was beginning to look as if he might pass out. Kathy reached forward to steady him.

'Suppose we get you a drink of water, or tea?'

Parsons nodded, sagging.

'Put your head between your knees. Go on. That's right . . . Better?'

The bowed head nodded.

Kathy called out to the patrol officer and sent him off to find some water. 'And tell Dowling to hurry up and report back to me,' she shouted as he ran off.

She had to contain her impatience as the minutes passed. Parsons remained stooped with his head between his knees. Eventually the doctor reappeared at the door. He examined Parsons briefly, then nodded to the patrol officer, who had followed him in with a flask. While Parsons drank, the doctor indicated to Kathy to step out under the portico of the temple.

'More police brutality?' he asked.

She smiled. 'That's right. But you won't find any marks on his body.'

'Unlike the one downstairs. I got through to Pugh. We were lucky. He'll make himself available right away. About twenty minutes, he says. I'd like to stay if you don't mind – see the Welsh Wizard in action.'

'He's good, is he?'

'By repute.'

'Can I continue with Parsons?' Kathy asked.

'Oh yes. It's just mild shock. I could give him something, but he's OK. I might go and wait for Pugh in the car park.'

Somewhat restored, Parsons completed his account of finding Petrou's body, running back to the house to tell Beamish-Newell, returning to the temple for the Director to see for

28

himself, and then remaining on the temple steps for the police to arrive. While he was talking, Dowling returned and gave Kathy a thumbs-up.

'All right, Mr Parsons, I'll let you get off and have a cup of tea. Just before you go, though, could you give me a quick run-down on this place? How big, how many people, and so on?'

'Well, the Director will have accurate figures, but the estate covers almost a hundred acres. It used to be much bigger, but most of the land's been sold off. The meadows that remain are leased to a farmer; the rest is the house and grounds – about twenty acres roughly.' Parsons had become animated, clearly relieved to change the subject.

'We have sixty-two guest rooms in the upper floor of the house and west wing, plus treatment and common rooms and kitchen and offices and so on in the ground floor and basement. There's six staff rooms in the attic of the house, and there's the four staff cottages – one for the Director, one for the family of one of the married staff, and one each shared by four male and four female staff.' It came out in a rush and he stopped suddenly, breathing heavily.

'So there are sixty-two patients here?'

'Well, that's the number of rooms. Some are double. The most we can accommodate is seventy-four, but at this time of year, I don't know, there might be fifty or sixty.'

'And how many staff?'

'In the brochure we say it's one to one.' Parsons phrased it carefully.

'What, seventy-four staff?'

'Well . . . maybe if you count all the part-time cleaners and cooks and gardeners and the like . . .'

'Come on. Realistically, how many staff have been in and out of this place in the last twenty-four hours?'

He shrugged, 'I don't know . . . Thirty? Forty? The Director or the Business Manager would be able to tell you.'

'Yes, I'll get to them. I just wanted an idea. And of those staff, what, about a dozen live in the grounds?'

Parsons counted in his head. 'Yes, six in the attic and nine or ten in the houses, plus the Director and his wife.'

'And what about you, where do you live?'

'In the attic.'

'And Petrou?'

'Yes, in the attic too.'

'So when did you last see him alive?'

Parsons' face clouded anxiously again. 'I don't know ... I've been trying to remember. Last night – Sunday night – staff often go out. There's always a recital or something for guests in the house after dinner. I had to spend all my free time over the weekend studying for this course I'm doing. I don't remember seeing Alex last evening at all, not at dinner or anything. Before that ... I don't know ... my mind's a blur.'

'Don't worry, relax, it'll come back to you. We'll be asking everybody that question, so give it some thought. What was he like?'

'Alex? Well ... we weren't close friends or anything. He hadn't been here that long.'

'About six months, the Director said. You'd been living next door to him for six months. Two single men. You were both single, weren't you?'

Parsons flushed. 'Yes, though I'm engaged. I tend to spend most of my spare time with Rose, except just lately when I've had all this studying. Of course, when he first arrived we chatted. But once he'd got settled ... We didn't have much in common, I suppose.'

'Did he have friends on the staff? Was he sociable?'

'Yes ... he was quite ... outgoing. Went out a lot. Several of the girls were interested in him. He was sort of ... glamorous, you know, him being a Mediterranean type, and with his accent and that.'

'He was foreign?'

'Yes. He came from Greece.'

Through the glass doors Kathy noticed a movement of lime-green Day-Glo jackets down the path. She turned back to Parsons. 'All right. We'll leave it there for the moment. What you might do for me now is go to the house, tell Dr Beamish-Newell that I may not get to see him for another hour or so, and ask him if he could start organizing a list of everyone who was in the grounds over the past twenty-four hours, in categories – staff, guests, others. OK?'

'Yes . . .' Parsons hesitated. 'Is this normal?' he asked timidly. 'I mean, all these procedures . . . for a suicide.'

'Any sudden death has to be thoroughly investigated. Don't worry, we'll be out of your hair soon enough.'

They stepped out under the portico. Head down, shoulders stooped, Parsons set off across the grass towards the house. A light drizzle had set in, making the rhododendron leaves glisten behind the two men pulling the generator up the path. Beyond them a second pair burst through the trees. Kathy recognized the doctor, pointing the way to a lean, hawk-faced man and having difficulty keeping up with his long stride.

Kathy looked back to Stanhope House.

A hundred people, she thought, *ninety-nine of them about to begin twittering about what happened to glamour boy.*

3

Professor Pugh looked closely at her as he shook her hand. There were little laughter creases at the corners of his eyes, and in his voice she heard the lilt of his Welsh boyhood.

'So you have something interesting for me, do you, Sergeant?'

'I hope so,' she replied, and led the way down to the lower chamber, where Dowling and the uniformed man were in a huddle around the body. Dowling looked shocked. She sent them upstairs to help get the lights fixed up and assist the SOCO team.

Until the floodlights finally burst into life, she held the torch for the pathologist, who peered at Petrou's head and neck through a pair of horn-rimmed glasses without touching any part of him. In the full light, the right side of his face, partly obscured by his glistening black hair, seemed distorted or squashed. It was impossible now to recognize any of the 'glamour' the girls had once seen in him.

Pugh stepped aside, folded the glasses and tapped them against his teeth, thinking. 'It's warmer in here than I would have expected,' he said, 'for such a damp place.'

'Apparently there's some kind of background heater installed in the organ chamber behind the console there, to keep the organ working.'

'Ah, the organ,' he nodded. 'Splendid. Well, now, has he been photographed?'

'No, sir. The photographer's due any minute.'

'Better get that done first.' He turned away and took his bag to a far corner of the room, where he pulled out some blue nylon overalls and a packet of surgical gloves.

The photographer arrived a moment later, manoeuvring his bag of equipment with difficulty down the spiral stairs. He nodded to the pathologist, who, after a politely deferential glance at Kathy, instructed him on the shots he wanted of the body. Kathy added her own requests, including the objects on the floor and general views of the room.

While they waited, Kathy was able to examine the other features of the place, now brightly illuminated by the temporary lights. The service door which Parsons had mentioned was visible now, on the side wall near the foot of the spiral stairs, its two bolts securely in place. The painting on the end wall was also clear and obviously in need of attention, with the canvas sagging in its frame. Otherwise the walls were bare, efflorescing with damp. On the floor below the other side wall a small panel of white marble had been set flush with the paving slabs. No inscription explained its presence.

'Now,' said Pugh when the photographer was done, 'let's have another look.'

He put on his glasses and gave the body a further close scrutiny, gently pulling the collar and hem of the tracksuit top away from the flesh, and then drawing the waistband of the pants down to look at the right thigh. He felt each of the limbs with his gloved hands and stepped back, nodding.

'Rigor is generalized,' he said, 'so between ten and forty-eight hours, say.' He turned to Kathy. 'Do we know if anyone saw him yesterday?'

'Not yet.'

'Mmm. I wouldn't like to risk losing this, you see.' He was talking half to himself, or to an imaginary tutorial group of students.

'Lose what, sir?' Kathy asked.

He turned and gave her a little smile, eyes bright. 'The pattern of compression of the muscles, you see? All down the right side as far as I can tell – the face, right shoulder, hip and so on. The flattening has been fixed by rigor mortis, which starts in the face and jaw, then the upper limbs, and finally the hips and legs. It disappears in the same order. I want to have a proper look at that pattern. Is that what you were concerned about, Anthony?' He turned to the doctor.

'Well, and the lividity,' he replied, stepping forward.

'Yes, yes, the lividity, of course.' Professor Pugh puckered his lips, staring at the drooping head.

'The bruising?' Kathy asked.

'Well, it's not bruising in the normal sense. When the heart stops pumping, blood gradually settles into the lowest vessels of the body, like oil settling into the sump of a car when you switch off the engine. That creates the dark patches you see; it's called hypostatic or congestion lividity. But if the flesh is pressed against something, the blood is excluded, which produces the white patches.'

'But . . .' Kathy hesitated, then decided to state the obvious. 'The patches are on the side of his head.'

'Exactly, and down the right side of his body. He's been moved, you see. For a time after he died, he was lying on his right side.'

'Ah.' Kathy felt the hairs stand up on the back of her neck.

Pugh moved forward again and squatted, peering at the right hand. 'At least, that's the way it looks at the moment. That's why he seems twisted. The muscles are holding the position he had on the floor, or wherever he was. Just to complicate matters, he's got dark skin, which tends to hide all but the most glaring lividity patterns. But there'll be others we'll pick up on the table. And of course, there may really be bruising, which the lividity may disguise.'

'Wouldn't the pattern of lividity change after he'd been moved into the new hanging position?' Kathy asked.

'Good question!' Pugh cried. 'After a period of time – a few hours, it varies – haemoglobin begins to diffuse into the tissues, and the pattern becomes fixed permanently. That's called diffusion lividity. So what have we really got here? It's tricky, you see, because each process – rigor, hypostatic lividity, diffusion lividity – they happen at unpredictable rates, depending on the temperature, the characteristics of the body, how he died, and so on.'

'So he may not have died by hanging at all?'

'Possibly not. Why were you particularly interested in bruising?'

Kathy indicated the two objects beside the organ console. She called over one of the civilian scene-of-crime officers, who had now arrived. Like Pugh, he wore overalls and gloves. He bagged the objects and handed them to Kathy. The second object, she saw, was a black leather hood, as the patrol officer had guessed, with slits for eyes, nostrils and mouth. She passed both to the pathologist, who put his glasses on again to examine them, wrinkled his nose and muttered, 'The impenetrable strangeness of the human mind,' and then, 'We'll have to wait for laboratory tests and the post-mortem to see what these have been used for, of course.'

He handed the plastic bags back to the SOCO.

'Would you check the pockets for me, please?' Kathy said to the man, who nodded and felt inside Petrou's tracksuit.

'Nothing.'

'That's odd.' Kathy frowned.

'Well now, let's get this chap down, shall we?' Pugh said. 'We'll need plenty of plastic sheeting. He mustn't touch anything at all, all right?'

They did as he directed, unfastening the bottom of the rope and lowering Petrou slowly down on to the sheeting. Pugh moved in again. 'Let's get his temperature now, shall we?'

He eased down the tracksuit pants and grunted. 'No shorts or singlet or anything under this. He's gay, is he, Sergeant?'

'I don't know.'

'Well, there are signs of recent anal intercourse, I'd say. Bruising. Almost sure.'

He straightened and with another instrument took a reading of the room temperature. 'All right, then. We have an ambient room temperature of 10.4 and an internal body temperature —' he peered at the first instrument '— of 11.2. What do you think, Anthony?'

'Getting close.'

'Too close to be much help.' Pugh turned to Kathy. 'After death the internal body temperature stays stable for a couple of hours, then begins to drop towards the ambient. It takes perhaps forty-eight hours to reach it, but the main drop occurs in the first twelve to fifteen hours; then the curve flattens and temperature change occurs slowly. But it all depends on so many things, you see — body weight, clothing, difference between body and air temperature — and we don't really know much about those, do we? We don't know for sure whether he's been here all the time, or whether he was wearing something else to begin with, or what.'

He looked around fiercely. 'All right. The best thing is to get him on the table as quickly as possible, before rigor starts to weaken.' He looked at his watch. 'I think . . . yes, I think I could do him at twelve. I'll have to check with the morgue and the coroner's office.'

'Midday?' Kathy said. 'As soon as that?'

'Yes, as soon as possible. Is that a problem? You'll be there, of course?'

'Yes, yes. Only I'll have to get things organized here.'

'You'll manage, I'm sure, Sergeant. Now, the tests in here . . .' He glared around the room and waved the SOCO over. 'I'll need scrapings and swabs of different areas of the floor, down here and upstairs. Fibre samples, of course, if there are any. Have a good look for human hair. What about a UV search?' He looked inquiringly at Kathy. She looked blank.

'Semen shows up under ultraviolet light. Sometimes. Worth a try?'

'Sure,' she shrugged, 'yes.'

'Try the whole building,' he commanded the officer, who nodded and said, 'I'll have to get the lamps in. We haven't got them with us.'

'All right. Anything else, Sergeant?'

'I'll talk to the fingerprint man. There are a couple of chairs upstairs that look as if they were disturbed recently.'

Pugh nodded. 'Better print the organ keys. Never know what they were up to.'

'They?' Kathy repeated. 'Was he murdered, Professor?'

'Who knows? Maybe we'll know more at noon. I'll see you then, unless I ring with another time. Are you coming, Anthony?'

Kathy followed the two doctors up the stairs. The building was alive with people now. She had the impression of a machine of which she'd pressed the starter button. The problem now was going to be to control it. She had very little time. It was essential she got more background before she left for the post-mortem. But how far beyond that should she go? If she waited till the PM was over, it would be mid-afternoon. People would have come and gone from the clinic, rumours would be flying around, memories confused by all the talk, evidence lost. On the other hand, if she launched a full-scale search of the grounds and interviewed a hundred people, the pathologist might turn up an innocent explanation and she would look as if she'd badly overreacted.

Either way, she had to decide now.

Dowling was standing under the portico of the temple, staring forlornly at the rain, now coming down steadily.

'Gordon, listen carefully. I'm going down to the house to interview the Director. I want you to begin organizing the next stage. It looks as if the body was moved at some point after he died, before he was strung up down there. You follow? That sounds like murder.'

Dowling looked intensely worried. 'Shouldn't we get help,

Sarge? Shouldn't we call Sergeant McGregor or Inspector Tanner?'

Kathy flushed. 'No, Gordon! *We*'ve been given this case to handle and that's exactly what we're going to do, at least until we've found out more about what's going on!'

'Yes, Kathy. Sorry.'

'Now listen to me.' She put as much quiet confidence into her voice as she could gather. 'I want the area around the temple secured and thoroughly searched. But coordinate closely with the SOCO team. You'll need half a dozen men, I should think. Start around the temple and work outwards, towards the house and the staff cottages. Then I also want to set up interview teams inside the house. Get as many as you reasonably can. I'll brief them when I'm finished with Beamish-Newell. I'll organize an incident room in the house. And see if you can get Belle Mansfield to come up here with them, too. Got all that?'

Dowling nodded, worried.

'Come on, Gordon! This is exciting!'

He was a foot taller than she was, and she was standing inches away from him, glaring up into his face.

'Yeah . . . yeah.' He gave a weak smile. 'It was just . . . seeing that bloke down there. It shook me up, I think. Don't worry. I won't mess up.'

'I know you won't.' She relaxed back on to her heels and gave him a big encouraging smile.

Kathy ignored the gravel path which led round the side of the west wing and out on to the main drive, and cut across the wet grass to the front of the house. The lowest floor of the original building was half sunk into the ground as a semi-basement, its windows tiny and deeply set into the heavily rusticated stone wall. Flights of steps on each side of the central portico led up to the main entrance at first-floor level. Tough on wheelchairs, she thought.

She paused at the top of the steps and shook her hair, now dripping wet. Far across the meadow the mist which had hung over the bridge and stream had been dissipated by the general drizzle. She turned and opened one of the tall glass doors, grander versions of the ones at the front of the temple.

She was enveloped by the warmth and by the smell of food – vegetable, institutional. A mixed collection of sofas and side tables filled most of the entrance hall. Beyond an archway, two bowed figures wearing dressing gowns and carrying towels shuffled away along a corridor. To her right, Kathy saw a counter through an open doorway. An elderly woman in a quilted dressing gown and fluffy pink slippers was leaning across it, speaking with suppressed intensity to the receptionist behind.

'But you don't understand,' she whispered urgently, 'I *have* to leave today. It's exceedingly important ... something unexpected has turned up.'

The receptionist flicked a page of the file in front of her.

'I'm sorry, Mrs Cochrane, your treatment doesn't finish until Saturday. You can't leave till then.'

'No, no, that's quite impossible ...' The woman looked over her shoulder and, seeing Kathy behind her, lowered her voice and tried again. 'The fact is, I just don't *want* to stay any longer.' She gave what she had intended to be a conspiratorial chuckle, but it came out as a whimper. 'This is the *twelfth* day. I've really had quite, quite enough. So if you would, *please*, just make the necessary arrangements ...'

The receptionist was unmoved. She had clearly been through this before, and she had the advantage over the other woman in that she was young, beautiful and had her clothes on. She fixed the old lady with a look that would have stalled a bulldozer and said firmly, 'Dr Beamish-Newell would never allow it, Mrs Cochrane.'

Kathy forced herself to be patient while this exchange continued. She turned to examine the titles of the books and pamphlets on sale in racks behind her – *Understanding Your Vital Organs*, *The Essence of Homoeopathy*, *Grains and Pulses*.

Come on! She took a deep breath as the old lady's fruitless appeal finally ground to a halt. The receptionist looked over the bowed white head to Kathy. 'Can I help you?'

'Dr Beamish-Newell, please. He's expecting me – Kathy Kolla.'

The receptionist checked on the phone, then nodded. 'I'll show you the way.'

Kathy followed her, leaving Mrs Cochrane still standing, head lowered, at the counter.

On the far side of the reception hall they entered a dark, carpeted corridor, where the smell of yeasty food was very strong and they could hear the clatter of metal pots from the basement and the sound of someone whistling. Past some stairs, the woman stopped at an unmarked door, knocked and showed Kathy into the Director's office.

The cold gripped her. Beamish-Newell was sitting at a desk in front of the open window. He raised his head slowly and again she was conscious of the eyes.

'Please sit down, Sergeant,' the voice soft.

His room was small, claustrophobic, barely large enough for the big desk set skew within it and the visitors' chairs. Against the dark-green wallpaper stood several mahogany bookcases, crammed with what looked like textbooks. On the wall to the right of the window hung a long chart showing the outlines of naked male figures in front and rear views with larger details of head, hands and feet, all covered with networks of red lines, like wiring diagrams, the junctions annotated with Chinese characters.

'So, you've finished your investigations.' A statement, not a question.

'Not quite, sir. The body is being taken to the County Mortuary. A post-mortem examination will be carried out later this morning.'

'So quickly?' he murmured. 'Who'll do it?'

'Professor –' Kathy began, and he completed the words for her, nodding, 'Gareth Pugh.'

'Sir, I wondered –'

Again he cut across her words. 'What do you hope to establish from the post-mortem?'

She blinked and clenched her fists on her lap. 'Time of death. Cause of death.'

'Cause? That's obvious, isn't it?'

'We'd like forensic confirmation. Do you have the information on Mr Petrou, sir?'

He stared at her for a long moment, his left eyebrow raised, then, without lowering his eyes, stroked his hand across a manila folder on the desk in front of him. 'This is his file. Not a great deal, I'm afraid.'

Kathy took it from him. There were only two pieces of paper inside. A copy of what appeared to be a standard form of employment agreement between the clinic and a member of staff provided his name, date of birth and a few other basic details. Next of kin was given as his mother, Mrs Ourania Petrou, of Apartment 114, 86 Souda Avenue, Athens. The signature at the end was dated 4 April 1991. A passport-sized photograph was stapled to the top corner of the page. Dark-eyed, startlingly attractive, with a thick thatch of black wavy hair, it took an effort to associate the face giving a racy grin at the camera with that of the mottled corpse in the temple.

The other document was a photocopy of an official translation into English of a diploma certificate in physiotherapy from the Academy of Health Sciences in Athens, awarded in 1987. The translation had been certified as accurate by the British Embassy in Rome, dated 10 March 1991.

'How did he come to be working here, Dr Beamish-Newell? Did he answer an advertisement?'

'No. He was on holiday, as I recall, travelling in Europe. He had an interest in naturopathic medicine and had heard of us. When he reached the UK he decided to pay us a visit. It happened we were short of a trained physio.' He shrugged. 'I didn't necessarily expect him to stay for long, but it suited us both at that moment. He seemed to settle in well enough.'

'He made friends easily?'

Beamish-Newell hesitated, choosing his words. 'I would say so, yes. His English was a bit limited at first, but he soon began to pick up colloquialisms. We've had a number of patients particularly ask for him over the months he was here, which is always a good sign.'

'I'd like their names.'

The Director frowned, opened his mouth to say something, then thought better of it.

'What about staff? Did he have special friends?'

'I'm not sure, really. I recall him going up to town one weekend with a group. Parsons may know – he lived next to him.'

'What about outside the clinic? Friends, clubs he joined, interests?'

'I really don't know. You'll have to ask other people about that.'

'And you say he gave no indication of depression, as far as you know?'

'That's right.' He turned his attention to a desk diary and then pointedly looked at his watch. 'My secretary is preparing the list of staff and patients who have been here over the past couple of days, as you asked.'

'Thank you. I'm going to have to interview them all.'

'All?' He looked incredulous.

'Yes. A team of detectives will be arriving shortly. Would

it be possible for us to have the use of a large room, or some small rooms, for talking to people individually?'

'No, I don't think that will be possible at all. It would be extremely disruptive.' Beamish-Newell's stare challenged her to disagree.

'I'm afraid it will be necessary to see everyone,' Kathy insisted quietly. 'If you can't find space for us, I'll arrange for some mobile accommodation to be brought, but that will take longer. I'd like to be out of your way as soon as possible.'

For a moment she thought he was going to become abusive. His eyes widened and his beard rose on his chin, like the hackles on the back of a dog. Then his expression abruptly softened to something almost like a smile.

'You eat too much junk food, Kathy. Full of poisons. You have good skin naturally. You should take care of it. I'll give you some pamphlets on diet – we have our own Stanhope recipes you should try.'

It was the lazy, almost intimate way he said her name that jolted her most. For the sake of his loyalty to his working-class accent she had suspended judgement on his contrived name, his black gloves and his fairground hypnotist's eyes. But no more. She decided he was manipulative, patronizing, a bully. She clenched her jaw, then said, in a voice as quiet as his, 'Did you remove anything from the body this morning, sir?'

It was the first time she had noticed him blink. For a moment her question seemed to stun him.

'What?'

'It surprised me that there were no keys on the scene.'

'Ah,' he smiled quickly, 'of course.' He reached into his pocket and brought out a small bunch of keys. 'I'm sorry, I forgot all about that. These were in the pocket of his tracksuit.'

Something else, Kathy thought. *Not the keys. He thought I was talking about something else.*

'He also had the key of the temple door which belongs on the office key board. I returned it there half an hour ago.'

She looked at him coldly. 'You did *what*?'

'I'm sorry, I would have told you. It just didn't seem important compared . . . well, to the fact of his death.'

'And why did you remove the keys?'

He shrugged. 'I wanted to have a look in his room. I wasn't sure if my master key would open it. Some of the staff rooms have non-standard locks.'

'So you've been up to his room?' Her eyes were blazing, but he seemed quite unabashed.

'Mmm. Nothing there. No note. That's what I was concerned about, of course. I felt I had a responsibility.'

'To whom?' Kathy exploded.

He leaned forward over the desk and said, his voice punching the words home, 'To those who have to go on living with what he did to himself, Sergeant.'

'And what else did you do for them, doctor? What else did you tamper with?'

'Tamper!' He glared at her, affronted, then sat back slowly in his chair, his face becoming expressionless. His hands rested on the desk top, balled into fists.

'I'd like you to take me up to his room now, sir,' Kathy said. 'I want you to show me exactly what you touched.'

Without a word he got to his feet and led the way out of the room.

They returned to the stairs which Kathy had passed before, and climbed up to the attic floor. The space under the roof had been subdivided and rearranged several times in its history, and the narrow corridor twisted and turned incomprehensibly. Beamish-Newell stopped in front of one of the doors and used the bunch of keys to open it.

'Don't go in, please,' Kathy said, and stepped past him into the small room. A tiny window had been cut into the ceiling, which sloped steeply beneath the roof on the far side of the room. Below it, an old cast-iron radiator gurgled fitfully. A miserable grey light illuminated the contents of the room – a bed, bedside cupboard and lamp, small wooden desk and chair, an empty bookshelf, a wardrobe, a chest of drawers. The only personal items visible were a Greek-language newspaper folded on the bed and a bright yellow Walkman on the desk. Kathy stood still by the door. She would come back later to see what was in the wardrobe and drawers when the SOCOs had been through the place.

'Tell me what you did when you opened the door last time.'

'Well . . . not much. I walked in . . . stood by the desk.' He shrugged.

'You came directly up here? With your gloves on?'

Beamish-Newell looked irritated. 'No, I left them in my office on the way up.'

'What then?'

'I saw there was no envelope or paper that seemed obviously like a note, and so I left, locking the door behind me.'

'So we won't find your fingerprints on the drawers or cupboards.'

He pursed his lips, exasperated. 'Oh really! This is absurd. Yes, you may find my fingerprints in one or two places.'

'Which places?'

'I really can't remember.'

'Every drawer?' Kathy persisted. 'Every cupboard?'

'I really think you're going a bit overboard on this, Sergeant. Your attitude seems unnecessarily . . . *aggressive*. I'm trying to cooperate with you, you know.'

He is firm, she is aggressive, Kathy said under her breath. 'All right, doctor. We'll leave it at that for the moment. Perhaps we could see about somewhere for us to work now, and you could prepare the list of patients who especially asked for Mr Petrou.'

As she went to follow him, he stopped suddenly and

turned to her within the narrow space of the corridor. 'It's possible to be too zealous, Kathy. Be careful, won't you? People make allowance for inexperience, but only so much.'

She was close enough that she could smell his breath, yeasty like the cooking. She pulled back abruptly and he turned and walked on before she could frame a reply. Thrown again by his intrusive use of her first name, she guessed she'd probably lie awake that night thinking of all the replies she should have made.

They began to hear the hubbub as they descended the stairs, at first a faint growl like a distant mob, then, more distinctly, confused voices interspersed with sharper cries.

'What the devil!' Beamish-Newell hurried down the corridor and was brought to an abrupt halt by the crowd which was backed up through the arch leading into the entrance hall.

Dowling had been uncharacteristically persuasive and had caught the police station at a time when two shifts had overlapped. The officers' arrival at the clinic had coincided with the mid-morning break, when all patients returned to the dining room next to the entrance hall for a glass of carrot or apple juice. As more and more patients surfaced from the treatment and exercise rooms in the basements they were met by a confused crush. Big men in dripping black raincoats squeezed together to let them through. Their good-natured banter ('Watch yer back, missus', 'Pull yer gut in, Jerry'), interspersed by the alien squawk of their radios, only underlined the grossness of this invasion from the outside world. Lowering their eyes, most of the patients pushed blindly forward, shrinking from body and eye contact, swallowing the indignity of their slippers and dressing gowns until they could reach the sanctuary of the dining room. Kathy noticed Mrs Cochrane pressed back against a wall nearby, her eyes bulging. The little woman suddenly lunged at the arm of another patient struggling past and squealed in terrified excitement, 'It's Alex, Gillian – the nice boy. He's been murdered!'

'Oh my God,' Kathy groaned, and at that moment Mrs Cochrane met her eye, blushed with embarrassment like a naughty schoolgirl caught spreading gossip, and then was swept away by the crowd. At her elbow, Kathy heard Beamish-Newell talking to her.

'The games room,' he was saying, 'you can have the games room. Over there.' He was pointing to a door back down the corridor. She nodded.

Some bolder patients were talking to the strangers, among them a tall, thin man in a towelling robe who was almost shouting at a detective Kathy recognized. She pushed forward and said, 'Excuse me, sir. Tom, will you move our lot into the games –'

'Who the hell are you?' the patient barked at her.

She flushed. 'Please go on through to the dining room, sir.'

'I asked who you were.' The man's voice was penetrating. People nearby turned their heads to see what was going on.

'I'm Detective Sergeant Kolla from County –'

'Are you responsible for this shambles?'

The bulk of the patients had now reached the safety of the dining room and the noise in the entrance hall had become more manageable. The man's angry words cut across the hubbub, and all heads turned towards him.

'Sir,' Kathy said, aware how conspicuous her voice was in the sudden silence, 'please join the others in the dining room.'

He glared at her, momentarily startled by the hush he had created. Then he spoke again, his voice low, teeth clenched together, in a vain attempt to be heard only by her.

'I, Sergeant, am Bernard Long, the Deputy Chief Constable of this county, and you will report to me in the Director's office. *Now!*'

Kathy blinked. The whole room had heard it.

'Sir,' she said at last. 'Tom, take all our people through to

47

the games room over there, first door on the left, and wait for me.'

'Do you mind, Stephen?' The tall, angular man in the white towelling robe deferred to the Director.

'Of course not, Bernard, be my guest. Take my chair. Do you want me to leave?'

'I'd rather you stayed, actually.'

He had regained control of his anger, and his voice had recovered a clipped public-school accent which had not been apparent in the exchange in the entrance hall. He indicated for Kathy to sit on the chair facing the desk, while Beamish-Newell stood back against a bookcase, hands clasped in front of him, regarding her with an air of detachment that implied 'I told you so'.

'What in heaven's name was going on out there, Sergeant? It was an absolute disgrace. I've never seen a more graphic example of insensitive policing.'

Now that he had recovered his composure, he had assumed an icy, patrician air. Kathy guessed he was in his early fifties. Though dressed as a patient, he managed to sustain an air of elegance that had escaped the others. She noticed the insignia of an expensive London hotel on his robe; his hair and nails were carefully groomed. She wondered if he went to the same place that trimmed Beamish-Newell's crew-cut and goatee.

'Uniform branch asked for CID assistance with a sudden death here, discovered this morning, sir. Apparent suicide.'

'Oh?' He looked with concern towards Beamish-Newell. 'I'm sorry to hear that, Stephen. One of the patients? I didn't see an ambulance. But even so . . .' He turned back to Kathy. 'A suicide hardly warrants such a gross over-reaction. This is a naturopathic clinic, not some illicit drug factory!'

The Director cleared his throat. 'One of the staff, in point of fact, Bernard. You've probably come across him in the course of your therapy sessions. Well, it's quite likely anyway. Young chap . . .'

Kathy was puzzled by his slowness in getting to the point. 'Alex Petrou,' she broke in abruptly.

Long looked as if she had slapped his face. For a couple of seconds which seemed to all of three of them to last much, much longer, he gawped at her in astonishment while his brain seemed unable to come to terms with the information. 'No,' he gasped, 'surely not. I saw him –'

'Well, as I said, Bernard, you would have done,' Beamish-Newell interrupted, speaking slowly, deliberately. 'All the patients would, at some time or another. It's a terrible shock.'

Long nodded, using the time to control the expression on his face.

'When?' Kathy broke in impatiently. 'When did you see him?'

He frowned, avoiding her eyes. 'Oh now, I'd need to think.'

Kathy was astonished. It seemed to her that she had never seen a more blatant demonstration of lying and confusion written across a witness's face. Beamish-Newell's attempts to deflect her attention only made it worse. He moved forward to the desk, opening his mouth to interrupt again, but she got in first. 'Doctor, I'd like to speak to the Deputy Chief Constable alone, if you don't mind. Would you leave now, please?' She was on her feet.

Beamish-Newell made as if to refuse. He looked down at Long, who glanced briefly at Kathy, then nodded. 'Yes, Stephen, as she says, thank you, if you wouldn't mind.'

As he left, Kathy sat down again, watching Long carefully. He seemed suddenly older. 'I'm sorry, Sergeant. I really don't know . . . I don't know why it hit me like that. I can only assume it's the diet. I've been here ten days now, on a strict

49

diet, water-only the first three days, then vegetable and fruit juices for the remainder. I believe it's made me light-headed.'

He took a deep breath and straightened his back. His voice was recovering some of its resonance.

'Yes, I can imagine, sir.' Kathy didn't try to sound convinced. 'Did you know him well?'

'No,' head shaking vigorously, 'no, no, no. I've had some massage treatment from him, this time and on earlier occasions.'

'You come here quite often, do you then, sir?'

'Yes, when I can find the time. I'm a member of the Board of Trustees, as a matter of fact. Where ... where was he found?'

'In the Temple of Apollo. Hanged.'

'Good God. But look, even so, it surely didn't need an army of storm-troopers ...'

He was recovering rapidly.

'There are some inconsistencies in the physical evidence. We won't know until the post-mortem is done whether they're significant or not. In the meantime I wanted to interview as many people as possible while their memories were fresh. I must admit, I didn't expect quite so much back-up so quickly.' She beamed at him brightly, and he permitted himself a hint of a doubtful smile in response.

'I'm particularly interested in when he was last seen alive, you see. You were about to tell me when you last saw him.'

He examined his even fingernails, and it seemed to Kathy that he was making a decision. 'I saw him yesterday afternoon, as a matter of fact. I suppose that added to the shock, having seen him so recently.'

'Sunday afternoon. Did you have treatment or something?'

'Not exactly. There's a small gym downstairs. I go there sometimes for a workout. He has ... had ... charge of the place. He opened it up for me at three, and was there when I finished.'

'What time was that?'

'Oh . . . an hour later, probably. Around about four.'

'Do you know if he'd arranged to meet anyone after you?'

'I really couldn't say.'

'He said nothing at all about his plans for the rest of the day? Please think carefully, sir.'

Long frowned, shook his head.

'Please let me know if you can be more precise about the time you left him. Were you aware of him being depressed at all, moody, worried?'

'No . . . I'd never have guessed.' Something seemed to occur to him, then he shook his head again. 'Good Lord.'

'You've thought of something?'

'No.' He blinked at her as if he'd momentarily forgotten she was there. 'No, no.'

Perhaps, she thought, *perhaps things are getting on top of you at work. Perhaps you're going through a bad time with your wife, or your teenage children. Perhaps you're not sleeping well, having difficulty concentrating. Who knows? But if you hadn't been who you are, I'd have said you were hiding something for sure. Something you don't want me to know about.*

'I'll have someone take a statement from you, sir. I'd be particularly interested in your conversation with Petrou. Anything he might have said. Any indications of his plans for the evening.'

'I'll try.'

4

Kathy broke off her account while Brock went to make a fresh pot of coffee. Now that she was well into the story, she was feeling much more confident and relaxed. The visitors got up from their seats round the fire and stretched their legs. When Brock returned, Dowling was casting his eye over the titles of the books piled on the worktop, keeping well clear of the live computer, and Kathy was having another look at the enigmatic little artwork on the wall.

'Mr Schwitters did me a big favour,' Brock said, setting down the pot. 'I'd never be able to get anything as good again, and I've never had the nerve to put anything second-rate beside it. If it hadn't been for that, these walls would have been a mass of flying ducks and faded Gauguin prints.'

Kathy laughed, but he saw the expression on her face and added, 'Really, it may just look like a mess of old tram tickets, but it is in fact a milestone of twentieth-century art. How I came by it is another story.'

It seemed to Kathy that it was very like Brock to own a treasure that you wouldn't recognize inside a house you couldn't find.

'Well, it's a great house,' she said. 'I love it.'

'I rented a room here many years ago, when my life was going through a change. Then later, when my landlady died, I bought the place from her estate. They were glad to get rid of it. It was a tiny, crooked little terrace house, and buyers couldn't find it. A few years later the one next door came on the market and I bought that too and knocked them together, and gradually it's just sort of grown. What about you, Kathy? Have you kept on your flat in North Finchley? I remember you had a very protective next-door neighbour and a splendid view.'

'Yes, I kept it on.' She smiled at the memory of his visit, when she had almost pushed the bunch of flowers he had brought, his peace offering, down the sink disposal unit. 'While I'm away, a friend is staying there. He'll move on when I return to London – if they're prepared to have me back at the Met.'

'Perhaps your friend will have grown attached to the place, like I did here. Not want to leave.'

She thought that remark was a little sly, and didn't respond. ·

'Well, you're welcome to use this place as a base any time you need to come up to town – both of you, I mean. There's plenty of room. Are you married, Gordon?' Brock asked.

'No, no.' He shook his head.

'Well, why don't you both stay over tonight? Return to the wild south tomorrow.'

'Oh,' Gordon said nervously, 'I think, if you wouldn't mind, sir, I really ought to get back today.'

'Of course, whatever. I just thought your tale may need plenty of time to do it justice. I must say I'm intrigued by the body in the Temple of Apollo. Whips and carrot juice. And the brass swastika, Kathy, you haven't explained that yet.'

Intrigued, and also a little worried. Kathy had become more confident, swifter in her decisions, than when he remembered her last. But he was concerned at her obvious antagonism towards Tanner, Beamish-Newell and Long – all of the main male characters in her account so far, apart from Dowling, whom she seemed to be mothering. He worried whether she was being objective enough in her assessments.

The building was brand new, the sharp smell of fresh paint and new carpets still strong in the air. They showed her through a door into a narrow viewing area separated from the examination room by a glass screen. She hardly noticed the three or four people present, as the sudden vision of Petrou's naked body on the stainless-steel tray just a couple of metres away leaped up at her. In the rush to get here, she hadn't consciously prepared herself for this. It was true that she had seen any number of corpses before, and with much more horrific injuries than this – her three years in Traffic Division had ensured that. But the immaculate *objectivity* of the setting gave the body a startling presence. Naked, blotched, its head thrust dramatically back by the block beneath its neck, eyes closed in the total self-absorption of the dead, it formed the focus of the brilliant lights overhead, of the silent attention of the watchers; the focus, too, of threat and danger, underscored by the plastic visors covering the faces of those who shared its space on the other side of the protective glass screen.

All except Professor Pugh, whose only head protection was his horn-rimmed glasses, which he continued to click absent-mindedly against his teeth when he needed to think.

'Ah, Sergeant!' he called to her, his voice distorted by the speaker system between the two halves of the room. 'Glad to see you.'

'Sorry I'm late, Professor. I came as soon as I could.'

'Don't worry. We haven't really started without you. We've undressed our friend, as you see, and we've been taking photographs and swabs and so on, as you'd expect. One or two interesting things for you. But tell me, any idea of a last sighting alive?'

'The best we have so far is around four o'clock yesterday afternoon. He was apparently fit and well then.'

'Excellent. That should give us plenty of time, then. Well now, definite recent anal intercourse, but his partner used a condom. We'll be able to identify the type by the lubricant. And the UV lights have given us suspected semen traces on his legs. The swabs will go for blood type and DNA analysis.'

Well, I'm not sorry I missed that bit.

'Nothing obvious in the finger-nails. We've been having a good look at the lividity, of course.'

'Can you say any more about that?'

'Not at this stage, I'm afraid. Our earlier impression is clearly confirmed – the pattern is unmistakable. What I can't do is put a timetable to any changes in the body position. Analysis of tissue samples may help us there.'

'What about cause of death?'

'There's quite a confused pattern of contusions to the throat – can you see? At present there's nothing to indicate a cause other than ligature strangulation.'

He took his glasses off, holding them in his gloved hand, and tapped them on his teeth. 'There are some marks on the torso which need some explanation. Difficult to see in this light, but clearer under UV. Like the marks of straps or bonds of some kind. We've got a photographic record for you. And the clothing has some points of interest. There are traces of a gritty dust on both the outside and the inside of the material of both top and bottom of the tracksuit. I'd guess the stuff on the inside has been transferred from the skin, where there are also traces, rather than the other way round. And I'd also be willing to speculate that it comes from the stone floor of the chamber where we found him.'

'You'll make tests for all the standard drugs, won't you, Professor?'

'Do you have something in mind?'

'Only that, if he was in that cold place in the middle of the night for fun, he must have been high as a kite.'

'Good point. But I'd say there has to be some doubt about that – I didn't mention the shoes.'

'The shoes?'

'Yes.' Pugh reached behind him for the plastic bag and

brought it over to the glass for Kathy to see. 'Look like new, don't they?'

Kathy looked at the sparkling white leather of the elaborate boots.

'Amazing what people put on their feet these days, eh?' Pugh raised his eyebrows. 'Pumps and valves and gadgets. Basketball baroque. Whatever happened to plain old plimsolls? Anyway, the point is, it doesn't look as if these have ever been out of doors, let alone walked through the wet grass and mud between the house and the temple.'

Kathy felt her skin crawl with excitement once more. 'He was carried there.'

'Well, that's for you to establish, Sergeant. I can only tell you what I see. Now, I think we might as well get on with the normal procedures, eh?'

He stepped back and nodded to his assistant, who had been hovering watchfully in the background. In a gracefully balletic movement the young man came gliding forward, raised a syringe over Petrou's upturned face, and plunged the needle down into his left eye.

Kathy swallowed and felt her eyes water in sympathy. It took her a moment to realize that something was wrong. The assistant was hesitating, frozen in position for a moment with the needle still in the eye. He glanced across at Pugh, then slowly retracted the needle, stooped and pulled Petrou's eyelid open. Pugh had moved to his side, wondering at this interruption in the smoothly predictable drill of collecting the first samples from eye and bladder. He stared at the eyeball, his brow furrowed in puzzlement. He reached forward and opened the other lid, then looked up at Kathy watching them through the glass.

'Someone's already taken a needle to this eye. It's punctured in several places,' he said. 'It's stupid of me. The lids have been closed all this time. I only examined the other eye. There was nothing wrong with that. The lids are intact.'

He turned and looked at his assistant.

'It just felt different – softer,' the young man said, consternation on his face.

'I don't understand,' Kathy said. There was an unpleasant constriction in her throat. 'What does it mean?'

'I haven't the remotest idea,' Pugh replied slowly. 'Someone has punctured his eyeball. God alone knows why.'

5

A hundred people, their paths crossing and recrossing during the course of the day. Kathy had thought that Belle Mansfield might have been able to help. A Canadian who had married an English engineer with IBM, she was a systems analyst who had been working as a civilian at County CID for the past year.

'This is a classic, Kathy! The English country house, with Miss Scarlet in the drawing room with the lead pipe. Only you've got just too many Miss Scarlets.'

Kathy smiled, buoyed by Belle's infectious North American optimism. She hadn't thought of it like that, but it was true. Sixty years ago the house and a dozen or so occupants would have made a perfect setting for Agatha Christie. Now both house and occupants had been recycled and it would take Belle's computer to sort it all out.

Before she had left for the post-mortem, Kathy had worked out with Belle a pro-forma sheet for each person interviewed, identifying where they were at each hour of the previous day, and who they were with or had seen. A separate sheet was to be used to note what the person knew of Alex Petrou. Photocopies of both sheets were run off, and by the time Kathy had left they were in the hands of half a dozen interview teams huddled over card tables around the edge of the games room, with Belle collating results on the table-tennis table in the middle. On her return from the autopsy Kathy found the games room empty apart from Gordon Dowling, who was sitting at the central table reading from the pile of interview reports.

'Where is everybody?' Kathy said, irritated. The rain was

falling heavily now, and she had been soaked again just running from the car park to the front door.

'It's the clinic's rest hour from two to three, and the Director didn't want people disturbed during it, so I decided to let everyone go and get some lunch at the pub and start up again during the afternoon treatment sessions.'

Kathy nodded, conceding the point.

'How did it go outside?'

Dowling shook his head. 'Nothing. The rain didn't help.'

'No signs of any similar rope?'

'No.'

'Wheelbarrow or trailer, or anything that might have been used to move a body?'

He shook his head doubtfully. 'We found a wheelbarrow, but it was full of water. Do we know the body was moved?'

'From the state of his shoes, it doesn't look as if he could have walked from the house across to the temple.'

'Ah. Well, we didn't come across any obvious footprints or tyre tracks, or signs of anything being dragged ... Sorry, Kathy.'

She smiled at him. 'Have you had anything to eat?'

'No. They offered me something, but I didn't fancy it. Just the smell of the food in here makes me feel sick. How about you?'

'No. Looking at other people's internal organs doesn't do much for my appetite.' She looked around. 'Where's the list of people we've seen so far?'

Gordon showed her a clipboard. 'We're concentrating on the patients, pulling them out of their treatment sessions individually without bringing the whole thing to a halt. They have two morning sessions, nine to ten thirty and eleven to twelve thirty, and one in the afternoon, from three to four-thirty. After that is free time until dinner at six, and we thought we should do the staff during that spell.'

Kathy nodded, studying the list. 'There are a few here I'd

like to see.' She marked a cross against some of the names and wrote a note at the bottom of the page. 'We might as well make a start, if we can get hold of them.'

Dr Beamish-Newell didn't get any easier. He accepted Kathy's apology for the morning's disruption with a dismissive gesture of his hand and leaned back in his chair, studying her down the length of his nose, silently inviting her, or so it seemed to Kathy, to fall flat on her face again.

'We're asking everyone to trace their movements yesterday, doctor.'

'So I understand. I should have thought there were much easier ways of doing this. We could have simply got everyone together, for example, and explained what had happened, and then invited anyone who saw Mr Petrou yesterday to remain behind and make a statement to you. I should have thought that would have got to the point much quicker, avoided a lot of rumours and inconvenience to us, and saved a lot of police time.'

Kathy took a deep breath. No doubt he had already given the Deputy Chief Constable the benefit of this advice. Out of the corner of her eye she noticed the creases of concern on Gordon's forehead as he waited, ball-point poised to take notes.

'Mr Petrou' now, not 'Alex'. Distancing himself.

'What were your movements yesterday, Dr Beamish-Newell?' she said evenly. He raised his eyebrows a little and continued to stare at her, unblinking.

His silent gaze went on for so long that Kathy began to wonder if he was going to refuse to say anything further. Then he suddenly spoke. 'Did the autopsy tell you anything?'

Several replies went through Kathy's head. She settled for 'Not yet; there are a number of forensic tests to complete,' and stared right back at him.

He finally shook his head in studied exasperation and,

looking down at his finger-nails, began to speak rapidly in a low monotone. 'Sunday, 28 October. I rose at about seven-thirty Read the papers over a leisurely breakfast with my wife Laura until perhaps ten. I came over to the house to see a number of new patients who arrived between ten-thirty and twelve-thirty.'

He broke off to refer to his diary and read out the names of half a dozen patients, then took a sip of water from the glass on his desk. 'I returned to my house between twelve-thirty and one, had lunch with Laura, sat with her for an hour in our living room, reading a book. At around three the sun came out and we decided to have a walk. I can trace our route if you wish – we saw a number of patients walking in the grounds. We returned to our cottage.' He drew breath. 'At around four I returned here to my office, to prepare schedules and do other paperwork for this week. I also did some work on an article I'm writing for the *Journal of Naturopathic Medicine*. Soon after six I joined Laura in the dining room for a light evening meal with patients and one or two visitors, after which we all retired to the drawing room for a recital she had organized, from seven till sometime after eight. She runs a programme of Sunday evening recitals for patients and friends. Last night it was a string quartet – students from the Conservatoire. She can give you details. There must have been thirty or more people there.'

'But not Mr Petrou?'

'No. At no time yesterday did I see him, and I have absolutely no knowledge of his movements.'

'Go on.'

He pursed his lips with irritation. 'We returned to the cottage together at around nine. Laura had a bath, retired around ten. I followed shortly after.'

'You share a bedroom?' Kathy was aware of Gordon's head bobbing up at her question. For a moment she thought she wasn't going to get a reply, then, 'No, as a matter of fact.

And if you're suggesting I got up in the middle of the night and went out . . .'

'I just like to be clear. You didn't, then . . . go out during the night?'

'No, Sergeant, I did not. Now,' he looked at his watch, 'if you don't mind, this morning's events have put me way behind.'

'That's fine,' Kathy said brightly, getting to her feet. 'I'd like to speak to your wife if she's available.'

Beamish-Newell lifted his phone and dialled.

'She's in her office. She'll come up and collect you.'

'Thanks. One thing. Why the temple, do you think? It seems a bizarre place for Petrou to choose, especially at night.'

'Yes.' Beamish-Newell hesitated, stared down at his blotter. 'It is . . . odd. I have no explanation. I must say I find it a rather chilling place. We have no real use for it.'

'Was it built by a Nazi sympathizer?'

'What? Oh, I see – the swastika grating. No, that was put there before the Nazis took the symbol over. It has an ancient history – the word itself is derived from Sanskrit. When the temple was built the broken cross would have signified something quite different – the wholeness of creation.'

Laura Beamish-Newell came into the room at this point. She took in Kathy and Gordon with quick, unsmiling glances and shook hands briefly.

'I'll take you back to my room so that Stephen can get on with his work,' she said. Kathy noticed a crease form momentarily between her eyebrows, and followed her gaze to her husband, who was seated again, staring fixedly at his blotter.

'Have you had lunch, darling?'

It took him a moment to reply. 'No . . . no, I didn't have time with all the disruptions this morning.'

'I'll have something sent up from the kitchen.' Then she

turned to Kathy, 'Come along,' she said, and led them out of the room.

Her office was in the basement. From the foot of the spiral staircase Kathy and Gordon followed her down a corridor with a vaulted stone ceiling, past cubicles, offices and treatment rooms inserted between the massive piers supporting the main floors above. They came to a door with a rippled-glass vision panel and she showed them inside to tubular metal-framed seats in front of her metal desk, on which stood a telephone and a VDU. An examination couch took up one side of the room and filing cabinets the other. Above her chair a semicircular window had been set in the thick wall, like an eye peering out at the dark sky above. A fluorescent fitting mounted to the underside of the stone vault cast a cold and functional light over the room.

At first, after Stephen Beamish-Newell, Kathy found Laura's curt, business-like manner refreshing.

'My husband works too hard,' she said. She had fine features, a long neck, good posture, blonde hair tied up neatly at the back of her head. Younger than her husband by at least ten years, Kathy guessed, her light-hazel eyes held no warmth and seemed dull with fatigue. 'He doesn't need this.'

'Has this happened at a particularly bad time, then?' Kathy tried to sound sympathetic, although the woman's apparent indifference to Petrou's fate was startling.

'There's never a good time, is there?'

'I just wondered if he'd been under particular pressure lately.'

Laura's eyes narrowed. 'By the end of the summer we're always a bit drained. We haven't been able to get a break this year.'

'What's your role in the clinic, Mrs Beamish-Newell?'

'I organize the treatment schedules. Stephen identifies the therapy regime for each patient, and I organize them into

63

timetables and so on. I also keep a general eye on what goes on down here. I've been a nurse for fifteen years.'

'So you knew Alex Petrou well.'

'Of course.'

'What was your assessment of him?'

'Not all that high. He was inclined to be a bit showy, lacked substance. Tended to lose interest when it came to the difficult bits. Left it to somebody else. But he was quite popular with a number of the patients.'

'Men and women?'

She shrugged. 'Yes, both.'

'Anyone special?'

'Special? I'm talking about some of the patients liking his . . . his manner, that's all. He was quite amusing, personable. Nothing more special than that, as far as I'm aware.'

'And staff? Any close friends, people he saw socially?'

'I wouldn't know about that. I was never aware of any particular friendships there.'

'When did you last see him?'

'Not yesterday. It would have been Saturday afternoon. He was exercising in the gym down the corridor there. I came in here to work. Some of the patients were coming and going.'

'Did you actually speak to him then?'

'Briefly.'

'Do you know what he did on Saturday evening?'

She shook her head. 'Sorry.'

'Were you aware of him being in any way depressed, down?'

'No, I didn't notice anything.'

Mrs Beamish-Newell described her movements on the Sunday, as her husband had done, confirming his account. Some time after he had left their house to go to his office in the afternoon she had also come over, at around five or five-fifteen she thought, to prepare the drawing room for the recital. Although she had come in through the basement

64

entrance and passed the door to the gym where Long had earlier been with Petrou, she had seen no sign of either of them.

Kathy asked to see the gym, and she led them back down the vaulted corridor to a doorway set in a recess. It was locked, and she took a master key from a pocket in her white coat to open the heavy door. The place smelt of damp mixed with the aroma of leather, talcum powder and sweat.

'Alex made this room his own,' Laura Beamish-Newell said, switching on the light. The room had the same low, vaulted ceiling as the corridor, and contained an assortment of weights, mats and exercise machines scattered around the floor. The grille of an extractor fan was visible high up in one corner, but there were no windows.

'Is it the lack of a note that's bothering you?' Mrs Beamish-Newell said suddenly. 'Only, you know they don't always leave one.'

For the first time Kathy felt that the other woman was trying to communicate with her rather than just fend her off. 'Yes,' she replied. 'But we haven't found anyone who even thought he was depressed.'

'Then again, it could have been an accident.'

'What makes you say that?'

'Oh come on, Sergeant.' Laura looked hard at her. 'In our work we've both seen stranger things. It happens, accidental hanging. Maybe he was doing it for kicks.'

From the corridor they could hear the muffled sound of patients returning to the basement for the afternoon treatment session.

'Would that seem likely to you, knowing him?'

'Yes,' she turned away. 'Yes, I think it would.'

She was reaching for the door when it abruptly swung open in front of her. Geoffrey Parsons was there, face flushed. He saw her and began gabbling rapidly. 'Laura! What are you doing? I thought we −' Then he noticed Kathy and Gordon standing in the background, staring at him. 'Oh . . .

I'm sorry.' He blinked several times. 'I'm sorry, I didn't realize. I'll catch up with you later.' He turned on his heel and hurried away. Laura Beamish-Newell glanced at Kathy with a bleak little smile, almost apologetic. 'We're all under pressure,' she said. 'It's all very upsetting.'

Ben Bromley came round his desk to shake Kathy's hand. He looked at her keenly.

'When they told me it was a woman in charge, I realized I'd never actually seen a woman detective in the flesh, so to speak. I mean, apart from on telly.'

'I hope I'm not a disappointment,' Kathy replied drily.

'Oh no, I'm sure you won't be. From what I hear you've made quite an impact with our senior management already, not to mention the punters.' He grinned at her, eyes twinkling.

'Is that right?'

'Enough said. I promised myself I wouldn't speak out of turn. Come on in and sit down. I think we can find room. It's a bit cramped in here, as you can see.'

It was true that the room looked no bigger than the storeroom it had indeed previously been, and all available surfaces, including the chairs, were covered with piles of computer print-outs, brochures and other papers.

'Yorkshire, is it?' Kathy asked.

'Lancashire – Bolton,' he replied.

She nodded. 'I was partly brought up in Sheffield, but I still have trouble telling the difference.'

'I saw the light six years ago. Company I'd been with for the previous fifteen years making window frames finally went the way of half the rest of the north of England, down the tubes. Taken over actually, by southerners. Asset-stripped and closed down. I decided if we couldn't beat 'em I'd better join 'em. Actually I was bloody lucky. Sir Peter Maples, chairman of the conglomerate that took us over, had just acquired a hobby –' he rolled his eyes around the room '– this place. He'd just rescued it from a fate worse than liquidation and was looking for a business manager to put in. I am he.'

He had managed to clear a couple of seats for Kathy and Gordon during this, and they all sat down.

'Would you like a cup of coffee?' he asked.

Kathy hesitated.

'No, no.' He waved a hand. 'None of that molasses muck or whatever it is they drink here.' He reached into a drawer in his desk and pulled out a tin of ground coffee with a triumphant flourish. 'Italian, smashing, what do you say?'

'Actually,' Kathy said with a deep breath, 'that's the best thing anyone's said to me all day.'

'Hear, hear,' Dowling muttered under his breath.

Ben Bromley had a kettle, jug and mugs tucked beneath a hatstand in the corner, and while he squatted to make the coffee, Kathy continued. 'I didn't realize the clinic didn't belong to Dr Beamish-Newell. I just assumed . . .'

'It did once. He bought this place in the seventies. It was a bit of a wreck, you know, needed a lot doing to it to return it to the glory you see today.' He gestured at the squalor around them.

'He must have had a bit of money.'

Bromley looked up at her and winked. 'Not him, luv, his wife. Behind every great man is a rich wife with an open cheque book.'

'Oh, I see. And then the cheque book ran out, did it?'

'Well, the great doctor is a brilliant man, of course. Learnt his acupuncture in Tibet or Timbuctoo or some such, and had this vision for a centre for holistic whatsit, but within these four walls he wasn't too good at keeping an eye on his cash-flow. So –' he straightened and placed the jug on the desk, spooning coffee into the filter '– when things got tricky he managed to interest some of his more influential patients

67

in the idea of setting up a charitable trust to take over the financial liabilities of the clinic and run it as a non-profit organization. They got Sir Peter interested, and he took charge. Should I be telling you all this?' He looked quizzically at Kathy. 'Why not? It's common knowledge. Not much help with what you're here for. What are you here for, anyway? I heard about poor old Adonis the Greek, but it's hardly a case for *Crimewatch*, is it? Or is there something I haven't heard yet?'

'In cases of sudden death we just need to make sure there aren't any loose ends.'

'Oh come on, luv! I give you all this background and ply you with coffee – how do you like it, by the way? – and you tell me nothing! Surely there's something you can tell me? Some titbit? In this house of rumour, one solid fact is worth its weight in red meat! I could have my way with half the lasses in the place if you'd just give me some little juicy thing – only joking, of course. I'm a happily married man and I'm not that desperate – nobody is.'

He was forty-something, rosy-cheeked and balding. His short and stocky build, inherited from undernourished forebears who had laboured for generations in pit and mill, didn't provide a particularly dashing framework for his more affluent diet. The thought of him daydreaming of having his way with the lasses of the clinic made Kathy smile.

'Well, for one thing,' she said, 'nobody seems to have had any idea that he might have been contemplating suicide. It just seems to have come out of the blue. In cases like that we try to establish some background.'

'Try to get to the *bottom* of it, eh?'

Kathy looked carefully at him and he beamed innocently back.

'Why "Adonis"?' she said.

'Oh well, he was another beautiful Greek youth, wasn't

he? And he died while hunting boars, I believe. There's plenty of old bores to hunt in this place, I can tell you.'

'You're suggesting that Mr Petrou preyed on the patients in some way.'

'Heaven forfend, officer!' He fluttered his hands as a disclaimer. 'Just my classical mythology carrying me away. Anyway, the human-relations side of this business is not my problem. I worry about the balance sheets.'

'But you look at what's going on with a pretty shrewd eye, I'd say. What made you think that Mr Petrou was gay?'

'Did I say that? I'm not really sure what he was. I had the impression *he* wasn't really sure what he was. But that may be completely out of line.'

'What gave you that impression, specifically?'

Bromley became vague. 'Oh . . . his appearance, manner.'

'What about his behaviour, with patients, say?'

Bromley looked at her with an angelic smile. 'Really, officer, I know nothing.'

'Well, how about the balance sheets, then. How have they been doing since Sir Peter took over?'

'Pretty well, as a matter of fact. Plenty of people want what our good Director has to offer. I've got a copy of last year's annual report if you want to have a look.'

'Yes, please.'

He pulled a copy of a brochure out from under a pile of other papers and gave it to her. While she turned the pages over, Bromley turned to Gordon.

'Talking about bottoms, have you heard the one about the lad with piles who goes to the naturopath and says, "Please doctor, help me for God's sake, I'm in agony," and the naturopath tells him to get a tea-bag and insert it in his back passage. So a week later the doctor sees the lad again and says, "How are you feeling now?" and the lad says, "Well, doctor, we haven't got a back passage at home, so I put it in

69

the side lane. But for all the good it did me, I might as well have shoved it up me bum!"'

Gordon sniggered. Encouraged, Bromley glanced at Kathy, who was thumbing through the report. She was surprised at how glossy the presentation was, in contrast to the rather spartan atmosphere of the clinic. Surprised also by the figures for annual turnover.

Bromley leaned confidentially towards Gordon and went on. 'Well, the lad uses the tea-bag as instructed, but it still doesn't do any good, and he's still having trouble with his piles, see, so he finds another naturopath and says, "Can you help me?" The naturopath says, "Drop your trousers, then, and bend over and I'll have a look," so he does that and after a long time the lad says, "Well? What can you see?" and the naturopath says, "I can see you taking a long journey and meeting a tall dark stranger."'

Gordon didn't get it.

'He was telling his fortune,' Bromley had to explain. 'With the tea-leaves . . .'

'Mr Bromley, maybe you'd like to tell us your movements yesterday,' Kathy broke in. 'We're trying to establish everyone's whereabouts on the estate during the course of the day.'

'Well, that's easy,' Bromley replied. 'I was at home with my family all day. You wouldn't catch me out here at the weekend if I could help it. I may be barmy, but I'm not mad.'

The interview teams finished off for the day at around six, and Kathy returned to County HQ with copies of the interview reports soon after. For a couple of hours she sat at a desk in the office reading them and making notes, until she started to nod off. She decided she should have something to eat, although she wasn't very hungry, and went down to the canteen in the basement. The whole building was quiet, the canteen deserted apart from three people she didn't know sitting over by the trolley with the sauce bottles.

She had her head down, poking with her fork at a plate of fish and chips, when someone sat down opposite her at her table. She looked up into Tanner's face. Her stomach lurched.

'Evening, Kathy,' he said quietly. It was the first time she had heard him use her first name.

'Evening, sir.' She put down her fork, preparing herself for trouble.

'Don't let me interrupt you.' He leaned forward till his head was only a foot away and picked up one of her chips. 'D'you mind? Haven't eaten myself yet.'

'Be my guest. I'm not very hungry.'

'Got to eat. Got to look after yourself. Nobody else will.'

'No, sir.'

'Hear you had a run-in with the Deputy Chief Constable today.'

'It was a misunderstanding really, sir. I think I sorted . . .'

Tanner waved his hand dismissively and took another chip.

'Bloke's a wanker. Know the definition of a wanker? Someone who'd rather read about it than experience the real thing. Mr Long reads reports. I'm told he's never actually run a criminal investigation himself in his whole career.'

'Is that right?' Kathy pictured the monogrammed towelling robe, the vaguely fretful tone in his voice. Tanner's voice, on the contrary, was a hard growl of experience and caution. Kathy wondered what was going on. She wondered why he was telling her this. She wondered if he'd been drinking, though she couldn't smell anything. Maybe he was just tired, as she was.

'What did you make of Dr Beamish-Newell?' he asked, chewing.

'You know him?'

Tanner stared at her, saying nothing, his expression unchanging.

'He told me I shouldn't eat junk food. Bad for my skin.'

'Looks good to me.'

The male gaze.

Kathy met his eyes. After a moment they creased at the corners in what might have been a smile, and he reached for another chip.

'I'll have to buy you another helping of chips,' he said.

'You certainly know how to treat a girl,' she said, and immediately wished she hadn't. It was a stupid remark, brought on by tiredness and by relief that he didn't seem to be hassling her.

His mouth, a tight, narrow line, widened. That was definitely a smile. He got to his feet and walked away. Kathy took a deep breath and went and ordered another cup of tea.

6

Kathy and Belle sat at the table-tennis table discussing the systems analyst's progress while the others stood by the tall windows, waiting for the morning sessions to begin.

'I'd really be better staying with the guys on the computers back at headquarters, Kathy. Why don't you fax the interview sheets through to me as they appear?'

In the background, Kathy could hear Gordon's voice: '"What can you see?" he asks, and the naturopath says, "Well, I can see that you'll be taking a long journey across the ocean and meeting a tall dark stranger."' He got some laughter, not uproarious.

'Would that be secure?' Kathy asked.

'Oh sure. Send it direct to the fax in my office. Here's the number. And have one of your people send it at this end – don't just leave it for the office staff here.'

From the background Kathy heard another male voice, louder and deeper.

'. . . packs his old dad off to a home. The first morning in the home the old bloke wakes up with an erection, see? A nurse comes in to give him his pills and when she sees his condition she leaps on top of him and has it off with him.'

Kathy said, 'OK, Belle, let's do that. I think I'd better get this lot into the right frame of mind for this morning.'

'. . . in the middle of the following night he has to go down the corridor for a leak. He's in the bog when one of the male nurses comes in, pounces on him, throws him to the floor, and rapes the old bugger. Well, next morning he phones his son. "Get me out of here," he begs, and explains what's happened. So the son tells him to be patient. "You win some, you lose some, Dad," he says. "That's all very well," the old bloke cries, "but these days I only get one erection a year, whereas I have to go to the bathroom three times a night!"' General laughter this time.

Kathy groaned.

'Good luck,' Belle grinned at her, making for the door.

Another voice began, 'What about the two nurses who . . .'

'Come on,' Kathy called to the group of police officers. 'Bring your chairs over here.'

Reluctantly they broke up and came to join her. She took them over the arrangements for the day.

'I've been through most of the interview sheets from yesterday and we haven't got a lot, as far as I can see. Everybody's so bloody polite. Nobody's got anything much to say about Petrou except that he was "nice", his death is "shocking", the Director is "wonderful", the clinic is "splendid". I want you to go back in your mind over the people you saw yesterday and try to identify anyone who might be able to tell us more about what's really going on here, anyone I can follow up on today.'

They thought for a moment and then someone spoke. 'I saw a Mrs Martha Price, Sarge. One of the patients, a widow, in her sixties. She practically lives here, been coming for years. I got the impression she knows the comings and goings, and what the staff get up to. You might try her.'

'OK. Anyone else? There was a woman complaining at the desk the first time I came here. Cochrane, I think her name was. She might not be as reserved as the others.'

'Doris Cochrane. I saw her. Hardly got anything out of her.'

Picturing the huge detective towering over the old lady, Kathy could imagine why.

'What about staff?'

'How about Rose Duggan? She's a physio like Petrou, and seemed to know him pretty well. She's engaged to the Estates Manager character that found the body.'

'All right. Now look, if there's anyone you come across this morning that you think could be telling us more, give them to Gordon when you're done with them. And for goodness' sake try to get them to tell you what they really think of all this.'

'Of course we all want to speak well of the dead, Mrs Price.' Through Ben Bromley, Gordon had managed to acquire a separate interview room for Kathy. Its small dimensions gave the meeting an intimacy which suited her. 'But it's very important that we form an accurate picture of what Mr Petrou was like. No one is perfect, after all, and we need to be aware of any of his failings as well as his good points.'

Mrs Price wasn't going to be rushed. The change from the usual routine was welcome, and she was going to make the most of it. She folded her hands on her lap and looked thoughtful. Kathy noticed that the finger joints were swollen with arthritis.

'What sort of failings did you have in mind, officer?'

'Well, I'd rather you told me. I imagine you must have got to know him and the other members of the staff pretty well over the past months.'

'It is true,' she conceded, 'that I've probably spent more time here in the last few years than anyone else, except staff of course. Since I developed my condition –' she glanced down at the walking stick beside her chair '– I've found it a great comfort to spend time here, and of course I've enjoyed the company of the regulars and the staff. I suppose I have got to know them quite well. But, as my late husband used to say, I see the good in people, and they respond to that. I wouldn't like to be thought of as someone who goes around talking about people's *failings*.' She looked disapprovingly at

Kathy as if she found her questions seriously lacking in good taste.

'Yes, of course. "Failings" is the wrong word, really. I suppose what we're trying to find, to understand, is anything in Mr Petrou's private life, in his relationships with people, that might have put pressure on him, caused him stress or anxiety, might even have driven him to take his own life.'

'Of course I've tried to think about that, as you can imagine. Tried to remember the poor boy's state of mind over the past week or two. The trouble is, he seemed perfectly as normal. Cheerful – he always had a bit of a joke with his patients, you know. And what the Americans call "laid back" – not tense or anxious at all. Suave, I'd call him, *suave*. I don't think he was any different lately.'

'Well, that is a mystery, then.'

'Yes . . .' She seemed to hesitate. Kathy waited patiently, letting her find the words.

'All I can think . . . It couldn't have to do with anyone in the clinic, you see. But he had friends outside. All I can imagine is that if he had a problem of some kind . . . perhaps it was to do with someone outside.'

'What do you know of his friends outside?'

She frowned. 'Nothing really. I remember one morning, the first treatment session of the day, he looked very tired, and I teased him, you know, said he looked as if he'd been burning the candle at both ends. And he laughed and said yes, he'd been out with his friends "up West". I remembered the expression because he seemed rather proud of it, as if he'd just learned it.'

'Did you take it that his friends were from London, or that they'd just all gone up to the West End for the night?'

'I . . . I'm not sure really. I suppose you could have taken it either way.'

Doris Cochrane was even less forthcoming, and as she tried

to get her to talk, Kathy realized that it hadn't been the other detective's fault that he'd been unsuccessful with her. She sat on the edge of her seat, a frail, bird-like figure, staring at Kathy nervously and mouthing as few words as possible.

'We met briefly yesterday morning, Mrs Cochrane, you may remember. You were at the reception desk when I arrived.'

She said nothing.

'You remember? You were trying to make arrangements to leave early. I couldn't help overhearing. Did you manage to fix things up in the end?'

An indistinct shake of the head.

'That's too bad. You obviously haven't been very happy here.'

The old lady's face frowned anxiously. 'I'm quite all right, thank you. It doesn't matter.'

'I wondered what particular things about the clinic hadn't agreed with you.'

'I told you, I'm quite all right.'

'Was it anything to do with Mr Petrou?'

'No!'

'I understand you liked him. You particularly asked for him rather than the women physiotherapists.'

'Please, I don't want to talk about this.'

'Why not? What's the matter, Doris? Can I call you Doris? My name is Kathy.'

It didn't matter what she called her. The old lady's lips were pressed tight shut as if they had been instructed to let out as little as possible.

'But even though you asked to have Mr Petrou again for your second week, I see that in fact you were given someone else. Is that the reason you were upset with them?'

'No! No! No!' she cried vehemently. 'It was nothing to do with that! I don't want to talk any more about this. Please stop it!'

'All right, Doris,' Kathy sighed. The woman was obviously distressed. 'I won't keep you any longer. If you think of anything you'd like to tell us, you will get in touch with me, won't you?'

The slight figure got to her feet. At the door she turned and looked back over her shoulder at Kathy.

'Dr Beamish-Newell . . .' she began, and then stopped.

'Yes? What about Dr Beamish-Newell?'

'Dr Beamish-Newell will be angry with you for pestering me.'

Rose Duggan was a welcome relief. Just a year or two younger than Kathy, she was open and frankly interested in what was going on. Thinking about the dispirited figure of the man who had found Petrou's body, Kathy found the contrast between the engaged couple extraordinary. Rose was sturdy and quick, her dark eyes sparkling, her face animated and expressive.

'Being called back to see the boss, does that mean I'm in trouble, then?' she grinned. 'Me and Doris Cochrane.' She rolled her eyes.

Kathy immediately felt better. 'She's not easy to get across to, is she?'

'I'm afraid Doris has one or two wires loose, poor dear. I wouldn't worry about her.' She spoke with a broad Ulster accent, tougher and more urban than the southern Irish, but still warm and companionable to the ear.

'I wanted to speak to as many of the people as I could who would have known Alex Petrou best,' Kathy said.

'I don't know what Doris has been telling you, then, because she didn't know Alex at all.'

'No, that was a mistake,' Kathy said. 'But you worked closely with him, didn't you?'

'Yes, I did.' Tears suddenly welled in Rose's eyes. She took a tissue from the pocket of her tunic and dabbed at them for a moment. 'I'm sorry. I had a wee cry for the man yesterday. It just suddenly springs up on you, doesn't it? It takes time to accept . . . that he's really gone.'

'You liked him.'

'Oh, sure. He was a charmer. You couldn't help liking him.'

'Somebody said that he wasn't very thorough in his work, though. You never found that a problem?'

'And I can guess who would have told you that, right enough. The ice queen. Oh no, he'd leave things for other people to sort out for him, but then he'd make it up to you. You couldn't be mad at him.'

'Did he have any special friends?'

'Not really. He liked to go out with a crowd. And he had friends in London. He did start to go out with one of the girls in the kitchen, right at the start when he first came here, but that didn't last long.'

'Is she still here?'

'No. She left months ago. Went up north.'

'Tell me about the friends in London.'

'I don't know anything about them, really. I never met any of them. I had the impression they might have been Greek. Just sometimes he went up to town. I don't think anyone from here went with him, though.'

'There's a suggestion he was gay.'

'Oh no!' Rose looked shocked, then laughed. 'Who could have said such a thing? I'll bet it was some old lady who thinks any man who has a pigtail or an ear-ring is queer. Honestly, this place!'

'You said in your interview that you saw him last on Saturday night. Could you tell me about that?'

'Yes, we – that is, the four of us girls living in the cottage together – we went out last Saturday night, just to get away for a couple of hours, you know, nothing planned. We went in Trudy's car to a pub in Crowbridge – there's nowhere in

Edenham – and while we were there we bumped into Alex. He was with another bloke, name of Errol.' She wrinkled her nose. 'He was older than Alex, bit of a wet blanket, I thought, and he left not long after. Alex stayed with us, and we all went on to a club he knew in Crowbridge. We left not long after midnight and came back here.'

'You're sure Alex came back at the same time?'

'Yes . . .' she hesitated. 'I came back with him, as a matter of fact. The other three girls wanted to leave first, so I said I'd get a lift back with Alex on his bike, which I did. It wasn't that long after they left. Maybe twenty minutes or half an hour. I shouldn't have, I know. I didn't have a helmet.' She shot Kathy a guilty little smile.

'When we got back it was about one. Dr Beamish-Newell doesn't like staff coming into the main house after eleven in case it disturbs the patients, so Alex slept on our sofa and was gone the next morning before any of us were up. I never saw him again.' Her eyes filled slowly with tears once more.

'You didn't go out with Mr Parsons, then, Rose? The two of you are engaged, aren't you?'

'Geoffrey's doing an Estates Management degree course by correspondence, you know. He's had a lot of assignments to do lately, and so he hasn't been able to get out as much. He had to get one finished by Sunday evening, to catch the post first thing Monday. He doesn't mind me going out with the girls when he's so busy.'

'So you didn't see much of him on Sunday either?'

'That's right. As I told the other officer, we all had a lie-in on Sunday – it was about eleven before we were up and about. Two of the girls left to visit relatives for lunch, but Trudy and Geoffrey and I had an omelette together in our house about one-thirty. Geoffrey had had to spend half the morning getting one of the drains unblocked, and he was in a bit of a lather about getting his essay finished. He went back to get on with it soon after two, and I spent the afternoon doing some ironing and writing some letters. Geoffrey came over again at five-thirty, after he'd done his rounds like he does each evening. He said he'd just about finished his work, thank goodness. I cooked him a steak and he went back to finish off his assignment about seven. Trudy and I spent the rest of the evening in front of our TV.'

'Rose, have you any inkling of what might have happened to Alex? How he came to be in the temple that night?'

She shook her head slowly, reaching for her tissue again. After a moment she got control of her sobbing and said quietly, 'I just don't understand it, I really don't. He was a lovely man. Not the moody type. It must have happened very suddenly, his decision. Could he have got some terrible news from home, perhaps? From his family in Greece?'

'We are trying to contact them. But why the temple? Did he ever express any interest in it?'

She shook her head. 'Horrible place! A dreadful place to do such a thing! All alone in the dead of night, poor man.'

Kathy made her way back to the games room feeling deflated, empty of ideas. The teams had almost finished the last of the interviews and only two patients were left in the room, an elderly couple conferring with a woman constable on some point of memory. As she came into the room Kathy saw them look up, interrupted by a burst of laughter from a group of detectives nearby. From among them a man's voice emerged, distinct and crude: '. . . and both of the old ladies are suffering from Alzheimer's disease.' The elderly couple exchanged a disapproving look as the voice continued. 'They're watching a dancing programme on the box, see, and one old dear says to the other, "Oh, ain't that lovely. Do you remember the minuet?" and the other replies, "Gor blimey, no. I can't even remember the men I *fucked*."'

A look of horror spread across the faces of the elderly

couple as the word sunk in. They struggled to their feet and scurried out of the room.

'Terrific, Kenny,' Kathy said, weary and angry. 'Next time, tell it with actions.' The group froze for a moment when they saw her face, then rapidly dispersed. Gordon came over to her. 'Would you like some instant, Kathy?' He sounded anxious. 'We got ourselves an urn. You take milk and sugar?'

She sighed. 'Just milk, Gordon. Then get everyone round here.'

He did as she told him, and then she began. 'So, what happened to Petrou on Sunday evening? No one saw him after Mr Long left him, around four. He just disappeared and turned up the next morning hanging by the neck in the temple crypt. No one had an inkling he might have been contemplating suicide. What now?'

Someone yawned, another stretched. They were tired; this stage of the operation was over, and they were reluctant to start pondering the next. Gamely, Gordon said what everyone was thinking. 'I reckon we've got to look outside, Sarge. Try to find his friends in London, the places he went to in Crowbridge and Edenham.'

'If he had a visitor that evening, I suppose they could have been mistaken for one of the people coming to the recital and not been identified by anyone,' Kathy said. 'But where would they have met? Parsons says he heard no sound from Petrou's room all the time he was working next door later that evening. Anywhere else he'd have been spotted, surely.'

'In the temple?'

'In the dark?' someone objected.

'Alternatively, could he have slipped off to meet someone? Visitors' cars were coming and going from about six forty-five. No one seems to have heard the motor bike leave, but it's possible he could have done.'

'The tank was full when we looked at it on Monday morning,' Gordon said.

'Although he was using it on Saturday night,' Kathy added. 'Maybe he filled it up on Sunday evening. We could check garages. Then the pub and club in Crowbridge that Rose mentioned, see if he went back there. And try to track down this Errol.'

'There's a gay pub here in Edenham,' someone said. It was Kenny, Kathy noticed, the comedian.

'Is that right?'

'Yeah, so my informants tell me.' Someone at the back sniggered. 'It's called the Jolly Roger.' Louder laughter. Kathy's eyes narrowed, wondering if he was having her on.

'No, straight up. It's on the other side of the High Street from the Hart Revived, down a side lane.'

'Is that a side lane or a back passage, Kenny?' a voice called out.

'I think you lot need some fresh air,' Kathy said. She set about organizing their tasks with Gordon.

It was after six that evening by the time Kathy left the clinic. She had faxed the last of the reports through to Belle's number, unsure whether anyone would be there at the other end to pick them up. As she handed over the keys of the interview rooms to the woman at reception, she saw the patients filing into the dining room for the evening meal, their routine now re-established. One man gave her a quick glance out of the corner of his eye, frowning as if willing the last of the intruders to go away.

The rain was holding off, but the wind was chill, giving the autumn smells the bitter edge of winter. She hurried to the car, turned on the engine, lights and heater, and drove off, her headlights swinging across the dark meadow towards the stone bridge. When she reached Edenham she drove slowly down the High Street and, sure enough, spotted the Jolly Roger off a turning to the right.

Formerly called the Plough, the brewery had tried to increase its modest turnover by transforming it from a rather drab little village pub into a themed bar. For some reason which no one could now remember, they had chosen a seafaring theme, and the interior was fitted out with timber-panelled walls punctuated with brass portholes, red and green navigation lights, framed charts and blackened fishing nets. The doorway to the former snug bar, now renamed the Poop Deck, was guarded by a replica cannon, which regularly caught the shins of customers when the place was busy. Kathy opted for the main bar, glad that it was almost deserted.

'What can I get you, luv?' The barman was young and good-looking. He wore a white collarless shirt and a black apron tied at the waist. He regarded Kathy with a severe expression, one eyebrow arched. Kathy didn't normally drink beer, but the overheated atmosphere of the clinic had dried her out.

'Half of lager, please.'

'Stella?'

'Fine. Maybe you can help me. I'm looking for someone.'

'Aren't we all, luv?'

'Yes, well. You ever see a foreign bloke in here, dark, in his twenties, your sort of build? I've got a picture.'

The man glanced at it over his arm as he drew the lager.

'Nice. What's he done, run off with someone?'

'He's had an accident. I'm trying to contact his friends. His name's Alex, Alex Petrou. Mean anything to you?'

The barman took his time to shake his head. 'What made you try here?'

'He worked at the Stanhope Clinic up the road. I just thought he might have come in here for a drink.'

The man looked at Kathy carefully. 'Well, I'll ask the regulars if you like. Want to leave the picture?'

'All right. I'll put my phone number on the back.'

Kathy handed it over and sat on a stool at one end of the bar. An evening newspaper was lying on the towelling mat.

The discovery of a murder on a suburban train was making the headlines. To date she had been happy that the press hadn't made much of Petrou's death, but maybe it was getting to the point where some wider coverage might help trace his movements on Sunday night, if he had left the clinic. Kathy sipped her beer and thought about it. She didn't take any notice of the customer who had arrived further down the bar until he ordered a Scotch. Then she looked up, surprised by the harsh Geordie vowels of Tanner's voice.

'Hello, Kathy,' he said, putting his wallet away, not even looking round at her. Then he turned towards her and smiled. There was something about his smile that made her feel even more uncomfortable than his hostility.

'Still hot on the trail, eh?'

He came over and sat on the stool next to her.

'What progress do we have to report today?'

'How did you know I was here, sir?' She heard her voice sound distant and tight.

'Maybe I didn't. Maybe I always drink here. Tasteful décor.' His lip curled in distaste as his eyes travelled round the room and fastened on the barman. 'Genial host.'

Kathy decided to play it straight. 'We finished interviewing everyone at the clinic today. Belle Mansfield is processing the data. I hope to hear something from the pathologist tomorrow. We're following up the possibility that Petrou left the clinic on Sunday evening and met someone. The tank of his motor bike –'

'Alternatively,' Tanner broke in, as if he hadn't heard her speak, 'I might just have heard that one of my sergeants had taken to frequenting gay bars. That sort of thing tends to get around, especially if the sergeant is a she.'

Kathy didn't reply. For several minutes they sat in silence. Eventually Tanner said, as if making idle conversation to a stranger, 'What's this Stanhope Clinic like, then?'

Kathy didn't really know how to reply. What was it *like*? It wasn't really *like* anything. It had its own peculiar personality, hard to describe. In fact, coming away from it, Kathy realized how strongly that personality had begun to form itself in her mind. She shook her head. 'I don't know. It's not a con. I think everyone there believes in it, the naturopathic thing, quite genuinely. You should ask the Deputy Chief Constable. He's on the Board of Trustees.'

'I did. He said I should take my next leave there. Do me the world of good, he said.' He drained his whisky. 'Get the poisons out of my system.'

Kathy smiled. 'What did you say?'

'I said I didn't think it would be that easy.' He got to his feet, buttoning up his raincoat. 'Come on,' he said. 'Show me.'

'Show you?'

'Yeah. I'd like to take a look.'

'But it's dark.'

'All the better. It was dark when it happened, wasn't it? Whatever *it* was.'

Kathy followed him out to the street. He had opened the passenger door of his Granada for her and was getting in behind the wheel on the other side. Reluctantly she got in beside him.

She directed him back through the dark lanes towards Stanhope. When they arrived at the house he pulled into a space in the front car park.

'They're probably still at their evening meal in the dining room,' she said. 'We can have a look round the rest of the house.'

'I don't want to go inside,' he said. 'Show me this temple.'

'There won't be much to see . . .' But he was already getting out of the car.

'What about a torch?' she asked. 'Do you have one?'

He ignored her, moving off between the trees towards the west wing. She followed. As they came to the building she pointed out features that were barely visible in the dark. There was the flight of stone steps leading down to the access door to the basement, from which Petrou might have come if he had walked from the gym directly to the temple. Here was the gravel path, one branch leading round the end of the west wing and up the rise towards the temple.

Tanner barely spoke, occasionally giving a grunt. His feet crunched on the gravel as he led the way. It was so dark that, even though their eyes had partially adjusted, they were almost at the foot of the temple steps before they could make out the dark mass of the building in its dense grove of foliage.

This is how it would have been. It was a night as dark as this, no rain till dawn, but heavy cloud cover, mist forming in the hollows.

Kathy watched the black outline of Tanner mount the steps. He was almost invisible between the columns. He muttered something.

'What?' she said.

'Come here.'

She went up the steps and found that he had parted the tape that the SOCO team had left across the front of the building to keep people out. She couldn't see what he had used to cut it.

'You got the key?'

'Yes.' She felt in her pocket and brought it out.

'Open it up.'

She did as he said, easing the door open. It scraped on the threshold, and the sound echoed in the cavernous interior.

'Go on.'

The darkness was so intense that moving forward felt like diving into black water. She took short steps, conscious of the sound of Tanner's breathing close behind. He had a smoker's wheeze, which she hadn't noticed before.

It seemed to take an age shuffling down the nave towards

the rail over the organ. All the time Kathy was thinking how stupid this was. Why hadn't he brought a torch if he intended coming here? The darkness was so heavy, so pervasive, that it was hard not to become disoriented, to feel panic. When they reached the end she seized the rail with relief, feeling her heart pounding, and said, 'There's a rail in front of you. Wait here and I'll go downstairs and turn on the light.' She sensed him just inches away, unseen.

She groped her way to the top of the spiral stairs, banging her shin once on a chair, then descended quickly and found the switch. After the darkness, the feeble organ light seemed remarkably bright.

'So,' Tanner said when he joined her, 'describe it for me.'

While she did so he strolled around, hands in pockets.

'Where were the things you found on the ground? The whip and mask?'

She showed him and he crouched over the spot.

'What did Pugh make of them?'

'Nothing yet. He said they looked clean, unused. But he won't know till they get the tests done.'

He stood up, thinking, silent.

Marooned together in that dimly lit pit in the darkness, Kathy had a sudden impulse to confide in him, to ask his opinion about the possibilities that had begun to form in her mind. But just as she was about to speak he turned his face towards her, and the chill of his expression choked the words in her throat. Then without speaking he strode away to the foot of the stairs and disappeared. She waited for a few moments to let him reach the top and then switched off the light. The darkness struck her blind and she hesitated before following him up the stairs. But waiting didn't bring any relief, and she began to climb.

She didn't know what had happened to him. She could hear no sound when she reached the top, no footsteps, no breathing. She shuddered and strode out, risking the chairs, judging the paces to the centre of the nave, then turning and making out the faint grey blur of the doorway at the far end. She moved towards it as fast as she dared, reaching it with a sigh of relief. Still no sign of him.

'Sir?' she called into the darkness.

Nothing. She closed the door behind her, stepped out into the night and hurried down the steps. Her eyes were fixed on the lights of the house across the lawn, when she suddenly became aware of a dark shape coming at her from the bushes to her right. She half turned as a hand came out of the darkness and grabbed her right upper arm hard. She was swinging round, about to scream, when she heard Tanner's voice.

'You didn't lock the door.'

She froze, knowing he had intended to frighten her. His face was close, and she could smell his smoker's breath.

'You should lighten up, Kathy,' his voice different, a hoarse whisper. 'You take things too seriously. Just relax.'

For a moment she was convinced he was going to do something – hit her or kiss her, she wasn't sure which – then his hand released her and his shadow slid silently away across the lawn. All her muscles were rigid and she began to shiver. *What the hell does he want?* She turned and paced back towards the temple, restraining the impulse to run. At the steps she stumbled, banging her head against one of the stone columns. She swore and forced herself to calm down, take her time. After locking the door she thought, *I can't face driving back to the pub with him.* But when she returned to the car park she saw that his car was no longer there.

The receptionist looked up in surprise.

'Oh! I thought you'd gone.'

'So did I,' Kathy said. 'I had some trouble with my car. Could you get me a taxi, do you think?'

'Certainly.' She peered at Kathy's forehead. 'You've had a scrape.'

'I bumped into something nasty.'

'Would you like Dr Beamish-Newell to look at it for you?'

'No,' Kathy said, too quickly. 'No. Thanks for the thought. Just order a taxi, please.'

7

Gordon was looking sickly pale, his brow crumpled with anxiety.

Brock cleared his throat. 'How about a break?'

Kathy nodded. She looked over at the window and was surprised to see sunlight reflecting off the snow on the branches of the trees outside. Brock was on his feet, stretching, rubbing his hand through his beard. 'It's lunchtime,' he announced. 'I'll get something organized.'

'Can we help?' Kathy offered, and they followed him out of the room, by a series of twists and bends in the passageway, to a small kitchen at the back of the house. Kathy heated tinned tomato soup on the stove while Brock gathered some things on a tray – cold meats, cheese, a pork pie, pickles and mustard, oatcakes and bread.

'What to drink?' Brock asked, and outlined some alternatives. Gordon opted for a can of Foster's, Brock a bottle of Guinness, and Kathy a cup of tea.

They returned to the sitting room, pulled a circular table into the projecting balcony and set places for themselves, Kathy and Gordon sitting on cushions on the window-seat, Brock pulling a chair over to face them. Golden sunlight was now streaming in from the south-west, enhanced by a dazzling white light reflected upwards from the snow-covered ground outside. The light caught Kathy's face, and for an instant Brock felt an involuntary sensation of immense regret that he wasn't twenty years younger.

'What are you working on at the moment, sir?' Gordon ventured, as they started on the soup.

'Oh ... I've got myself side-tracked a bit, a dead end I

think.' He sucked a steaming mouthful from his spoon. 'I made the mistake of writing an article for *Contact* a while ago – that magazine the Met Forensic Science Lab brings out from time to time.'

'I read it,' Gordon said. '"New Directions for Offender Profiling".'

'Really? Well . . . unfortunately, so did one or two other people, with the result I got dobbed in to represent the Met at this international conference that's coming up on the subject.'

'Somewhere nice?' Kathy asked.

'Rome.'

'Well, that sounds wonderful. I've never been to Italy.'

'Haven't you?' Brock poked gloomily with his spoon at the soup. 'I had accumulated a lot of leave, and Personnel and Training were insisting I take some of it, so the deal was that I would go into hibernation for a month or two and do some research in preparation for this conference, where I have to present a paper. In my paranoid moments I wonder if they aren't trying to ease me out gently – you know, all that stuff about early retirement that's been going around the Met recently.'

Kathy didn't remind him that they weren't in a position to know what was going round the Met.

'More to the point,' he continued, 'the conference is at the end of this month, and I still don't know what I'm going to say. To tell the truth, I'm finding the whole thing a bit of a pain.'

Brock returned to his soup for a while before speaking again. 'The Americans from Quantico will have masses of data of course, much more than I can lay my hands on. The Germans will be proposing some kind of European standard for systematic evaluation. I'm told the French will be contributing a philosophical/cultural/historical perspective, would you believe. No doubt they'll prove that Fourier or some other Frenchman invented the whole thing centuries ago.'

'I don't think I've read him,' Gordon said.

'He had a theory that human nature was formed by twelve passions,' Brock explained, 'the particular mixtures and variations of which determine each individual character. From the twelve passions he derived 810 basic human personality types – profiles if you like. He designed ideal communities around the idea of getting together precisely the right mixture of these personalities. Quite mad, of course.'

He peered at Dowling, as if reassessing him. 'You *read*, Gordon. I'm delighted. You're not one of these new breed who seem to get everything they need from videos.'

Gordon smiled shyly, pleased with the compliment, and got on with his soup.

'So what line are you taking, Brock?' Kathy asked.

'As you probably saw' – Brock nodded his head back towards the computer on the bench – 'I'm supposed to be taking apart all my old cases and as many others as I can claim some familiarity with.'

Gordon choked on a piece of bread: the old man had spotted the screen after all.

'I'm interested in the way the serial offender's behaviour is *changed* by his experience of the previous crime, learning and developing the pattern in the light of what happened last time, you see. In other words, not seeing his profile as something fixed, so much as an evolving thing, becoming more violent perhaps, more formalized, more ritualistic, or whatever. The unfolding of his internal obsession against the experience of the reality of the act. At least, that was the idea. The people at the University of Surrey have been trying to help me, but, I don't know ... it's much harder than I thought it would be. God knows what I'm going to say in Rome. There's no chance that your murder could have been one of a series, I suppose?'

Kathy smiled. 'I hope not. One was trouble enough.'

'So,' Brock said, picking up some cheese and pickle with

an oatcake, 'we move on to the Wednesday, then. Is that right?' Brock said. 'The post-mortem had been on the Monday. Weren't you getting some lab test results back by this time? That seems to be the crucial area.'

Hang on. Let me tell it. 'We did get something later that day.'

'Pugh – I've heard the name before. I just can't remember the connection.'

'Wednesday was the sort of day when things suddenly go flat. You've gone through the first panic, done all the obvious things, and then suddenly you're on hold, just waiting. I had people trying to check Petrou's activities outside the clinic, but I didn't really believe it would lead anywhere. Then Belle came up with something.'

'Aha!' Brock settled back in his chair. The light caught his hair and beard in a kind of halo, and Kathy smiled. *What a luxury to have a good listener*, she thought, *like a hot bath at the end of a long, cold day.*

'This is the schedule of discrepancies, Kath.' Belle had handed her two pages with about forty numbered items.

'That's great. I didn't expect them so soon,' Kathy said.

'I thought you'd be in a hurry, so I worked through the night and all morning on it. I'm going home now for some sleep.'

'Thanks, Belle, I really appreciate it. There seem to be an awful lot of discrepancies.'

'Well, most of them are trivial, I'd say, just lapses of memory – A says she left the sauna at quarter past three when B says she was already in the dressing room at five past – that kind of thing. But there's one that's kinda interesting.'

She pointed to number twenty-three on the list. 'Late in the afternoon a patient went to get something out of his car in the car park and noticed the utility van that belongs to the clinic come out of the stable courtyard where it's kept, and drive away. It was soon after four-thirty, he reckons. It was light enough to identify the vehicle clearly, but dark enough for it to have its side lights on.'

Kathy nodded. 'Dusk was at four-forty and it became overcast towards evening.'

'Yes. The thing is, no one claims to have been driving it that afternoon, and everyone is accounted for at that time.'

'Except Petrou! Did the patient see anything of the driver?'

'The statement says not, but I guess you could ask again.'

'That's great, Belle. We should have picked that up ourselves.'

'There are just too many things to cross-check. I hope it helps.'

'Oh yes. It's exactly what we needed.'

While Gordon organized a new search in Edenham and Crowbridge, this time looking for sightings of the van rather than of Petrou's motor bike, Kathy returned to the clinic. She spoke to the patient who had seen the vehicle leave on the Sunday evening, but he was unable to add anything useful to his earlier statement. He had a clear picture of the van driving past, but absolutely no recollection of the driver.

Kathy then spoke again to Geoffrey Parsons, who was responsible for the security and maintenance of the vehicle. He said he hadn't been aware that it had been taken out on Sunday. When he opened up the stable block on Monday morning, it had been parked in the courtyard as normal. He held a set of keys in his office in the stable block, but another set was kept in the office in the main house.

When Kathy said that she wanted to take the van away for forensic examination, Parsons became agitated. 'We need it to collect groceries and things from town. We use it all the time. I don't think we can do without it.' He wiped his thin sandy hair back from his brow. 'I'm sure the Director won't agree to it.'

He was right. Dr Beamish-Newell evidently considered

Kathy's request the final straw. He slammed his diary down on the desk and stood up, turning away from Kathy and glaring out of the window. She watched him clasping and unclasping his hands behind his back. When he finally turned round to face her, he made no attempt to hide his anger. 'What possible reason could you have for wanting the van?'

'It was seen leaving the clinic on Sunday afternoon, soon after Mr Petrou was last seen here. It's possible he was the driver. We are trying to trace his movements, and the van may be able to help us.'

'Was he identified as the driver?'

'No.'

'This is getting way, way beyond a joke, Sergeant Kolla. You have done everything possible to disrupt the workings of this clinic, and I have had enough.' His eyes held her with an almost physical force. She could imagine the effect on patients.

'We will return it as soon as we possibly can. But if you don't agree to surrender the vehicle voluntarily, I shall apply for a warrant, sir.'

It was clear he wasn't used to having people talk back to him. He weighed her up for a moment before shaking his head.

'You'd better know what you're doing,' he said. 'Have it back here by tonight.'

At four o'clock that afternoon Kathy kept an appointment with Professor Pugh, made in response to her phone call earlier in the day. She was shown into his office and accepted the offer of a cup of tea. The pathologist left his desk and came and sat with her on the low chairs arranged round a coffee table in the centre of the room. He seemed preoccupied as he thumbed through a sheaf of papers.

'Any developments?' he asked, and listened with head bowed, nodding from time to time.

'Well,' he said when she had finished, 'I don't know that I

can help a lot at this stage, but I can tell you what we've got so far from the tests. Blood tests now . . . First of all, he wasn't HIV positive.'

He searched for a particular sheet and pulled it out. 'Blood group . . . He was an O secretor. PGM group $(2-2+)$. The blood group of his sexual partner, on the other hand, was AB secretor. Unfortunately, the semen stains weren't strong enough for a successful PGM grouping. Unlikely anyway after more than six hours . . .'

As he droned on about different classifications of the blood groups, Kathy found herself listening to the tone of his voice rather than what he was saying. The lilt had gone, his voice flat. He seemed worried.

'. . . and until they get an effective PCR technique up and running it's taking six to eight weeks to get a DNA profile. I've sent the semen samples anyway, though the profile won't be much use unless you have someone to match it to – if it's relevant at all. You particularly asked about drugs. We think we've found traces of MDMA.'

All these initials were beginning to go over Kathy's head, and it took her a moment to register. 'Ecstasy?'

'Yes.' He shrugged. 'It suggests he wasn't short of money, or the person who gave it to him wasn't.'

'I'm not up to date with this. Is it very expensive, then?'

'It's not so much that it's very expensive as that in the past year it's become so much more expensive than the alternative drug of choice – good old-fashioned LSD. About twenty-five pounds a unit as against five for LSD, so they tell me.'

'Are they similar, then?'

'To tell the truth, I'm not really sure. There's damn-all scientific data on the effects. MDMA's supposed to be softer, more pleasant, somewhere between a stimulant, like amphetamine, and a hallucinogen, like LSD. But in the high doses, 100 to 150 milligrams, it's probably much like LSD. If you want to try it, let me know. I could write a paper on it.'

For a moment his face brightened, then reverted to a frown.

'I was about to fax my preliminary report to you this afternoon anyway,' he said. 'You and the Deputy Chief Constable.'

Kathy blinked. He was looking down at his papers, avoiding her eyes.

'The Deputy Chief Constable?'

'Yes . . . I understand he has a personal interest in this case. Didn't you know?'

'I didn't know he was asking for copies of your reports.'

'Perhaps I've spoken out of turn, then.' He looked up at her carefully, letting her know he was trying to help. 'Perhaps you'd best forget I told you.'

Gordon Dowling found Kathy standing at a window in the office, staring out at the darkening sky. The street lights were coming on, some orange, others still cold and red. She was wondering why she was doing this. For three days she had been trying, trying hard, and had got nowhere. At the clinic she had been an outsider, attempting to get people to talk to her, help her understand. No one had. She remembered the look on the face of the last patient she had seen as she left. It was the same sensation she had had in the Jolly Roger, of being an unwelcome visitor, an alien. And it was the same sensation she had here in the force. And now Professor Pugh . . . All the time, she felt as if she had been charging around the outside, trying to find some way in.

'Cheer up, Kathy,' she heard Dowling say at her back, 'I've got something for you.'

She turned and saw him standing there like a big puppy, holding two mugs of tea. She smiled. 'Thanks, Gordon. Just what I need.'

'I've got something else, too.'

'What's that?'

'I found where the van went.'

He beamed in triumph at the look on her face.

'Where?'

'A greengrocer's shop in Edenham. Two blokes own it – Jerry and Errol.'

'Gordon! That's terrific!'

'Yeah. It was the barman in the Jolly Roger put me on to them. He knew they were friends of Petrou's.'

'What? He never said anything to me. How come he told you?'

Gordon looked sheepish. 'I don't know. He guessed you were a copper.'

'What about you?'

'I told him straight off. He said I might have a word with them.'

Kathy was peeved. 'Well . . . and did you?'

'I spoke to Jerry. You'll want to see him yourself. I said we'd meet him in an hour, after he's closed up the shop. He wants to meet in the Hart Revived. More discreet, he says.'

Kathy raised her eyebrows.

'So Petrou visited them at the shop on Sunday evening.'

'No. That's the thing – it wasn't Petrou. The driver of the van was Dr Beamish-Newell.'

8

They sat in one of the ingle-nooks by the blazing fire in the snug of the Hart Revived. Jerry had style, Kathy decided. He was telling them a story about the unfortunate interior décor of the Jolly Roger and a biker who had become entangled in a lobster pot and fishing net after importuning an uncomprehendingly straight workman who had come in for a quick drink while repairing the road outside. He was very amusing and talked as if he were sitting with a couple of old friends instead of two police officers seeking his help with their inquiries. His large, round glasses reflected the firelight as he underlined his more telling phrases with languid movements of his hands and head. His complexion seemed ageless, although from the creases in his hands Kathy thought he must be at least forty.

'So,' she said eventually, steering the conversation back, 'how do you come to know Dr Beamish-Newell?'

'Dr Fiendish-Cruel?' They laughed. 'Oh, that's what they call him up there, you know. That and a few other things. He's a customer of ours. We supply the clinic. All organic, no pesticides.'

'I thought they grew their own in the walled garden.'

'No, they can't grow a fraction of what they use. They're not set up for it.'

'He's just a customer, then?'

Jerry looked at her pointedly, pursing his lips. 'I didn't say he was *just* a customer, dear. Unfortunately, my partner in life, Errol, has a great talent for attracting such *shit*, which is why I'm talking to you, isn't it? From what Gordon tells me, it sounds as if Errol has been dancing a bit too close to the flame again, not for the first time.'

'How long have you two been in partnership?'

'We've had the business for fifteen years. But we've been together much longer. Next year is our twenty-fifth anniversary, as a matter of fact.'

'Anniversary of what?' Kathy couldn't help asking, revising his age upwards.

'Of when we were married. Yes, it's true. Twenty-five years ago next spring, Errol and I were married in a church, on the quiet, by an obliging vicar we knew. I sometimes wonder why, but we've lasted longer than most of the straight couples we know. Are you married, luv?'

Kathy shook her head.

'No, well. It has its ups and downs, but I think we're getting to the stage when it's just too much like hard work to look elsewhere. At least, *I* am. Sometimes Errol needs reminding.'

'So what happened on Sunday?'

'I thought something was going on when he said he was going to the shop to take stock of the non-food items for the VAT return. He *never* does that – leaves it all to me, the lazy bitch. After an hour I decided to go in and see if he really was there. Well, he was, and so was the doctor. They were having an argument about something, I don't know what. They shut up when I walked in, and Fiendish-Cruel just glared daggers at me – at *me*! Then he marched out. I asked Errol what the hell was going on, and he got all sulky and said I was spying on him, which I was. He *claimed* Fiendish-Cruel just called in out of the blue with an order for fruit for Monday, but I could tell that wasn't true – Fiendish never does the running around himself and, besides, Errol had that hurt, innocent look he always has when he's telling lies. Anyway, I thought I'd made my point. But when Gordon came into the shop this afternoon and told me about this police investigation, I began to wonder if Errol was being *used* by that man and getting himself into deep water. He's an innocent, you see, contrary to appearances.'

'You knew Alex Petrou?'

'I recognized the picture Gordon showed me, but I didn't know his name. I'd seen him in the shop once or twice. Well, you couldn't help noticing him. I'm not too old to *look*.'

'So you never met him socially?'

'No, never. I'm sure Errol never has, either.'

'I'll have to talk to Errol. Is he at home?'

'Must you? Yes, he'll be home now. Probably wondering why I'm not there cooking his tea.'

Errol was in a belligerent mood. As Jerry closed the front door he shouted angrily, 'Jerry? Is that you? Where the hell have you been?'

'Scoring points,' Jerry muttered softly.

Errol appeared at the end of the hall, his scowl changing reluctantly into a smile as he saw the strangers. He came forward to greet them.

'This is Sergeant Kolla and Constable Dowling, Errol. They want to talk to us in connection with someone up at the clinic who died at the weekend.'

Errol stopped dead in his tracks.

'Come through into the lounge,' Jerry said, apparently not seeing the stunned look on his friend's face.

They followed him and sat on a pair of old leather chesterfields.

'You remember that Greek boy came into the shop a few times a couple of months ago? He's the one who's died. You hadn't seen him since, had you, Errol?'

Jerry asked the question as if it was the most ordinary thing in the world, but they all heard the accusation underneath.

'Jerry, we should speak to Errol on his own, if you don't mind,' Kathy said gently. 'It's standard procedure, you see.'

'Oh.' His lips tightened, then he swung to his feet. 'Would you like a cup of coffee, then, or a drink?'

'No, thanks all the same.'

'Well, I think I will.' He marched out, closing the door pointedly behind him.

Errol was shorter than his partner, more pugnacious in build and appearance, and without any of his easy charm. He glared at Kathy defensively.

'You had seen him since, hadn't you, Errol?' she said.

'Had I?' He adopted a look of wide-eyed innocence, which she took to be the symptom of guilt that Jerry had described.

'Jerry assures us that you've never met Alex Petrou socially, but we know that isn't true.' She let it sink in. 'Well?'

He took a deep breath, shrugged in resignation, raised his eyebrows as if it wasn't a matter of importance anyway.

'I bumped into him once or twice in pubs.'

'Which pubs?'

He mentioned the Jolly Roger and the names of two places in Crowbridge.

'You became close friends.' Kathy phrased it as a statement rather than a question, and he flushed and puffed his cheeks.

'Absolutely not! God, if you're trying to insinuate . . .'

'You weren't ever worried about him being HIV positive?'

It was an unforgivable tactic, she knew, and deserved to fail miserably, but she was tired of being spoken to as if she were a robot.

He turned white and for a moment looked as if he might topple from his seat. 'Oh Jesus,' he gasped. 'Holy Mother of God! He wasn't? Say he wasn't!'

She stared at him, holding his eye for a long while, then said quietly, 'He wasn't.'

Colour rushed up his face from the neck. 'You bitch,' he hissed, tears spurting in his eyes. 'You fucking, fucking bitch.'

They waited for him to recover, and then he told them of his affair with Petrou, a 'passing fancy', he said, which had come to a definite end two weeks before when he had discovered that the Greek had another lover.

'Who?'

'I don't know. He just mentioned it casually one evening. I got upset.'

'How did you meet him without Jerry knowing?'

Errol bowed his head. 'I go to a gym in Crowbridge couple of times a week. Jerry likes me to keep in shape. I used to meet Alex there. I don't want Jerry to know about this, Sergeant. It would make him very . . . unhappy. Does he have to?'

Kathy shrugged, suddenly feeling depressed. 'I'm not sure. Tell us about Sunday afternoon.'

'Stephen Beamish-Newell rang me at home on Sunday morning. He insisted on meeting me, and I suggested the shop that afternoon – there was an old movie on TV that Jerry particularly wanted to see, so he wouldn't offer to come with me.'

'You knew the doctor?'

'Yes, I do the deliveries for the shop and often go up to the clinic. I'd met him a few times over the years. Anyway, it turned out he'd heard about me and Alex. He wanted me to promise to stay away from him. At first I thought he was worried about the reputation of the clinic or something. But he got very emotional, wouldn't believe we'd broken up. Then I realized he was jealous.'

'Jealous?' Kathy repeated.

'Yes. I told him so to his face, and he went berserk. That was when Jerry came in. Just as well, even if it did cause me more trouble with Jerry. Beamish-Newell was getting violent.'

'Really?'

'God, yes. I reckon he'd have killed me. Manner of speaking.'

'Errol, I want you to come back with us to County HQ

and make a statement. I'll also want your permission to take a sample of your blood.'

'Shit. He did have Aids, didn't he?' Errol's hand began trembling again.

'No, nothing like that. We're using blood tests to cross-check witnesses. It's a scientific procedure. You have nothing to worry about if you've told us the truth. Of course, you don't have to agree to this. It's quite voluntary, at this stage.'

It was well after eight that evening when they finished with Errol. Gordon and Kathy had a quick meal in the canteen, then returned to their office to check his account against the earlier statements of people at the clinic. It didn't take long to confirm the information they needed.

'Beamish-Newell left the shop at around five-fifteen, certainly no later than five twenty-five,' Kathy concluded. 'It's a ten-minute drive to the clinic, but he wasn't seen by anyone until he appeared for dinner in the dining room towards six-thirty. He had plenty of time to find Petrou and have a fight with him.'

'You think he did?'

'Why did he lie to us? I'll tell you what, I'd love to know if he's an AB secretor – only two per cent of the population is, Gordon. Only two per cent!' Kathy's eyes were bright. 'No wonder he didn't want us to take the van. I'd better tell them we're looking for his prints inside now.'

'Do you want to speak to him tonight?'

Kathy hesitated, looked at her watch. It was fourteen hours since they'd come to work. 'He's not going anywhere,' she said. 'We'll get him in the morning.'

She smiled. 'Relish the prospect, Gordon. You did well.'

He grinned back.

They met early the next morning, but Kathy had to wait to find out what had happened with the van. It was nine-thirty before she was able to get hold of the sergeant in charge, and she was tapping her fingers impatiently on the phone as she spoke to him. 'They returned it yesterday evening, Gordon. They're sorting the fingerprints now. It'll take them a few hours yet, he says, so we won't wait. Come on.'

She got up and reached for her coat just as Tanner walked through the door. It was the first time she had seen him since their visit to the temple, and she froze inwardly at the sight of him. He ignored her and spoke abruptly to Gordon. 'Where are you going?'

Gordon hesitated and half turned his head towards Kathy, expecting her to answer. When she didn't, he said, 'To Stanhope Clinic, sir.'

'What for?'

Gordon looked back at Kathy again, not understanding. Still she made no move to step in. 'Er ... we want to interview the Director again, sir. It appears ...' he searched desperately for the right words. 'It appears he lied to us in his earlier statement.'

Tanner glared at him, then barked, 'My office!' and turned on his heel.

Gordon looked appealingly at Kathy. She shrugged and hung her coat back on the hook. 'My mistake, Gordon. We should have gone last night.'

They sat facing Tanner across his desk. It was untidy, piled with files and document trays. He lit a cigarette and blew smoke impatiently out of the side of his mouth. The ashtray beside the telephone was already half full. 'Tell me,' he said.

'What, sir?' Gordon said.

'Everything. The whole thing.'

Gordon paused, then with relief heard Kathy begin to speak. Yet, unnervingly, Tanner continued to glare at him, snorting smoke from time to time, as if it was Gordon's words coming out of her mouth.

She gave a full account of the development of their investigation over the previous three days. Her voice was expressionless, which Gordon found almost as alarming as Tanner's strange eye-contact. When she'd finished, Tanner said, still staring fixedly at Gordon, 'Your paperwork is shit.'

Gordon blinked. Was he supposed to respond?

'I want all of this written up. A detailed report. Before you do anything else.'

'Sir!' Kathy protested, 'It's not that incomplete, apart from yesterday. We'll write it all up later today, but right now it's important we see Beamish-Newell immediately.'

'You'll do exactly as I say.'

Gordon hesitated, then offered, 'I'll write up the reports, Kathy. You can take someone else.'

'Dowling, you sleepy bugger.' Tanner's voice was low and withering. 'Why don't you keep your fucking suggestions to your fucking self. I said, you'll do exactly as I say. Both of you.'

It felt like being back at school on detention. They sat on opposite sides of the table while people came and went, Kathy writing longhand drafts, Gordon typing with two fingers. Her face was white, her lips tight with anger.

They finished soon after eleven and together took a photocopy along the corridor to Tanner's office. He tossed it carelessly on to a brimming paper-tray. 'There's going to be a Senior Officers' Case Conference on this investigation,' he said.

'A what?' Kathy asked.

'Senior Officers' Case Conference,' he repeated. 'New management procedure. There was a memo about it a couple of months ago. Don't you read the memos that come to you? To familiarize senior officers with significant cases and to help investigating officers deal with sensitive cases.'

'Help?' Kathy stared at him. 'We don't need any help.'

'That doesn't seem to be the general view, Sergeant.' He lifted his eyes and looked her in the face for the first time. 'Not the general view at all.'

She took a deep breath. 'When . . . when is this conference going to be, then?'

'Today. You'll be called.'

'And meanwhile?'

'Meanwhile, you sit in your office and do nothing.'

Towards one o'clock Kathy got one of the departmental secretaries to check with Tanner's office and was told that they should get some lunch. When they returned there was a phone message taped to her door, saying the meeting would be convened at three o'clock in one of the small conference rooms, room 407. At a quarter to three another message arrived to say that it would be delayed for an hour and moved to room 518. At three-fifty they picked up their files, took the lift up to the fifth floor and found that room 518 was next to the Deputy Chief Constable's secretary's office. She showed them into the empty room, offered them tea which they refused, and left, closing the door behind her.

At four-fifteen the secretary returned and told them that the meeting would now be held in the Deputy Chief Constable's own office. She showed them back through her room just as the door on the far side opened. Kathy was stunned to see Dr Beamish-Newell sitting inside. He was talking to someone out of view, and another man whom she didn't recognize was standing nearby, looking down at him. He was tall, heavily built, with silver hair, wearing a silver-grey business suit. He was eyeing the doctor with a stony expression, and Kathy knew that she had seen his face before. A lawyer, perhaps. The man said something she couldn't catch, then picked up a slim briefcase and came through the door, glancing briefly at her with a cold eye as he passed.

As they went into the room, Kathy saw that Beamish-Newell had been talking to the Deputy Chief Constable. Next to him was Inspector Tanner.

Long waved them to seats and waited for his secretary to

leave. The chairs were low, designed for informal discussion around a coffee table, and made Kathy feel uncomfortably at a disadvantage.

'I don't propose to keep minutes at this stage,' Long began. 'We are here to review the investigation into the apparent suicide of Alex Petrou at the Stanhope Naturopathic Clinic, sometime during the night of 28 and 29 October. The aim is to dispel some of the confusion which appears to have accumulated around the conduct of this case.'

Kathy had not intended to speak until she understood better what was going on, but Long's choice of words stung her.

'Sir,' she broke in, 'if we are to review the investigation or conduct of the case, it is surely improper to have Dr Beamish-Newell present.'

Long raised his eyes to let her see his irritation, then lowered them again to his papers, letting the silence hang in the air for a moment. 'Dr Beamish-Newell,' he said quietly, 'wishes to make a statement which will hopefully clarify matters a good deal. I was about to say that our aim is both to dispel confusion and to reach a resolution of the matter. I take it you would welcome that, Sergeant?'

'Sir.'

'Good. Now, doctor, perhaps you would repeat to the investigating officers what you told Inspector Tanner and myself earlier.'

Beamish-Newell said nothing for a moment, eyelids lowered, then his nostrils flared and he nodded. 'Thank you, Deputy Chief Constable. I am very glad of the opportunity to set the record straight.' His voice was sonorous. 'I must confess to some embarrassment. I had no idea that such a matter – tragic certainly, but essentially rather straightforward, one would imagine – that such a matter could become so overcomplicated ... take on the character of a major criminal investigation in fact.' A faint, pained smile flitted across his face. 'As it unfolded before my eyes, the simple tragedy was transformed into a nightmare. The peace of mind of dozens of people for whom I am responsible, the very balance and stability of the clinic, were threatened. I didn't think as clearly as I should, and as a result I find I have placed myself and another member of my staff in an invidious position. I should like to clear up any possible misunderstandings now, and bring this whole matter to the simple conclusion that it should have reached on the very first day.'

He cleared his throat, adjusted his position on the chair and fixed his eyes on Kathy.

'In my statements to you, Sergeant, at the beginning, I made certain simplifications, which in retrospect were counter-productive. I see that now, although at the time it seemed prudent to gloss over some matters which could stain the otherwise impeccable reputation of Stanhope Clinic. The fact is that Geoffrey Parsons and I did not call the police immediately after Mr Parsons found Alex Petrou's body. At my instigation – and it was entirely my responsibility – we delayed in order to make certain adjustments to the circumstances in which we found him, which were, frankly, of an unpleasant and compromising nature.'

Kathy thought what a good salesman he was. He was immensely persuasive, using everything – his voice, his hands, his body and, above all, his eyes – to engage his audience and make them believe. The phrases were carefully prepared but delivered with an intensity that seemed spontaneous, straight from his soul.

'When we found him, Petrou was wearing – I hesitate to call it "clothing" – a bizarre costume composed of straps and belts and the like. It apparently had some sort of perverse erotic significance – his genitals were exposed – although I must say we found it difficult to make that association at the time. The effect was quite grotesque and made more so by the fact that a leather hood covered his head, so that at first we didn't know who it was, hanging there.

'I simply felt that I couldn't leave him to be discovered and exposed in that condition. One need only reflect upon the distress to his family and the unmerited taint upon the clinic if the tabloid press were to get hold of such a thing. I decided that it was my responsibility to save his, and our, reputation, even if I could not save his life. Together, Mr Parsons and I lowered his body to the floor and removed the things he was wearing. In the pocket of his tracksuit, which was lying on the floor with his sports shoes, I found his keys. I returned to the house and went to his room, to see if he had left a note. There was none, but I did find other things which I felt should be removed. There were a number of pornographic magazines – German, I think – showing pictures of people dressed much as Mr Petrou had been when we found him. I gathered all this together and put it into a sports bag which I found there in his room. Then I returned to the temple, where Mr Parsons had remained guarding the body. We re-dressed the body in the tracksuit and shoes and hanged him again, as best we could in the position we had found him in. It was an unpleasant task and we were in a hurry, anxious to get it over. I packed all the incriminating material into the bag, and when we had finished I put it in the boot of my car until we could dispose of it with the general refuse collection on the Tuesday. I returned to the house and called the police.'

He paused and looked around at his audience. 'I realize we were wrong to do what we did, but I believe any normal, decent person would understand our motives and would have done the same.'

Kathy watched the Deputy Chief Constable nod sagely. Tanner's expression said nothing.

Beamish-Newell spoke again. 'There is something else. On the day before this tragedy, I became aware that Mr Petrou might be bringing drugs into the clinic for his own use. You can understand how shocked I was to learn of this. The whole purpose of the clinic is to promote natural therapies, health without medical drugs of any kind. To discover the possibility of narcotics being brought on to the premises was appalling. When I confronted Petrou with my suspicions on Sunday morning, he was quite open about it and unrepentant. He was in many ways naïve to the point of childishness, and seemed oblivious to the legal and other repercussions of his folly. He told me the name of the person from whom he had obtained the drugs, which he described as an "amusement". I contacted that person and went to see them late on Sunday afternoon in order to ensure that the supply was terminated and that no other members of my staff were involved.

'Again, Sergeant, I omitted information to you in describing my movements for that afternoon, in order to avoid having to implicate my dead employee in another unfortunate ... vice. What didn't occur to me until today was the possibility that his two peccadilloes might be connected – that his bizarre appearance in the temple and his accidental death by hanging might both have been the result of his being under the influence of drugs.

'I should like to make a sincere apology to you, Sergeant, as I have to the Deputy Chief Constable, for any possible prolongation of your investigation which may have resulted from my reticence. As I said at the beginning, I had no idea that a straightforward case of suicide would be pursued in such a ... may I say, obsessive manner.'

He leaned back in his chair, erect, and looked at Long, who nodded.

'Thank you, doctor,' he murmured. 'I rather think we can let you retire at this point. Is there anything you would like to raise before the doctor leaves, Sergeant?'

Kathy hesitated, then looked Beamish-Newell in the eye.

'Were you and Petrou lovers, doctor?' she said.

There was a snort from Tanner, a stutter of protest from Long. Beamish-Newell's eyes widened.

'There's no need to respond to that,' Long said quickly, getting to his feet. He indicated the door and led Beamish-Newell away.

Kathy sat motionless, feeling numb.

When he returned, Long took his seat behind his desk, rather than with Kathy and Gordon around the coffee table. His eye-level was now eighteen inches above theirs. With his slender pink fingers he straightened two files on his otherwise empty desk, one the case file for Petrou, the other a green file from Personnel and Training.

The sense of unreality which had gripped Kathy from the moment she had seen Beamish-Newell sitting in the Deputy Chief Constable's office intensified as Long now launched into a monologue that appeared to have no connection whatsoever to the Petrou case. Listening for some cue to link his words with what had just occurred, she found herself losing track of their meaning. She was conscious of the emphasis placed on certain phrases, *best practice policing*, *quality assessment procedures* and *quality audits*, *desirable outcomes*, *client satisfaction* and *institutional goals*, though quite what all this had to do with the body of a young man hanging in a deserted building in the middle of the night, with a hood over his head and semen stains on his legs, was not immediately obvious. Only at the words *facilitated counselling* did a small alarm bell begin to go off in her head.

Suddenly she realized that he was talking about Petrou. 'Inspector Tanner and I are satisfied, however, that the account of events now tendered by Dr Beamish-Newell provides a complete and adequate explanation for the circumstances of his death.'

Kathy seized upon this glimpse of something solid through the verbal fog. 'Well, I'm not satisfied, sir. Dr Beamish-Newell has now lied to us on at least four occasions – concerning the removal of keys from the body, concerning his search of Petrou's room, concerning his movements on Sunday, and concerning his actions when the body was found. He is completely unreliable. His statement does not provide a complete, let alone adequate, explanation of Petrou's death at all. It is highly improbable, for example, that Petrou died alone, whether his death was accidental or, as seems more likely, given the amount of covering-up that's been going on, murder. Then there's the forensic evidence –'

'Inspector Tanner has thoroughly reviewed the forensic evidence with the pathologist, Sergeant . . .' Long hesitated in his angry response, regretting being provoked into an explanation. His fingers gripped the green file as if trying to choke it. 'Let me make this quite clear, Sergeant. You don't seem to have been listening to what I said earlier. Whether *you* are satisfied with Dr Beamish-Newell's explanation is now irrelevant. What is more relevant is whether *we* can be satisfied with *your* conduct.'

He took a deep breath, consciously relaxing his fingers. 'Inspector Tanner has my instructions to conclude this matter immediately and to prepare a report for the coroner. You and DC Dowling are to be assigned to other duties. You are to undergo counselling in investigative procedures and community relations. Now . . . you will please go with Inspector Tanner and conclude this briefing. I wish to hear nothing further on this matter.'

Stunned, Kathy and Gordon got to their feet and followed Tanner out of the room, along the corridor, into the lift down to level 2 and along to his office.

Tanner sank into the chair behind his desk, lit a cigarette, then indicated that they sit. He looked at Kathy expectantly. 'Did you follow all that, Sergeant?'

'No, I can't say I did,' she said carefully. 'I didn't follow how a case could be resolved without the participation of the two investigating detectives who were most familiar with it. I didn't follow how a senior police officer who was himself a witness and involved in the financial affairs of the institution under investigation could assume control of the investigation and close it down without consulting the investigating officers. I didn't follow how a principal witness who had lied to the police on a number of occasions could be privately briefed by that senior officer. And I didn't follow how, after all that, I'm the one who needs counselling in investigative procedures.'

Tanner exhaled smoke upwards. 'The fact is, you haven't followed very much at all. Not from the very beginning of this case.'

'Sir! I won't have snide remarks about my competence used as a smoke-screen to mask a cover-up.'

Tanner smiled, pleased that she was so angry. 'The only cover-up going on around here is the attempt by the Deputy Chief Constable and myself to hide the incompetence of an officer who can't handle her job. In just three days you expended –' he made a play of consulting some figures written on a memo pad '– 214 man-hours of police time. Yeah, 214!' He raised his eyebrows in mock amazement. 'And at the end of it the only thing you've proved conclusively that wasn't obvious at the bloody start is that you couldn't organize a piss-up in a fucking brewery.'

He gave her a big grin of satisfaction.

'Oh, I tell a lie! There were other *outcomes*. We've had a small mountain of complaints. From Mrs Doris Cochrane, for example, alleging that you harassed and bullied her in order to get her to say that Dr Beamish-Newell was a monster. Her son is a QC, interestingly enough. In fact there were a number of distinguished members of the legal profession and senior public figures among the clientele of the clinic when you mounted your assault on the place on Monday morning, many of whom have written personally to the Deputy Chief Constable in support of the Director and expressing concern at the heavy-handed tactics of the police. I think "crass insensitivity" was the phrase one of them used. Apparently they didn't appreciate all those little jokes at the expense of sick people.

'Then,' he shook his head wonderingly, 'alongside your incompetence, there's your homophobia, your obsessive – yes, that word suits you very well – your *obsessive* pursuit of some kind of gay plot. We're still not sure whether we can persuade one gentleman not to go public on that – you know, the one you reduced to tears by pretending that his boyfriend had Aids?

'You look pale, Sergeant. Not feeling well? Can I make a suggestion? And this applies to you both, because however much we may privately feel that Sergeant Kolla is the prime mover in all this, you, Dowling, you dozy bugger, are also up to your ears in shit. If either of you still thinks you have a future in the police force, *any* police force, then you have some very serious rehabilitating to do. You will do what you're told; you will go to counselling; you will keep very, very low; you will be very, very quiet and humble. Because if I see or hear one cheep from either of you again, I am personally going to insert all the paperwork from this case into your private orifices and set fire to it. Do I make myself clear?'

9

There was a little municipal park whose narrow entrance was squeezed between two buildings facing on to the long market-place which formed the heart of Crowbridge. It had been built on the site of the only building to be bombed in the town during the Second World War, a narrow-fronted terrace with a large rear garden which rolled down the long slope of the hillside. In the earnest spirit of the late forties, the town council had turned this single casualty into a public amenity, transforming a pleasant eighteenth-century garden into the functional patchwork zoning of dahlia beds, herbaceous borders and rose gardens which signified the beneficent arrival of the Welfare State.

Kathy sat on a bench watching a gardener tending the roses. In her present circumstances she felt a sharp envy for the simplicity and satisfaction of his work, which involved the severe pruning of a year's exuberant growth to a foot or two of stunted stalk. There were a number of men upon whom she would have liked to practise similarly drastic surgery.

She sat for over an hour until the cold and gloomy atmosphere of the afternoon had soaked into her sufficiently to restore a sense of proportion. Then she climbed back up the winding path to the iron gates facing the market-place and returned to her car. She drove to Edenham and parked in the High Street, right outside the greengrocers'. Jerry wasn't pleased to see her. She waited while he finished serving his customer.

'I'm just closing. What do you want?' he said.

'I'd like some grapes, if they're sweet and juicy.'

He stared at her through his big lenses, which gave his face a surprised, innocent expression even when he was scowling, as now. 'They are. How many do you want?'

'Couple of big bunches. How's Errol?'

'*You* should ask! He's off sick as a matter of fact, thanks to you.'

'How come?'

He stared at her for a moment and his lip curled. 'I don't want to talk to you. Take your grapes and eff off.'

'I'd like to speak to Errol. I suppose I could call round to your place now.'

'Don't you dare! Errol's under doctor's orders. I'm warning you, you leave him alone! You've given us both quite enough grief.'

'But you haven't said how. What's happened, Jerry? Did someone else come round to visit him? Today? Who was it?'

Jerry was becoming quite agitated, cocking his head from side to side, adjusting his glasses on his nose as if something had happened to their focus. 'He's been told to speak to nobody, and so have I. If you try to pester him again I'm going to make an official complaint. I warn you, one more try and I'm on to my solicitor.'

He turned away, looking towards the shop window, blinking rapidly.

Kathy sighed. 'I'm sorry, Jerry,' she said finally, shook her head and left.

She found a phone box and rang the County Mortuary. She was told that Professor Pugh had left for the day. She found his home address in the phone book and returned to her car, where she identified his place on a street map of Crowbridge.

The road was lined with horse-chestnut trees, but most of their big leaves had fallen. The houses were large, red-brick, built fifteen or twenty years before, when Crowbridge had been discovered by commuters from the metropolis. Pugh's house was in darkness, and Kathy waited in her car in the street, eating the grapes. Jerry had been right: they were succulent.

Towards seven a large white Volvo pulled into Pugh's drive, and the boot swung up. The professor and his wife got out of the car and began carting plastic carrier-bags of shopping from the boot to the front door. It took them two journeys each, and then Pugh opened the garage doors and drove the Volvo inside. Kathy gave them ten minutes to get themselves organized, then went to the front door and rang the bell.

Mrs Pugh came to the door, a small, grey-haired woman in a thick cashmere jumper and tweed skirt.

'I wondered if I might speak to Professor Pugh. My name is Sergeant Kolla, from County CID.'

The little woman looked intently at Kathy for a moment, then said, 'Yes, come in, Sergeant. Funnily enough, we were just talking about you. Gareth was wondering if you might get in touch with him.'

Kathy stepped into the warm hall, which smelled of furniture polish and pine-scented air-freshener.

'Let me take your coat. It looks a bit damp. I'll hang it beside the boiler. Perhaps it'll be dry by the time you leave. Gareth is in the living room with the evening paper. Come along.'

The pathologist was sitting in front of an imitation-log gas fire. He looked up at her, peering over the top of his glasses. 'Ah!' He got to his feet. 'We were just talking about you, Sergeant! Come in, come in.' He seated her opposite him beside the fire, in a plump, floral armchair. 'Now, am I to take it that this is an unofficial visit?'

'That's right. I would really appreciate a few minutes of your time on an informal basis. If it isn't too much of an imposition,' she added uneasily.

He nodded. 'So, it's as if, let us say, we had met in the supermarket just now by chance, and my wife had said, as she well might, that you must come back with us and share the mug of hot chocolate which she always makes after our weekly expedition to Sainsbury's. It's surprising how enjoyable these little rituals become as one gets older. You do like hot chocolate?'

'Really, I'm fine.'

'Nonsense. Anyway, the hot milk is on and Megan will be making you one regardless.'

'This is very kind of you. I should really have rung first.'

'But you were afraid I'd say no, eh?' He smiled. 'What it is, see, we have a daughter, about your age. She's an engineer, and I suppose watching her progress has brought it home to me how difficult it is for a young professional woman to make her way – well, for all young people these days it's so competitive, but particularly for girls. And I would like to think, were she to encounter a problem of some kind, that some old duffer like me, familiar with her work perhaps, might spare her the time of day, see?

'Of course, she could hardly expect him to talk to her about, say, the senior partners in the company she works for. They might be rogues for all I know, but all the same it wouldn't be right for him to comment on that to her. But if some of the technical details of her work were to come up in discussion – things he might expect her to be familiar with anyway – well, there would surely be no harm in him talking them over with her, now, would there?'

Kathy smiled at this elaborate preamble. She noticed that the lilt was back in his voice.

'I'm sure she'd very much appreciate that, sir.'

'Good. And here is Megan with our hot chocolate. I was just telling Kathy here about our Marion, cariad.'

'Yes, that's her picture over there. We're very proud of her.' Mrs Pugh pointed up to a framed graduation portrait in the centre of the mantelpiece. 'I'll go and get on in the kitchen, then.'

'You don't need to go. Stay with us, cariad.'

'No, I don't think I will. I don't have Gareth's professional detachment, see, Sergeant. When he talks about body fluids and the intimate parts of people, he might as well be talking about bits of his car. But I can't help seeing it all in my mind and picturing the horrible things that people do to each other. It makes me feel quite sick, I'm afraid. I can't help it.'

Pugh chuckled indulgently and settled back with his mug. 'Well, you're wondering about Dr Beamish-Newell's new story, is that it? He is a real doctor, by the way, in case you were wondering. I looked him up when I first came across him and that clinic of his. Interesting man, in fact. He did his medicine at Cambridge, stayed on for a while at Addenbrooke's, then went to one of the London hospitals – Guy's, I think. While he was a student he was quite radical. That was normal for those days, the late sixties, though not necessarily for a medical student. He was actually arrested at the Garden House riot, do you remember? No, of course not, you'd only have been about ten, I suppose. Anyway, while he was in London he became increasingly interested in alternative medicine, and in the early seventies he threw in his job and went to China to study acupuncture. He wrote an article for the *Lancet* about alternative medical procedures in China, and when he came back he wrote a book, *Holistic Therapies* or something like that, which was quite well received. Then he managed to turn his theories into practice, I suppose, at Stanhope. He's been back to China a few times since, I believe, and he's lectured widely about his ideas.'

'You approve of the clinic, then, Professor?'

'Ah, I didn't say that. I'm not one of those medics who pooh-pooh alternative therapies as hogwash, not at all. I'm only too well aware of how little we know about how our bodies work – good lord, half the time I can hardly tell why one of them has stopped working, let alone how the rest of them manage to continue. So if someone can cure the rheumatism in your arm by sticking pins into your big toe, I say good luck, boy, so long as it works. And if someone else can take some substance that causes the same symptoms as you're presenting, and then dilute it until there's barely a molecule or two left in the glass, and have you drink it and cure you, even though the whole procedure seems absolutely bonkers, well, again I say good luck.

'But what bothers me about Dr Beamish-Newell and his clinic is the arrogance of the man. He doesn't believe he's practising an *alternative* form of medicine at all – he believes his is the only way. It may be fine for encouraging people to stop smoking or think more about their diet or take a bit more exercise. A week or two at Stanhope for those who can afford it may be just the thing. But what about the poor fellow who's got something seriously wrong and is persuaded to abandon his conventional treatments, his drugs and surgery, for the sake of some will-o'-the-wisp that has no scientific basis at all? That's what bothers me and I've said so. Dr Beamish-Newell and I had a fairly vigorous exchange of letters on the subject some time ago in the *Daily Telegraph*. The local paper took it up and did an article on the clinic which Beamish-Newell wasn't best pleased about. So, you see, in his eyes I'm a hostile witness. I am *against* him – probably trying to blacken his name. That's how he will think. I have to bear that in mind when it comes to this business with Petrou, and so should you, Kathy.'

Kathy nodded. 'Yes, I see. I felt something of that atmosphere of . . . of conviction, although I didn't really understand what it was. That's what made someone like the Business Manager seem so out of place. He was so normal he seemed weird.'

Pugh laughed. 'Yes, but it would be a mistake to dismiss them as cranks. There is a lot of sound stuff in what they practise. As usual it's the human element that complicates matters. And the man has powerful friends, don't forget that. Plenty of important people have gone through Stanhope and been very impressed by its Director.'

'Yes, that point has been brought to my attention.'

'Ah, right. So, best that we just stick to the physical evidence, eh?'

Kathy nodded. 'How does it square with the new story, would you say?'

'Well, according to what Inspector Tanner put to me this morning, Parsons actually found the body soon after six that morning. He fetched Beamish-Newell from his house, and together they went to the temple and lowered the body to the ground. Beamish-Newell delayed returning to the temple until he was certain he had thoroughly searched Petrou's room and removed anything he didn't like the look of. Working back from the time of calling the police, it could have been ten or quarter past eight before they lifted the body off the floor again, so he might have been lying there for over one and a half hours. That could explain the patterns of lividity and flattened muscle, provided we assume that diffusion lividity was already occurring but that rigor had not yet fully set in. That would put the time of death at about 2 a.m. Beamish-Newell has also provided a rough description of the things Petrou was wearing when they found him, and it does correspond pretty well with that other pattern of marks I found on the body, which I mentioned at the post-mortem.

'So the picture we get is of Petrou, in a disturbed or hallucinogenic frame of mind, under the influence of ecstasy, dressing himself up, coming to the temple around 2 a.m., stringing himself up for some kind of weird thrill, kicking away the chair by mistake, and hanging himself.

'As far as I can see, this explains quite a few of the mysteries of the forensic evidence. It explains the marks on the body and the patterns of lividity and muscle distortion fairly well; it explains body fluid traces we found on the floor beneath the body; it explains the floor dust on the body and inside the tracksuit; and it explains the presence of those peculiar things you found in the corner.

'So far, so good. All of those puzzling things are now clear.' Pugh paused and sipped thoughtfully at his hot chocolate.

Kathy waited. 'But you're not completely happy.'

'The trouble is that the things I'm uneasy about are the very things it's hard to be precise with. If he died at around 2 a.m. – and it couldn't have been much earlier according to this account, or rigor would have set in before he was laid on the floor – I was taking his temperature not much more than eight hours later. I wouldn't have expected it to be as close to ambient in that time. But . . .' He shrugged. 'Body temperature is always a dodgy guide to time of death.

'Then there were the shoes, being so clean. We did find stone dust on them, but then they had been sitting on the floor of the temple all night. But there were no mud or grass stains to suggest they had been used outside. Again, though, the absence of evidence is problematic. Inspector Tanner pointed out that you can get from the house to the temple on a gravel path, and though we found no signs of gravel on the shoes, it could explain the absence of other stains.'

Pugh lapsed into silence.

Eventually Kathy said, 'There are other things too. You said before that you thought you'd found traces of ecstasy – it didn't sound as if he'd had very much.'

Pugh nodded. 'But that's something else I can't be precise about, you see? There's simply nothing available on what you'd expect to find in a body ten or twelve hours after taking MDMA, let alone relating it to quantities. I've put out an inquiry to see if data is available from fatal car accidents involving users, but even then, with the variables of time, quantity, body weight . . .'

'Yes, but either way it doesn't work.' Kathy insisted. 'If he was fairly sober, the cold and the sheer inconvenience of going out to the temple on his own would surely put him off. Whereas if he was high enough to be oblivious to all that, it doesn't seem very likely he could manage the mechanics of getting out there without waking up half the clinic – he had to get into the office for the temple keys, find his way out of the house and across the grounds, find some rope from somewhere, open up the temple and make his way down to the crypt, all in the pitch dark, without a torch. You see? He didn't even have a torch.'

Pugh nodded. 'Yes, put like that . . .'

'That's why there had to be someone else, the AB secretor or whoever,' Kathy said. 'Whether it was an accident or murder, there had to be someone else. What about the semen stains on his legs?'

'I can't put an accurate time to that, Kathy. He could have acquired those any time that previous evening.' The pathologist shook his head. 'People do strange things, Kathy. The longer you live, the less surprised you become by anything, especially in our jobs.'

'They gave you a hard time,' Brock said. He got to his feet and slowly stretched his back.

'Maybe they were right,' Kathy said. 'Maybe I did get it out of proportion. Maybe I was determined that this was going to be a murder case from the start. When Tanner brought up the jokes and accused me of homophobia . . . I felt terrible when I thought about it afterwards. I couldn't sleep properly for weeks.'

'But you knew he was trying to intimidate you. He was just good at his job.'

'Do you think so?'

'You know it, Kathy. Deep down, you know it. Otherwise you wouldn't be here now.'

'Yes.'

'So, why are you here now?' He sat down again and faced her across the table, folding his big hands in front of him.

'The inquest was held later in November,' Kathy replied. 'A verdict of accidental death while under the influence. I wasn't required, and I didn't go. I was sick of the whole thing, actually. Just wanted to forget about it. Then around Christmas I got a letter from the clinic, from Rose Duggan, Parsons' fiancée. The one who was out with Petrou on the Saturday night.'

Kathy handed Brock two sheets of pale-blue writing paper. The lettering immediately took him back to the blackboard of his primary school, where the teacher could make a's and b's and p's with perfect circular forms. Rose Duggan's lettering had retained this perfection, unspoilt by speed or lazy habits.

Dear Sergeant Kolla,
I hope this letter reaches you in confidence. Everyone here is busy writing Christmas letters and cards and I thought I would write to you as I have thought of doing many times this past month.

They told me what came out in the Coroner's Court and the verdict on what happened to poor Alex. You can imagine the whispers in a place like this. It makes me very sad to think of him gone and his memory no more than a dirty joke. I knew the man better than any of them. He loved fun and liked to enjoy himself. But he would never have done what they say unless he was made to do it by people in positions who should know better.

I beg you to clear the filth from the memory of a darling man.

Yours truly,
Rose Duggan

'What did you do?'
'Nothing. Rose Duggan was the one who laughed at the

idea of Petrou being gay. It seemed to me she didn't know him as well as she thought. I guessed she might have had a bit of a crush on him. And anyway, what could I do?'

'So?'

'Just that . . . doing nothing didn't do me a lot of good. I've kept thinking about that letter. It was like an accusation that I'd given up.

'Anyway, I did nothing. And then earlier this week I heard a rumour about Long. His secretary is a friend of Penny Elliot's sister and told her that Long has put in for a top job at Scotland Yard – she said the Assistant Commissioner. I couldn't believe it, and then I wondered: what if it's true? I remembered how he'd interfered in the Petrou case, and then I thought about Rose's phrase "people in positions who should know better", and I thought, what if she meant *him*? The only thing I could think to do was see you, Brock. I wondered if you could find out anything about Long. Maybe check if the story was true about him applying to the Met.'

'Oh, I already know about Long, Kathy,' Brock said. 'It wouldn't surprise me in the least if he lusted after a position like that. I'd hate to believe it was anything more than fantasy, but you never know . . . worth a phone call, I suppose.'

He got to his feet and went over to the phone on the work-bench beside the computers. While he thumbed through a small notebook, Kathy and Gordon set about clearing the lunch things, taking them through to the kitchen and washing them in the sink. They took their time, not speaking, wanting to leave Brock alone while he phoned his friends. When they returned he was sitting deep in thought, a frown on his face.

'He's got it,' he said at last. 'The bugger's got it. Apparently the process has been going on for months, and he's come out on top. They're currently in the final negotiations over the package – the knighthood, I suppose. The position is a direct appointment of the sovereign. There probably won't be a public announcement for several weeks.'

'Oh God!' Kathy looked sick.

'I can't believe it. It seems he has important friends. But still . . . he's such a . . .' He searched for the word, failed and paced up and down, shaking his head.

'We went through Bramshill Police College together in the early sixties,' he said at last. 'I remember being impressed by the fact that he was the first person I'd ever met who had already planned his whole life – he would have been, I don't know, twenty-five, twenty-six. He'd done a first degree at Manchester, then gone to America to get an MBA – ahead of his time, you see. He wasn't in the least interested in what the police *do*. The force for him was simply a structure to be climbed according to a prearranged plan. It might have been the Foreign Office or the Inland Revenue, it didn't really matter. He chose the police because he'd read that a new spirit was afoot, sweeping away the old types, the ones who'd come up slowly through the ranks. A new culture was to be nurtured, a culture of young, tertiary-educated, managerial types who would be given accelerated promotion so as to bring about the sweeping changes necessary. Well . . . you know the sort of thing. It makes me tired to think about it.

'Anyway, he was right in a way. He did rise quickly, despite the objections of one or two absurd old reactionaries who felt that policemen should probably know something about solving crimes. I thought when he reached Deputy Chief Constable, five or six years ago, that he must have finally reached the level of his incompetence. But I was wrong, it seems.'

'It isn't only him,' Kathy said. 'Tanner made Chief Inspector last month.'

'Well, now, they're all doing fine, aren't they? I did wonder about Tanner, why he went along with Long's interference.

Perhaps that's the explanation: he knew what was in the wind.' Brock collected his thoughts for a moment.

'Anyway, the heart of the matter is Petrou's death. If you were wrong to smell a rat there, then there's nothing to be done. But if you were right . . .'

Kathy nodded. 'But there's no way I can get the case reopened, Brock. Nobody could now, not without some real evidence.'

'And if there's any of that, it's hidden away in Stanhope Clinic.'

Brock got stiffly to his feet and stretched his back. He started talking again as if on a completely different tack. 'I've been feeling a bit out of shape lately. And this damn shoulder has been getting worse. It's been playing up all winter. I wonder if a spot of acupuncture would help.'

Kathy and Gordon stared at him. 'You're not serious?' she said.

He beamed. 'Do you know, Kathy, I've been worried over the past couple of months that I was about to turn into one of those old men sitting in their armchairs, tapping out their reminiscences, pontificating to the young. I do believe you've saved me. Anyway, I can take my laptop with me, write my paper for the conference while they're cleaning the poisons out of my system. Do you have the phone number? I could be down there tomorrow.'

Part Two

IO

Brock set off late on Monday morning with an expansive sense of freedom and anticipation. He hadn't realized what a relief it would be to get back to the investigation of a crime again. The novelty of working on his own, without the need to report to or organize anyone else, was exhilarating. As if to highlight his mood, the sun came out as soon as he reached open country, bringing a blinding sparkle to the snow-covered fields. As he made his way down the Kentish back roads, he lowered the window to catch the smells in the sharp country air and listen to the shrieks of rooks wheeling out of the copses. He stopped at a quiet country pub and had a light lunch of bread and cheese and beer, in deference to the simple but wholesome diet he expected to enjoy over the next two weeks that he was booked into the clinic.

The sun disappeared shortly before he reached Edenham, and by the time he reached Stanhope the sky was dark and heavy. He pulled up under the trees in the car park and walked to the front of the house. At the top of the steps he stopped to recover his breath, admire the view and kick the snow off his shoes. He stepped into the warmth of the entrance hall and was immediately confronted by the pervasive smell which Kathy had tried to describe – earthy, institutional, yet not quite like anything he had ever smelled before.

The woman at the desk checked his name against a schedule and told him he had an appointment with the Director in just over an hour, at three-thirty. Before then he should go up to his room, get changed into the clothes he'd been told to bring and fill in the questionnaire she gave him. She took a print of his credit card and gave him a key, and on a photocopied diagram of the layout of the house she marked out for him with her ball-point the route he should take to his room in the west wing. He felt like a new boy at school, making his way in his outdoor clothes and carrying his small suitcase past the patients he met in the corridors.

The room was spartan, with basic furniture and a wash-basin simply mounted in one corner. A large window looked directly out to the gardens on the north side of the house. And there in the centre of his view, brooding in its dark grove above the swell of white ground, was the Temple of Apollo.

The sense of pleasurable anticipation with which he had set off from London was evaporating. He changed into shorts and T-shirt and sat on the edge of the bed in his dressing gown and slippers. He felt absurd. The few belongings he had brought with him – the laptop, a box of disks, a couple of books – looked pathetically out of place on the small table. He picked up the file of information about the clinic which had been left for him on the bedside cabinet and flicked through it, wondering how he would pass the time until his appointment.

He turned to the questionnaire and began to fill it in. When he came to 'Occupation' he entered 'Civil Servant', a half-truth. In response to 'What do you most want to achieve from your stay at Stanhope?' he wrote 'General physical well-being and relief from shoulder pain', a lie.

At three twenty-five he went downstairs and followed the photocopied plan to the room marked 'Director's Office'. Dr Beamish-Newell looked sombre and impressive as he shook Brock's hand. He held it just a little longer than might be expected, fixing Brock with his dark eyes, his expression slightly distant as they exchanged pleasantries, as if his mind was concentrating on making a diagnosis through his hand and eye contact. He offered Brock a seat and examined his responses to the questionnaire. 'A civil servant, Mr Brock,' he murmured.

Brock smiled absently. 'Yes.'

'We've had quite a few people from various parts of Whitehall visit us in the past. What kind of work do you do?'

'Home Office,' Brock replied. 'Statistics.' Another lie.

'Sedentary work?'

'I'm afraid so.'

'Do you take any form of exercise?'

'Well, not much, really. I used to walk a neighbour's dog until a year ago, when she died. The dog, I mean.'

'And you're a single man. Divorced. How long ago?'

'Oh, ages. 1970.' Brock wondered if this was really necessary. He was beginning to feel like a suspect.

Beamish-Newell questioned him at length about his diet and eating habits and then moved on to his health record, confirming that he hadn't smoked for ten years and querying his estimate of his alcohol intake. 'Did you bring any alcoholic drinks here with you?'

'I did as a matter of fact.' Brock felt absurdly guilty. 'A bottle of whisky.'

Beamish-Newell nodded. 'Many people do, the first time they come here, David.' The confession seemed to have earned the use of the first name. 'But I don't want you to touch it. What you drink is part of your diet, and diet is central to what we do. Abstinence is an important tool in the control of diet, as in the control of self. I shall invite you to embrace abstinence willingly, David. Forgoing the whisky will be the first step. All right?'

Brock nodded. This was going to be more serious than he had thought.

'You say you want to achieve general physical well-being. Apart from the shoulder, how do you feel about your physical state, would you say?'

'Oh . . . a bit flabby, I think. Need to lose a few pounds.'

'How many?'

'I don't know. In fact I'm not sure how much I weigh normally. But I'd say I'm up a bit at present.'

Beamish-Newell went on at some length, discussing sleeping patterns, headaches, stiff joints, until he returned to Brock's shoulder.

'I got it a long time ago, when I was in my twenties. Had a fall.'

'Sporting accident?' He was adding notes on the back of Brock's questionnaire.

'No. I was in the army. Malaya.'

'Really?' Beamish-Newell looked up. 'Wouldn't have taken you for the military type.'

Brock smiled amiably, the picture of an unmilitary civil servant. 'I took a short-service commission when I finished university, rather than do National Service. More eventful than I expected. Malaya, Cyprus, Aden.'

'Did you enjoy that?'

'Yes, I did as a matter of fact. Why do you ask?'

'Just curious. Did you kill anyone?' He was staring at Brock intently.

Brock looked back at him, surprised. 'No. Not directly, at any rate. But then the hand that pulls the trigger isn't the only one that kills, is it, doctor?'

'Indeed. Does it ever trouble you, what you were involved in doing then?'

'Only my shoulder. As I said, I had a fall. Broke the collarbone et cetera, and was laid up for a couple of months. Ever since, it plays up from time to time.'

'Take your dressing gown off, will you?'

Brock did as he was told and made to get up.

'It's all right. Sit down.' Beamish-Newell came round the desk, moved behind Brock and began to probe his shoulder and spine. Brock winced.

'Here?'

'Yes, and closer to the spine . . . Yes, there.'

'Which university did you go to before the army?' Beamish-Newell continued feeling as he spoke.

'Cambridge.'

'Really? So did I. Which college?'

'Trinity.'

The fingers stopped prodding and Brock began to relax.

'I was at King's.'

Suddenly Beamish-Newell's arms came round Brock's head, gripping it hard and violently twisting it to the left. For a moment Brock thought he was trying to kill him. Then the arms abruptly released him.

'Try moving your head and arm now,' the doctor said, as if nothing had happened.

Brock did. 'It feels . . . different.'

Beamish-Newell nodded and returned to his seat. He began writing again. 'Should relieve it a bit. But you'll need physiotherapy. And acupuncture – ever had that?'

'No, never.'

'Well, it'll be a new experience. But not for the first few days. First we're going to get rid of some of the accumulated poisons in your system.'

He began writing rapidly on another sheet, which looked like a chart of some kind. When he had finished he looked up.

'What's your real reason for coming here, David?'

Brock wondered if the surprise showed on his face. He had been finding it unexpectedly difficult to lie, something he had assumed that, having studied so many experts, he would have no problem with.

'I, er . . . I mentioned the reason on the form there. My health . . .'

'Is that the real reason?'

'I'm not sure I follow you.'

'People come here for many reasons, David. Not always the ones they put on the form. Companionship, perhaps, or time to get away, resolve some problem.'

'Ah, yes. There may well be something of that. Sometimes one's motives aren't altogether clear, even to oneself.'

'Exactly. And if we are to help you in any real way, we must come to an understanding of what it is you are really seeking here.'

Brock nodded solemnly. 'Yes, yes, I see that.'

'How did you come to choose us, by the way?'

'Someone at work told me about you.'

'Oh really? Who was that?'

'A colleague. Not one of your patients, but they knew of you through people who had been here. I wouldn't have thought of it except I was suddenly told by Personnel to take some of my back leave, and when someone mentioned Stanhope I thought, why not?'

'Interesting. Some of our most important decisions are made spontaneously, you know. Let's hope you find that this is one of them. Many of our patients have found exactly that, and they've then wanted to become more involved in the clinic, feel more a part of it. If you came to that view, you would find many advantages in talking to Ben Bromley, our Business Manager.'

'Really?'

'Yes. He has developed a number of highly tax-effective packages for people who would like to support what we do here and at the same time invest in their own health.'

'Well, I'll certainly do that.'

'Good. Now, I'll introduce you to my wife. She'll be supervising the treatment regime which I'll work out for you, and she'll want to meet you and show you round the treatment facilities.'

He lifted the phone. While he waited, Brock looked around the room. Near the door he spotted a small framed picture, and he got to his feet to have a closer look. It was a coloured etching, the view of a classical house in a parkland landscape. Beneath it was a title: *The Malcontenta*.

'You recognize it?' the voice said behind him.

'It looks familiar.'

'You just walked through that portico. It's this house, when it was first built, in the eighteenth century. Without the west wing, of course.'

'Ah yes. And the title?'

'That's the name of an Italian house it was modelled on. You'll find a history of the place in the library if you're interested.'

Beamish-Newell tried another number. 'Laura's probably still tied up with the afternoon sessions. Hello? ... Ah, Rose, is Mrs Beamish-Newell with you? ... No? Well, I wonder if you could come up to collect a new patient ... Yes, my office.' He put down the receiver. 'Are you interested in architecture, David?'

Brock shrugged. 'I sometimes wonder how we manage to persuade ourselves to go to all the trouble of making such permanent things, knowing our own time is so limited.'

'That's a particularly apt observation as it happens. The gardens here were laid out as a kind of architectural discourse on the theme of mortality, a sort of eighteenth-century conceit about life and death. If you look closely at the etching, you'll see a small ruined pyramid under that tree to the right. It's actually out there, if you search for it, at the end of the avenue of cypresses. And there are other things scattered about, reminders of what's in store for us.'

'From my room just now I could see a rather forbidding-looking temple hidden among the trees at the back. Is that one of the reminders?'

'In a way. At least it was originally. When the garden was set out they built just the four columns and the pediment on that little hill as a folly, a ruin. Then much later, early this century, the owner of the house had the temple building constructed behind the ruined front. Resurrecting the imaginary original building, if you like – the building that had never been there.'

'You make it sound like a Frankenstein monster.'

Beamish-Newell gave a thin smile. 'Buildings aren't people. You can do things to them – hack them to bits, reconstruct them, bring them back to life – that wouldn't be acceptable, on the whole, with people.'

There was a tap at the door. The Director called 'Yes', and a young woman in a white coat and white shoes came in. Beamish-Newell introduced Brock to Rose, who impressed him as being bright and alert, eager to please her boss. She shook his hand, gave him a big smile and led him off for a tour of the basement treatment areas.

By the time they reached the gym, Brock was feeling a bit more comfortable about what lay in store for him. Most of the rooms they looked into were occupied by small groups of patients and staff, all of whom seemed absorbed and content. Rose had a knack of making the oddest-sounding procedures sound quite appealing, and even the empty room with the acupuncture couch seemed almost commonplace by the time she had explained it.

'There's more space down here than you'd think,' he said, as he watched her trying to unlock the heavy door in front of them.

'Mmm, it's a bit of a rabbit warren, really,' she agreed, in her strong Ulster accent. 'But you'll soon know your way around, David. Is it all right if I call you David? Most of the patients prefer first names, you know.'

'Of course. Which part of Ireland are you from, Rose?'

'Belfast. Sandy Row, if you know the place.'

'I do,' Brock smiled, then immediately regretted it as the inevitable question followed.

'How come?'

He recalled his short visit several years before, during the course of a murder investigation of an Irish girl in London.

'I visited some friends in Belfast once. They showed me round the area.'

'Then you'll know why I left.'

He smiled vaguely and decided to change the subject, conscious again that he was going to have to work harder at telling lies or avoid having to tell them at all.

'What's this chamber of horrors, then?'

The door swung open at last, and he saw the exercise machines and recognized Kathy's description of the gym which Petrou had been in charge of.

'I don't know if you'll be needing this place. Patients have to use it under instruction because it's just too easy to pull a muscle or do yourself some other injury, and we don't want your family to see you hobbling home in worse shape than when you came.' She had a full, warm laugh. 'Do you have any muscular problems?'

'A bit of a sore shoulder. Dr Beamish-Newell said I'd be needing physiotherapy and acupuncture.'

'Oh well, we'll see whether he wants you to exercise in here, then.'

'Do you look after the gym, Rose?'

'No, Mrs Beamish-Newell has overall charge, of course, but one of the men, Tony, usually supervises.'

Brock surveyed the room. It seemed constricted by the low brick vaults supporting the house above, and the air smelled musty with old sweat as if it was rarely aired.

'I should have mentioned it before, Rose, but I think we may have a friend in common.'

'Really?'

'Yes, her name's Kathy. I met her unexpectedly in London not long ago, and when I told her I was coming here she said to say hello to you.'

'Kathy, you say?' Rose frowned, puzzled.

'Kathy Kolla. She's in the police.'

Brock saw Rose's expression freeze.

'She mentioned that you had written to her a while ago and she felt guilty that she had never replied. Something about her having been taken off the case and not able to do much to help. She did say, though, that, off the record, she shared your concerns, and if there was any new information she'd like to hear about it. You could either contact her direct, or you could tell me about it and I'll pass it on. That's what she said.'

'I see.' Brock caught the reserve in her eyes and voice. Outside in the corridor he could hear the sound of people leaving the afternoon therapy sessions. 'It was to do with the young man who died suddenly here, wasn't it? I read about it in the papers, I remember.'

Rose hesitated, the vivacity gone from her face. Brock scratched his beard and pressed on, trying to get some response before they were interrupted. 'That must have been a terrible thing. Did you know him well?'

'Quite well,' she said after a pause, then added, 'This was his gym – he was in charge of it before Tony.'

'Ah. What was his name?'

'Alex ... Alex Petrou,' she said, and at that moment the heavy door swung open and Brock met the eyes of another woman in a white coat standing staring at them.

'Rose?' she said sternly.

'This is a new patient, Mrs Beamish-Newell. Mr David Brock.'

The Director's wife nodded and offered her hand to Brock. She had the same cold look of detached appraisal as her husband, but was taking less trouble to put a friendly front on it. 'Come to my office, Mr Brock.' She turned on her heel. Brock gave Rose a little smile as he followed. She made an effort to respond, but her face was troubled, her dark eyebrows lowered in a frown.

Laura Beamish-Newell closed her office door behind Brock, went round the desk and picked up a file. They both stood while she read from it in silence. Through the small semicircular window above her head the afternoon light was dying. When she finally looked up at him, he almost felt disposed to make a full confession. She had intelligent eyes and he noticed they were lightly made up to cover some premature creases. She considered him steadily for a moment as if weighing up whether he was a fraud. 'Take off your dressing gown, Mr Brock, and your slippers. Get on the scales, please.'

She noted his weight, fourteen stone six, and his height, six foot two, then told him to sit down on the metal office chair facing her desk. Remaining standing, she wrapped a strap around his upper left arm and took his blood pressure. Then she took the file back round to the other side of the desk and sat down.

'Are you interested in exercising in the gym?'

'Well, I thought it might be a good idea.'

'It should be all right. But only under Tony's instruction. I'll have a word with him.' Her accent was difficult to pin down, Home Counties probably, but with a trace of something underneath, from the north perhaps. She continued writing, filling in boxes on what looked like a timetable and making notes on a page in the file.

Eventually she made a number of copies on the small photocopier in the corner of the room, put them into a plastic folder and handed them over to Brock. 'This is the information you need for your first week here. We'll review your progress at the end of that time. That is the schedule of your therapy sessions.' She leaned across the desk and indicated with her pen on the timetable. 'There are three sessions each day, at nine, eleven and three; in between you have the morning break, lunch and rest hour, and afternoon free time. A notice of evening talks and other events is posted in the entrance hall outside the dining room. All sessions start promptly, Mr Brock. Please bear that in mind.

'This is information on your dietary programme for the first week,' she continued, indicating another sheet in the folder. Brock stared at it for a moment, trying to make sense of it. It didn't look much like a menu, more like a chemical analysis. The numbers of grams listed in the right-hand column didn't seem very large.

'The first week is crucial. At each meal-time you will find a tray with your name on it waiting for you on the long table in the dining room. Please don't supplement your diet in any way, apart from water and lemon juice. Is that understood?'

There was none of Dr Beamish-Newell's invitation to set out on a great dietary adventure. These were orders, not requests. This was going to be serious.

II

Brock realized just how serious when he collected his tray for dinner that evening and opened the lid. There was a woman in a white coat standing at one end of the long table, a cook perhaps, and he took his tray to her.

'I wondered if there had been some mistake,' he said.

He opened the lid and showed her the solitary glass of water and slice of lemon. She smiled and looked at the label on the tray.

'Mr Brock? No, no mistake, dear. You're on total fast for three days.'

'Three days!'

'That's right, dear. Seventy-two hours. You can look forward to dinner on Thursday night for a real treat.'

'My God. What will it be?'

'Oh, I don't know,' she laughed. 'Something special. Maybe a glass of carrot juice. Sit down anywhere and make some friends.'

Somewhat stunned, he wandered over to a table at which a couple were sitting and asked if he might join them. The man rose stiffly to his feet and extended his hand. He was tall and willowy, and there was an air of exhaustion about him.

'Sidney Blumendale,' he said. 'And this is Martha Price.'

Brock introduced himself and sat down.

'Are you all right, old chap?' Blumendale asked. 'You look a bit pale.'

'I've just had a shock, actually,' Brock said. He lifted the lid of his tray and showed them the glass of water. 'Apparently this is my dinner.'

The two diners smiled. 'Your first day?' Blumendale asked, and Brock nodded.

'You'll feel wonderful after you've got over the first week,' Martha Price assured him.

'You sound as if you've got plenty of experience of the place,' Brock said, eyeing their plates. 'What are you eating? It smells good.'

'It's a vegetable casserole,' Martha told him, 'with a delicious nut crust topping and fresh green salad. But don't think about it.' She was enjoying herself. 'Oh, and this is freshly made carrot juice from the vegetable gardens here. And after the casserole we'll get some stewed apples and cream bran – that's bran with yoghurt and honey.' Of a similar age to her companion, in her sixties, she appeared to have twice his energy and her voice crackled with mischief.

Brock groaned. 'I'm told I can look forward to the carrot juice in three days' time, if I behave myself. How long have you been here to deserve all that?'

'Oh, we practically live here. I started coming five or six years ago, when I was first seriously bothered by this.' She held up a hand with joints swollen by arthritis. 'You wouldn't believe, but I could hardly move with it, and I was only sixty-three. Now it hardly bothers me at all, and that's all due to exercises and acupuncture and, above all, the diet. In the last six months I've even been able to do without my walking stick. So you must behave and do as you're told, David. No cheating!'

Brock guessed he was getting the pep-talk she gave all newcomers and he played along with it, pulling a face and muttering, 'Good for the soul, I suppose.'

'Now, why did you come here if you weren't ready to take it seriously?' she scolded him. 'This isn't a holiday camp, you know. Honestly, some of you men are like little boys. You don't know what real hardship is.'

Brock was beginning to think that Martha Price was a pain, but he nodded ruefully and sipped his water, and after a moment Sidney Blumendale gave a dry little cough and said, 'I first came here in '89, the year after my wife died. Getting a bit run down, you know. Spend ten months of the year here now.'

'The other months he visits his children for as long as they can put up with him,' Martha added, 'and this winter we had a fortnight out of season in Majorca, which we'll be doing again, won't we, Sidney?'

Sidney nodded agreement. From the look of him Brock guessed he didn't dare do otherwise.

'What about you, David?'

'This is my first time. Got a bit of a bad shoulder. Thought they might be able to help.'

'Oh, if anyone can, Dr Beamish-Newell will. He's a wonderful man.' Martha Price's eyes filled with the light of enthusiastic faith.

'Is he? I only met him this afternoon for the first time. He's certainly got an impressive way with him.'

'Bit of a showman,' Sidney murmured, and then, as if he might have been overheard blaspheming, hurriedly added, 'but brilliant, of course, brilliant.'

'His wife's pretty formidable too, isn't she?' Brock tried not to stare at them eating.

'She doesn't put on the kind of pretence you often find in the private health sector,' Martha said with her mouth full, since she was determined to respond immediately to the scepticism she heard in Brock's voice. 'But she's very competent and she cares deeply for her patients, the genuine ones, that is.'

'Sound,' Sidney nodded in agreement. 'Very sound.'

'Isn't everyone genuine, then?' Brock asked. For a moment Sidney was inclined to speak, but seemed deterred by Martha's unexpected silence. She chewed thoughtfully for a moment, then said, 'You'll get the hang of the place after a while.'

Brock saw that he was going to have to be patient, and let the conversation move on to questions about himself, what he did for a living, and where he lived.

'Not far from Dulwich,' he said.

'That's where Mrs Thatcher lives, isn't it?' Martha said. 'What a wonderful woman.'

'Can't say I've ever bumped into her in Boots.'

She shot him a look to see if he was being disrespectful, then went on at some length about her husband, who had been active in local government for a number of years before his death. Her voice was sharp with resentment, above all at the injustice of the stroke which had interrupted his inevitable progress towards becoming mayor and taken him when so many less adequate men had been spared. She also showed Brock a photograph of her only son, Ralph, pronounced *Rafe*, a man of around forty with shoulder-length hair, whom she described as artistic. Sidney waited patiently through this account of her family, although he must have heard it many times before, and at the end rose to fetch them their desserts.

The dining room had been the principal reception room of the original house, with tall glass windows overlooking the gardens, an ornate ceiling and pilastered walls, and a huge central chandelier. On one wall long gilt-framed mirrors flanked a marble fireplace, making the space seem deceptively large. The air resonated with the murmur of conversations at the dozen or more tables.

Brock felt uncomfortable sitting alone with Martha Price. He felt irritated by her and suspected the feeling was mutual, yet she had been there the previous autumn and was just the sort of person whose confidence he should be cultivating. He decided to try again. He thought for a moment and then asked her about her arthritis and how it had been helped by the treatments at the clinic. She told him about her first symptoms and the progress of the disease, at first imperceptible and then frighteningly fast, and her increasing desperation as the relief provided by drug treatments was followed by relapse and further deterioration. While she was speaking, Sidney returned with their puddings but neither of them touched their plates as she went on to describe the painful but steady progress of her recovery after she had discovered Stanhope. Brock was moved, and when she finished and asked him about his own problem with his shoulder, he shook his head, embarrassed, and admitted that it was rather trivial compared to what she had been through. She put her hand on the sleeve of his dressing gown and insisted that he tell them, so he shrugged and made his story sound as interesting as he could.

At the end she smiled and patted his hand, as if she'd just heard a confession, and nodded at Sidney. 'There are two types of visitors here, David,' she said. 'We call them the sheep and the goats. The genuine ones, who are here because they need help like us, we call the sheep. But you'll come across others who are really only here for a break, to lose a few pounds perhaps, because they've heard it's a fashionable place to come or some other reason best known to themselves. They are the goats. They don't really believe in Dr Beamish-Newell's work; in fact you'll hear them laughing at him behind his back. He tolerates them because they bring income to the clinic which he uses to subsidize genuine patients who couldn't otherwise afford to come here. Of course' – she leaned forward and lowered her voice – 'Dr Beamish-Newell is under pressure from the *business* side of the clinic to take them in, to make more money.'

'Ah,' Brock nodded. 'That's Mr Bromley's department, isn't it? I haven't met him yet.'

'Come, come, Martha,' Sidney protested half-heartedly. 'Ben Bromley has his part to play. Place like this needs to be run efficiently, just like any other business.'

'Well,' Martha said, changing the subject as if his remarks

weren't worth the effort of contradiction, 'we'd better get in now if we want good seats.'

'Get in?' Brock asked.

'To the Director's fireside talk. He holds them three or four times a week after dinner. You must go, of course.'

He followed them out of the dining room and across the hallway to another large public room, set out as a sitting room with armchairs and sofas arranged around a blazing fire, and a variety of bentwood chairs behind them making up seating for fifty or more. A more intimate atmosphere than the dining room was created by a lower level of lighting from a few table-lamps around the perimeter of the room. Martha and Sidney made straight for a sofa in front of the fire, but Brock felt he'd had enough of their company for the time being and excused himself. When he returned five minutes later, all the comfortable seats at the front in the glow of the firelight had been taken, so he sat in a chair in a corner at the back. He watched the remaining patients filing in, a few of them young but mainly middle-aged or elderly.

The buzz of conversation died away at the sound of Beamish-Newell's voice outside in the hall, and then he entered, his dark suit conspicuous among the assorted dressing gowns of his audience. He made his way to the fireplace and stood to one side of it. The light from a low table-lamp shone up into his face, and he looked slowly round the room before speaking.

'Tonight,' he said, 'I shall talk about what we mean by the idea of balance in diet.' He paused, letting the warmth of his voice soak into them like the heat from the fire.

After five minutes Brock found his attention wandering. The content of what was being said seemed amateurish science, and the voice was mildly soporific. He looked around the room, examining the attentive faces, trying to decide which were the sheep and which the goats.

After a while he forced his attention back to the figure by

the fireplace. The Director was saying something about grains and pulses, and as Brock tried to pick up the line of argument again, the talk came to an end. For a moment there was silence as Beamish-Newell's dark eyes travelled around the room from one rapt face to another.

'I expect you have some questions.'

No one moved at first, and then a woman towards the back put up her hand. The gesture seemed tentative, but the voice was loud and firm. 'Yes, I do understand about that as a theory, doctor. But the fact is, I've been following this diet for ten days and I feel worse now than I did when I arrived.'

An excited murmur rippled across the chintz chairs. Beamish-Newell showed no reaction.

'I mean, I felt all right before. Now I feel ... well, not right at all. I seem to have no energy. Quite often I feel nauseous.'

Several heads were nodding surreptitious encouragement. 'Yes, yes,' their eyes said, 'that's how it is with us too. Tell him!' Still the Director said nothing, and the murmur stilled into an expectant hush which became tenser as the silence persisted.

Then he spoke. 'That's good,' he said, slowly and firmly, and their eyes widened in surprise. 'That's exactly how it should be.' His gaze was locked on her. 'Did you drink tea, Jennifer?' he challenged her gently, an iron cadence in his velvet voice. She nodded.

'Coffee?'

'Yes, I ...'

'How many cups a day? Five, eight, ten? ... And meat? ... Processed food with a hundred preservatives, colourings, additives? For years you have been filling your body with poisons, Jennifer. It has become a toxic vessel. Your body is *addicted* to poisons,' he accused softly, and the other patients focused on her as if her arms were covered in needle marks. 'And you are surprised that after ten days it is still suffering from the shock of withdrawal. It *must* suffer. If it didn't suffer, you would be getting nowhere.'

Then he turned his gaze away from her and his face filled with immense warmth and charm. 'Champagne for my sham friends,' he said, 'real pain for my real friends.' And a wave of relief and laughter followed his smile around the room.

As soon as Beamish-Newell left, some of the patients started to shuffle out of the room, while others stayed chatting in small groups. Brock made his way across the entrance hall to the reception desk, now closed for the night. On the noticeboard beside it he found the list of current patients which he had spotted earlier when he checked in. Looking round to make sure he wasn't being watched, he unpinned the list, folded it up and put it in the pocket of his dressing gown.

The pay-phone in a converted cupboard down the corridor was unoccupied, and he went inside and dialled. Kathy's voice sounded wonderfully normal. 'How is it, Brock?'

'Dreadful,' he said. 'I'm not sure how much of this I can take.'

'But you've only just got there.' She sounded a good deal less than sympathetic.

'Do you know what they've just given me for dinner? A glass of water! Oh, it had a slice of lemon in it, too.'

She laughed. 'Well, it'll do you good. Anyway, I haven't had time for anything to eat all day.'

'Yes, but that's your choice.' He found himself extremely irritated by her lack of sympathy. 'Look,' he snapped, 'get out that list of who was here last October and I'll read you the names of who's here now.'

'I've got it.'

He began to read through the names. At the end of it they had found only three which appeared on both lists: Martha Price and Sidney Blumendale, plus a Grace Carrington.

'And Martha Price was on the list that Beamish-Newell

gave me of patients who had particularly asked for Petrou,' Kathy added.

'Right, I've met her. There's a Jennifer someone . . .' Brock scanned his list. 'It must be this one, Jennifer Martin, who stood up to Beamish-Newell this evening. Are you sure she wasn't here then?'

'Sorry, no, she wasn't. What do you think of him, Brock?' Kathy's voice was serious.

'I don't know, Kathy. He's quite a performer. I imagine he could be a bastard if he didn't get his own way. Did anyone say anything to you about sheep and goats when you were here?'

'What?'

'Never mind. I'd better go.'

'See you Thursday?'

'If I survive that long.'

As he slammed down the receiver he realized he was still annoyed with her, and he recollected his earlier irritation with Martha Price. He thought of Beamish-Newell's sermon and wondered if the poisons were already preparing to leave his toxic vessel.

I2

Whether they were or not, he slept remarkably well, having
resisted the temptation of the bottle of Teacher's in his
suitcase. Next morning he made sure he was one of the first
in the dining room for breakfast, and went down the line of
trays on the long table, identifying the one marked for Grace
Carrington. He sat himself beside the tall windows and gazed
out over the gardens while he waited to see who took up the
tray. He was directly on the central axis of the original
house, an imaginary line which was acknowledged a couple
of hundred yards away by an obelisk, a ghostly needle
floating on the undisturbed white surface of the ground. On
each side the snow-laden shrubs and hedges shone in the
early morning sunlight, which glittered on the icicles suspended from the upper branches of trees and for a few
moments flashed in reflection from the glass doors hidden
among the dark foliage on the hillock over to the left.

Brock sipped at his water and lemon, and allowed himself
a little glow of self-righteousness. The feeling didn't last long,
as his mind turned to the first session marked on his timetable:
'Hydrotherapy' and, ominously, 'Room B52'. His mind again
returned to his first day at big school, waiting for the first
fearful Latin lesson, and the sudden anxiety that he wasn't
dressed properly or had come without some essential item
that everyone else would certainly have.

It was half an hour before Grace Carrington finally claimed
her tray. She was in her early forties, he guessed, a slender
figure in a lime-green tracksuit, with a lean, attractive face,
one which he didn't remember seeing the previous day. Her
hair was brown, cut to her jaw-line and lightly curled, and

her eyes were intelligent and sad. They met his briefly as she turned from the long table, and then she moved to a corner table and sat alone, fingering a glass of orange juice, preoccupied. He didn't feel inclined to disturb her.

Room B52 seemed to live up to its explosive name when Brock opened the door, as clouds of steam burst out and enveloped him. He stripped as he was told, and after the first numbing shock found the alternating hot and cold hip-baths of the Sitz bath treatment surprisingly bearable. He was moved on to soak for a while in a warm mineral bath, and finished the session in a Scottish douche, with jets of hot and cold water pulsing over his spinal column. At each stage his supervisor explained the theory of what was happening to him, the opening and cleansing of the pores of his skin, the improvement to his circulation and stimulation of the underlying muscles. By the time he got dressed again and went upstairs for the mid-morning break, his body was tingling all over in a remarkably pleasant way.

'How are we this morning?' Martha Price's voice piped out from the huddle around the long table where herbal tea was being poured, and he found himself sounding extraordinarily cheerful as he waved a greeting and said he felt good.

'Physiotherapy, B16' came next. At first Brock thought it might be in the subterranean gym he had visited with Rose the previous day, but instead found a bright, sunlit room at the far end of the basement, below the west wing. Couches, a couple of exercise bikes and some exercise frames were arranged round the edge, and there were two physiotherapists who ran the session for half a dozen new patients, beginning with breathing and mild stretching exercises for the whole group, and then going on to individual massage on the couches.

He saw Grace Carrington again in the dining room at lunch-time. He began to make his way towards her with his pathetic tray, but was stopped by a call from Martha and

Sidney, whom he hadn't noticed as he threaded between the tables.

'Sorry, I didn't see you there,' he muttered, taking the chair they offered him.

'Perhaps you were wanting to sit with someone else,' Martha said coquettishly, raising her eyebrow suggestively in the direction of Grace Carrington's corner.

'Not at all.' Brock felt his spleen return. It was hard to decide which of her little acts was more aggravating, the Tartar or the tease.

'You seemed to be more cheerful today, when we saw you earlier.'

'Yes, I feel reinvigorated,' he said. 'I had hydrotherapy first, then physiotherapy. Stress management this afternoon.'

'They're breaking you in gently, David. Will you be having acupuncture later, do you think?'

'Ah.' Brock's sense of well-being suffered a further deflation. Somehow, every time the word 'acupuncture' was mentioned, his mind jumped to Kathy's description of the punctured eyeball of the corpse on the mortuary table. 'Yes, it's on the timetable for later in the week. Thursday, I think.'

'And osteopathy for your shoulder?'

'Yes, that too. Why? Is it uncomfortable?'

'No, no, no.' She patted his arm with the reassuring smile of a veteran, exaggerated enough to raise serious doubts. 'And the fast, how are you coping with that now?' She stared fixedly into his eyes.

'Oh, fine. I think I've more or less come to terms with that.'

'That's splendid. You'll find your stomach will shrink and you'll lose your appetite after a while.'

She smiled winsomely and lifted her fork to her mouth.

'What have you got there?' Brock regretted hearing himself say.

'Golden Slice. It's quite delicious, and so very simple to do yourself. Some finely grated carrot and cheese, and some rolled oats, about equal quantities of each to make up to about a pound in all, then an egg, a couple of ounces of margarine and a little rosemary. Mix them all up with seasoning to taste, but only a little salt of course, and press the mixture into a greased tin and bake at gas mark four for twenty minutes or so until quite browned. Then cut it into slices and serve with a parsley sauce. Isn't it good, Sidney?'

Sidney nodded, scraping up the last of the sauce on his plate.

'And he's a very fussy eater. You must buy some of the Stanhope recipe books before you go, David, so you can try them all at home.'

Brock cleared his throat and sipped at his glass of water. 'The name Stanhope . . .' he began slowly, then paused.

'Yes?' she chirped.

'It was familiar to me, before I came. I wasn't sure why, but then I remembered: it was in the papers last year. Didn't a member of staff have a nasty accident or something? You must have been here then, weren't you?'

'Oh yes, we were here.' Martha lowered her eyes for a moment as if contemplating whether he was yet enough of an insider to be confided in. Mrs Thatcher took over from Mae West as she made up her mind and continued. 'I will not encourage prurient gossip, David,' she said sharply.

'Prurient?' He raised his eyebrows in innocent surprise. 'Was there something . . . unsavoury about it?'

'I sometimes think that Stanhope is like a ship in many ways, don't you? Self-contained, somewhat detached from the everyday world, especially at this time of the year with the countryside so silent and white all around.'

Brock wondered if the thought of prurience had made her lose track of the conversation, but she continued. 'And on a ship, it is not uncommon for gossip to get out of hand, to become . . . overheated. I'm afraid there was some of that here. You may hear stories about Alex Petrou's death which you must simply ignore.'

'Really.' Brock shook his head sadly. 'What sort of stories?' He looked at Sidney encouragingly.

'Well,' Sidney spoke up for the first time since Brock had arrived, 'he was found hanged in the Temple of Apollo, out there in the grounds. Have you been there? Spooky sort of place. And the story is that he not only did it in the middle of the night, but that he first dressed himself up in these –' Sidney cast around for a term he might use '– fetish sort of clothes.'

'That's the sort of unseemly gossip –'

But Brock broke in before Martha's scathing voice could entirely dampen Sidney's prurient imagination. 'That's right, I remember now. It was mentioned in the papers. So he was involved in some kind of sexual perversion, then?'

Martha gave a squawk of protest. Sidney raised his eyes towards the chandelier as if to say, man to man, what would you think?

'With the patients, do you mean?' Brock persisted.

'David!' Martha's outraged voice stopped the conversations at the surrounding tables. 'That is *precisely* the sort of speculation that makes for an unhappy ship!' she spluttered, then registered the puzzled expressions on the faces turned her way.

'But, Martha,' Brock said, in a reasonable tone, 'what was the explanation, then? It seems an odd sort of thing to do to yourself.'

With an effort she brought herself under control and spoke with suppressed indignation. 'Drugs,' she hissed. 'The poor man had come under some very bad influence, outside of the clinic of course, and had taken drugs. He didn't know what he was doing.'

'Ah.' Brock noticed the sceptical pursing of Sidney's mouth. 'Didn't I read that he was gay?' Martha's nostrils flared again and he hurriedly added, 'Nothing wrong with that, of course. So,' he beamed, 'you don't think he was making a bit of extra cash selling drugs and bizarre sex to the patients, then?'

Martha brought her fork down so hard it nearly broke her plate. She rose to her feet.

'How *dare* you' – she struggled to keep her voice down – 'suggest such a vile, *vile* thing, about a *Stanhope* person you never even met!'

She tossed back her head and marched towards the door. Sidney half rose from his seat as if to follow her, then thought better of it and sank down again.

'You're a game sort of chap, aren't you?' he said after a moment.

'Oh dear. As bad as that, eh?'

'Martha's very strong on loyalty, especially to the dead, I've noticed. And to the clinic, of course.'

'I went too far. I'll apologize to her.'

'I'd leave it for a bit if I were you. Just my advice.'

Brock nodded. 'Thanks.'

'I never liked him, myself. Couldn't stand him touching me, for some reason. Wouldn't really have surprised me if he had been up to something odd.'

'Could that have had anything to do with the "goats" among the patients that Martha was talking about yesterday, do you think?'

Sidney's eyes, invariably watery and distant, snapped suddenly into focus, and a worried expression passed across his face. Then he looked away and began to push himself to his feet again. 'No idea,' he muttered. 'Best to drop the subject, old chap, eh?'

Brock smiled and watched him walk stiffly out of the room. Looking round, he saw that Grace Carrington had already gone.

A one-hour rest period was scheduled for the clinic after

lunch each day, and Brock, having no postcards to write or good books to read, was uncertain what to do. The nagging deadline of his forthcoming paper in Rome was making him increasingly uneasy, but he found it hard to think about it in the present circumstances. He wanted to visit the Temple of Apollo, but wasn't sure how to go about getting there across the snowy gardens, dressed as he was. He crossed the hall to the reception desk and asked if he could see Ben Bromley, the Business Manager of the clinic, but was told he was away that day. Brock settled for an appointment on the following day and made his way to the library instead.

This was a much smaller public room, next to the dining room and also facing north across the gardens. It was lined with glass-fronted bookcases, and a leather-topped table occupied the centre. Most of the shelves carried well-worn paperbacks donated by past patients, but one bookcase was marked 'Reference – Not to be Removed' and contained a collection of hardback books, among them a black-bound volume with the title *A History of Stanhope* on its spine. Brock took it from the case and sat down with it at the end of the table.

Though not old – the dedication was dated July 1978 – it belonged to the days just before photocopiers and word processors became ubiquitous, when people still used carbon paper and foolscap sheets, and it had a prematurely dated air about it. It comprised the yellowing carbon-copy pages of the typewritten account of the history of Stanhope House, and more recently of Stanhope Naturopathic Clinic, as compiled by one Felicity Field. It had clearly been a labour of love. Chapter headings such as 'A Herb Garden is Born' and 'The Invalid is Nursed Back to Health' brimmed with coy enthusiasm, and the text was illustrated by many black-and-white photographs glued into the pages. The first was a picture of the south front of the house, with a small figure of Stephen Beamish-Newell just visible between the columns at the top of the entrance stairs, chin up, like Mussolini surveying a party rally. It accompanied the dedication by the Director, which commended the unflagging efforts of Miss Field to record the past of a great landmark of English social and architectural culture at this moment standing at the threshold of an exciting new future.

Miss Field had begun with Stanhope House itself, originally the home of Sir William Stanhope (1698–1752), a member of Lord Burlington's circle. Like Burlington, Stanhope had visited Palladio's buildings in Italy and had determined to promote the revival of his work in England by designing his own Palladian house in the Weald. Where Burlington had taken the Villa Rotonda as the model for his house at Chiswick, Stanhope had chosen the Villa Foscari, known also as the Malcontenta, as Miss Field explained:

> Some would have it that the name *Malcontenta* was local to the site long before Niccolò and Luigi Foscari built their house there. Much more romantic is the story of an ungovernable daughter of the family who was exiled there from the temptations of Venetian society, and whose ghost is said to haunt the house still. Lord Stanhope certainly preferred this latter account. Whichever explanation you choose, the name seems to evoke perfectly the spirit of its setting in the Veneto, so often wreathed in mists and vapours, and it may have been this which persuaded Lord Stanhope when he came to build upon the meadows beside the River Strood.

Stanhope had begun his version of the Malcontenta shortly after Isaac Ware published his translation of Palladio's *Four Books on Architecture* (as Miss Field noted, 'from Scotland Yard, in 1737'), which was dedicated to Richard, Earl of Burlington, and for which Stanhope was one of the original subscribers. After Stanhope's death, his son commissioned Humphry Repton to landscape the estate in 1796, and followed his father's taste for things both classical and elegiac by instructing Repton to include in his scheme a series of monuments, 'modest yet sublime', on the theme of *memento mori*. Miss Field helpfully provided a list of these, and a little map showing where they might be discovered about the grounds. One of them was to be a ruin of four Ionic columns standing on a knoll to the north-west of the house, based on Palladio's drawing of the ancient Temple of Fortuna Virilis in Rome. These columns later became incorporated as the front of the Temple of Apollo, built, along with the west wing, by the architect Albert Fusy in 1910 for the industrialist who then owned Stanhope House. Miss Field obviously relished the quotation which she provided from Pevsner's Buildings of England series concerning these additions, as 'unfortunate efforts which, taken with Fusy's contemporaneous remodelling of much of the interior of the original house, can only be described as mutilations of what had been one of the finest neo-classical houses in the country'.

Brock skimmed to the end of Miss Field's account of the history of the building, with its decline into neglect after the Second World War, 'a home for spiders and mould'. At this point the library door opened and a man came in. He nodded to Brock and went over to one of the bookcases. His hair was longish and wavy over a pugnacious, fleshy face, and his dressing gown looked as if it had been tailored in Savile Row, a piece of double-breasted power-dressing which gave him none of that air of comfortable domestication that most patients quickly slipped into. From the top pocket he drew out a pair of spectacles which he brought up to his face with a flourish, accompanied by a frown of concentration and thrust of the chin, all of which looked to Brock more like a display of male dominance than a serious attempt to focus on the paperback titles.

Brock resumed his reading, skipping through the herculean efforts of Dr and Mrs Beamish-Newell to restore the house, to clear the jungle which they found within the walled garden and re-establish the organic cultivation of vegetable and herb beds in soil which had never known modern chemical herbicides or pesticides, and to rationalize the land holdings around the house.

'Interested in ancient history, eh?' The voice from behind his left shoulder was deep and sonorous, as if its owner was a heavy cigar smoker or had just woken up. Brock looked at him.

'Just browsing, really,' he said, and offered his hand. 'David Brock.'

'Norman de Loynes,' the man introduced himself and sat down beside Brock. 'You're a new boy, I gather. Overheard your little contretemps with Lady Martha at lunch just now. Couldn't help it, I was sitting at the table behind you. She's an impossible cow, isn't she? I call them S & M, the two of them, although they're the wrong way round of course, Sidney being an irredeemable masochist. Have to be, to put up with her. I sometimes amuse myself, when I have to sit through some tedious discussion about fruit and nuts or how to defecate in a bio-friendly way, by imagining her in the role of Madame Lash. Frightening thought, eh?'

De Loynes chuckled playfully until he had raised a grin from Brock. Then the smile vanished from his face and he said abruptly, 'What's your interest in Alex Petrou?'

Brock stared at the book in the man's hand and noted the title, *Showdown at Purple Gulch*. 'Who?'

'The fellow who died here last year. You were asking about him.'

'Oh, yes. Just curiosity. I remembered reading the newspaper reports.'

'They had a field day, of course.'

'Martha Price seems to feel he was maligned.'

'Oh, he pandered to her, I expect. He was good at amusing the ladies. He was a charmer when he wanted to be.'

'You're a regular here, obviously.'

'Mmm. I knew him quite well, if that's what you mean.

Great shock when he went, of course.' He didn't sound greatly disturbed.

'Yes, it must have caused quite a stir. Were you here at the time?'

De Loynes nodded. 'Police turned the place upside down. They were very thorough – remarkably so, really. Since then we've been the poorer without young Alex,' he added. 'He brought a certain something that we lack. There's a fatal streak of the moral puritan in most of the people who come here. Makes them dull as weak tea. Or perhaps that appeals to you?'

It seemed to be a challenge, and Brock smiled. 'No, no. I think I know what you mean. But maybe it's the diet. After a couple more days on water and lemon juice, I'll be taking to weak tea like strong meat.'

De Loynes laughed, a braying sound, head back. 'My dear chap, we'll have to look after you. After the initiation period, Stephen will start you on a few vitamins, get you going again. Then we'll have to find you something more satisfying to get your teeth into.'

He got to his feet. 'Glad to catch up with you, David. We'll meet again . . . Oh.' He stopped on his way to the door and looked back. 'Have you spoken to Ben Bromley yet? He's worth having a chat to, if you're interested –' he gestured at Felicity Field's book in front of Brock '– in what goes on in this place.'

'As a matter of fact, I've got an appointment to see him tomorrow, Norman.'

'Good, excellent. Entertaining fellow, our Ben. Small, but perfectly formed.' He smiled maliciously. 'See you.'

Brock watched the door close behind him, grimaced and took a deep breath. He lowered his head, staring at the book but not seeing it. *De Loynes wasn't on Kathy's list. He was here last October, but he wasn't on her bloody list.*

Brock shook his head and blinked. Focusing on the page in

front of him, he noticed a photograph captioned 'Dr and Mrs Beamish-Newell soon after the opening of Stanhope Clinic to the first patients – September 1977'. The Director looked considerably more youthful, his face leaner and beardless, his hair thicker and longer. Standing beside him was a dark-haired beauty not remotely similar to Laura Beamish-Newell.

Frowning, his mind still preoccupied by de Loynes, Brock thumbed back through the book, looking for further references to what presumably was Beamish-Newell's first wife. Eventually he found her name, Gabriele, and a short account of their meeting and falling in love when he was a medical student at Cambridge and she an Italian studying English at one of the language schools in the city. From her subsequent comments, Miss Field gave most of the credit for selecting Stanhope House for the new clinic to Gabriele, and invited the reader to note how wonderfully appropriate this choice was, given that the Director's young wife originated from the same region of northern Italy from which Palladio himself had come.

Brock shrugged and snapped the book shut, his face still set in a frown as he thought about de Loynes. When he returned the history to its place among the reference books, he searched for and found a copy of *Who's Who*. The de Loynes family had three entries: a brigadier, an MP, and their nephew Norman, aged forty-six, an orthopaedic surgeon. *Norman the goat*, Brock thought, and swung the glass front of the bookcase closed.

Stress management was run by an intense, wiry, middle-aged woman who made her class very nervous by insisting that they begin by opening up individually to the group, sharing some particular fear. Brock confessed that he was haunted by the thought of standing in front of a huge, expectant audience and discovering that both his mind and the pages of notes he had brought were inexplicably blank.

The therapist nodded vigorously and told him that he had a fear of exposure.

After this awkward beginning there was a period of theory on the causes of stress and the biochemical effects of flight-or-fight conditioning. One by one the patients' faces went politely blank, until they were each given a questionnaire to assess their own stress level. 'Have you tried to track a murderer during the past few days?' didn't figure among the questions, and since he hadn't recently divorced, moved house, lost his job or a close relative, Brock's score was shamefully low.

Finally there were techniques for stress management, particularly relaxation, and this at least was outstandingly successful. Each patient lay still on the floor, head on a small pillow, eyes closed, following the instructions on breathing, then muscle relaxation, and finally calming the mind, and before long the woman's mellifluous voice was accompanied by first one, then several nasal murmurings, which grew steadily in volume as she led the patients who remained awake through an idyllic summer woodland of the imagination.

As he came out of the room, Brock caught sight of Grace Carrington's lime-green tracksuit disappearing down the basement corridor. He followed her and came at last to the door at the end of the west wing, which led outside to the gardens. He noticed the sharp smell of fresh air in the corridor, something he had become unused to in the overheated atmosphere of the house. On the doormat was some snow, blown in when she had left. A pair of white slip-on shoes, still warm from her feet, lay beside the mat, and next to them half a dozen pairs of wellington boots, together with a collection of umbrellas and walking sticks, all presumably available for casual use by patients. Hanging from a row of pegs above were a number of bright orange anoraks.

Brock helped himself to the largest size of boots and coat

he could find, selected a round-handled walking stick and stepped out into the cold afternoon. The lungful of crisp air made him dizzy, and he had to blink and adjust to the outdoors, as if shaking himself awake after a deep sleep. Her footprints were quite clear, curving away along the snow-covered gravel path which led up towards the knoll and the Temple of Apollo.

13

Brock crunched through the snow after Grace Carrington, all the way to the front steps of the temple, and saw where she'd kicked her boots clean at the threshold. The tall glass-panelled doors, their timber frames slightly twisted through years of neglect, creaked complainingly as Brock pulled them open, and he heard the sound echo within. There was no sign of her in the upper chamber and, as his eyes grew more accustomed to the dim light, Brock moved forward, his boots clumping on the marble floor panels until he reached the swastika grille. Still .no indication that she was there, except perhaps the faintest trace of soap or perfume in the dank air.

He found the small spiral staircase leading to the lower chamber and made his way awkwardly down, his clumsy rubber boots too large for the triangular stone treads. When he reached the bottom he didn't notice her at first. She was standing motionless in front of the organ console below the grille, exactly where Alex Petrou had been found. In the shadow of the recess her face was very pale, a hand raised to her mouth, her eyes wide with fright, and she looked as if she were about to scream.

'Good lord!' Brock said. 'You gave me a start.'

'Who are you?' she whispered.

'Brock, David Brock. I'm new here. Only arrived yesterday. I was just exploring. Are you all right?'

She took in his orange anorak and wellington boots, just like hers.

'Yes.' He heard her take a deep breath. 'You scared me. I heard the sound of the front door, then your footsteps and the tapping of your stick. And then I heard you coming down the stairs. I suddenly felt very frightened. Stupid . . .'

'Oh no, I can imagine exactly what it must have sounded like. This is a very spooky sort of place. Mind you, I'm finding everything a bit strange at the moment.'

'I'm sorry –' she stepped out of the darkness towards him '– my name is Grace Carrington.' They shook hands formally. 'Actually, I have seen you. I think your room is close to mine.' She sounded faint, a wraith that might fade away at any moment.

'Ah. I was in the library after lunch,' Brock said, trying to fill the chill space around them with the confidence of his voice, 'and I found a history of the house and the estate. It mentioned this place, so I thought I'd take a look. The Temple of Apollo.' He gave a snort, as if to dispel any lingering miasmas with his scepticism.

'He was the god of music,' she said, indicating the organ console behind her.

'Yes, and of the healing art – appropriate for a clinic, I suppose. Identified also with the sun, both as the giver of life and the destroyer. It's amazing how many jobs they were able to hold down in those days.'

She managed a smile. 'You're finding it a bit strange here, you said.'

'Yes. It's my first time. It all seems quite odd.'

'You'll soon get used to it. And when you come to leave, you'll find that the world outside seems equally strange at first.'

'In what way?'

'I found I'd become . . . detached from it.'

'So you've done this a few times?'

Grace shivered suddenly. 'Let's go upstairs,' she said, and made for the foot of the stairs. 'This is my third visit. I'm not as much a regular as Martha or Sidney – I saw you talking to them at lunch-time today.'

'Yes.' Brock's voice became muffled as he climbed the

spiral staircase. 'I think Martha decided to take me under her wing.'

Grace was standing at the top, waiting for him, and smiled again at the expression on his face. 'She has a habit of doing that with new people. She'll let you go after a bit.'

'I think I may have already exhausted her patience. I got her a bit upset today.'

'Did you? How did you manage that?' They began walking slowly back up the nave.

'I recalled seeing something that was reported in the papers last year, about one of the staff here who was found hanged. In this building.'

Grace stopped and turned towards him, looking carefully at his face. 'Yes. What did you say?'

'I was just trying to find out what she thought really happened. I'm afraid she was offended, thought I was casting aspersions on the man.'

Grace turned away, saying nothing at first. Then, 'I was here, too.'

Brock waited for her to say more, and when nothing came he spoke carefully, pitching his voice lower. 'Just now, Grace, when I came upon you down there, it occurred to me that you must be standing in the actual place where he was found.'

She didn't acknowledge his comment for a long while. Eventually she turned towards him again and said, 'I think many of us . . . would like to know what happened.'

'Martha said drugs.'

'That's what they said at the inquest. But you've seen what it's like down there . . . Knowing him, it's hard to believe.'

They paused for a moment outside the doors, in the space behind the four Ionic columns of the temple front.

'These columns were here for a hundred years before the temple was built,' Grace said, resting her hand on the fluted surface of one of them, picking at some lichen with her nail.

'They were meant to be a ruin, you see, something to be contemplated from the house, or while strolling in the gardens. To remind you of the passage of time, of your mortality.'

'Yes, that was mentioned in the book I was reading in the library,' Brock said. 'And you know about the other things, too?'

'No. What other things?'

'The ruin was just one of a series of *mementi mori* – is that the plural? According to the book, the others should still be around somewhere in the grounds. I thought I might mount an expedition at some point to try and track them down.'

She smiled. 'That's a nice idea. You must tell me what you find.'

'Why not join me? In this weather it might be safer to explore in pairs in case one of us gets lost in the drifts.'

She didn't answer and they set off towards the house, the silence broken only by the sound of their footsteps until Brock said, 'I met someone else today who said he was here last October when that chap died. Norman de Loynes. Did you meet him then?'

'Yes, I do remember him. He made himself unpopular with some of the staff. A cleaner, I think. He was quite arrogant about something, as far as I remember – he's not a friend of yours, is he?'

'No, no.' Brock's eyes had been studying their original footprints as they retraced their steps, the deep grip of the soles of their boots showing up as two different patterns. He noticed that there was also a third pattern of footprints, with a distinctive diamond-shaped heel mark, heading towards the temple and in some places obliterating the tracks which Brock and Grace had left. Brock stopped and stared back towards the knoll, but he couldn't see anyone. As they approached the door to the west wing, this third set of tracks could be seen curving in towards them from the direction of the car park, its origins lost in the slush of the roadway.

'All right,' Grace said as they closed the door behind them and started pulling off their outdoor clothes. She was quicker than Brock and finished while he was still wrestling with his anorak. 'I'll come on your expedition. When do you want to go?'

'What about tomorrow afternoon?'

She nodded. 'I'll meet you down here,' and she walked quickly away down the corridor.

After dinner that evening a video, *On Golden Pond*, was shown in the drawing room for the patients. Brock skipped both dinner and video and, tucking into yet another glass of water, forced himself to do some work on his paper.

The following morning's treatment sessions were a repeat of the previous day's, with hydrotherapy followed by physiotherapy and massage. He had little opportunity to talk to the staff involved, and saw no sign of Rose, whom he had been hoping to meet again.

At two, after the lunch hour, the patients dispersed, some to their rooms to rest, others to the drawing room to read the morning papers or to the games room to play a hand of cards. Brock went to the reception desk to keep his appointment with Ben Bromley. The receptionist lifted the counter flap for him and led him to a door at the back of her office, knocked and showed him in. Expecting the converted storecupboard that Kathy had described, Brock was surprised by a generous office, with a large window overlooking the gravelled terrace at the front of the house. The furniture and fittings appeared to be recently delivered and, unlike everywhere else in the building, were coordinated with each other. There was a pungent smell of new carpet, and another smell as well, elusive and enticing, which Brock couldn't quite identify until he saw, incongruous in the middle of the large executive desk, a hot meat pie and a bottle of beer.

The receptionist, taking no notice of them, said, 'Have a seat, Mr Brock. Mr Bromley has just stepped out. He'll be back in a sec.'

Brock sat down, mesmerized by the shockingly blatant display on the desk. He wondered if this was some kind of test, if Beamish-Newell might be watching him on a hidden camera, waiting to see if he would break down and hurl himself at the forbidden fruit.

Bromley bustled in after a while, cheerfully shook Brock's hand and went round to sit in the large, pneumatically operated chair behind the desk. His aftershave was powerful. 'Sorry about this,' he said, gesturing towards the pie and beer. 'I got held up in town, negotiating with the stoats and weasels at the bank. Went on much longer than I'd expected, and I missed my lunch. You've had yours, I suppose?'

Brock nodded. 'Please, go ahead. Don't let it get cold.' He tried to drag his eyes away.

'Well, if you really don't mind, I might just do that. I'm ravenous, as a matter of fact. Always does that to me, talking about money.' Bromley grinned and bit a large chunk out of the pie. While he chewed, he carried on talking. 'Well now, David, mmm, mmm, what can I do for you?'

Brock coughed, clearing the saliva in his throat. 'Well . . . it was Dr Beamish-Newell who suggested I might speak to you. About the possibility of investing in the clinic. Then I was speaking to Norman de Loynes, and he suggested the same thing.'

'Mmm, mmm.' Bromley nodded vigorously, licked his lips and took another bite of pie. Gravy oozed down his chin. 'Good idea. Stephen did mention you to me. This is your first visit, I understand.'

'Yes. I must admit I'm pretty new to all this. I really don't know a lot about it. I only arrived on Monday.'

'Mmm. Well, I imagine the Director has been painting the picture, mmm, of the health side of things. Obviously, what

Stanhope has to offer in that respect is a very superior product. Maybe unique. What has probably also become apparent to you is that Stanhope is a community of like-minded people. That's a very important part of the philosophy, mmm; it's not just some sort of sterile out-patient facility or a commercial fat-farm.'

Bromley nodded at his own words and paused briefly to take a swig from the beer bottle and another bite from the remains of the pie. 'But the third aspect of Stanhope, mmm, mmm, which may not be so apparent up front, David, is that it is also a very sound business enterprise. I'll show you figures in a tick. Three things, you see — health, community and enterprise. Together they create a really special investment context.'

He let that sink in while he finished the pie, screwed up the foil tray and tossed it into his waste-paper basket. 'Smashing,' he said.

Brock regretfully tore his eyes away from the piece of foil and returned his attention to the man swallowing beer behind the desk. He noticed that Bromley had some kind of skin trouble around his nose and eyebrows, which gave his chubby face a slightly inflamed look. 'But isn't the clinic a charity? Can you *invest* in a charity?'

Bromley wiped the back of his hand across his mouth and gave Brock a cunning smile. 'Good point, David. Good point. The Stanhope Foundation is a registered charity, yes. The Stanhope Naturopathic Clinic and the Stanhope Trust are not. It's a matter of allowing people to participate in the affairs of Stanhope in many different tax-effective ways, according to their needs and inclinations — as patient, trustee, donor, shareholder or Friend.'

'Friend?'

'I imagine that may be what Stephen and Norman had in mind when they suggested you speak to me, David. We have a limited class of membership of the Stanhope community which we call "Friends of Stanhope". You might say they are all the other categories rolled into one. They pay an annual fee, which makes them shareholders in the enterprise, and also partly goes to support the charitable work of the Foundation. In return, the Friends have access to the range of Stanhope facilities on a privileged basis. They can come here for short stays, for example, at discount rates, and have access to the therapeutic treatments they require, on a one-off basis or not, as they wish. It's like a club, David. They can drop in for a weekend, unwind, meet their pals. That might suit you quite well, a single man – a retreat from the stresses and strains of the city? They have their own lounge upstairs,' he chuckled and winked at Brock. 'The dumb waiter that serves the dining room from the kitchen downstairs goes on up to the Friends' lounge, you see. They make their own arrangements with the kitchen.'

'Ah, yes, I can see the merit in that. Well . . . as I said, Ben, I'm still finding my feet here at the moment, but it certainly sounds an interesting concept. I think I should find out a bit more.'

Bromley nodded. 'Health, community and enterprise, David. It combines the three essential ingredients of Stanhope in a unique way.'

'I would have thought the business enterprise side might have been at odds with the other two aspects, though? I mean, I didn't get the impression from Dr Beamish-Newell that making money was a priority.'

'What did you think of him?' Bromley tilted back in his chair and eyed Brock over the neck of the bottle with a mischievous, and maybe slightly sly, grin.

'He was very impressive, from the one meeting we had. "Charismatic" is probably the word.'

'Charismatic.' Bromley nodded solemnly. 'Yes, you're right there, David. He's a brilliant man in his field, a wonderful asset to the clinic. That's his role. The money side isn't of great concern to him. That's left to drones like me. But we're all part of a team, some of us more visible than others, but all with our roles to play.'

'Ye-es.' Brock sounded doubtful. 'I'm sure you do. But in the end, this place really *is* Dr Beamish-Newell, isn't it? I just wondered about that, when the idea of investing came up.'

'How do you mean, David?'

'Well, what would happen if something happened to him? I mean, supposing it turned out one day that he'd killed someone, Ben?'

'Eh?' Ben froze, and then came upright, as if his chair were ejecting him, but in slow motion. He stared at Brock, and, when Brock didn't offer anything more, said, 'What the hell does that mean, David?'

'Well, that sort of thing can happen to doctors, can't it? Some unfortunate accident, a patient with a weak heart and aggrieved, litigious relatives. It happens all the time these days, doesn't it?'

'Oh . . . yes, I get your drift. I thought for a moment there you were suggesting . . .' He leaned back and his seat sighed under him. 'I take your point, David. As a potential investor, you would naturally be worried about a one-man organization that could fall apart overnight if that one man got fed up with the whole thing, ran off with the milkman's wife or, as you say, had some kind of accident. Am I reading your mind?'

He wasn't, but Brock nodded anyway.

'That would have been the case until five or six years ago, David. I certainly wouldn't have been interested in throwing any of my hard-earned cash into this place before that.' Bromley gave a knowing smile, rotated the beer bottle to make sure it was quite empty, then sent it flying into the basket.

'Absolutely no financial control,' he continued. 'What passed for books were a joke. I'm saying this in a spirit of openness, David, not by way of criticism of Stephen. That just wasn't his forte. His strengths lay elsewhere, and he had the good fortune to meet up with Sir Peter Maples at just the time when he most needed him. Sir Peter was able to harness his business acumen to the good doctor's vision and set the clinic up on a sound, long-term footing, one that others can feel comfortable about participating in. Dr Beamish-Newell is part of a team now – an important part, of course, responsible for the health programmes, just as I'm responsible for implementing the business plan and for the ongoing financial management. But not an indispensable part.

'That's what I meant just now about the team,' Bromley went on, staring up at the ceiling pensively. 'I've learned, from my experience of many different kinds of businesses, large and small, that charismatic people, essential as they may be to provide the initial dynamic, in the end are only as strong as the team they are able to form around them. And we have a very strong team here, David.'

Bromley frowned. 'In any organization, after a certain stage is reached, the enterprise can do without the charismatic leader, but the charismatic leader cannot do without the team. That's my point, David. Believe me, it's true what they say about no one being indispensable. I've learned that the hard way.'

'True enough,' Brock remarked sadly. 'Well, is there a prospectus for the Friends, Ben?'

'Not exactly, David, but I do have some information on the financial side.' He swung his stocky figure out of the chair, went over to a filing cabinet and extracted a file. He passed Brock a single sheet of paper. 'That's the current figure for this year.'

Brock read the top line and blinked. The annual fee appeared to be about equivalent to what he earned in two months.

'Part of the fee can be designated contributions to a charity and so attracts tax relief, David, and part is a share purchase, attracting future dividends. The calculations give an illustration of the bottom line for a typical contributor, but you'd want to go through that yourself with your accountant.'

'Yes, yes. That's interesting. And how does one apply?'

'As I said, it's like a club. An existing member has to nominate you, and the membership as a whole has to accept you. It's a small group, like-minded.'

'Do you have a list of members?'

Bromley smiled. 'Only for members' eyes, David. But I think you can take it that you've already met one of them.'

'Aha. What about women? I got the impression when you were talking just now that the Friends were predominantly men?'

'They are all men, as it happens. No reason why there shouldn't be a woman, of course. Just haven't been any nominated so far. Stephen mentioned you work in the Home Office, David.'

Brock nodded. 'You've given me plenty to think about, Ben. I'd better get off to my afternoon therapy session now and let you get on with your work.'

Bromley relaxed in his chair. 'What's the torture this afternoon, David?'

'Yoga.'

Bromley grinned. 'Did you hear what happened to the india-rubber woman who went out with the pencil salesman?'

'No, I can't say –'

Brock was spared by the receptionist, who put her head round the door to remind Bromley of his next appointment. They shook hands and Brock was given another folder of brochures on his way out.

When the afternoon session was finished, Brock collected his overcoat, gloves and scarf from his room in preparation for his walk with Grace Carrington. She was waiting by the basement door and laughed when she saw his gear.

'I did the same.' She showed him her woollen mittens, scarf and hat, all striped in bright rainbow colours. 'I hope you've got a map or something.'

When they had pulled on their boots, Brock produced a piece of paper from his coat pocket with a flourish. 'Copied it myself. The locations are marked by the crosses and numbers.'

'Very impressive. Come on, then.'

She pushed the door open. Cold air caught their nostrils and turned their breath to steam.

'Oh, it's wonderful!' Grace called back over her shoulder to him. Sunlight came pouring out of a blue sky and was reflected blindingly from every snow-covered surface. Brock pulled the door shut behind him and crunched after her.

They walked round to the front of the house, where the drive broadened into a forecourt in front of the entrance steps. On the far side of this area, two rows of cypress trees formed a narrow avenue, now unused and overgrown, leading to the east.

'Along this avenue somewhere,' Brock called, puffing to keep up with her, 'there should be some fragments.'

They found them half-way down on the left: several large stone capitals tilted at odd angles, partly buried in snowdrifts.

'Looks as if the builders of the house had a few left over,' Brock said, but Grace shook her head.

'Wrong type. These are Corinthian, whereas the ones on the columns of the house and the temple are Ionic. They're too big, as well. It's disturbing, seeing them scattered on the ground like that,' she added, 'knowing that they belong high up on top of columns. You feel as if some catastrophe has happened.'

They walked on to the end of the avenue, where a stone pyramid, about the height of a man, blocked their route.

'Well, this one seems clear enough,' Brock said. 'Egyptian monument to the dead.'

'Or Roman: the Pyramid of Cestius, for example.'

'You're good at this.'

'I used to teach art history. Long ago.'

There seemed only one way forward, through a gap in a hedge, and they found themselves in a garden of overgrown shrubs whose snow-laden branches barely gave them room to pass through. The bushes thinned out, and they came to a clearing with a stone bench facing an old sprawling yew tree. Beneath it stood a large block of stone, tilting slightly where the roots of the tree had unsettled it.

Grace brushed the snow off the bench and sat down while Brock went forward to examine the monument. 'It looks a bit like an altar,' he said, ducking his head under the branches of the yew to get closer to it. Then, noticing that in fact it wasn't a solid block but had a heavy stone lid, he said, 'No, it's more like a sarcophagus. There's some lettering carved into the front.'

'What does it say?' Grace called to him.

'*Et in Arcadia ego.*' Brock spelled it out to her. '*And in Arcadia I.* What is that supposed to mean? I can't believe that anyone actually ever spoke this language. It's like trying to decipher a crossword puzzle. This doesn't even have a verb.'

'That's the point.' Grace's voice came softly from behind him. 'The ambiguity adds to the meaning.'

Something in her tone made him pause and look back at her. Through the branches of the yew he saw tears streaming down her cheeks. He hurried back and sat beside her on the bench. 'Grace, whatever is the matter?'

She shook her head and quickly brushed her face with her glove. After a while she took a deep breath and spoke. 'My first visit to Paris was with my husband, before we were married. It was a wonderful trip, just the way it should be – it was spring, we were in love, you know . . . Anyway, in the Louvre we saw a famous painting by Poussin. It shows a group of shepherds in Arcady standing around a tomb which they've just discovered, like us. On the tomb are the words *Et in Arcadia ego*.'

She shrugged and her voice became more businesslike, matter-of-fact. 'You could imagine the verb in the past tense, *And I was in Arcady*, as if the person in the tomb was speaking to us from the past, you know, *Think of me; I used to live here too, just like you*. On the other hand, the verb could be in the present tense, in which case it isn't the dead person talking, but death itself. *Remember, even in Arcady, I am here*.'

'Yes, I see,' Brock nodded. 'You *are* good at this. But why does it upset you?'

She said nothing for a while, and he watched her stubborn profile staring fixedly at the snow at her feet.

'I'm going to die,' she whispered at last.

He was stunned. 'What do you mean?'

She struggled to compose herself. 'Everyone's going to die, of course, we all know that. Only we don't, not really. We just don't believe it's ever really going to happen. But I know it's going to happen to me. I've been picked.'

'Picked?' Brock was conscious of how tense and still their bodies were.

'When I was a girl, a teenager,' she whispered, and she suddenly sounded very weary, 'I remember reading about a village in Spain during the Civil War. Was it in Hemingway? I don't know, I was reading him about then, I think . . . Anyway, this village was high up on the side of a mountain, and there was a sheer cliff on one side of the village square. When one side won control of the village, all the people who had supported the other side were picked out, and one by one they were carried to the edge of the cliff and thrown over.'

She paused as if watching the scene projected on to the white surface of the ground.

'I was horrified, imagining what it must have been like, waiting for your turn, watching the others lifted up, struggling and begging and screaming, and then disappearing over the edge. And then seeing the eyes turning on you, realizing it's *you* now, feeling their hands on *you*, carrying *you* towards the void.'

Grace stopped for breath, trembling, and Brock waited, silently.

Another deep breath, like an immense sigh. 'I have cancer, David. That's it. I have cancer.'

'Oh, Grace, I'm . . .'

'They first detected it last June. A tumour in my side. I had chemotherapy through the summer and it seemed to work. I lost all my hair and felt like a wet rag, but I was in the clear. I knew it was going to be all right. I came here a couple of times to help with the recuperation.

'Then last month I went for a check-up. My hair had been growing back and I had more energy, though I still kept feeling exhausted. In a way I enjoyed that. It reminded me of what I had overcome, and made me feel that my body was recovering. But they discovered that the cancer had survived after all, and it had spread all over, deep, malignant. And I began to realize, from what they said and the way they said it, that it wasn't going to be all right after all.'

She half turned her head and looked into his eyes. 'I shan't be here for summer. I shall be gone, into the void.'

Brock turned away, unable for a moment to meet her gaze. 'Grace . . . I'm so sorry.'

'The thing that really brought it home to me, that really made me feel so terrified, was the way Winston and the boys took it. Winston is my husband.'

She took another deep breath. 'We have two boys – Richard, who's eighteen, and Arthur, who's sixteen. Anyway, they were very sympathetic and caring and everything, just like the first time. Only ... I began to see that they were taking it in their stride. They'd already had a dress rehearsal, thinking they were going to lose me, and now they knew how to deal with it. It was as if they just went straight to the recovery stage, as if they'd already gone through denial, grieving and all the rest, and didn't need to do it again.

'For me it was the complete opposite of the first time, when I'd been distracted from worrying about myself by worrying about how they would cope without me. That first time I'd told Winston he mustn't feel guilty about marrying again when I was gone, because I didn't see how he'd manage on his own. He told me not to say things like that, but now I realize that he did think about it, and now I don't think I like it any more. Oh, it's not that he wants me to die or anything. I'm sure he'd do anything to save me, if he could – it was he who suggested I come here. It's just that in his mind he's already moved ahead to when he'll be a single man again, and I think he doesn't find the idea all that unbearable. I find it difficult to face my women friends now, especially the single ones, without wondering if their being so solicitous has something to do with the fact that there'll be an attractive spare man in my house in a month or two who'll need helping out.'

She sighed. 'Doesn't that sound dreadful? I even imagine them asking me if I'll leave him to one of them in my will. It isn't really jealousy exactly. I feel as if I were sitting in a train in the station, and Winston and the boys are alongside me in another train, and we can talk to each other through the open windows, just as if we were all together. But pretty soon our trains will leave the station and continue their journeys, and we all know that the tracks will separate and go off in different directions. I have a terrible sense of panic, of loss, that I won't be with them any more, that they will go their way without me. Maybe that's what jealousy is, really, the thing that makes it hurt so much. It's also fear. I'm absolutely terrified, David. It wasn't like this the first time at all. I was brave, or at least I seemed to be able to act bravely. Perhaps I was just in shock. Now I seem to have completely lost my nerve. And the calmer and more considerate they become, the more I panic. That's why I had to get away from them for a while.'

It occurred to Brock that, for someone who had spent half his life investigating sudden death, supposedly an expert in the subject, he had absolutely nothing useful to say to her.

'Grace, I feel so stupid suggesting we come out here . . .' He waved his arm at the sarcophagus.

'No,' she put her hand on his arm. 'I'm glad you suggested it. It isn't morbid. I really want to come to terms with it. That's why I was in the temple yesterday. I wanted to try to understand what had been in Alex Petrou's mind.'

Brock had originally planned to turn the conversation to this. It was the reason why he had suggested their walk. Now he no longer wanted to pursue it with her. Yet it took them on to slightly easier ground, away from the impossibly oppressive facts of Grace's story. 'Do you feel he could have known what he might be facing?' he asked.

'That's what I've been trying to decide. Did he know? He had such style! He made everyone else seem timid, tongue-tied, rather provincial, as if he belonged to a wider, more expansive, more exciting world. I've been trying to imagine, if he had known that he was at risk in some way, would he have behaved differently? Or would he have gone on being the same, risking everything, daring the fates?'

'You felt he was a risk-taker?'

'Oh yes, I'm sure he was! I remember some old dears driving back to the clinic one day and arriving in a terrible state because they'd met Alex on the road on his motor bike.

He drove like a bat out of hell – that was his expression. He'd picked it up from someone and it appealed to him. "I am the bat out of hell," he would say. He'd had several speeding tickets.'

'Well . . . maybe that's the best way to go.' Brock muttered the words before he could stop himself, then immediately bit his tongue. But Grace didn't appear to have heard. She was staring past his shoulder, eyes wide, her expression rather as he had seen it first in the lower chamber of the temple.

Brock turned in the direction of her stare and saw a dark, hooded figure standing motionless, watching them, about thirty yards away towards the high hedges which surrounded the north lawn of the house. They remained immobile, the three of them, for a long second, and then the figure turned abruptly and disappeared behind the nearest hedge.

'Stay here,' Brock said. He ran as fast as he could towards the other end of the hedge, jumping over flower-beds and clumps of dead foliage. He threw himself around the end of the hedge and slithered to a stop. There was no sign of anyone else. Chest heaving from the sudden exertion in his heavy boots and coat, he trotted along the hedge, back towards the spot where the figure had been standing. Before he reached the place, he saw the footprints and recognized the diamond heel pattern. The track came a few paces down the line of the hedge, then crossed back through a gap and headed towards the clearing where he'd left Grace.

'Shit!' he muttered, and pushed through the gap, his eyes fixed on the footprints. They detoured round a cluster of bushes, and looking up he caught a glimpse of the dark figure through an opening in the shrubbery ahead. Whoever it was had reached Grace, was standing over her, and Brock could see her pale face turned upwards.

He decided to cut directly through to them rather than follow the path, and found himself floundering up to his thighs in deceptively deep mounds of pristine snow. The two motionless figures seemed unaware of his approach as he struggled towards them. Finally, Grace nodded and turned her face towards Brock, and he realized she had known he was coming but had been listening to something the other figure had been saying. It, too, turned, and Brock saw a peaked cap projecting under the hood of the black parka, and beneath the cap a male face.

'David! You'll give yourself a heart attack,' Grace said, with genuine concern.

It took him an embarrassingly long time to bring his heaving lungs under sufficient control to speak. 'Who . . .? Who . . .?'

'This is Geoffrey Parsons, David. He's the Estates Manager.'

Parsons offered his hand and Brock was obliged to pull his glove off and shake it.

'What were you doing, lurking over there?' he asked truculently.

'I saw you, but I didn't want to interrupt . . .' Parsons sounded anxious. And looking at him close up, at the wisps of sandy hair falling untidily across his eyes, and listening to his weak voice, Brock felt foolish at having expended so much effort pursuing him.

'What about yesterday? You followed us up to the temple, didn't you?'

Parsons nodded. 'I've been wanting to ask Mrs Carrington something. Sorry, I didn't want to disturb you.' He smiled wanly at Grace, then nervously at Brock, and turned and walked away.

'What did he want?' Brock asked.

'He's worried about his girlfriend, Rose. Wanted to know if she had been speaking to me. She works here too, and we got quite friendly the last time I was here.' She sighed. 'Perhaps I should speak to her, try to find out what's wrong. It's the last thing I want to do, but of course he doesn't know about . . .' She looked up at Brock sharply. 'You won't say anything to anyone, David, will you? I didn't mean to tell anyone.'

'Of course not. Can I help in any way – with Rose, I mean?'

She shook her head. 'I'm not even sure that he wants me to approach her. He's so tense. I wonder if her problem is *him*.'

14

Brock met Rose the following morning, although the circumstances were such that her problems were not uppermost in his mind. She was acting as assistant to Stephen Beamish-Newell for Brock's first acupuncture session, the thought of which had been making him feel unreasonably apprehensive.

'Any side-effects from the fasting, David?'

Beamish-Newell had sat Brock on the edge of the couch, really a kind of trolley, waist high, and was now taking his blood pressure before beginning the treatment. The room was one of a series of small, sparsely furnished rooms which ran down one side of the corridor in the basement and were linked by connecting doors with frosted-glass panels.

'No, I seem to have coped with it all right, after the first shock.' Brock suddenly thought about Ben Bromley's meat pie, and his stomach gave a small gurgle. He looked up at Rose, standing waiting in the corner, and she shot him an automatic smile of encouragement. There was a stainless-steel trolley beside her, and on it were rubber gloves, some folded hand-towels and a block of sponge into which a number of acupuncture needles had been stuck. Whether it was the thought of the meat pie or the sight of the needles or the combination of the two, Brock felt suddenly nauseous. He took a deep breath and tried to think of something else while Beamish-Newell took his pulse.

'All right, good. Lie face down on the couch now, David, and we'll get you started.' The doctor went over to a small basin and washed his hands.

The large cast-iron radiator beneath the tiny window was oversized for the small room, and with the doors closed it was even more oppressively hot than elsewhere in the house. Brock lay on his front, folded his arms under his head and tried not to think about pierced eyeballs.

He felt something soft dab at a spot on his upper left hip, then a pause, and then a slight tingling sensation in his flesh.

'You'll be finishing your fast tonight, David.' Another soft dab, this time on the right side. 'The grosser poisons should pretty well have drained from your system. Takes time for them to leach out completely, but you'll soon notice the difference. Hope you've been drinking plenty of water?'

No reply.

'David?'

Silence.

'Haven't fallen asleep on us, have you?'

Beamish-Newell moved to Brock's head and touched his cheek, then pulled his eyelid back. 'Passed out.'

The doctor swore quietly under his breath and checked Brock's pulse. Rose wet a cloth under the cold tap and offered it to him. He nodded but didn't take it, and she came forward and wiped Brock's face. He didn't stir.

'Come on!' Beamish-Newell slapped the back of Brock's hand and waited. Nothing.

After five minutes the doctor withdrew the two needles he had inserted. After ten he shook his head impatiently and told Rose to keep a close eye on the totally unresponsive figure on the couch while he got started on the other patients in the adjoining rooms. While she waited Rose turned down the valve on the radiator, and then stood up on a chair and with difficulty tugged open the little window under the vault. She chatted to Brock reassuringly as she did so. 'Sure it's awful hot in here. Isn't it just? It's no wonder you passed out. I had someone pass out in the sauna just last week. Heat can take you that way. No warning, especially if you're short of fluids. Could that be the way of it, do you think?'

But no sound came from Brock until over half an hour had

passed since the first needle had gone in. Then he suddenly gave a snuffling grunt and scratched his beard.

'Well, thank the Lord!' Rose helped him sit up and offered him a glass of water.

'All done?' Brock asked, disoriented.

'All done, indeed! We never even began. Do you feel all right? I'll fetch the doctor.'

Beamish-Newell came bustling in and gave Brock a quick check-over.

'You seem to be all right. Maybe you'll do better after you've taken in some nutrition. You have another session scheduled for tomorrow morning, don't you? Well, we'll try again then. You'd better go and lie down in your room now for an hour or so. What's your second session this morning?'

'I think it's the exercise bicycle or something.' Brock found it hard to focus his thoughts.

'Better give it a miss.'

'I'll see Mr Brock to his room,' Rose said, helping him on with his dressing gown.

Walking seemed to revive him, and by the time they reached the lift he felt considerably better. He shook his head as they waited. 'Stupid,' he said. 'I don't know what brought that on.'

'You'll feel just fine after a wee lie-down.'

'I met your fiancé yesterday, Rose, while I was walking outside with Grace Carrington.'

'Is that right?' The professional solicitude faded from Rose's voice. 'Are you a one for the ladies, then, Mr Brock? I hear you tried to take on Martha Price, no less. And then there's your friend Kathy Kolla.'

'Chance would be a fine thing, Rose.'

The lift arrived, a tiny box squeezed into the width of a cupboard in the old masonry structure, barely big enough to take the two of them.

'You wouldn't be in the same line of work as Kathy, would you, Mr Brock? A policeman?'

Brock smiled. 'Do I look like a policeman? Anyway, would it matter if I was?'

The lift wheezed to a halt and they stepped out.

'I don't know,' she said as they walked down the deserted corridor. 'I've been thinking about what you said, about you taking her a message. I'm not sure. I'm in an awkward sort of position, you see. And it may do no good anyway. After all, the poor man's dead, isn't he? Nothing can alter that.'

'Depends how you feel about that. Sometimes it's harder to live with than it should be. When something hasn't really been sorted out, for example, or when a cloud hangs over a person's memory that shouldn't be there.'

They were at Brock's door. Rose didn't reply, and to keep the conversation going Brock added, 'Martha Price seems to guard his memory quite jealously.'

'What does she know about him!' Rose's voice was low but suddenly fierce, and Brock saw that her eyes were glittering with tears. 'She doesn't know a damn thing about him, interfering old bitch!'

Brock nodded. 'My sentiments entirely.' He waited for Rose to go on, and for a moment it seemed she would, but then she turned abruptly on her heel and walked quickly away.

Brock stayed in his room through the rest of the morning, listening to the sounds of activity come and go from below as the patients gathered for the mid-morning break, and then disappeared for their second therapy sessions. The sun was back again and warmer this time, as if encouraged by its success on the previous day. A wood pigeon up on the parapet nearby began cooing complacently in the background as Brock lay on his bed, tapping at his laptop.

At twelve-fifteen he got up and dressed himself in the outdoor clothes he had arrived in three days before. They felt unfamiliar and looser than they should. He took the fire escape at the end of the west wing down to the basement level and left by way of the door where the boots and coats were kept. The snow had been melting fast and he had to detour and jump puddles to avoid getting his shoes full of water as he made his way to his car. Along the edge of the drive, bluebells which had been caught by the late snow were beginning to poke their heads out again into the brilliant sunlight.

The car splashed along the wet lanes to Edenham, and when he reached the High Street he turned through the archway of the Hart Revived to park in the yard at the rear. He found Kathy at a small corner table in the deserted snug bar. She gave him a big grin, and he sank into the seat beside her and sighed deeply. It took him a moment to speak.

'Kathy, you have no idea how wonderful it is to see you again.' He sighed once more. The log fire crackled in the big stone fireplace and an electronic games machine in the far corner bleeped plaintively for attention. 'Normality, the real world. I never thought I'd be so pleased to get back to it.'

Kathy laughed, 'Oh dear, is it as bad as that?'

He nodded. 'Worse. Much worse.'

'But you've only been there a couple of days.'

'Time means nothing. It feels like an age.'

'Well, you'll appreciate that.' Kathy indicated the pint of bitter she had ready for him. He looked at it apprehensively and said, 'No, no. I'd better not.'

'Oh, come on. You can relax in here, can't you? I mean, it's not as if you're really there for your health.'

'Kathy, you have no idea. They take you over, body and soul. I swear, if I drank that he'd know about it. He'd just look at me and see the poisons oozing out of the pores of my skin and the guilt written all over my face.'

Kathy thought this was hilarious. '"He" being Dr Fiendish-Cruel? So you agree he's scary.'

'Oh yes, I agree. This morning I passed out while he was sticking his damned acupuncture needles into me.'

'Yuck! What's the food like?'

'What food? I haven't had a thing apart from water and lemon juice since I arrived. They put me straight on a seventy-two-hour fast to purify my system. When I come off it tonight, I might be allowed a glass of carrot juice.'

'Well, since you've already been wicked and gone over the wall, you might as well make it worthwhile and give yourself a treat. The steak-and-kidney pie looks pretty good. It's home-made.'

Pleased as he was to see her, Brock was finding Kathy's response to his tale of suffering a little flippant. He was reminded of Grace Carrington's remark about the difficulty of adjusting to the outside world again. The thought of Grace and her problems made him suddenly ashamed. It was almost as if the processes of the clinic had reduced him to childishness.

He shook his head, 'No, no,' he muttered. 'You go ahead.'

'OK. I'm ravenous, I didn't have time for breakfast this morning.'

She caught the look on Brock's face and added, 'Sorry. Really I am. You must be wishing I'd never got you into this. Let me ask them if they've got something mild for you, break you in gently from your fast.'

'It's all right, Kathy,' he smiled at her. 'Get me a glass of mineral water if you like.'

'With ice and lemon?'

'Yes, why not. The works.'

He settled back into his seat, slightly dizzy from the cigarette smoke and the smell of frying that hung heavy in the air.

After a moment Kathy returned, holding a ticket for her meal in one hand and Brock's drink in the other. She waited while he removed the straw and lifted his drink and sipped at it, letting him begin his story in his own way.

'Well,' he said at last, 'I'm not sure I've really marshalled my thoughts, but I'll give you what I have. Yes, Beamish-Newell is quite a formidable character. But not necessarily the dominant force he once was. He had to get outside finance to keep the clinic going five or six years ago, and the financier, Sir Peter Maples, has clipped his wings somewhat. Ben Bromley, the Business Manager, is Maples's man, he's there to keep the Director under control.

'Beamish-Newell has been married before, by the way. The name of his first wife was Gabriele. She was Italian, from a wealthy family, and gave him his start at Stanhope. I haven't really formed much of an impression of Laura Beamish-Newell, the second wife. She seems distant, efficient, not a very endearing bedside manner, but the regulars like her, think she's good at her job and cares for them.' He shrugged.

Kathy nodded. 'Yes, my impression was much the same.' She had her notebook out and was writing as Brock spoke.

'Number eighteen?' a voice called from the bar, and Kathy held up her ticket. 'Yes, over here, please.' The barmaid approached them with a large plate heaped with battered plaice and chips.

'Oh my God,' Brock groaned.

'Ketchup, dear? Tartar sauce?' The woman gave Kathy some cutlery wrapped in a paper napkin and sauntered back to the bar.

'Anyway . . .' Brock made a superhuman effort to recall where he'd got to. 'Rose. Yes, she certainly knows something. She almost came out with it this morning. Her boyfriend, Parsons, is worried about her. He's a nondescript sort of character, isn't he? I caught him creeping around; he followed us twice when I was out walking in the grounds with Grace Carrington. She's one of your regulars, you remember? Along with Martha Price and Sidney Blumendale. I really don't think they know anything about what happened to Petrou.

They seem baffled, disoriented by it; and they won't hear a word said against Beamish-Newell or the clinic. Now, the interesting bit. Norman de Loynes. Ever heard the name?'

Kathy shook her head. 'I'm never going to finish all this. Are you sure you wouldn't like some of it? The fish is good. So are the chips, actually.'

'Forget your stomach, Kathy, and just concentrate on what I'm telling you.' Brock reached over for her notebook and printed de Loynes's name.

'Lower case "d". You sure he wasn't there when your storm-troopers took the place apart?'

'Certain. I'd have remembered a name like that.'

'Well, he says he was. And Grace Carrington remembers him being there too.' Brock watched the startled look on Kathy's face with satisfaction. Keeping his eyes on her, watching the surprise turn to perplexity, he reached forward for his glass and had taken a big swallow before he realized he was holding the pint of beer.

'Oh hell!' He licked his lips. 'Nice, though.'

'How could he have been there?' Kathy said.

'There's a class of patrons of Stanhope Clinic called "Friends". They pay a large sub every year and have the place as a sort of private health and social club. They enjoy privileged terms and can make use of the therapeutic facilities. I get the impression that their diet is somewhat more interesting than the one the ordinary patients endure. I suspect, although I don't know for sure, that they were invented by Ben Bromley as an entrepreneurial initiative to raise funds for the clinic. They have their own private lounge somewhere in the house, which no one else uses, and half the time you wouldn't know they were there.'

Brock took another mouthful of beer. 'Bliss,' he murmured.

'You mean he might actually have been in the building all the time we were carrying out our investigation?'

'It's conceivable. Or maybe he was tipped off to leave as soon as there was a hint of trouble or scandal.'

Kathy shook her head. 'The office staff, Beamish-Newell – they would all have had to lie to us, cover up. They provided the lists.'

'Yes. And if there was one of them there at the time Petrou died, there could have been others.'

'Hell!' Kathy pursed her lips with annoyance. Brock admired her mouth – a strong mouth, he thought, determined.

'That would completely undermine the whole of my investigation, Brock. Are you sure?'

'Well, it wouldn't hurt to have a look at their files, look at their bookings, find out the names of the Friends.'

Talking had restored Brock somewhat, and he was beginning to feel almost normal again.

'You mean, break into the office? Could you do that?'

'I'd rather not,' Brock said. 'I thought you might be able to have a go. Their records will all be on the computer. Ben Bromley's keen on that sort of thing, I should imagine. The office has two new machines, and he has another on his desk. Couldn't your systems analyst hack into them?'

'Belle Mansfield? I've no idea.'

'Why don't you give her a ring and find out?'

'Now?'

'Finish your lunch first, Kathy, before it gets cold.'

While she ate, Brock pulled the sheaf of Stanhope brochures that Bromley had given him out of his pocket and began thumbing through them. One of them, an annual report, had photographs of some of the principal figures: Beamish-Newell, Bromley and, above them at the top of the page, the Chairman of the Stanhope Foundation and its associated companies, Sir Peter Maples.

Kathy pointed with her fork. '*That's* the one who was in Bernard Long's office with Beamish-Newell and Tanner that time when Gordon Dowling and I were pulled off the case. I knew I recognized him from somewhere.'

'Really? So he's not just a figurehead. Bromley certainly implied that he took it all very seriously.'

'Should I know about him?'

'If you read the business section of your paper. He's what the *Express* likes to call a "Eurotycoon". Interests in lots of areas, seriously rich.'

Kathy put down her knife and fork. 'That's as much as I can manage,' she said. 'I'll see if I can get hold of Belle.'

When she came back she saw that Brock was clutching a ticket. She smiled to herself but made no comment.

'Any luck?' he asked.

'I got her. She isn't sure if she can help. The computers would have to be connected to a phone line, you know, to receive electronic mail or fax messages. Then any computer outside with a modem could communicate with them. And then it would depend on how the system had been set up, how security-conscious our comedian was.'

'Comedian?'

'Mr Bromley. Didn't he try to tell you any of his awful jokes?'

'He began to. So, is she going to have a go?'

'Apparently, it's possible the Stanhope computer would record the number of anyone calling in. She doesn't think it would be a good idea to use one of the police computers or phone lines.'

'Ah.'

'Number forty-two?'

Brock glanced up at the call from the bar and signalled. The barmaid came over and placed in front of him a plate of steak-and-kidney pie, chips and mushy peas. 'Brown sauce, dear?'

'Please.' He looked at Kathy. 'Might as well be hung for a goat as a sheep.'

'Sheep as a lamb, isn't it?' Kathy grinned.

'Whatever. So what's the answer?'

'Belle says her marriage is in need of a boost. She suggests she gets her mother-in-law to come and look after the baby at home while she takes her husband away to have a night of wild sex at some hotel, in the name of Mr and Mrs Smith of course. She'll take her laptop, which has a modem, and which she can plug into the hotel's phone line.'

'That sounds good. Tell her it'll be my treat.'

'She can't go tonight, but maybe tomorrow if her husband and mother-in-law are free. But anyway, she says access to the files will probably be protected by a password. She wondered if you could find out before she tries to break in.'

'How?'

'Each operator probably has their own password, maybe their initials or something like that. She wonders if you could watch them when they open up the computer first thing in the morning.'

Brock nodded, munching away.

'Good?'

'Wonderful. It restores your perspective on life. I think Beamish-Newell uses starvation to exercise personality control over his patients. One other thing, Kathy. Did you ever find out about Petrou's financial situation? If he was doing rich people favours, presumably he was doing it for money.'

Kathy shook her head. 'We never got that far.'

'His estate may have been wound up by now. Maybe something could be found out about it discreetly.'

Brock drained the pint glass, wiped his mouth with the paper napkin and got to his feet. 'I'd better be going,' he said. 'I'll ring you tomorrow morning. What have they got you working on this week?'

'There's a tyre-slasher on the loose in Crowbridge. It makes a great start to the day to have to interview another dozen or so angry people who've had their cars done during the night. Best if you ring me at lunchtime, say between one and two. I'll make sure I'm in the office.'

The cold air outside was like a sharp slap in the face. Brock took a deep breath and hurried across the street, ducking into the bookshop he'd noticed opposite the Hart Revived. At least no one from the clinic had seen him coming out of the pub. The doorbell tinkled behind him and he looked around. The shop was newly painted and some of the shelves were bare. A woman at a small counter was talking energetically on the phone at the same time as she was wrapping a book for a customer. A man wandered through from the back of the shop and languidly said as he passed her, 'The van's arrived, dear.' She covered the mouthpiece and urged, flustered, 'Couldn't you deal with them, darling?' but he ignored her and moved to the shop window, where he shuffled one or two of the books on display.

Having found it impossible to find any words of his own in response to Grace Carrington's tragedy, Brock had hoped to find someone else's words to say to her instead, but as he looked along the shelves his heart sank. He recognized one or two titles which dealt with the subject of death, but doubted whether he would have got much comfort from Waugh's *The Loved One* or a collection of the metaphysical poets, were he in her situation.

'Can I help you?' The man at the window had come over to him, presumably to avoid having to deal with the van. His wife finished with her phone conversation and customer, and hurried out to the back.

'I'm having difficulty finding a present for someone. She's not going to be around long.'

'Going overseas? How about something on scenic Britain?'

'No, she's going to die.'

The man blinked and looked appalled, as if Brock had said something in very poor taste. 'I . . . I'm not sure I can be of much help. Our religious section is over there.' He waved a hand and hurried off to the counter, where he busied himself with a publisher's catalogue.

Brock was about to abandon his search when he saw a long-forgotten title. He pulled it down from the shelf and turned to the opening words.

> *The Mole had been working very hard all the morning, spring-cleaning his little home. First with brooms, then with dusters; then on ladders . . .*

Kenneth Grahame's evocation of his particular Arcadian dream brought a smile of recognition to Brock's face. He read some more, then went over to the man at the counter.

'Found something?' He looked doubtfully at the cover of *The Wind in the Willows*.

Brock shrugged. 'I'd like you to wrap it in some decent paper if you would. And I'd like to write a message on a card.'

'Well, here's a card. But my wife does the wrapping. I'm useless, all thumbs. She'll be back in a minute.' He returned to the catalogue.

Brock wrote: 'From a fellow-inmate in Arcady. Best wishes and good luck. David Brock.'

He tucked it inside the book and they waited for the woman to return. She did the job briskly and smiled at him as she took his money, wiping her hair back from her forehead.

'Family business?' he asked.

'Yes, we're just starting. It's difficult getting established, especially in a small place like this. But we're really keen. We'll make a go of it.'

'All the best,' he said.

She smiled her thanks. Her husband ignored him.

The road out of Edenham was so winding that Brock was

forced to concentrate on the way ahead and didn't notice the white car behind until its blue lights started flashing. He slowed down, but it took him a while to find a place where he could safely pull over in the narrow lane.

The uniformed man asked him if he was the owner of the car, demanded to see his licence and took a slow and careful walk around the vehicle, looking at tyres and lights.

'Have you had a drink recently, sir?'

Brock nodded. 'I've just had a pint in the Hart Revived. One pint.'

'I'd like you to blow into this, please. Don't touch it with your hands.' The policeman produced a breathalyser and inserted the mouthpiece.

Brock said nothing and did as he was told.

The officer seemed to take an age examining the result, and as he did so Brock was suddenly overtaken by a wave of nausea. The interior of the car seemed suffocatingly hot and short of oxygen. He pushed the door open, ignoring the look from the policeman, and ran through the slush of the verge towards the hedge behind his car and abruptly brought up his lunch into the ditch.

He stood for a while, leaning his weight against the car, waiting to see if there was more to come. In the background he could hear a large truck slowly manoeuvring round their parked cars.

'You all right, sir?'

He didn't reply.

'Do you want some help?'

There didn't seem to be any more. His stomach, empty again, seemed quite settled. He shook his head and stepped back through the mud to his door. He looked at the policeman as he took hold of the handle. 'That was a daft place to pull me over. Narrow road like this.'

The man held his eyes. 'You were driving erratically, sir. Just go carefully now. You got far to go?'

Brock shook his head again and got into the car.

That evening at dinner-time he slipped the book on to Grace Carrington's tray and then went searching for his own, when he heard Sidney Blumendale cough unobtrusively at his shoulder. 'Over here, old chap.'

Brock followed him to his table, where Martha was waiting.

'Since this is your night to celebrate finishing your fast, David, we thought we should all try to be friends together again. I told cook to do something special for you.'

From her tightly pursed lips it was clear that Martha was still very much in two minds as to whether she was doing the right thing in giving Brock a chance to redeem himself. He decided to play it with a very straight bat.

'Martha, how very thoughtful of you. I've been very unhappy about the way we left things the other day. I think it's extremely gracious of you to make this gesture.'

She looked closely at him, searching for any hint of sarcasm, but, detecting none, she smiled generously and tilted her head forward intimately. 'Look what you've got for being a good boy.'

He lifted the lid on the tray which they had waiting at his place.

'What is it?'

'Stanhope lentil soufflé. It's cook's speciality. Normally she wouldn't do it, but I persuaded her. Red lentils, onion and garlic cooked gently in stock until tender, than add some cheese and beaten egg yolks. Whisk up the whites and blend into the lentil mixture, then bake in a moderate oven for half an hour. She does it with such *flair*. We were worried you might not come down straight away and it would be ruined.'

'Well, it looks splendid. And carrot juice, too.'

Brock was worried as to how his stomach would react, but in the event it behaved as well as he did. Sidney Blumendale seemed particularly relieved.

15

On the following day, Friday 22 March, the vernal equinox, Brock was waiting by the locked door to the office when the receptionist arrived.

'You're early, Mr Brock,' she said cheerfully. 'Had your breakfast already?'

'Yes, my first breakfast in four days, Joyce.'

'Jay,' she corrected him. 'I hope it was something nice.'

'Orange juice and cereal. Look, I'm sorry to be so early, but I got in a bit of a panic last night, and I wonder if you could help me out. My sister rang to say she'd arranged a meal with friends for me when I get out. She said Sunday the 31st, but I was sure I'd booked till the Monday. I was wondering if you'd mind checking for me, and I'll ring her straight back now, before she goes off to work.'

'Yes, that's no problem.'

He followed Jay into the waiting room with the book-racks of material for sale, and watched while she unlocked the inner door to her office and raised the roller shutter over the counter. She took off her raincoat, which was dripping wet from the short distance from the car park to the front entrance to the house, for the day had begun dark and wet. The desk with her computer was set at right angles to the counter, and Brock positioned himself at one end to get as wide a view of the screen and keyboard as he could.

She sat chatting about the foul weather after the beautiful couple of days they'd had, and he watched as she switched on her terminal. The machine gave a ping and the screen lurched into life. Almost immediately a box came up requesting a password, and Jay pressed three keys. The letters appeared only as stars on the screen, but Brock had been watching her fingers: something in the middle of the centre row, then extreme centre-left, then top centre.

She waited while the hard disk whirred into action and icons began appearing on the screen, and then started using the mouse and keyboard to open them. After a minute of this she said, 'Your sister's right, Mr Brock. Sunday the 31st is your last day.'

'Oh, marvellous. Thanks very much, Jay, I really appreciate that.'

Up in his room he opened his laptop and considered the letters of the keyboard. It didn't take him long to work out that Jay's access code was most likely the three letters of her name.

Again feeling like a doomed schoolboy, he reluctantly made his way down to the basement for a second attempt at acupuncture.

'How was your first meal, David?' Beamish-Newell looked keenly at him as he sat on the couch, offering his arm.

Avoiding his eye, Brock replied, 'Good. Stomach's been feeling a bit shaky, though.'

'Diarrhoea?'

'No. I just felt a bit nauseous after breakfast this morning. Nothing serious.'

'Let me know if it persists. We must look after you. Ben Bromley tells me you've been to see him. You think you might be interested in joining us?'

'Yes. I found it all very interesting.' Brock caught Rose staring at him. She quickly looked away and busied herself at the trolley.

He forced himself to think about something else while, one by one, a dozen needles were inserted into his back, from shoulder to hips. He imagined going through his house slowly, from room to room, checking that everything was in its place, as if he were spring-cleaning it like the Mole, drawing up an inventory of all that he owned.

Rose's role was to move the needles gently once Beamish-Newell was satisfied with their placing. He murmured something to her that Brock couldn't make out, and left the room.

'Well, Rose.' Brock cleared his throat. 'How are things with you?'

'OK.' Perfunctory, preoccupied.

'Why don't you talk to me while you're doing that? Might be the best chance we get. Tell me what's bothering you.'

'You're sounding like an amateur psychiatrist today, Mr Brock. Just what are you?' She was belligerent now.

'You were the one who contacted Kathy, Rose. I just want to help.'

'Do you? How do I know I won't just make things worse for –'

She stopped mid-sentence and tugged at one of the needles. He winced.

'For whom?'

She didn't reply.

'I really don't think you've got a choice, Rose. I believe, in your heart, you know you're going to have to talk to someone.' Brock was finding it hard to make his point when all he could see of her was the toe of her shoe.

'Never you mind about what's in my heart, mister,' Rose leaned over him and hissed in his ear.

He sighed. 'Look, you'd probably be more comfortable talking to Kathy. Why not give her a ring? I can give you her home phone number.'

She didn't reply until they heard Beamish-Newell's voice outside the door, and then she said quietly, 'I'll think about it.'

'Well, you survived this time, David.' Beamish-Newell came back in and looked him over. 'I think we can get down to things in earnest next Monday.'

205

Brock waited while the needles were withdrawn, then got unsteadily to his feet and headed for the door.

It seemed everyone wanted to use the pay phone that lunch-time, and it was almost two o'clock when Brock eventually got through to Kathy.

'How's the tyre-slasher?' he asked.

'Another eight cars last night. How's the human pincushion?'

'Thoroughly punctured, thank you. The closest I can get to the computer password is that the receptionist's name is Jay, and she typed in three letters that might have been J, A, Y, or something close to those.'

'Upper or lower case?'

'I don't know. I didn't see her touch the shift key, but she might have.'

'Right, I'll tell Belle.'

'And you can tell her that she's not allowed to start any sexual gymnastics until she's found out what we want. Not while I'm stuck like a monk in this place and paying for her room.'

'Yes, sir. Anything else?'

'I had another word with Rose. She's being very reluctant. I believe she's worried for someone else, protecting them.'

'Her boyfriend?'

'That's the obvious choice, I suppose. I suggested she might be more comfortable speaking directly to you on the phone at home. She said she'd think about it.'

The corridors had cleared by the time he rang off, the patients all tucked away in the various corners of the house for the rest hour. Brock went up to the first floor and worked his way back along the corridor to what he estimated to be the area above the dumb waiter in the corner of the dining room below. Two doors were possible and he tried their handles, but both were locked.

He was beginning to head back to his room when he heard

206

one of the doors open. He turned and found Norman de Loynes staring round the jamb at him.

'Oh, hello, Norman,' he said.

'Looking for someone, old man?'

Brock strolled towards him and he stepped out into the corridor, pulling the door almost closed behind him. He was dressed, Brock saw, in a flamboyant, brocade smoking jacket, black silk pyjama trousers and gold slippers, like some character from the circle of Oscar Wilde.

'I was hoping to catch a bit of the racing from Newmarket on the box actually, Norman. They're watching some woman's programme downstairs, and someone mentioned they thought there was another sitting room up here with a telly. I was trying to find it.'

'Nothing on this floor, David.'

'Ah, too bad.' Brock smiled and didn't move.

De Loynes paused as if in doubt, then shrugged. 'See you later, David.' He slipped back through the door and clicked it firmly shut.

Brock rang Kathy at home immediately after breakfast next morning, impatient.

'I haven't heard from her yet,' she said. 'They're probably having a lie-in.'

'Let's hope they've earned it,' he said testily.

The clinic seemed to be in limbo, the normal routine suspended for the weekend as some patients departed and others arranged outings for the day. Brock waited an hour and tried again.

'No luck, Brock. I'm sorry. She couldn't do it. Apparently the clinic is in some kind of electronic bulletin-board network, and she was able to get into that all right, but not into their private files.'

'I thought even schoolkids could break into anybody's computer these days.'

'She was very apologetic, but they did have a nice evening, anyway. She says thank you for that. It seems you saved their marriage!'

Brock grunted ungraciously. 'Well, that only leaves the old-fashioned manual method, I suppose.'

'Brock, I've been thinking. I reckon you've done about as much as you can down there. I think you should let it be. Come home.' She sounded worried.

'What's the matter?'

'The last thing we need is a Detective Chief Inspector from Scotland Yard caught red-handed breaking into their files. Anyway, if we're right, there's a high probability that a particularly nasty murderer is still wandering around down there. I think you've done about as much to stir him up as you should.'

'Or her.'

'Pardon?'

'Him or her.'

'Oh yes, well . . . but they had to be strong enough to carry Petrou's body out to the temple and string it up.'

'Maybe. Anyway, your point is taken. All the same, who-ever specified the internal locks in this place wasn't too bothered about security.'

'Oh God. Please, Brock. I'm getting a bad feeling about this. And I feel responsible.'

'It was entirely my idea to come here, Kathy, and I'd like to have something to show for my pains. But I won't rush into anything, don't worry.'

Brock spent the morning working in his room. Towards lunch-time he made his way down to the library to see if he could find a dictionary. As he stepped out into the corridor to leave, he almost bumped into Grace Carrington. She didn't seem pleased to see him.

'Are you all right?' he asked, puzzled.

'Yes. Thank you for the book, but I don't want it.' She

fumbled in her shoulder bag, pulled it out and thrust it at him. She sounded furious.

'What's the matter? Was it a bad choice?'

She glared at him.

'Look, come into the library for a moment,' he said. 'There's no one here. Tell me what's wrong. Please.'

Reluctantly she followed him in and he closed the door.

'No,' she said at last. 'I suppose it was quite an appropriate choice, in a way. I thought it was a touching thing to do, actually. Then I spoke to Rose this morning.' She looked at him, challenging him.

'So?'

'She was very upset. She said you had been putting pressure on her to tell you about what went on in the clinic when Alex Petrou died. She said she was frightened of you, of your questions. And I thought of all the questions that you've been asking *me*.' She paused, controlling her anger. 'She thinks you're a policeman. Is it true?'

'Ah.' Brock turned away, avoiding her accusing stare.

'It's hard when you start off by lying to people,' she said, her voice tight and low, 'hard to stop, and hard for anyone to accept anything from you at face value.'

'I don't believe I lied to you, Grace.'

'Maybe not in so many words. Anyway, I don't want your gift.'

She made for the door.

'I'm not on duty here, Grace. But what happened to Alex Petrou was never resolved, was it? And I think it's important that it should be. Don't you think that?'

'What I think is that you should leave Rose alone. I think you should leave me alone. And above all I think you should leave Stephen Beamish-Newell alone. Because that's what this is really about, isn't it? You just can't stop yourselves trying to get at him, at people like him. You hate the fact that he *cares*, when all you can do is *punish*.'

He let her go. Out of the window the rain had dissolved almost all the snow, and the knoll brooded dark and threatening over a sodden landscape. Brock left the copy of *The Wind in the Willows* lying on the table and made for the door, feeling sick.

He stayed in his room through lunch-time, then went down to the games room and sat by the window, pretending to read a paper. The window looked west towards the stables and the gravel road leading round to the staff cottages. At about two-thirty he saw Rose and another woman come down the road and head for the door into the basement. He got to his feet, went out into the hall and took the stairs. He met them at the foot.

'Ah, Rose. Could I have a quick word?' He saw her look of antagonism, and saw that her companion had noticed it too. 'Only for a second.'

She looked annoyed, then said reluctantly, 'Go on, Trudy. I'll catch you up.'

Trudy stared at Brock, then moved on.

'I just wanted to apologize for pestering you, Rose. Grace Carrington had a word with me and said I'd upset you. I'm sorry. I won't mention the matter again.'

She looked doubtfully at him. 'Oh . . . well. That's fine, then.'

He nodded and she seemed to accept that he was genuine. 'I probably overreacted. I've been a bit tense lately. You only wanted to help, I suppose.'

She turned to follow her friend.

'That's right,' Brock said. 'I did think I might have a word with Geoffrey Parsons. You wouldn't know where I could find him, would you?'

She spun back to face him. 'No! I don't want you to do that! I –'

She stared at him, at a loss for words, her bottom lip clenched between her teeth.

'Please,' she said finally, her voice tense and urgent, 'don't do that. Don't speak to Geoffrey. Will you promise me that?'

He looked quizzically at her and scratched his beard.

She put out her hand and touched his sleeve. 'I need . . . I need time to think. Just give me a little time. Will you? Please?'

'Of course, Rose. Whatever you say.'

He was suddenly conscious of a movement in a doorway nearby and they both turned their heads at the same time to see Laura Beamish-Newell standing staring at them. Her eyes were focused on Rose's hand on Brock's sleeve. Rose turned abruptly and ran down the corridor after her friend.

'Could I have a word with you, Mr Brock?' The Director's wife fixed him with a cold look. 'In my office?'

He followed her to the small room and sat on the metal chair as he had on his first day while she closed the door and came round behind her desk. She sat down, put her elbows on the desk and examined him without speaking.

The interrogator's initiative, Brock thought to himself. *I couldn't stare at you like this unless we both knew you were guilty as sin.*

He placidly examined his fingernails, not attempting to meet her eyes.

'I am very protective of my staff, Mr Brock,' she said finally. 'The work that they do inevitably brings them into close physical contact with patients. This intimacy is necessary for them to do their work properly, for the health and well-being of their patients. Unfortunately, a patient may occasionally – very occasionally, I'm pleased to say – try to take advantage of this.'

'I beg your pardon?' Brock looked up at her in surprise. 'Are you suggesting that my behaviour has been in some way improper?'

'I am suggesting that you have been putting pressure on Rose for some reason of your own.' Her voice was deadly calm. Brock wondered if it was significant that she used the same phrase as Grace. 'I am suggesting that you have been upsetting her. Do you deny that?'

'Mrs Beamish-Newell,' Brock replied, rising slowly to his feet, 'I can assure you that I have absolutely no wish to take advantage of Rose in any way whatsoever. I think if you speak to her she will confirm that.'

He waited to give her the opportunity to say that she had already spoken to Rose, but instead she said, 'I understand that you were extremely belligerent with another member of our staff, too.'

Brock stared at her, puzzled. 'Who?'

'Mr Parsons. Outside in the grounds, when you were walking with Mrs Carrington.'

Brock was stunned. 'Belligerent?'

'He told me that you ran after him. He thought you might be going to attack him. I understand very well how new patients sometimes have difficulty at first in adjusting to a different way of life here, Mr Brock. I would simply ask you to remember that the harmonious atmosphere of Stanhope is something we all have to work at, staff and visitors alike.'

As Brock returned to his room he thought how odd it was that Parsons had reported his encounter with Brock and Grace to Laura Beamish-Newell. It was clear that there was little chance of privacy at the clinic. He was also struck by the protective way that she had spoken of the other staff, and in particular of the Estates Manager.

A video, *Ruthless People*, was shown in the drawing room after dinner that evening. The audience generally seemed to warm to the idea that Bette Midler became a pleasanter human being the more she lost weight, while Brock was more taken by the thought of Ben Bromley as a Lancastrian Danny de Vito. It finished around nine-thirty, and the patients drifted slowly away to their rooms for the night. Brock went to the games room, where a few card-players remained, but they too broke up after a short while, and by ten the public rooms were deserted. He went up to his room and lay on his bed in the dark, watching the strip of light beneath his door. It went off at ten-forty. He waited half an hour and got to his feet.

That afternoon he had collected the jack handle from his car, and he now wrapped it, together with a flat-bladed dinner knife borrowed from the dining room that evening, in a towel. In his pocket he had a small notebook and a ball-point pen.

The corridor and stairs were lit by dim green emergency lights, and, looking like some ghostly eccentric hunting for the showers, he made his way silently down to the entrance hall. The door to the reception area and office was fitted with a cheap, modern, aluminium knob set, with the lock housed in the knob. Brock slid the blade of the knife into the crack of the jamb and held it against the corner of the panelled door to protect it from being damaged as he forced the sharp end of the jack handle in behind the blade. He gave a jerk and the lock burst open with a bang. He slipped inside and pressed the button down on the inside knob to relock the door. He repeated the process on the inner door into the office area which held Jay's computer.

There were no windows here, and he could see nothing in the pitch darkness. Eventually, moving very cautiously towards the centre of the room, he felt Jay's desk and found the lamp. He pressed the switch and settled into her chair.

The musical ping of the computer as it came to life sounded remarkably loud in the silence of the night. He waited for the demand for the password, then typed in the letters JAY and watched the screen clear. He soon found what he was looking for in a folder labelled 'Mailing Lists'. Inside were separate files: 'Patients', 'Staff', 'Executive', 'Newsletter' and, finally, 'Friends'. He opened 'Friends' and began scrolling through a list of names and addresses.

Not wanting to contend with the printer, Brock began copying the list by hand into his notebook. Two names were as expected — de Loynes and Long — and others seemed familiar though not immediately placeable. When he had finished he closed the file, then the 'Mailing Lists' folder, and began a second search. Inside a folder marked 'Admin General' he uncovered a large number of files devoted to correspondence of various kinds, and among them a series of spreadsheets marked 'Bookings', each covering a specific year. He opened the one for the previous year and scrolled through to October. De Loynes was booked from 21 October to 3 November, the two weeks straddling Petrou's death on 27 October. In the listing for the second of the two weeks his name was misspelt 'de Loyns', and, without thinking, Brock corrected it.

He now began to cross-check the list of Friends with the list of patients booked in at the Clinic on 27 October. After a few minutes he found one: Simon Mortimer, booked from 21 to 28 October. He was writing the details in his book when a sound made him freeze.

It was a metallic click and, though muffled, was uncomfortably distinct. It was hard to place where it had come from. He held his breath, waiting, but nothing more disturbed the stillness. Hurriedly now, he continued scanning the names on the screen and comparing them with those in his notebook.

There was another click.

This time Brock rose slowly to his feet. As he did so, his line of sight cleared the back edge of Jay's desk and took in the pale line of light from the bottom of the connecting door to Ben Bromley's office. At the same moment he heard the murmur of a voice beginning to speak in the next room. It was Bromley's voice, and it was answered by another that he recognized, a woman's, Laura Beamish-Newell.

It occurred to him that if he could see their light under the door, it was possible they could see his. Very carefully he rolled the jack handle and knife back into the towel and reached for his notebook and pen. At that moment the computer in front of him gave a loud ping and the message 'Save Now?' flashed up on the screen. Immobilized by the sudden noise, he hesitated long enough to realize his stupidity in correcting the spelling mistake, and so provoking the computer's question. He was conscious of the abrupt silence from the next room as the murmur of voices stopped.

Then Bromley spoke, his tone quiet, incredulous.

Brock grabbed at his things, switched off the desk lamp and flew for the door. He banged his shin against something as he reached it and wrestled the knob open. As he swung it closed, a shaft of light from behind him flashed against the jamb. He could hear their voices as he reached the outer door, and then he was through and dodging between the armchairs in the entrance hall. He made the corridor and sprinted to the far end of the west wing without pausing to hear if he was pursued. On to the fire stairs, then up to his floor; he peeked through the fire door to make sure the corridor was empty, then made the last dash to his room. His chest was heaving with the sudden exertion. From the direction of the main stairs he could hear a faint voice, and the glow of the stair light coming on suddenly reflected along the corridor wall. He felt in his pocket for his bedroom key and immediately knew, with complete certainty, that it was still lying on his bedside cabinet on the other side of the door. Leaving his room in the dark, he had forgotten to pick it up.

The voices in the stairwell were growing. He reached for the knife and jack handle and fumbled to get them into the door jamb. The handle slipped out of his grip and landed on the floor with a thump. As he groped for it in the gloom, the main lights in the corridor blazed alive. He grabbed the jack handle again, slammed it into the gap and wrenched. With a splintering crack the door flew open and he stumbled into the dark room. Recovering, he swung the door closed again and clicked the lock. He pressed his forehead against the cool surface of the paint and took a deep breath, feeling his heart pounding in his chest.

Suddenly the light in the room snapped on. A voice behind him said, 'What are you doing?'

16

Brock turned and was startled to see Grace Carrington in his bed. She was staring at him wide-eyed over the edge of the blankets. Then he noticed that the curtains were different, the wardrobe in a different place.

'Oh no,' he groaned. 'The wrong door.'

'What?' She was looking at him as if he were mad. Behind him Brock could hear voices approaching.

He took another deep breath. 'I was trying to break into my own room. I locked myself out. But in the dark I thought your door was mine.'

Her eyes moved from his flushed face to the jack handle in his hand. Then she too heard the voices outside. 'What's going on, David?' she whispered.

He hesitated. 'I've been misbehaving, Grace. And I very nearly got caught.'

She watched him, then said, 'Do you want to leave now?'

'I'd rather hang on a moment – if you don't mind.'

'Then you'd better sit down and explain what you're doing in my room in the middle of the night.' She seemed calmer now.

So he sat on the end of her bed and told her about Kathy, and about her visit with Dowling to his home. He described some of Kathy's frustrations with the case, and his offer to spend some time at Stanhope. And he spoke of his reasons for breaking into the clinic's computer that evening.

'I can't believe that a senior police officer would do such a thing,' she said. 'What if you'd been caught?'

He nodded and hung his head. 'You're right. Kathy said exactly the same.'

'If you believe Alex was murdered, then who do you suspect?'

'I don't know. The problem is that the motive is unclear. It might have been blackmail, or sexual jealousy. Or perhaps it was an accident in which others were involved who would prefer to keep their names out of it. I find it hard to come to grips with Petrou. He seems to have been so many different things to different people.'

She nodded, thinking back. 'I suppose that's true. He had a surface charm, which he could adapt to the people that he came into contact with. There was a certain intimacy almost immediately you met him; he seemed soft, yielding. But I always felt that underneath he was quite hard, that he had a very strong sense of self-preservation and self-interest.'

'He was manipulative, then.'

'Yes, I think he was.' She looked hard at Brock, who was nursing his breaking-and-entering tools. 'I'm sorry I flew off the handle at you earlier. I thought *you* were being manipulative.'

'Well, I suppose I was. Until I got to know you, anyway.'

'What are you going to do now?'

'Right now? Well, if the coast is clear, go back to my room, I suppose.'

'You're going to smash another door in?'

He smiled, shrugged.

'Maybe it was fate, David, that you broke into this room. Maybe it was even intentional – subconsciously, I mean.'

He reddened.

'Alternatively,' she said, 'you could just stay here and in the morning I'll tell Jay that I've locked myself out again and she'll lend me the master key – she does it all the time for the patients.'

Brock looked at the chair by the desk. It seemed the only possibility, but he'd already found from the one in his own room that he was too big for it. 'Well ...' He sounded doubtful.

'Don't be daft,' she said. She wriggled over in the narrow bed to make room for him, and then reached up to turn off the light.

'You are real, then.' He opened his eyes at the sound of her voice and saw her gazing at him. A weak silver light leaked in around the curtain, and the hot water gurgled in the old cast-iron radiator under the window.

'Yes.' He felt their bodies pressed together in the narrow bed. 'I'm real, and a bit ... surprised.'

'Don't you do this much, then?' She smiled at him, and he thought how very nice a smile it was, and how much poorer the world was going to be without it. He kissed her cheek and stretched as much as he could in the confined space. 'I just didn't expect to find myself waking up here with you. I'm very glad I have, though.'

'In half an hour I'll go downstairs and get someone to give me the key. But not yet.' She slid her hand across his chest and gave him a squeeze.

'No,' he agreed, and eased his arm under her shoulders. For the first time he noticed that his automatic wince was unnecessary, for there was no pain from his shoulder.

'You think Stephen Beamish-Newell killed Alex, don't you?' she asked.

He hesitated. 'I have no real reason to. I think Kathy does.'

'I can understand that. He can seem intimidating, even terrifying, I suppose. But he would have the most to lose if someone was murdered at the clinic.'

'And perhaps the most to lose from someone who was threatening the reputation of the clinic in some way. You like him, don't you?'

'It's not *liking*. More *trusting*. I just don't believe he would do it.'

'How about his wife?'

'Laura?' Grace looked at him in surprise, then frowned. 'Of course not! How do they train you to think like this?'

'It comes from having to *punish* people all the time, I suppose.'

'I'm sorry I said that, David. It must be very hard, doing what you do. Not allowed to forgive anyone.'

'That's what makes it bearable, Grace. It would be too difficult to have to forgive as well. Someone else gets that job.'

A wood pigeon had settled on their window-sill and began cooing reassuringly. Then a blast of the gusting north-easterly wind sent it fluttering away out of earshot.

An hour later Grace returned from her visit downstairs. 'Jay doesn't come in on a Sunday, but the girl who opens the office for her gave me the key. She didn't seem to know about any goings-on last night.'

'There's no way they couldn't have heard me. And I left the computer on. Still, it doesn't sound as if they called the police. Not yet, anyway.'

'What have you got planned today?'

'Not a lot. I'm supposed to be writing a paper for a conference . . .' Brock's voice trailed away. Talking with her about anything happening in the future was so difficult. He thought how much he would have liked to take her to Italy.

'Go on,' she said.

'It's not important. Not in the least. What about you?'

'Can I spend time with you, David? It doesn't matter, if you feel awkward about it.'

'Of course I don't feel awkward. I'd like that.'

'It isn't that I don't love my husband. But this . . .' She gestured hopelessly round the bare little room.

'I know,' he said. 'It isn't Paris in the springtime, but it's a comfort. It's a comfort for me too, Grace, believe me.'

She moved up against him. 'I arranged to meet Rose this

afternoon,' she said. 'If you like, I'll try to persuade her to talk to you.'

They went for a walk in the grounds after lunch and looked in the library when they returned, to see if they could retrieve Brock's gift to her, but it was gone.

Grace went off to keep her appointment with Rose. 'She says she will talk to you, David,' she reported back later. 'I gather it has something to do with her fiancé, Geoffrey Parsons. Apparently, there's something he kept from the police, and he's been worrying a lot about it. He doesn't want Rose to speak to anyone, but she feels he's going to have a breakdown if he doesn't do something. She's tried getting him to speak to Stephen Beamish-Newell, but he says there's no one he can talk to.'

'Does she have any idea what it is that he's hiding?'

'I'm not sure if she knows or just suspects. It's strange – sometimes she sounds very protective and concerned about him, and the next minute she becomes quite aggrieved and annoyed. I got the feeling that their relationship hasn't been very happy lately, almost as if she's only keeping it going because he's dependent on her.'

'It's funny you should say that. I got a lecture from Laura Beamish-Newell yesterday about harassing her staff. Apart from Rose, she said I'd been belligerent towards Parsons, who'd told her about the time he approached you while we were out there in the snow. He claimed I almost attacked him.'

'You were very protective.' She smiled at him. 'I thought that was sweet.'

'Well, the thing that surprised me was how protective Laura was towards Parsons. More so than towards Rose. It almost made me wonder if there could be something going on between them.'

'What? Oh no,' she laughed. 'I'm sure there isn't. She's probably just noticed that he's been under a strain lately. I really do think she worries about people she feels responsible for, David.'

'Maybe. When can I see Rose?'

'She says that's difficult. Laura has been questioning her about you, and she thinks Laura has asked the other girls in the house to keep an eye on her. She says she'll be seeing you anyway tomorrow afternoon for acupuncture, and she'll talk to you then.'

'Oh no,' Brock groaned.

'What's the matter?'

'Acupuncture. I don't know what it is about it. I passed out in the first session I had.'

'You didn't? Really?'

'Yes. I don't know why. I barely made it through the second one. I've been feeling a bit groggy anyway for the last couple of days. I'd say I was going down with flu, except for what that patient said to Beamish-Newell the first night I was here, about feeling much worse after a week than when she arrived. He said it was to be expected.'

She looked at him with concern. 'I'm sorry, I've been selfish. You should be resting this weekend.'

'Don't be daft,' he said.

17

If it hadn't been for Rose, Brock would have abandoned his afternoon therapy session. The morning osteopathy had left his back aching, barely able to bend. Worse were the headaches and nausea which had been recurring in waves over the past days, and he was convinced he was going down with flu. His stomach felt as if it belonged to someone else and his vision kept blurring. The thought of another acupuncture session filled him with dread, but if Rose was going to talk to him, he would have to be there. Beamish-Newell had brought the time of his session forward to two o'clock, during the rest hour for the other patients, and he suspected that this was to avoid alarm and inconvenience if he passed out again. His sense of gloom was heightened by the darkness of the day, the light of the sun overwhelmed by a motionless mass of black cloud.

Rose was waiting for him, looking nervous. She avoided his eyes as Beamish-Newell swept in and went through the preliminaries. He seemed distant to Brock, even abrupt, and if it hadn't been for the fact that Rose had asked for the meeting, he might have wondered if she had complained to the Director about him. Perhaps his wife had.

He said conversationally, trying to get Beamish-Newell to talk, to hear the intonation of his voice, 'How many needles today, Stephen?'

Beamish-Newell took a long time to say anything, and when he did the reply sounded ominous. 'Let's see how many you can take. It's probably time we stopped mollycoddling you.'

Brock rolled on to his front and closed his eyes, feeling dizzy even before the first needle went in.

When he opened them again he was completely disoriented. He groaned inwardly. *I've blacked out again.*

He blinked, trying to make out what had happened, but it was so dim. *My eyes are dim, I cannot see, I have not brought my specs with me.* His head was spinning, half waking, half trying not to. He felt an agonizing cramp in his legs, but when he tried to move them he couldn't. *They've paralysed my spine, for God's sake.* He struggled desperately to make them work, and suddenly there was a thump and the trolley shifted slightly and he found he was able to move them at last. *Thank Christ for that.* He realized that it was so dim because the overhead light was off, and although it was only mid-afternoon it was so dark outside that little light was coming through the small high window. Or was it mid-afternoon? He really had no idea. His back was so bad after the manipulation that he could hardly raise his head and turn his wrist to look at his watch. When he finally managed it he saw it was only two-forty. He'd been out for twenty minutes or so.

Where was everybody? Surely they wouldn't have left him to come round by himself? Or had Beamish-Newell finally given up on him? Rose too? He lowered his head down on to his forearms again and waited. Faintly, in the distance, he could hear some music. An exercise class perhaps, or relaxation. Maybe just cook in the kitchen, preparing another lentil soufflé. Nausea swept through him, and he knew he wasn't going to be able to stay lying there. *At least they could have left the bloody light on.*

He sat up with difficulty, cursing his back, and swung his feet to the floor. When he tried to put his weight on them they buckled from the cramp, and he leaned back against the trolley, but only for a moment as he felt the sharp stab of a needle in his back. *Oh shit.* He reached behind him with a tentative hand and felt ten or a dozen needles, maybe more, in two neat rows down his lower back.

He waited for a moment for his legs to recover, moving his

weight from one to the other, then reached for the towel lying across the end of the trolley. It felt heavy – and odd somehow. Everything felt odd. He shuffled to the door, and found it was locked. A large key was sticking out of the mortice. He turned it and opened the door, blinking from the sudden bright light of the corridor.

Waiting there a moment in the doorway, shaking the cotton wool out of his head, he saw two elderly ladies approach from the direction of the west wing. They stopped and stared at him, open-mouthed. One of them began to scream, the other crumpled to the floor in a dead faint. A moment later a male therapist came running down the corridor in response to the shrieks and saw Brock. In his subsequent statement to the police he described how he had noticed Brock's posture, stooping as if he had been in an accident, and the small acupuncture needles covering his back. But before that he saw the blood, lots of it, all over Brock's hands, drenching his legs, dripping from his towel, staining the carpet around his feet.

18

Word of another killing at Stanhope rippled through County Police divisional headquarters at Crowbridge, running fast through some parts of the building, more slowly through others. Kathy was sitting in an office on the fourth floor typing up her fifth report on the tyre-slasher, when the word reached the level below her. A uniformed WPC picked up a pile of papers and headed for the stairs, intending to speak to her friend in the next room to Kathy, but at the same moment Kathy's phone rang. It was three-thirty, perhaps an hour after Rose's throat had been sliced open.

'Kathy, have you heard? There's been another killing at Stanhope Clinic,' Penny Elliot told her. 'It looks as if war's broken out on the second floor.'

'No! I hadn't heard. What's happened?' Kathy felt her heart start thumping with panic, as if she already knew the worst.

'Hang on.' Kathy heard her talking to someone nearby, then, 'Apparently, someone's been found down there with their throat cut.'

'Oh God! Brock!'

'What's that?'

But Kathy had already jammed down the receiver and was running for the door, just as the woman in the next office looked in and said, 'Have you heard . . .?'

Kathy skidded to a halt under the trees before the car park, full of marked and unmarked police vehicles. An ambulance had backed across the grass verge by the west wing and was standing with its rear doors open beside the door to the basement. The two ambulance men were waiting, smoking, chatting to a uniformed constable who challenged her when she got out of the car. She opened her wallet for him, barely slowing as she came down the steps, and raced along the corridor, sensing her way to the epicentre of the disaster from the increasingly strained expressions on the faces she met along the way.

Scene-of-crime and forensic were already well into their routine as she came to a halt, eased her way around a knot of crouching men and looked into the room from which the photographer's light was flashing. She saw the dark blood everywhere, across the trolley, the walls, and all over the white coat of the body on the floor. She recognized the sheen of Rose's black hair, wedged into the angle between the floor and wall.

She stepped back and took her bearings, looking around her, heart racing. Further up the corridor a man in blue overalls and wearing surgical gloves came out of a room carrying several plastic bags containing blood-stained items. She walked quickly up the corridor and looked inside. Brock was sitting motionless on a metal chair facing the door. He was wearing only a pair of boxer shorts, originally white but now stained, like most of his body below the elbows, with blood. His face was as grey as his beard and his eyes seemed to be looking at something far, far away. One man was taking scrapings from his finger-nails, another swab samples from the blood on his feet, and another – she recognized Professor Pugh squinting through his glasses – was removing acupuncture needles from his back. For a moment Kathy was struck by the image of a grotesque beauty parlour.

'Ah, Sergeant Kolla! How nice to see you again!' Professor Pugh beamed at her. Brock looked up and his eyes met Kathy's. Almost imperceptibly he shook his head, then lowered his eyes again.

'I wondered if you might be coming along to the party,'

Pugh went on, stooping to retrieve a needle from Brock's lower back. 'I thought Chief Inspector Tanner must be calling upon your extensive experience of this place.'

As if on cue, a voice, low and cold and hard, growled in Kathy's ear. 'You – outside!'

Kathy turned and he indicated the corridor with a jerk of his head. She started walking and sensed him following half a step behind and to one side. She retraced her steps back below the west wing until the door at the end came into view. The uniformed man standing there straightened up as he saw them. Tanner's hand on her arm stopped her and she turned to face him.

'Go back to Division, clear whatever you've got on your desk in ten minutes, no more.' He was speaking quietly, his face less than a foot away from hers. Round his shoulder Kathy could see the constable looking curiously at them, straining to hear what they were saying. 'Speak to no one. Then go directly home and wait to be contacted. As from this moment you are suspended from duty.'

Part Three

19

It was strange how different the place was in daylight in the middle of a weekday afternoon. In theory it should have been the same as at the weekend, but somehow it wasn't at all. The sounds were different: the cries of small children coming home from the primary school round the corner; heavy traffic on the main road at the front; complete silence indoors. The house seemed more squalid for being empty. She sat at the small table in the middle of the kitchen and saw all the things she'd never had time to notice before. She wondered whether she should try to do something about the deposits of black grease which had formed around the feet of the old gas cooker, but then saw the state of the lino, curling and cracking wherever furniture wasn't pinning it to the floor-boards. Without people rushing through it on their way to work or out for a date, the room was forlorn.

Especially forlorn was the cupboard on the opposite wall, with grubby stickers on all the doors identifying whose was which. Someone had done that several generations ago, someone with a tidy mind, or upset at having their stuff pinched. The names had remained the same, although the tenants had all changed. She was 'Eric', the girl on the ground floor who worked at the building society was 'Monty', and 'Sylvester' was a creepy little man in the attic. She didn't know the other two tenants.

'We never meet for the best part of a year, and suddenly we keep bumping into each other.'

Kathy jumped at the unexpected sound. 'Oh yes. Hello again. So you're "Mary".' She nodded at the name on the door he was reaching across to open. 'Mary' was a six-foot-two, fair-haired man with a boxer's face whom she'd passed as he was talking on the pay-phone in the hall that morning.

'My other name is Patrick. And you are "Eric", I believe.'

'Aka . . . Kathy.'

'How do you do, Kathy,' he shook hands formally. 'You're the detective, aren't you? We never meet because we both work odd hours. I'm a rep with Whitbread's.'

'I was just realizing how little I know about this place, even though I've been living here all this time. I'm probably one of the longest-serving tenants by now.'

He smiled, a pleasant, battered, gentle smile, she thought, the asymmetry of the nose and the larger left ear potentially engaging, if that sort of thing appealed to you. 'Not quite. You're a figure of considerable mystery and speculation, though.'

'Why's that?' Kathy asked.

'Because of what you do, I suppose. And the fact that hardly anybody has spoken to you or seen you, except occasionally being picked up by bulky men in unmarked cars.'

'I haven't participated much in the community of number twenty-three, you mean? I honestly didn't think there was one.'

'Oh, you might be surprised. It's helped me out from time to time.'

'Well, maybe I'll get the chance to find out. This place is pretty grimy. Maybe I should do something about it.'

'That would be wonderful. None of us likes cleaning. Want some?' He offered her some of the instant coffee he was making.

'Thanks, I'm OK.'

'Taking some time off?'

'You could put it like that.'

'You make it sound pretty bad.'

Kathy got to her feet. 'Yes.' She turned and made for the

door. When she reached it she stopped to think. 'Look. If you hear the phone any time over the next few days and it's for me, would you make sure and bang on my door, no matter what time it is? It's just that I don't always hear it, being at the back of the house. My room is –'

'I know where it is.' He smiled again. 'Yes, I'll do that, of course.'

'Thanks.' She strode off down the threadbare hall carpet, avoiding the pedal and oily chain of the padlocked bike parked at the foot of the stairs.

A couple of hours later Kathy was lying on her bed, hands behind her head, staring at the ceiling, when there was a soft tap at her door. She jumped to her feet and yanked it open.

'Hi.' Patrick grinned shyly at her in the gloom of the landing.

'Is it the phone for me?'

'No, no. I was just thinking, I have to go out to pay a call on someone. It's a nice quiet place, not far away. I wondered if a drink might brighten your day.'

'Thanks, it probably would. But I'd better stay here, just in case.'

'Jill just got back from work. Her room's right next to the phone, you know. She says she's going to be here till her friend picks her up at eight, and she'll ring the number I give her if any calls come in for you.'

Kathy hesitated. 'I suppose it would look pretty bad if I refused, in view of my non-participation in the social life of the household so far.'

Patrick shrugged and nodded agreement. 'Pretty bad.'

The 'place' was a drinking club called PDQ, for some reason that Kathy never learned. It was so dark that its actual extent was indeterminate. The darkness also had the welcome effect of suspending real time, so that it became difficult after a while to recall what hour of the day or night it was outside. They sat on stools at the bar and Patrick introduced her to

Carl, the blond Swede who owned the place, whose forearms were as massive as the joint of cold beef he proceeded to carve for them for sandwiches with their drinks. After an initial altercation when Kathy tried to order mineral water, they both settled on lager. While Patrick took Carl's order for the brewery and tried to interest him in a new strong beer, Kathy sipped her lager, munched on her sandwich and stared at the tiny silver stars glued to the midnight-blue ceiling. She thought of Brock, now more than twenty-four hours in Tanner's hands. She thought of his grey face and the stoop of his shoulders. And she rehearsed once more the responses she would give to their questions, although the longer they took to call her in, the more difficult it was becoming to believe in her replies.

'Looks to me like a case for a rusty nail, Carl,' she heard Patrick say.

'What?' she said, bringing her attention back to the two of them. Patrick was looking at her with concern. 'What's a rusty nail?'

'A liqueur folded into the spirit that forms its base. I suggest Lochan Ora and Scotch.'

'Nah.' Carl was shaking his head. 'She needs a walkie-talkie, that's what she needs.'

'And what's a walkie-talkie?'

'You don't need to know, but after I give you two of them, you can't walkie and you can't talkie.' He roared with laughter.

'Yes,' Kathy said, imagining herself attending her interrogation in a state of alcoholic paralysis, 'that's all I need.'

The call came the following morning just after eleven. A secretary from administration told her to report to Interview Room 247 immediately. In the taxi, Kathy recalled Tanner's earlier instructions to Dowling and herself. *You will do what you're told; you will go to counselling; you will keep very,*

very low; you will be very, very quiet and humble. Because if I see or hear one cheep from either of you again, I am personally going to insert all the paperwork from this case into your private orifices and set fire to it.

She wished she knew what had happened to Dowling. She had tried a number of times to ring him at work and at his home, but without success. By the time the cabbie pulled in to the kerb outside the building, her heart was pounding badly. She fumbled the money and looked closely at the man's face while he searched for change, as if he was the last normal human being she was ever likely to see.

Tanner kept her waiting another hour, sitting alone in the windowless interview room with her back to the door, facing an empty chair across the table. At least it gave her a chance to bring down her heart rate and stabilize the adrenalin in her bloodstream, although when the door eventually did fly open she nearly leaped to her feet.

A woman detective came in after him, closed the door and took a seat behind Kathy's right shoulder. Tanner took the chair facing her. He laid down a plain manila file, lit a cigarette and considered her for a moment through the blue smoke. Imagining what she would do in his position, she had decided he would begin with that last interview he had had with them, and his words of warning. Then, having established the *threat* with that recollection, he would begin the *questions*.

She was wrong. He had no questions. Instead he opened the file and withdrew a single typed sheet of paper and laid it in front of her. Beside it he placed a ball-point pen.

'Read and sign,' he said simply, his tone distant, indifferent.

She blinked with surprise, then leaned forward, not wanting to touch the piece of paper, and read what it had to say.

STATEMENT BY DETECTIVE SERGEANT K. KOLLA

On 16 March last, I, together with DC G. Dowling, visited the private home of DCI D. Brock in London. The latter was known to me from professional contact during my previous attachment to the Metropolitan Police. My intention was to persuade Detective Chief Inspector Brock to use his influence as a senior officer with the Metropolitan Police to reopen the case of the death of Alex Petrou at the Stanhope Clinic during the night of 27/28 October last. I was fully aware that the police and coroner's investigations had been completed on the circumstances surrounding the death of Mr Petrou, that the case was closed, and that my superiors had explicitly instructed me to make no further inquiries into the matter. I made these facts known to DCI Brock.

After discussion, DCI Brock agreed to undertake a private investigation of his own into the affair, and to this end registered himself as a patient at Stanhope Clinic, without disclosing his intentions or his identity as a police officer to the owners of the clinic. He entered the clinic on 18 March last.

On 21 March I met DCI Brock in Edenham to review his progress. During this meeting we discussed the possibility of illegally gaining access to the private computer files of the clinic. Subsequently DCI Brock did in fact do this, during the night of 23 March, by forcibly breaking into the clinic offices.

This statement is freely made and witnessed.

Kathy felt a cold, nauseous lump rise from her stomach towards her throat as she reread the document. She forced herself to concentrate, think clearly.

Some of this must have come from Brock . . . All of it? . . . No mention of Belle . . . And not a word about Rose.

'No' – she sat up and met Tanner's eyes – 'I can't sign that.'

'You'll notice that there's no mention of Rose Duggan's name.' Tanner spoke casually but slowly, letting her think it through. 'No mention of your and Brock's role or share in the responsibility for her death.' He leaned back in his chair and studied her face as he might a television screen, waiting for some information to come up, impersonally.

Kathy stared back at him, then lowered her eyes and read the page a third time.

'Take out the last paragraph,' she said finally, 'about the files.'

Tanner gave a little smile and shook his head. 'There is another version of that paragraph,' he said. 'I'm still not sure which to go for.'

He reached forward and drew out a second sheet of paper from the file in front of him. At first it seemed identical to the other. Kathy ran her eye quickly down it until she spotted the difference. A further sentence had been added to the last paragraph, after 'forcibly breaking into the clinic offices'.

He did this after an unauthorized attempt by STO B. Mansfield to gain access to the clinic computer, using a private phone line, was unsuccessful.

Kathy swallowed, forcing the lump back down. Then she reached forward, picked up the pen and signed her name to the first version of the statement, without the reference to Belle.

Tanner kept her waiting in the interview room for a further forty minutes. Then he reappeared. 'How did you get here?' he asked.

'Taxi,' she said.

He nodded and left. Ten minutes later a uniformed WPC put her head round the door. 'Chief Inspector Tanner says you can go now. There's a taxi waiting downstairs.'

Kathy made her way down to the front entrance. The taxi was standing at the kerb, engine running. She opened the rear door to get in, then hesitated, seeing another passenger on the far side of the back seat. She didn't recognize him for a moment.

'Brock!'

She was shocked by his face, haggard, with dark circles under his eyes.

'Where to?' the taxi driver asked, looking at her in his mirror.

'Do you want to get something to eat?' she asked Brock gently.

He shook his head. 'Wouldn't mind ten minutes' kip,' he said, his voice sounding husky.

She hesitated, then gave the man the address of her bedsit. When they got there she paid off the taxi and led Brock up to her room on the first floor. He seemed not to notice his surroundings as she opened the door and showed him the single bed over by the far corner.

'The bathroom's first on the right outside.' She pulled the curtains closed, found him a towel and left him to it.

She went out to the small supermarket two streets away and bought some groceries, then lingered at a newsagent's on the way back, flicking through magazines, to give Brock time to get himself organized. When she finally put her head round the door, the room was dark and silent. She tiptoed across to check the motionless form under her duvet, collected a sweater from the wardrobe and went back downstairs to the kitchen.

Around eight she cooked a couple of steaks with onions and baked potatoes, and went upstairs to wake him, but he was so unresponsive to her touch that she decided to leave him be. She knocked on Patrick's door to see if he was interested in a steak, but he wasn't there.

By eleven she was flagging. She returned to her room and attempted to make a nest for herself in the armchair. For a couple of hours she shifted uncomfortably from one position to another, overtired and sleepless. Throughout this time there was neither sound nor movement from the figure on her bed. Around one o'clock she got out of the chair and went back down to the kitchen with a paperback, a blanket wrapped round her shoulders. Patrick was there, making a cup of instant.

'Hello again!' he beamed.

'Hi. Just back from work?'

'Sort of. How about you? Did you get your call?'

'Yes, it came finally. Now I've had to put someone up in my room for the night and I can't get to sleep myself.'

Patrick thought. 'You could use Mervyn's room. Up in the attic. He's gone to stay with his parents for a couple of days.'

'Mervyn – he's "Sylvester", isn't he? He seemed a bit odd.'

'Oh, not really. He has some personal problems – well, BO actually, as you must have noticed. He's very sensitive. But we're working our way round to helping him sort it out.'

Kathy wondered what their strategy was. 'That's the social welfare committee of number twenty-three, is it?' she asked.

Patrick smiled.

'Well, I couldn't just use his bed without asking him.'

'Oh, it would be all right. I have his key. Everybody leaves a spare key to their room with one of the others. Everybody except you, that is.'

Kathy began to see the extent of the social web of the house, of which she had been totally oblivious.

'We couldn't rely on Dominic, you see.'

'Who's Dominic?'

'The landlord, of course.' Patrick was shocked at her ignorance.

'Oh, right. I did meet him once.' Kathy sighed with tiredness.

'Look, I'm absolutely sure that Mervyn would be very upset if you didn't make use of his room.'

Kathy nodded. She no longer had much confidence in her own judgement as to what was proper. She followed Patrick up to the top of the house and fell exhausted into Mervyn's bed.

Brock finally awoke next morning at eleven, his 'ten-minute kip' having lasted twenty hours. Kathy made them both bacon and eggs while he had a bath and shaved, and they sat and ate it on their laps in her room in front of the electric fire. Brock was certainly more like his old self, complimenting her on the food and trying to work out where they were from the view out of the window. But she found his sporadic conversation aggravating. It seemed as if he was refusing to think about what had happened. Finally, the thought she had been resisting refused any longer to be suppressed.

He's given up. He just doesn't want to know any more.

She had intended to let him begin, but now she decided to broach the subject herself. 'Do you want to see the papers? I've kept them all from Tuesday morning when they first carried the story.'

'What do they tell us?'

'Not a lot. No arrests. No clues mentioned. Inquiries continuing. A lot of patients leaving the clinic. Regurgitation of the Petrou case. An interview with Rose's parents.'

Brock's frown deepened at the mention of Rose's name, but he said nothing. Kathy broke into his silence with what was uppermost in her mind. 'I signed a statement, Brock.'

He wiped his plate clean with a piece of bread and chewed it thoroughly before replying. 'Yes, he showed it to me. You had no choice, I'd say.' He reached for the mug of tea.

'Do you think so? I didn't tell him any of those things. He didn't ask me anything.'

'No. He didn't get them from me either, if that's what's worrying you.'

'But . . .?' She stared at him perplexed.

He took a sip of tea and placed the mug carefully back down on the tray. 'He knew it all already.' Brock straightened his spine against the back of the chair and flexed his shoulders. 'I'm afraid I seriously underestimated our problem, Kathy. I shan't do it again. The only thing to say on the positive side' – he turned his neck slowly – 'is that they do seem to have cured my bad shoulder.'

20

'The other good thing,' Brock said later, when they were washing their plates in the kitchen, 'is this conference. They feel inhibited about disgracing me while I'm supposed to be representing the cream of my profession at an international conference. They feel bound to wait until I get back.'

'You're still going to Rome?'

'Have to. I'm booked to fly out on Saturday. What day is it today? I've lost count.'

'Thursday.'

'That means it's Good Friday tomorrow. Is that right?'

'I suppose so,' Kathy said. 'I'd forgotten it was Easter. When will you get back?'

'Well, it might be advisable for that date to become a little uncertain. The formal business of the conference finishes on Friday, but I suppose, if my paper was brilliant enough, my Italian colleagues might feel it necessary to ask me to extend my stay. I don't actually use up all of my back leave until the middle of April.'

Kathy stared at the soapy water in the bowl, again wondering if he was telling her he was bowing out.

'I don't think,' he said, wiping the last plate with the tea-towel, 'that they'll go for you until they've made up their mind what to do with me. I may be wrong, but that was the feeling I got. There were one or two interruptions, phone calls, in the course of their inquiries, concerning relations between forces. You are still formally on secondment from the Met, which makes it a little more awkward for them. And, of course, it now looks as if you were right about

Petrou being murdered. Embarrassingly so. They won't forgive you for that.'

Brock took the dishes over to the cupboard. 'Let's see, you're "Eric", aren't you?'

'How on earth did you know that?' Kathy looked at him, astonished.

'Jill told me. Nice girl. Patrick's a pleasant fellow too. You're lucky to have such good neighbours.'

'And when did you meet them?'

'About four in the morning. I woke up with a foul headache and went searching for an aspirin. Jill and Patrick were down here. They fixed me up.'

'They were down here then?'

'Mmm. Jill had just got in from some disco. She offered to take me next week, but I had to tell her I'd be in Rome. They did say they were a bit concerned about you.'

Kathy shook her head in disbelief. 'You think ... you think Division will just leave me in suspense for a while?'

'Yes. They don't need to rush. I think you should keep very quiet. Not do anything to attract anyone's attention. Trust no one.' It reminded her of Tanner's earlier advice. 'On the other hand, if you knew of ways to stay in touch – indirect, inconspicuous ways – it would be very useful to know what was going on.'

'You haven't told me what happened to Rose,' she said.

Brock frowned and lowered his head. 'I feel like some fresh air. Is there anywhere around here we can walk?'

They put on their coats, crossed the main road at the front of the house and followed a lane opposite that led down to the banks of the stream which flowed through the centre of Crowbridge. There was a path along the bank, wide enough for them to walk side by side, and they followed it slowly, watching the heavy current swirl past between clumps of willow and hawthorn.

'Poor Rose,' Brock said at last.

'Tanner said we shared the responsibility for her death.'

'Perhaps he's right. It makes it worse that I was there and couldn't prevent it. Hell, I don't even know what happened! One moment I was feeling the first needle going in, and the next thing I remember was trying to get my legs out from underneath her body – twenty minutes later. I can't blame them for being sceptical. I wouldn't have believed it myself if a witness had told me that.'

'But you'd passed out in similar circumstances before – Beamish-Newell could confirm it.'

'Yes. I wonder if he did.'

'Anyway, if you had been awake you'd have received the same treatment as Rose. How did they do it?'

'Those treatment rooms are linked to one another by connecting doors. They must have been in one or other of the adjoining rooms and waited for Beamish-Newell to leave, then stepped in, cut Rose's throat, locked the door to the corridor and switched off the light. Then back into the next room, take off the protective clothing – there was a hell of a mess, it must have been all over them – bundle it up and march off down the corridor.'

'Pretty cool – and chancy. It would have to have been someone in the clinic who knew the routines. God, the more you think about it, the more difficult it sounds.' Kathy shook her head. 'And why do it anyway?'

'Because they knew she was going to tell me something crucial. Something worth taking a risk for.'

'Who knew she was going to talk to you?'

'I don't know. Grace Carrington, certainly, but I don't know who else. Rose might have spoken to her boy-friend about it. Maybe even Laura Beamish-Newell.'

'They couldn't know that you would pass out. And they couldn't know when Beamish-Newell was going to leave. Well, that's not quite true, is it? One person could have known both those things: Beamish-Newell himself.'

'Yes. He rearranged the time of my session. And it seems odd if he left the room knowing I'd passed out. I imagine he's been giving a fairly detailed account of his movements after he left the room.'

'As he did the first time – all lies. And anyway, people would only be able to vouch for him once he had left the room. They wouldn't be able to say what he'd been doing before that, when he was alone with Rose and –'

'And one ever-alert undercover detective,' Brock muttered bitterly.

Later, when they turned to retrace their steps along the river bank, Kathy asked, 'How about your paper to this conference? Did you get it finished?'

'All but. It seems pretty spurious now, though. If it were any good, it should tell me how to solve this one.'

'It was about serial crimes, wasn't it?'

'The hidden thread,' Brock said without much conviction, 'that links the actions of the serial killer. I've had plenty of time to ponder that over the last few days. But it's amazing how much easier it is to spot in retrospect.'

Brock was anxious to get back home to London. Kathy could understand, but all the same she didn't relish the prospect of being left in limbo without a future or a plan. Later that afternoon she walked part of the way with him to the vehicle yard attached to Division, where Brock's car was being held. Rain was beginning to fall as they shook hands on a street corner and wished each other luck.

That evening she came upon Patrick in the kitchen.

'I think,' she said, 'that it's time I had a rusty nail.'

Over the following days she followed Brock's advice, keeping a low profile and approaching no one at Division. On Tuesday the morning papers carried the news that an unnamed male employee of the clinic, aged thirty-three, had been taken to Division headquarters the previous evening, exactly one week after Rose's murder, and was helping police with their inquiries. The local radio news repeated this through the day, but by evening had added nothing to it. At seven Penny Elliot rang.

'Kathy, how are you? I thought you might have rung me.'

'I wanted to, Penny, but I thought I'd better leave you alone.'

'You sound depressed. Have you heard the news?'

'Only what's been on the radio.'

'They've charged someone. Someone called Geoffrey Parsons. Do you know him?'

'Yes. He was the victim's fiancé. What has he been charged with?'

'Murder, I understand.'

'One murder, or both?'

'I'm not sure – just one, I think. Anyway, it vindicates you, doesn't it?'

'Maybe. Do you know what evidence they have?'

'Well, not really, they're being very tight-lipped down on the second floor. But one of my people claims to have heard that the girl was pregnant.'

Kathy shook her head. 'Oh God. But it doesn't make sense, Penny. Why would he have killed her, especially if she was carrying his child?'

'Well, that's the point, apparently. The rumour is that it wasn't his. The blood group of the foetus was wrong. But it would have been right for the previous victim to have been the father.'

'Petrou?' Kathy was startled. 'But she would have to have been at least five months gone.'

'I imagine they won't know for sure till they've done the DNA tests. Kathy, this is just hearsay. The place is buzzing with rumours. Can't you get back in here and demand that they come clean with you about what they've found out? It was originally your case, after all. It isn't right that they should put you in this position.'

'Thanks, Penny. I'll think about it. Maybe I should just wait awhile.'

'You know best. Anyway, I just wanted to let you know the good news. Is there anything I can do to help?'

Kathy hesitated, then said, 'Do you know the DC I had on the original investigation – Gordon Dowling? I'd like to get in touch with him, but I can't seem to track him down.'

'I know him, but I haven't seen him around for a while. I'm not sure if he's part of Tanner's team at present.'

'Very unlikely. He's probably on suspension, like me.'

'Oh, well, I'll try to find out where he is.'

'What about Belle Mansfield, in technical support? Have you seen her lately?'

'The systems analyst? Yes, she came up in conversation the other day. She's leaving, apparently. Handed in her notice.'

'Oh shit.'

'Was she involved?'

'I'm not a good person to know at present, Penny. That's why I didn't want to contact you.'

The line was silent for a moment, and when Penny spoke again Kathy could hear the hesitation in her voice. 'But Kathy, surely now . . . now they've caught the girl's killer . . .'

'If I'd done as I was told, she'd still be alive, Penny.'

'You can't think like that! You didn't kill her!'

Kathy didn't reply.

'Kathy,' Penny's voice sounded worried, 'you need help, somebody to talk to about this. I could speak to someone.'

'No! No, Penny. I appreciate you ringing, but I just want to keep out of the way at present. If you could find out about Dowling, that would be a help. And if you do learn of any new developments, I'd really appreciate hearing about them.'

The days dragged. Kathy took to visiting the supermarket just to hear the sounds of normality and get away from the deathly silence of the house, but she always came back within an hour in case someone rang.

On the Thursday of that week, she decided in desperation to take the only positive step she could think of that wasn't likely to get straight back to the investigating team at Division. She drove the twelve miles to Edenham, parked her car in the council car park behind the main street and walked into Jerry Hamblin's greengrocer's shop.

Jerry finished serving his customer with some remark, obviously catty, which Kathy didn't catch but which had both Jerry and the woman cackling with laughter. Then he turned and his face dropped as he recognized her. 'Oh my God! I thought I'd seen the last of you. It's this business at the clinic, isn't it? That's what's brought you back, like a bad smell.'

'Hello, Jerry. No, I'm not involved in the investigation at all.'

There was a flatness to her voice that sounded genuine to Jerry and made him hesitate. 'Why're you here, then?' he said, marginally less aggrieved.

'I was just passing. Thought I'd have some more of your juicy grapes, if you still have them.'

'It's not the season, dear. Just passing, were you?' He stared at her sceptically, and she looked back for a moment and then dropped her eyes.

'Well . . . there was something. I'd hoped to see Errol, really.'

'He's not here, as you can see. What did you want him for?'

'You are still together, then?'

'Of course we are. Why shouldn't we be?'

'I hoped you were. I was afraid our investigation must have –' she shrugged '– caused trouble for you.'

'Yes, well, don't bother yourself about that. Just leave us both well alone.'

'When I was leading that inquiry, I said something to Errol that was unforgivable. I wanted to apologize to him.'

Jerry looked at her, incredulous. 'The copper wants to apologize! Bloody hell! Whatever will they teach you next? And what was this thing you said?'

'It doesn't matter.'

'Was it about Alex Petrou having Aids, by any chance?'

'Something like that. He told you?'

Jerry nodded. 'Actually,' he said, fiddling with the avocados on the tray in front of him, 'your interfering probably did our relationship a bit of good. Brought a few things to the surface. We decided to make a fresh start. Went away at Christmas for the holiday of a lifetime, to the States – like a second honeymoon, you might say.'

'I'm glad. I hope it works.'

'God, you do sound pessimistic. Have you been having a rough day or something?'

'Sorry.' Kathy smiled briefly and made to turn and leave.

'Here,' Jerry said, 'fancy a drink, do you?'

'What about the shop?'

'It's half-day closing. Come on, I'll come back later and clear up properly.'

Jerry untied his apron and took a leather bomber-jacket from the hook behind the door to the back of the shop. They stepped out into the cool afternoon and walked down the High Street to the Hart Revived.

Jerry brought two glasses of white wine over to their table near the fire. 'I want to hear what the latest is on this new killing,' he said.

'I told you, Jerry, I'm not involved. You heard they charged Geoffrey Parsons?'

'No! When was that?'

'Tuesday. It was in the papers this morning.'

Jerry frowned. 'Parsons. I wouldn't have thought he could kill a rabbit!'

'Yes, I agree. You thought Beamish-Newell killed Alex Petrou, didn't you?'

'Did I?' Jerry adjusted his glasses and looked coy.

'Of course you did. So did I.'

'Yes, well, we all make mistakes. Why would Parsons have done it?'

Kathy hesitated. 'The suggestion is that Rose was pregnant and Petrou may have been the father.'

Jerry's eyes widened and his mouth formed a shocked O. 'The bitch!'

'I wouldn't describe her as that,' Kathy said.

'Not her, him! That bitch Petrou! I knew he was a slut, but *really*!'

Kathy nodded. 'He certainly seems to have got around.'

'So all that about Fiendish-Cruel coming round to see Errol was completely irrelevant, as it turned out.' Jerry rolled his eyes and shook his head. 'I could have saved us all a lot of pain by keeping my trap shut.'

'Maybe. Did you know that he told us Errol was supplying Petrou with ecstasy?'

Jerry flinched. 'What are you up to, Kathy?'

'Nothing. I just wondered if our lot ever followed up on that with Errol.'

'No, they didn't.' He shuddered. 'God! That's the last thing we need.'

'And they haven't been back to see you this time?'

Jerry shook his head.

'Finish your drink,' Kathy said, 'and I'll get you another.'

When she sat down again, Jerry was contemplating the flames flickering in the grate. 'I really did the dirty on old Fiendish, when you come to think of it,' he said.

'How do you mean?'

'Well, there was me thinking he was a murderer, that he was using Errol and getting him into trouble, when really it was Errol who'd been letting Fiendish down, playing around with Petrou, selling him stuff, all that. He didn't need to do that, especially not to Fiendish-Cruel.'

'As a good customer, do you mean?'

'What? Oh, well, not only that. Fiendish had been good to Errol before. One of the reasons I was willing to make allowances for Errol was that he lost his mother last summer. It really upset him: they were ever so close. She was a funny old duck. Do you know that it was only the Christmas before last that she realized that we were gay? We'd been living together for almost twenty-five years, and she hadn't the faintest idea! My Mum and Dad came down to have lunch with us on Christmas Day, 'cause really my Mum's a terrible cook, and Dad's always saying I'm twice as good as she is. Anyway, we invited Errol's old dear over as well for a real family occasion – she was a widow – and she and Mum were sitting together sipping their sherry in the living room while Errol and I were in the kitchen cooking, and my Dad was out in the garden smoking his pipe, and suddenly she said to Mum, as if it'd been on her mind quite a bit, "Evelyn, do you think our boys are quite, you know, normal?" and my Mum said, "No, of course not. They're both queer as coots, you silly old bat."'

Jerry broke into peals of laughter, Kathy joining him, until there were tears running down both their faces.

'Anyway, she got cancer soon after, poor old thing. They tried all sorts, but in the end they couldn't do anything for her. Errol was ever so upset. He told Fiendish-Cruel one time he was out at the clinic, and Fiendish was good with him. That's how he got to know him well, really. Fiendish even went to see the old duck in hospital and afterwards when they sent her home. He gave her some of his organic medicines, but of course they didn't do no good either.'

'That's interesting, that he would do that. He really must have cared.'

'Yes, I think he does care. I kind of think of him as a bully, you know? But he's more complicated than that. I think he likes you to be in despair – oh God, that sounds really bitchy, doesn't it? No, I mean, if you're in despair and are prepared to hand the whole thing over to him, put him in control, then I think he'll really go out of his way for you. And Errol was in despair. Only afterwards, when he started fooling around with that Petrou, it must have seemed to Fiendish like a right slap in the face.'

'Yes, I see.'

'Anyway, I reckon that was Errol's mid-life crisis, brought on by his Mum's passing. There won't be any more Alex Petrous in Errol's life.'

Kathy raised her glass. 'I'll drink to that, Jerry.'

'You haven't told me why you're down in the dumps, Kathy.'

'Oh . . . I think I screwed up. And got a friend into trouble in the process.'

'Not that nice boy who got on to me in the first place, was it?'

'Gordon Dowling? No, not him.' Kathy laughed. 'You thought he was a nice boy?'

'Sure of it, Kathy. Can't see him making a go of it in the police, though. Can you?'

'Well, he's not all that bright.'

Jerry chuckled briefly, then checked himself. 'Sorry, Kathy, but I didn't think that would be a disqualification. No, I meant his being gay.'

'Gay?'

'Yes. Didn't you know?'

Kathy looked at him, surprised. 'No, I had no idea.'

'That's how he got on to me, you see. At the Jolly Roger.'

'Of course, yes. I should have thought.'

'Well, it's not important anyway. Unless some of those butch bastards he's got for workmates cottoned on to it.'

Kathy was aware of a sick feeling in the pit of her stomach.

*

Kathy had two phone calls on Friday evening. She was sitting in the kitchen with Jill, Mervyn and Patrick, all eating a Lancashire hot-pot which Patrick had cooked, when Penny Elliot rang. She had little new to tell Kathy. According to one of the clerks in Personnel, Gordon Dowling had left for three weeks' leave about ten days before. No one seemed to know where he'd gone. Penny had a couple of addresses of next-of-kin taken from his file. She had discovered next to nothing about the progress of Rose's murder investigation, beyond a rumour that rope identical to that used to hang Petrou had been found somewhere – the stories were conflicting as to precisely where – that appeared to incriminate Parsons.

Kathy, puzzled, thanked her and returned to the kitchen. She chewed a mouthful of stew, then said suddenly, 'Patrick, this is really good. Maybe we could do a deal: you cook and I'll clean the kitchen.'

'Done.' He smiled.

A few minutes later the phone rang again. Jill ran out to the hall, hoping it was her boy-friend, with whom she'd had a quarrel. She reappeared a few moments later, barely hiding her disappointment, to tell Kathy that it was for her *again*. It was Brock.

'He sounds happy,' she added.

He did sound cheerful, and the line was so clear that Kathy assumed he must have returned to London until he corrected her.

'No, no, I'm still in Rome. You sound a bit flat, though. Things difficult?'

'Oh, just frustrating. Have you heard that they've arrested Geoffrey Parsons?'

He listened for a few moments as she started to tell him what she knew, then interrupted her. 'Kathy, I can't talk long. Look, I'd like you to come over here, tell me everything.'

'Over there?' Kathy didn't get it. 'There's not a lot to tell –'

'Your passport in order, is it?'

'I think so.'

'Look, get down to Heathrow tomorrow morning, terminal two. You're booked on an Alitalia flight to Rome leaving at 8.35 a.m.'

'I am?'

'You can pick up the ticket at the check-in counter.'

'Brock, I –'

'You sound as if you could do with a change of scenery. It's splendid here. The spring's arrived in earnest. I'll be waiting for you at the airport. OK?'

The line went dead.

Kathy returned to the kitchen, bemused.

'All right?' they asked her.

'I don't know,' she said. 'I think my friend's gone round the twist. He wants me to meet him in Rome tomorrow morning.'

'Wish I had friends like that,' Jill said wistfully.

After they had cleared up, they dispersed to their rooms, the other three to prepare for a Friday night out. Kathy hesitated at her door, then called out after Patrick. She pulled something out of the pocket of her jeans and gave it to him.

'I had a spare key cut,' she said. 'Maybe you'd look after it for me, would you? In case some waif needs a room while I'm away.'

He grinned and gave her a peck on the cheek. 'Have fun,' he said.

21

Brock was right about the spring. The sun was blazing down over Rome and sparkling on the aircraft bodies on the tarmac. The sense of unreality, of not knowing what she was doing there, whether on a treasure hunt or a wild-goose chase, was heightened by the sight of Brock waiting for her beyond the barrier, beaming in shirt-sleeves and a pair of dark glasses like one of the Blues Brothers or a mafioso.

'Any bags?'

'No, just this. I wasn't sure how long I'd be staying.'

He gave her a big smile and led her out to the short-stay car park, where he fished out the keys for a Polo convertible and threw her bag in the boot. She noticed his cases were in there too. From the airport they drove out towards the autostrada and on to the A1, heading north.

'We're not staying in Rome, then?' she shouted.

He shook his head. The open top discouraged conversation, so she settled back in her seat to enjoy the unfamiliar countryside sliding past in the bright sunlight, happy to substitute the Autostrada del Sol for the usual Motorways of Murk.

After less than an hour he signalled right and took the exit for Orvieto, and she sat up and watched as the little city, perched on the flat top of its volcanic plug, came into view. They wound their way up the surrounding cliff and parked behind the cathedral.

'I thought you might be ready for some lunch before we go any further. Let's stretch our legs.'

They walked through the cathedral with its blue-and-white candystripe nave, and then down a narrow lane until they reached the main street in the city centre, and finally found a table outside a small restaurant, overlooking the stream of people passing by.

Brock rubbed his hands. 'We must try the local wine.'

He ordered a bottle while they examined a menu. Kathy settled for *lasca*, a speciality from nearby Lake Trasimeno, and Brock chose cannelloni. He asked her about her flight, her flatmates and half a dozen other unimportant things until the wine arrived. Then he raised his glass in a toast: 'To absent friends.'

He didn't offer an explanation, and she sipped at the wine, cool and fragrant.

He set down his glass and sighed. 'Well, you'd better tell me what's been going on,' and she told him what she knew.

He shook his head when she had finished. 'You can never be sure, I suppose, but I wouldn't have thought him capable of it. Not like that. Dear God, it was savage, Kathy, the way her throat was cut. One single stroke, hard, decisive, absolutely unflinching. Her head was almost off. That's not Geoffrey Parsons in a month of Sundays.'

She nodded agreement, and they sat in silence for a while until the waiter approached.

'How did your paper go down, anyway?' Kathy asked, brightening with the appearance of the food.

'Oh, quite well. I'd been dreading the whole thing actually, but it was quite fun, as it turned out.'

'Fun? A conference on catching serial killers?'

He managed a laugh, even though his mouth was full of pasta.

'There was a good paper from a young American on chance and coincidence. I suppose somebody had to work chaos theory into it somehow, but he did it very well. He went back to Jung and Koestler and so on, and he had the most fascinating case-studies from America in which completely convincing but quite inexplicable coincidences appeared, which either misled or guided the police. With a long series of murders, of course, you get more opportunities for random things to creep in. But some of them were extra-ordinary, almost as if a third hand were at work. That's the thing about life, I suppose, as against fiction. Quite strange but innocent coincidences do happen. You're trying to con-struct a logic to lead you along the hidden thread, and you have to remember that sometimes the most beautiful align-ment of events may actually be quite meaningless.'

Brock paused for another sip of the Orvieto wine, then continued.

'Like the fact that the translation of Alex Petrou's physio-therapy certificate was authenticated by the British embassy in Rome, not Athens – do you remember that? I thought at the time, What a coincidence, that's where I'm going in a few weeks. Of course that was a meaningless coincidence, except that it did mean I could ask one of the Italian people I got to know here to try to find out what Petrou had been doing in Rome a year ago, just before he came to England. It wasn't likely to be important, except that, when he came back with the answer, it suggested all sorts of other coincidences that were so beautiful, just like in the young American bloke's paper, that I couldn't resist finding out more.'

And finally Kathy realized that Brock wasn't just wasting time, and with an enormous sense of relief she put down her knife and fork and stared at him. 'You've found something out.'

'Well, now, try this one. Petrou had been in Italy for six months. He had come from Greece and before that from the Lebanon, where his family had businesses. They finally quit Beirut about four years ago and moved back to Athens, where Alex trained as a physio. I don't know why he came to Italy originally, but he got a job at a clinic, not in Rome but in Vicenza, up in the north. Now that is a rather promising coincidence, wouldn't you say?'

Kathy shook her head, 'Not off-hand.'

'Vicenza was the home of Palladio, the sixteenth-century architect of the Malcontenta, the house which was the model for Stanhope House, the place where Alex was next going to show up.'

Kathy frowned doubtfully.

'Too thin?' Brock asked. 'Well, let's go on. The reason why Stephen Beamish-Newell established his clinic in the English Malcontenta was that his first wife found the place for him and was attracted to it because she recognized its source. And she recognized its source because she herself came from . . .'

'Vicenza,' Kathy whispered, feeling a prickling along her spine.

'Right, Vicenza. Her family has lived in the city for generations. When she was eighteen they sent her to polish up her English at one of the language schools in Cambridge, and there she fell in love with a charismatic medical student. They married and eventually her family, being well off, provided the funds for them to set up their clinic. When her marriage fell apart, Gabriele returned to her family home and reverted to her maiden name, Montanari.'

'And she was there when Alex Petrou was there?'

Brock nodded. 'She still is.' He took a folded sheet of paper out of his pocket and spread it on the table. It was a photocopy of a newspaper photograph of an attractive middle-aged woman in evening dress climbing the front steps of a building, accompanied by an older man in black tie. 'Gabriele Montanari and her father, at their last public appearance, for a charity ball in Padua last Christmas.'

'Do we know if she met Petrou?'

Brock shook his head. 'No, we don't know that. But, there's a final coincidence: Papa Montanari turns out to be a shareholder of the clinic where Petrou was working.'

Kathy smiled. 'They *must* have met.'

'We do know that Petrou was getting himself into trouble

in Vicenza. There were complaints to the authorities, suggestions of extortion. He lost his job at the clinic and would probably have been picked up by the local police if he hadn't suddenly left Italy of his own accord. So what do you think of those coincidences?'

'Compelling.'

'I made a call home to Immigration and discovered that Petrou entered England at Dover, on a cross-Channel ferry from Calais. I'm also told that he bought the ticket at Calais, which suggests he didn't have a through ticket on a train. In other words, someone might have driven him up from Vicenza and put him on the boat.'

'What date was that?'

Brock consulted his notebook. 'April Fool's Day, last year. He started at Stanhope Clinic two days later.'

'Quick work, if he didn't have any contacts.'

'Quite. And Stanhope isn't exactly just off Piccadilly. It's not the sort of place you'd run into by chance.'

They finished their meal and prepared to make a move.

'Was she the absent friend you toasted?' Kathy asked suddenly.

'Who?' Brock looked startled.

'Gabriele Beamish-Newell.'

'Oh no. Someone else.'

'Someone you'd like to be sharing a bottle of Orvieto with in some Italian hill-town.'

Brock gave a little nod and turned to go.

They reached Vicenza in the late afternoon. Brock had some scribbled notes by means of which he got them to the west gate of the old city, the Porta del Castello, and into the Piazza del Castello just beyond. There Kathy was introduced to her first Palladian building, the unfinished Palazzo Giulio Porto, in front of which they left the car and went in search of their hotel on foot. The owner of the Albergo Tre Re, when they eventually found it, advised them of a more suitable parking spot, and by dusk Kathy was unpacking her small bag in a tiny but charming room with a partial view of the dome of the cathedral. She thought of the elegant woman in the photograph and wished that she had brought more clothes.

The following morning they strolled down the main street, the Corso Andrea Palladio, until Brock, consulting his notes, led them down a side-street to a small square. There they established themselves at a table outside a small café and ordered breakfast. Brock pointed to a dark-brown building on the far side of the square. 'The Palazzo Trissino-Montanari. The family home.'

'A palazzo?' Kathy was impressed, although the dour mass of the building didn't stand out from its neighbours. 'What do we do?'

'We wait, I think. I'm rather afraid,' he added regretfully, 'that I'm going to have to tell lies again, Kathy. I didn't realize how difficult it is pretending you're not what you are. I thought I'd enjoy it, but it'll be a great relief to be able to come clean with people again.'

'Can't you just tell her the truth?'

'I think she'd clam up and call the old family lawyer in ten seconds flat. No, it's got to be lies, unfortunately. And I'm afraid we're going to have to be somewhat unfair to Dr Beamish-Newell.'

'Play the "hell hath no fury" angle, you reckon?'

'Very possibly.'

They spent the whole day, singly and together, in and around the café, without catching sight of anyone leaving the Palazzo Trissino-Montanari.

'She could be anywhere,' Kathy said, as the puzzled café proprietor finally presented their bill.

'Yes. But it's Sunday today. Maybe tomorrow will be different.'

'If we're doing this again, I'm going to bring a cushion. These metal chairs are all right for half an hour – no more.'

Brock nodded. 'They design them that way on purpose.'

By the following mid-morning they had finished the previous day's *Sunday Times* which Kathy had found on sale at a kiosk nearby, and were beginning to have doubts. Not a single person or vehicle had passed through the stone archway into the palazzo. And then, suddenly, she was there, stepping out into the sun.

She looked elegant and poised – a simple skirt and silk blouse, cashmere jumper loose over her shoulders, to which her auburn hair just reached. She paused and felt for the dark glasses resting on the crown of her head and brought them down on to her aristocratic nose.

'I knew I should have brought more clothes,' Kathy muttered.

'Keep on her tail while I settle up with Gregorio,' Brock said, and disappeared into the café.

A couple of minutes later he was hurrying along in the direction he had seen them take. At last he spotted Kathy standing at a shop window, staring at the clothes inside.

'They're lovely,' she said, 'but I couldn't afford a single thing.'

'Where is she?' he puffed.

'Other side of the street, in the hairdresser's.'

'Oh no, she could be hours.'

They found another café and resumed their watch, this time insisting on paying as soon as they were served. Towards one o'clock Gabriele reappeared, her hair not noticeably shorter, and they set off again, following her into the great Piazza dei Signori, through the colonnades of Palladio's Basilica and into a small piazza on the other side. Here, outside the Ristorante del Capitanio, she found an empty table with a white linen tablecloth, inside an area enclosed by neatly clipped, boxed hedges. It was the last free table.

'What now?' Kathy joined Brock at a postcard stand beneath the colonnade.

'Follow me,' he said, and set off towards the restaurant.

At the door the proprietor vaguely indicated that he might be willing to attend to them in due course. Brock began to speak, then paused. '*Momento*,' he said, and approached Gabriele's table. With a little bow he said, '*Scusi* . . . excuse me. It isn't Mrs Beamish-Newell, is it? Gabriele Beamish-Newell?'

She looked up, surprised at first, then doubtful.

'Brock,' he beamed, 'David Brock. You remember? I was one of your patients, years ago, at Stanhope! Must have been '80 or '81.'

She removed her sunglasses slowly and looked at him coolly. Her eyebrows were fixed in that half-way position when you're not sure but don't necessarily want to give offence – yet.

He laughed. 'Of course, I didn't have the beard then.'

'Ah.' Her face lightened a little, but not much.

'You look wonderful, if you don't mind me saying, Mrs Beamish-Newell. What an amazing surprise to see you like this! But then this is your part of the world, isn't it? I've often thought of you, you know, and what a wonderful job you did for us all at Stanhope. I was thinking that only last week in fact, when I was there, and considering how much things had changed since your day.' He shook his head a little sadly.

'You were there last week?' Some genuine interest registered.

'Indeed. I go back from time to time. But . . .' He frowned. 'Oh dear. Have you been back at all recently?'

She shook her head slightly, her immaculately shaped hair brushing across the collar of her blouse. 'No. There have been many changes?' she asked.

'Oh yes. And especially in the past year, since . . . well.' He shrugged and smiled vaguely.

'Since what?'

'Oh, maybe I shouldn't comment.' Then, apparently changing the subject, 'You know, I could say that you're responsible for my being here. I became quite interested in the architecture of Stanhope, and through that in the work of Palladio. That's the reason my niece' – he indicated Kathy still standing at the doorway of the restaurant – 'and I are here. To see it in the flesh.'

'Your niece?' Gabriele looked politely in the direction of his hand.

'Yes. I'll introduce you. Do you mind?'

He called Kathy over. 'Isn't that a marvellous coincidence, us looking for a restaurant for lunch, and who should I spot but Mrs Beamish-Newell, whom I've spoken of many times. Do you remember, Kathy?'

'Of course.' They shook hands.

'I use my family name now – Montanari, Gabriele Montanari. Perhaps –' she looked undecided '– perhaps you would care to join me?'

'Are you sure? How marvellous! We'd love that. Just for a bit. We don't want to be in the way.'

'Not at all. My life is very boring these days. It will be interesting to hear of Stanhope. I am expecting a friend, but . . .' She shrugged.

'Well, you just let us know when you want us to go, Gabriele. May I call you that?'

She tilted her head gracefully. 'I'm sorry, I don't recall your –'

'David. And this is Kathy.'

'Your niece, yes. How nice.'

She looked carefully at Kathy, who tried not to show her surprise.

'So, what is the latest gossip from Stanhope?'

'It isn't the same, Gabriele. I always believed it was you who brought the humanity to the place. These things are

263

intangible, I know, but so important. And when you left, I was proved right. It seemed to have less . . . soul. More like a business. But perhaps I shouldn't speak out of turn about your former husband.'

'Oh, speak out of turn as much as you like, David. And his wife, what do you make of her?'

'Mmm.' Brock appeared to struggle to find an appropriate word. 'What would one say? Efficient?'

'Yes, one might say that.'

'A trifle . . . cold?'

'Efficient and cold. Yes. A bitch, in other words.'

Brock gave a little splutter and looked down, nodding his head vigorously.

'You are smiling, Kathy. Have you met her?'

'Yes, I have. I thought she was a bitch, too.'

'Good, we are getting somewhere. Now, I see my friend coming. Before she arrives, tell me what happened a year ago.'

'Oh well, there were some new staff changes. One in particular. Quite a disruptive influence, one would have to say. Charming, but . . .' Brock raised his eyebrows suggestively.

'Tell me.'

'Well, perhaps you would rather we left you to have lunch with your friend in peace, Gabriele. In any case, I don't really like to speak ill of the dead.'

Her face drained of colour and she froze in her seat. At that moment a dark-haired woman in an expensive but overworked costume with gold accessories arrived at the table.

'Gabriele, *cara*!'

'*Ciao*, Violetta.' Gabriele half rose, still looking shocked, brushed checks with her friend and murmured introductions.

'You are most hospitable, signora,' Brock said, 'but we don't want to intrude. We should leave you in peace.'

'Please sit down, David. I insist.'

'Well, in that case *I* insist on buying us a bottle of champagne to celebrate our fortunate meeting. Would that be in order?'

'As you wish.' She sat back and explained in a low stream of Italian to Violetta, who evidently spoke no English.

Violetta did enjoy champagne, however, and by the time they opened the third bottle, and the waiter had still not appeared with any food, her enjoyment of the company wasn't in the least inhibited by the fact that Kathy spoke no Italian and Brock's stock of phrases was pretty well exhausted. Gabriele maintained her poise, rather distant, joining in only when her friend demanded a translation of something. Kathy watched Gabriele out of the corner of her eye. She was smoking American cigarettes and building a small pile of white stubs smeared with her brown lipstick in the ashtray in front of her. Only her fingers were restless, the long nails perfectly manicured and coloured to match her lipstick.

At one point, while Brock and Violetta were deep in confused conversation, she turned suddenly to Kathy as if she knew she was being studied and said, 'I don't remember your uncle at all, you know.'

'He's usually a very quiet man,' Kathy replied. 'Self-effacing.'

'Have you ever been to Stanhope?' Gabriele asked.

'Yes, I was there last October.'

'Do you know what he was talking about just now? A death?'

Kathy wasn't sure how Brock wanted to play it. 'It was very strange,' she replied. 'Shocking.'

Gabriele fixed her with her dark eyes, letting Kathy see that she was used to having her way. 'He said a staff member. Who was it?'

'His name was Alex Petrou.'

Gabriele continued staring at Kathy.

'I'm sorry,' Kathy said sympathetically. 'Did you know him well?'

'Know him? Why do you say that?'

'I could tell from your reaction it was a shock. I'm sorry.'

Gabriele shook her head, momentarily uncertain. 'How did he die?' she said quietly.

'He was hanged.'

The gleaming brown finger-nails no longer moved.

The waiter's arrival broke the silence which had suddenly descended on their table. 'Food at last,' said Brock.

Violetta ate energetically, apparently now concerned about the time, and finished her *saltimbocca* while Gabriele was still toying with hers. They exchanged words, Violetta urging, Gabriele irritated. Finally Gabriele pushed her plate away and said to Brock, 'I am sorry, I must go. I will speak to the waiter.'

'I'll take care of it.' Brock looked carefully at her.

'Will you remain in Vicenza long?' She was staring across the square, apparently more interested in the teenage boys on their scooters.

'Probably not. We had thought of driving out to see the Malcontenta tomorrow. I don't suppose you'd be able to join us? Perhaps in the afternoon?'

'I'm sorry,' she said coolly, 'I am occupied.'

She got to her feet, ignoring Violetta's fulsome goodbyes to Brock and Kathy. Then she lifted her cigarette packet from the table and said, 'In the morning I am free.'

As they watched the two of them walk away, Kathy said, 'You seem to be quite good at picking up strange women, Uncle.'

Gabriele appeared precisely ten minutes later than the time arranged. She smiled as she watched Brock try to explain to a pair of uniformed policemen why he was parked illegally within the old city walls. Then she stepped forward and came to his assistance, dismissing the officers with a couple of phrases. 'Is this your little car? How sweet,' she remarked to Brock. She settled herself elegantly in the passenger seat in front of Kathy and they set off.

'It is a beautiful day for a drive,' she said. And it was a beautiful day, the spring sun starting to dissolve the silver morning mist over the fields as they sped eastward along the autostrada towards Padua and then Venice. Gabriele waved for him to take the Dolo exit, and he slowed and followed her instructions as she directed him along quiet roads across the flat countryside. The mist became heavier and more persistent as they neared the coast, and several times Brock was forced to slow to a crawl as they came upon a particularly thick patch.

Finally they turned on to a gravel drive and, with dramatic effect, the stone bulk of the Malcontenta loomed before them. Whether it was the quality of the light or the rugged character of the stonework and pantiles, it seemed more archaic, more powerful, than its English offspring at Stanhope, which by comparison appeared fastidious and neat, a polite copy without the brooding presence of the original. Brock stopped the car and they approached on foot. The place was quite silent and deserted; no sound of a dog, voice or motor disturbed the morning quiet. They walked all round the house, seeing no sign of anyone, and returned to the car, where Brock opened the boot and took out a bag and a rug.

'Let's sit over by the willows and have our picnic,' he said.

'A picnic?' Gabriele smiled.

'I try to think of everything,' he replied.

'Yes, I rather think you do. Are you a tax inspector, Mr Brock? Or a policeman?'

Brock looked at her in surprise.

'I am sure you were never a patient at Stanhope when I was there. I have an excellent memory.'

'Ah.'

'I much prefer people to be honest with me.'

'Thank goodness for that,' Brock said.

They walked over to the willows and found a stone bench, and the two women sat down. While Brock was unpacking his bag on the rug and offering them rolls and coffee from a vacuum flask, he explained to Gabriele something of who they were and what they were doing there. He outlined the circumstances of Petrou's death but didn't mention Rose's murder.

After a lengthy silence Gabriele finally said, 'This coffee tastes strange.'

'I added some fortification,' Brock admitted. 'Brandy.'

'My former husband would not approve of your drinking habits.'

He smiled. 'Nor of your cigarettes.'

She shrugged. 'I still have dreams about him. It took him only, oh, I don't know, a few months, to control me. I was young, I was in love with him. I let him take control. It took me many years to recover myself again. In my dreams he still comes to claim my obedience. Every cigarette I smoke is a message to him.' She gave a tight smile. 'A smoke signal of disobedience.' She opened her packet and lit up.

Kathy, sitting by her side, asked quietly, 'How did you break away?'

'I didn't – he did. He had an affair with one of the nurses. I knew about it but did nothing. I thought, how *banal*, the doctor and his nurse, it would blow over. But she was greedy to have him and she became pregnant. We had no children – it was the one thing I hadn't been able to give him. And when he discovered that she was having his baby, he decided that was the most important thing for him.'

She sucked in a deep lungful of smoke before going on. 'He was very ruthless. That is the way he is when he has made up his mind about something. He made things impossible for me until I agreed to return to Italy and let him get a divorce. My father was very angry but he could do nothing – Stephen had found a new business partner to give him money to keep the clinic going. The irony was that they lost the baby at birth.'

She glanced over her shoulder at the Malcontenta and frowned. 'I sometimes felt that it was the house that made us barren for him. She has never given him a child, I think.'

'Laura?' Brock asked.

She nodded, 'Laura Parsons.'

'Parsons?' Both Brock and Kathy echoed the name.

'Yes. She now takes his name, according to English law. But I am Catholic. In my family's eyes he is not divorced.'

'Laura is related to Geoffrey Parsons?' Brock asked.

She looked blank.

'The Estates Manager at Stanhope,' Kathy urged.

'I know no one of that name,' Gabriele said. 'That must be something else she has arranged since I left.'

They sat in silence again. Kathy thought of Laura Beamish-Newell, her brother and her lost child, and adjusted her perception of the woman in the light of these new facts. If Rose was pregnant when she died, would Laura have been aware of it? And how would she have reacted?

Brock said quietly, 'Tell us about Alex Petrou, Gabriele.'

She shrugged. 'He was not a nice man. He was working here in Vicenza at a private clinic in which my father holds an interest.' She laughed bitterly. 'I had forgotten that it was Stephen who first made Papa consider investing in such a place. Anyway, my father mentioned this man who was causing difficulties for the clinic, a scandal. He said he was like a virus, contaminating everyone he came in contact with – men and women. And when he said that he must be made to leave, to go far away, before the reputation of the clinic was fatally damaged, I thought what a fitting present it would be for Stephen and Laura to receive such a person. It could be my final message to them both.'

She ground out her cigarette with her heel and lit another. 'I met him and told him that he would be in big trouble if he remained in Italy. I said that, for the sake of my father, I could help him get a new job in England.'

'And he agreed to that?' Kathy asked.

'I gave him some money and I insisted that I drive him to France to make sure he crossed over. He had to go to Rome first to get his papers from the British embassy. I told him things about Stephen. I knew that Stephen wouldn't be able to resist him.'

'You mean Stephen is bisexual?' Kathy said.

Gabriele looked uncomfortable. 'He ... I knew that he found young men attractive.' The corners of her mouth turned down with distaste. 'I don't think he ever ... But perhaps these things become more difficult to deny, to control, as one gets older.'

'You don't believe it likely that Petrou could have killed himself?' Kathy asked.

She stared at her beautiful finger-nails for a moment. 'I think suicide was probably the only thing that he would not have been capable of.'

When Kathy mentioned on their return to the car that she had never visited Venice, Gabriele insisted she couldn't leave without having done so, since it was so close. As they drove through Mira they found a pay-phone and Gabriele made a call to some friends and arranged to meet them for lunch.

Mists still shrouded the distance when they caught their first glimpse of the golden city, magically suspended in the lagoon, the unreality of its presence only heightened by the heavy odour of the oil refineries in the still air. They drove across the causeway and found a parking place in one of the *autorimesse* by the Piazzale Roma, then took the *vaporetto* along the Grand Canal as far as the Accademia, where the queue for the gallery waited patiently around the perimeter of the little square. They crossed back over the canal on the Accademia bridge and followed Gabriele through a labyrinth of narrow lanes until she brought them to an inconspicuous doorway in the sheer wall of a building. They entered and found themselves in a restaurant with a terrace overlooking the Grand Canal. Two people, a man and a woman, were waiting for them at a table on the terrace, greeting Gabriele and her companions with great warmth.

Gabriele came to life in their presence, her face glowing with enthusiasm and the formerly stiff movements of her fingers expanding into flowing gestures of her whole body as she talked to them. Kathy sat back, soaking up the warmth of their company and of the spring sunshine. She turned to Brock and said, 'This is magic.'

He peered at her over the top of his mafioso sunglasses and nodded, sipping contentedly at his vodka and tonic. 'Yes. Better enjoy it while we can. It's back to the real world tomorrow.'

Later that afternoon in Vicenza, after they had parked the Polo near the West Gate and walked with Gabriele back to the piazza where they had first waited for her, she stopped at the doorway of the Palazzo Trissino-Montanari and turned to Brock, offering her hand. 'Do you think I was very bad, sending that man to Stanhope?' she asked.

'I think it was fate,' he replied.

And to Kathy, after Gabriele had shaken hands and disappeared into the shadows of the courtyard, he added, 'A Greek tragedy.'

22

They drove down to Rome the following morning, catching an Alitalia flight back to Heathrow in the early afternoon. As if to ram home the contrast, the Home Counties were once again blanketed by ominous black clouds, into which the plane's passengers descended reluctantly. The world below was struggling through darkness, drenching rain and a baggage handlers' dispute. Brock and Kathy finally emerged from the arrivals concourse and tried to work out where they had left their cars in the medium-stay car park. When they had found them, he turned to her. 'I think you should follow me back to my place, check what's been happening before you go to Crowbridge. You never know.'

She did as he suggested, trying to keep him in sight through the spray and heavy traffic on the M4, then across the river and through the inner boroughs until they reached Matcham High Street and the archway into Warren Lane. They parked in the courtyard and ran for Brock's front door, leaving their dripping coats on the pegs inside and taking the stairs up to the study. Brock lit the gas fire and went to make a pot of tea, while Kathy stood in the window bay looking out over the lane and the railway cutting. It seemed much longer than three and a half weeks since they had made toast here and watched the snow swirling outside this window. If she had been able to go back to that Saturday morning in the car with Gordon Dowling and elect to abandon the search for Brock's house and leave well alone, she thought, sadly, that she would have done it. Not because she thought she was wrong, but because the price had just been too high. She began to tick off in her mind all the people who had paid for her unburdening herself to Brock – Brock himself, Gordon, Belle Mansfield and poor Rose. Four people, and herself – five lives disrupted. Not to mention Rose's killer.

'Just bills.' Brock had been opening his mail while he'd been waiting for the kettle to boil. 'Why don't you ring your place and see if there've been any messages? Will there be anyone there at this time?'

Kathy looked at her watch. It was half past four. 'Hard to say. I'll try.'

The number rang several times before Patrick, out of breath, answered. 'Kathy, you're back! How did it go?'

'Magic. I brought the social committee something to cheer them up. Have there been any messages, do you know?'

'Yes – three, I believe. A woman rang yesterday. I think the name's on the pad here, hang on . . . yes, Penny Elliot.'

'Oh yes. Did she say anything?'

'Just to ring her when you got back. Your aunt also rang.'

'Aunt Mary?'

'Yes, from Sheffield. Same message, to ring her when you got back.'

Kathy sighed. 'Anything else?'

'This bloke called round at the weekend. A real hard man, a Geordie. Wouldn't give his name.'

A chill went down Kathy's back. 'What did he want?'

'Well, he wanted to know where you were. Jill answered the door, and when she said she didn't know, he came out with this story that you were looking after something of his that he really needed right away. She said she couldn't help and pretended we didn't have your key, but he said you'd given him a key and told him to go on up and find the thing he wanted. He just pushed his way past Jill, but I arrived at that point and stopped him. He was pretty bloody arrogant, in point of fact. We weren't sure what to do for the best. He went away eventually.'

Kathy's heart was pounding. What did she have in her

room? 'You did the right thing, Patrick. He isn't a friend of mine, and I haven't given him a key.'

'Christ!'

'Has he been back?'

'Not as far as I know. But there's been a car parked across the street for a couple of days now, with a bloke inside reading the paper. Not always the same man.'

'Patrick, would you do something for me? Go to my room and put any notebooks and papers you can find into a carrier bag. I think there's a couple of files and several spiral-bound notebooks, and maybe some loose – yes, there's a wad of loose typewritten reports in one of the drawers of the desk. If you could put them all in a bag and hide it somewhere till I get back – under your bed or something.'

'Jeez! All right, good as done.'

Kathy put the receiver down and sat staring at the bench top.

'Problems?' Brock asked quietly.

'Tanner's been round to my place and tried to talk his way into my room.'

'What's he after?'

Kathy shrugged. 'All I can think of are my notes on the Petrou case. That's about all he'd be interested in.'

Brock grunted. 'Anything else?'

'Penny Elliot rang.'

'Sounds as if it would be a good idea to talk to her. We really need to know what's been going on. You'd better not tell her where you are, though.'

Kathy agreed and dialled the number of Division, asking to be put through to Detective Sergeant Elliot. 'Penny, it's Kathy. I'm not coming back to Crowbridge just yet, but I heard you'd been trying to reach me.'

'Yes, yes. Are you all right? You got me worried disappearing like that. I thought you might have fallen under a bus.'

'I just needed to get away for a few days. What's been happening?'

'Hang on a minute.'

Kathy heard some murmuring and sounds of movement, then Penny came back, whispering so low and fast that Kathy had to press her ear to the receiver to pick out the words. 'Tanner and his boys have been trying to find you! Didn't you know? They had a go at me for a while, thought I should know where you were. They said they just wanted to talk to you. I've got the impression that the Rose Duggan case has bogged down. Have you been reading the papers?'

'No.'

'Well, her boy-friend is still under arrest, but the lads on the second floor don't seem very happy. I believe he hasn't confessed yet. The wife of the Director of the clinic has been here a few times creating a scene, apparently. I don't know the background, but I'm told she had the front desk in uproar the other day until the Deputy Chief Constable agreed to see her.'

'Is there some suggestion she's related to the boy-friend, do you know, Penny?'

'No idea, sorry. What's going on, anyway, Kathy? Shouldn't you be back here?'

Kathy hesitated. 'I think they may have got it all wrong, Penny. But I don't have anything concrete to offer. Do you think Tanner was looking for my help?'

Now it was Penny who hesitated. 'To be honest, Kathy, when he came at me I felt like the woman who runs the refuge in town, when the men come battering on the door looking for their runaway wives. He didn't strike me as a man who wanted some friendly advice from a colleague. Why does he hate you so much?'

'I don't know, Penny, I really don't.' She sighed. 'I just wish I could get a clearer idea about what's going on.'

'I'll try to do what I can and ask around. But the risk is it'll get back to him straight away.'

'What about files? Can you get access to them in the normal course of things?'

'You're joking! Past Medusa?'

Kathy remembered the formidable woman clerk who guarded the CID file room. 'Oh yes, of course.'

'Probably the best way is through the clerical staff. Keep well clear of the investigating officers.'

'Mmm.' Kathy sounded doubtful. 'I don't want to get anyone else into trouble over this, Penny. Especially you. Have you heard any more about Gordon Dowling?'

'Not a thing.'

'How about Belle Mansfield?'

'She cleared her desk a week ago. I've got her home number if you want it.'

'Yes, OK.' Kathy wrote down the number Penny dictated, thanked her and rang off.

'Apparently my aunt in Sheffield has been trying to get hold of me, Brock. I'd better ring and make sure she's all right.'

She dialled and heard her aunt's voice answer tentatively, 'Yes?'

'It's me, Aunt Mary – Kathy. How are you?'

'Oh, Kathy! Have you been away, dear?'

'Yes, for a few days. I got your message. Are you all right?'

'Oh, I'm fine. Your Uncle Tom's had a bad cough this past week, though.'

Uncle Tom's cough and its remedies took a few minutes, then, 'No, I just wanted to make sure your friend had been able to get in touch with you.'

'Friend?'

'Yes. He phoned here yesterday. Was it yesterday? No, I tell a lie. It must have been Monday, because Effie was here at the time. A nice man, he sounded like.' Aunt Mary's judgement was cautious, which Kathy knew meant she really wasn't too sure. 'He sounded ever so keen to see you again.

Is he an admirer, dear? He seemed to think you were staying with us for a holiday. I don't know how he could have got that idea, it's been such a long time since we saw you. The way he was talking, I think he'd have got in his car and come straight down to Sheffield there and then if I'd given him any hope of seeing you.'

'Down?' Kathy repeated. 'You said he'd have come *down* to Sheffield?'

'Aye, well, he was a Geordie, wasn't he? From Newcastle, I'd say. Don't you know him, then, dear?'

Kathy brought the call to an end as soon she could and told Brock this new discovery.

'Persistent, isn't he,' Brock said. 'I wonder if he's been here too.'

Kathy dialled Belle Mansfield's home number next. She sounded philosophical about what had happened.

'I was ready for a change anyway, Kathy. Don't worry about it.'

'Belle, I don't know what to say. I feel terrible, getting you involved.'

'I knew that what we were doing was out of line, Kathy. I guess I just didn't expect the boys to be quite so smart.'

'How did they get on to you?'

'You remember I told you the clinic's computer might record the numbers of incoming connections? Well, it did – Tanner was able to trace a call from our hotel that night I tried to break into the computer. And while we were at the hotel we used a credit card. I guess that was stupid, but it's all very well being Mr and Mrs Smith until you want to pay for something. We never carry much cash around.'

'All the same, it was pretty clever of Tanner to put all that together.'

'Yeah. And so quickly. He's a tough customer, Kathy. You should be careful where he's concerned.'

'I know that, Belle. Was he rough on you?'

'Oh, not really. He just came straight to the point once he'd worked out what I'd done. I had a choice, he said. I could stay and fight, face disciplinary action, then the sack and probably prison, and my husband would probably lose his job at IBM too, given how sensitive they would be to this kind of crime in the family. Alternatively, I could sign a statement and resign gracefully, without retribution. I'm sorry, Kathy, I had to sign.'

'Of course you did.' Kathy felt her throat constrict as if a noose were being tightened around it. 'What did it say?'

'Oh, just about everything. What I did, whose idea it was, your friend's offer to pay for the room. Everything.'

Neither of them spoke for a moment. Kathy's hand was aching from gripping the receiver so tightly.

'I'm sorry, Kathy,' Belle repeated at last.

Kathy took a deep breath. 'There was nothing else you could do, Belle. I had to sign something similar. It doesn't matter.'

'Yeah, well, good luck.'

'What I really need is information. I feel as if I'm blind.'

'What kind of information?'

'About Rose Duggan's murder. What evidence they have against the man they've arrested, what statements other people have made, things like that. I'd hoped that Penny Elliot could have found out something for me, but they're keeping everything on the second floor locked up very tight. She doesn't know much more than is in the newspapers.'

'Has she tried her computer?'

'How do you mean?'

'The CID computers on the second floor are networked. Some of the ones on the third floor are in the same network. Hers will be. She could look at their case files.'

Kathy bit her lip, hesitating. 'What will be there? Would there be investigating officers' reports? Forensic reports?'

'I doubt it. Those things are still going on to paper and

into the manual files in the CID file room. But some useful stuff goes on to the computer files. Transcripts of taped interviews, for example.'

'Of course!' Kathy remembered the print-outs.

'I have to go, Kathy. I hope it works out.' Belle couldn't hide the doubt in her voice.

'Something?' Brock asked.

'Maybe.' Kathy explained about the computer files, then described the way in which Tanner had traced Belle's involvement. 'Rose died on the Monday, and by the Wednesday, when he pulled me in, he knew all about Belle. I can hardly believe it! He couldn't even have known that we'd tried to break into the clinic computer, and yet within – what? – thirty-six hours, he had it all worked out and had traced telephone numbers and credit cards.' Kathy shook her head. 'It's scary, Brock.'

The phone began ringing as she said it.

It was Patrick. 'Didn't have much luck, Kathy. I couldn't find any of those things in your room. Er . . .'

'What?'

'Well, your room's pretty untidy. I just wasn't sure if it's always like that.'

'Like what, Patrick?'

'Well, the drawer on the floor, you know? And the stuff all over the bed.'

'Oh . . .' Kathy bowed her head and ran her fingers through her hair. 'Don't worry, Patrick. It doesn't matter. Just lock the place up again and leave it. Is the car still outside?'

'Hang on.' The phone banged on the table and she heard his footsteps echo down the hall, then return. 'Yep, still there.'

'Well, just ignore them. Thanks for your help, Patrick. I'll see you sometime soon.'

She turned to Brock. 'The bastard. He got in anyway.'

Brock shook his head. 'Kathy . . .' he began slowly, 'who

else knew about us meeting at the Hart Revived that day when we talked about getting Belle involved?'

'No one. The only way anyone would have known is if the phone you used at the clinic was bugged. Isn't that the only possibility?'

'Mmm. It seems a bit elaborate to monitor the patients' phone calls, but –'

'Oh shit.' Kathy suddenly froze on the stool where she was sitting beside the phone. She was pale. 'Gordon Dowling. I saw him the next day. I'd forgotten all about it. I was in a terrible rush when I bumped into him. He looked so bloody sad and I gave him something to cheer him up. I told him about our meeting in the pub and how we planned to get into the computer at the clinic.'

She closed her eyes and groaned. 'Oh Brock, how could I be so dumb. Gordon Dowling – poor, dozy, gay Gordon Dowling.'

They sat in silence for a moment. Then Brock said, 'Maybe there was another way Tanner could have found out.'

But Kathy shook her head, her shoulders sagging. 'No. That's it for sure. That's just about the end, isn't it? Gordon betrayed us.'

Brock said nothing but got to his feet and went over to a cupboard under one end of the long work-top. From inside he fished out a bottle of Johnny Walker Black Label and a couple of glasses.

'I suppose,' Brock thought aloud as he poured the drinks, 'it would be interesting to know *when* he betrayed us.'

'How do you mean?'

'Did he talk to Tanner only after Rose was murdered, or did Tanner already know I was at the clinic? Had Gordon already told him about his visit here, with you, to this house?'

'Oh yes. And before that, Rose's letter to me.' Kathy groaned, and then suddenly stiffened. 'And if he knew then, why not last October when he put me on the Petrou case with Gordon in the first place? There was something about that – the way Tanner always seemed to know what I was doing, even though he didn't seem much interested in my reports.' She screwed up her forehead in thought, sipping absent-mindedly from the glass.

'So you think Dowling could have been reporting back to Tanner all the time?' Brock frowned. 'Pretty devious. I didn't really imagine him leading a double life.'

'Perhaps he had no choice. The greengrocer, Jerry, spotted him as gay right away, but I don't think any of his mates in the force know it. Jerry was fearful of what kind of treatment he would get if they did find out. Maybe Gordon wasn't ready to face that. Maybe Tanner found out and used it. I imagine that's the kind of working relationship that Tanner likes to have with subordinates.'

Brock shook his head. 'Poor Gordon.'

'I'll break his bloody neck!' Kathy drained the glass and slammed it down on the work-top.

'Well, how do we get even?'

'Penny Elliot for a start.' She dialled the number and explained what Belle had told her.

'The CID computer files? I never use them. Hang on, I'll try.'

Kathy waited for three or four long minutes before Penny came back. 'Yes, there is something. The files have got number codes. There's quite a lot of them. I don't suppose you know the case number of the Duggan murder?'

'No, sorry.'

'Well, I could just go through them until I find it. Or perhaps I could sort them by date. When do you want this?'

'Oh, Penny, you know . . .'

'Tonight, you mean. Well, I suppose I could stay on a bit. Do you want a print-out or a disk?'

'Either would be great.'

'I'll ring you back in an hour and tell you how it's going.'

She did exactly that. 'It'll take another half an hour, then I'll be going home. Do you want to pick it up there? I live in Tunbridge Wells. I'll tell you how to find the house.'

Kathy took down the instructions, then turned to Brock. 'I'd better get moving. What's the quickest way to the A21 from here?'

'I should come with you. Tanner's got me feeling nervous for you now. Maybe he's got something on your friend Penny, too.'

Kathy smiled, suddenly weary. Was it only this morning they'd had breakfast in Vicenza? 'I shouldn't think so, Brock. I'll be fine. But maybe I could come back here to sleep tonight? At least it's out of his territory. I just wish I could go home to my flat in Finchley.'

'I wonder if your fellow tenant has had a visit from Tanner too.'

'Yes, very likely.'

It was almost midnight before she returned. Brock was waiting up for her, although he had given her a key. The study smelled of toast, and Brock indicated a plate of bread and cheese and pickles. 'Hungry?' He took the toasting fork from its hook beside the gas fire and set to work.

Kathy collapsed into the chair, clutching a fat envelope. Brock eyed it. 'Looks as if she came up trumps.'

She nodded. 'I haven't had a chance to go through it yet, but it looks promising.'

'We'll get to work in the morning. You look all in.'

'Yes,' she sighed, 'but it isn't just that. That day you rang me from Rome, Penny gave me addresses for Gordon Dowling's next of kin. I remembered when I was talking to her that I'd written them down in my diary. So when I left her this evening I thought I might look them up. His mother lives not too far from Crowbridge, and I wondered if he might be there. He was.

'She didn't want me to see him at first. She's a formidable woman. Small, but tough as old boots and very protective. She said he was ill, and when he eventually appeared at the front door he certainly looked it. They let me in and I had a chat with him alone for a while.'

Kathy took the toast Brock offered her and began cutting slices of cheese. 'We were right, Brock. He's been spying for Tanner for a couple of years. It seems Tanner has been monitoring the gay scene in Crowbridge, and when Gordon's name came to his attention he decided to use him to keep an eye on things. Gordon's terrified of Tanner. Tanner's told him he's moving back to the Met with Long when his promotion is confirmed, and he's going to take Gordon with him, but frankly I don't think Gordon's going to make it. He told me he's thought of running away to sea or taking his own life. He broke down when he was talking to me. Burst into tears. He's a mess.'

Kathy shook her head, 'So Tanner knew everything, all along the line. What a farce! I led you straight into it, Brock. I just don't know what to say.'

He shrugged. 'Such is life. If we both end up selling hamburgers at the gates of Stanhope Clinic, so be it. We'll probably make a fortune. The thing I'm more interested in is who killed Rose and Petrou. Tanner wasn't smarter than us, just better informed. I wonder how much better informed he is about Parsons? Let's hope there's something, in there' – he nodded at the envelope Kathy had brought back from Penny – 'because I still can't see it.'

'It has to be Beamish-Newell.' Kathy surprised him with her sudden vehemence. 'We've been going round and round this,' she went on, 'but in the end he's the only one who fits. He told us all those lies about his movements when Petrou was killed, he was on the spot when Rose was killed and, as Gabriele said, he's ruthless in getting what he wants.'

'What motive?'

'He's a closet gay. Petrou tried blackmailing him, having

been pointed in the right direction by Gabriele. He murdered Petrou, and then Rose discovered something from Parsons that would incriminate Beamish-Newell, and he had to kill her too.'

'Come on, Kathy,' Brock objected. 'These days you don't kill people who threaten to reveal you're bisexual. All right, Dowling – a young lad just starting out in the police force – might be intimidated by a bully like Tanner, but Beamish-Newell would never have been panicked by Petrou. He'd have told him to get lost.'

'Maybe he was blackmailing other people too – the goats, important people who would have been embarrassed to appear in the tabloids wearing what Petrou died in.'

Brock shook his head, unconvinced. 'They'd pay up, buy him off. He'd have accepted, I'm sure. Murder's far too risky.'

'Perhaps it depends how greedy he was.'

They sat a while longer in front of the hissing gas fire, talking over the possibilities, until Brock offered to show her to her room. Although she'd grown used to sleeping under a duvet in her own bed, the crisp white sheets were freshly laundered and tucked in tight, the way a nurse would have done it, and Kathy fell quickly into a deep sleep. By the time Brock started roaming around in the kitchen next morning, she had already showered and made a pot of coffee, and was working in the study on Penny's material.

'While you get on with that,' Brock told her over a bowl of cornflakes, 'I think I'd better go up to the Yard and snoop around. Try to find out discreetly how we're placed before I make an official entrance.'

It was late morning before he returned, looking preoccupied and carrying a bulging briefcase.

'How did it go?' Kathy said, and had to make do with the muttered reply, 'Don't ask.'

He took off his jacket and tie and cast an eye over the

paperwork sorted into piles on the bench. He grunted abstract-edly, hands deep in his pockets, and Kathy had the impression his mind wasn't taking anything in.

'Is something wrong?' she asked. 'I mean, even more wrong than we thought?'

'I don't know.' He shook his head. 'Look at this.'

He turned to the armchair where he'd thrown his briefcase and pulled out a small brown-paper parcel. It had been neatly wrapped and just as carefully opened. 'Security thought it was a bomb.'

He spread the brown paper open and showed her the paperback book inside. The pages were dog-eared and yellow-ing with age. Its title was *Meaning in the Visual Arts*, and the author Erwin Panovsky. Brock opened the cover and pulled out a folded sheet of plain white paper, on which there were a few lines of handwriting. He handed it to her without a word, and she read,

Dear David,
Chapter 7 is for you.
Forgive me.
Forgive those who helped me, please, please, for my sake.
Remember me. I *too* was in Arcady.

  G.

Puzzled, Kathy picked up the book and turned to chapter 7, an essay on a group of paintings and their common theme, entitled '*Et in Arcadia Ego*'. She looked up at Brock for an explanation.

'One of the patients who was at the clinic, both when Petrou died and when I was there, was Grace Carrington.'

Kathy nodded, remembering the name.

'Because of that, I befriended her. We talked about paint-ings, about the subject of that essay. She was suffering from cancer. She said she was going to die.'

'You want to find out what happened to her.'

He nodded heavily. 'Yes.'

He phoned Stanhope Clinic, but they would only tell him that she had checked out on 27 March, which was two days after Rose was murdered. They refused to give him her home address.

'I think she said her home was in Essex. The postmark on the parcel is Chingford. I've been trying to remember her husband's name, but I can't.'

'Winston,' Kathy said.

'Yes! How the hell did you know that?'

'It's here, on the flyleaf.' She showed him the book. 'Almost faded away; "With love from Winston, Christmas 1968".'

Brock took a deep breath, then reached for the first volume of an old set of Greater London telephone directories on the shelf above the bench. There was only one entry for 'W. & G. Carrington' in Chingford.

'Well,' Kathy said, 'can I come? Or would you rather go on your own?'

'Please do,' he said, 'if you don't mind taking a break from that.'

They found the house without difficulty. The street was quiet, private, with spring blossoms beginning to flower from decorative shrubs and trees.

A man in early middle-age answered the door, wearing an open-neck shirt, sweater, jeans and trainers.

'Mr Carrington?'

He nodded.

'I wonder if I might speak to your wife?' Brock's voice, never loud, was now almost inaudible.

The man seemed to brace himself a little. 'No, I'm afraid you can't. What do you want her for?'

'We're police officers. It's concerning the murder that took place at Stanhope Clinic a couple of weeks ago. Your wife was a patient there at the time. We just wanted to ask her a couple of things.'

'Well, I'm afraid you can't.' The muscles around his mouth were taut, so that an involuntary smile seemed to cross his face. 'She died last weekend.'

Brock just stared at him. After a moment Kathy broke the silence. 'We did understand that she was ill. We didn't realize it was quite so . . . critical.'

'Yes.' Winston Carrington cleared his throat with a dry little cough and rubbed his mouth. 'Yes,' he repeated.

'It must have been a terrible shock for you.'

He nodded and began to speak very rapidly. 'She'd been on remission for some while and had been doing remarkably well, but we knew it couldn't last. She phoned on the Tuesday, that's the week before last, and said she was starting to feel ill again and wanted to come home, so I went down to Stanhope the next day to pick her up. All that following week she went downhill very quickly. The doctor had arranged for her to go into hospital last Sunday, but in the event she didn't make it. She had a bad night on the Friday, and I phoned the doctor the following morning. She was dead by the time he arrived.'

'I'm so sorry,' Kathy said and looked at Brock uncertainly. He still didn't seem able to speak.

'The funeral was on Wednesday,' Carrington added.

'I don't suppose she said anything to you about what happened at the clinic in the few days before she came home?'

He shook his head. 'That was the last thing on her mind.'

'Of course. Well, we won't disturb you further,' Kathy said, again looking at Brock for a lead.

Suddenly he spoke, his voice very low. 'What was the official cause of death?'

'I beg your pardon?' Carrington looked startled.

'The official cause of death – of your wife, for our records.'

'Oh, I see . . . It said coronary failure on the death certificate, I think.'

'Was there an autopsy?'

'No, no. It was expected, you see. It just came much quicker than we had thought. Which was a blessing, really – she was in pain.'

Brock nodded and made as if to go, then stopped and turned back. 'Did she leave letters to be sent to people after she died?'

'Yes, she did. After she passed away I found letters she'd written to us – that is, the boys and me.' He hung his head and hesitated a moment. 'Also, half a dozen letters and packages she wanted me to post to friends and relatives and so on after the funeral. I sent them off on Wednesday. I didn't take a note of the names. Why?'

Brock shook his head. 'Her will,' he said. 'Was there anything unexpected about that?'

Carrington was beginning to look exasperated. 'What on earth do you mean?'

'I was thinking of the clinic, Mr Carrington. A legacy to someone connected with the clinic? Or a donation to the place, perhaps?'

'No, nothing like that. I don't quite see what you're implying.'

Brock shook his head again. 'Nothing, really. It doesn't matter. We just have to make sure there are no loose ends.'

As they came back down the drive, a car pulled up at the kerb. A woman got out and gave a little wave towards the front door. She reached back into the car for something, and as they passed her they could make out the golden crust of a home-made pie.

They drove back in silence. Dusk was falling as they turned into Warren Lane and trudged back to Brock's front door. He climbed straight back up to the study, still wearing his outdoor coat, sat on the stool at the bench and picked up the letter that had been inside the book.

'It's a suicide note, Kathy,' he said heavily.

'Yes.'

'She died on Saturday morning, while we were driving up from Rome.'

Kathy suddenly recalled his toast to absent friends in the café at Orvieto.

'We talked about forgiveness. She said it must be hard for us, the police, not being able to forgive the guilty people we have to catch. I said, on the contrary, that was what kept us sane. I think I was just being glib.'

He sighed and lowered his head on to his hands, rubbed his forehead and eyes. 'Dear God, why should she ask my forgiveness?'

'What about *those who helped me*?' Kathy said.

'Well ...' He spread his hands in a gesture that might have been assent or despair. 'She needed all the help she could get.'

'Brock, you remember I told you I visited Jerry Hamblin last week, the greengrocer? He told me that his partner, Errol, had been very upset last year because his mother died of cancer. He said Beamish-Newell had been very kind to her, visiting her and giving her medicine. Helping her.'

Brock stared at her, stunned. 'Helping her to die, you mean?'

'Errol started his affair with Petrou after that,' Kathy continued. 'It would be natural for him to talk to his lover about what had happened. Then Petrou would really have had something on Beamish-Newell. Remember that Beamish-Newell went to see Errol the day that Petrou died, perhaps to find out how much Petrou really knew.'

'Grace must have thought *that* was the reason I was at Stanhope in the first place – to nail Beamish-Newell,' Brock said. 'When she first suspected I was the police, she was very angry. Beamish-Newell had probably already told her he would help her when things got bad, and she thought I was there to trap him, to stop him. It was only when I convinced her it was the Petrou killing I was interested in that she talked to me again.'

'It's a motive, Brock. If he was helping good people to go through a difficult death, Petrou's life must have seemed pretty worthless by comparison.'

'It's possible, I suppose.'

'Well, I'll tell you this much: I've been through all this' – she waved her hand at the papers on the bench – 'and there's no way that Parsons did it.'

'You're sure?'

Kathy nodded. 'I'm hungry too. We haven't eaten since breakfast. I know you're used to all this fasting, but I wouldn't mind a bite. Let me buy you dinner, and then I'll explain what I mean about Parsons.'

He smiled at her chiding. 'I'm sorry, I wasn't thinking. There are a few places we could get a take-away from in the High Street.'

'Right. I'll go and get something.'

He shook his head, 'No. If Tanner's out there looking for you, I'd rather not give him any opportunities. I'll phone and get them to deliver. What do you want? Pizza?'

While they waited for the food, Kathy outlined what she had made of the documentation that Penny had provided. 'That pile is the transcripts of interviews with Parsons since the time he was brought in to Division on the evening of Monday 1 April, through to last Sunday, the 7th. I can understand Tanner's frustration. Parsons has said almost nothing. The transcripts are practically monologues. Look.'

She picked out a sample for Brock to read.

DCI TANNER: You're going to have to let go, Geoffrey. What's done is done. It has to be brought out into the open. You're going to crack up if you don't let it out.
(PARSONS coughs)
DCI TANNER: What? . . . I said you're strung up like a fiddle.

You have to talk to us . . . I want you to begin with what Rose was going to tell Mr Brock. What was it that was so terrible that you had to kill her? Had you confessed to her that you had killed Alex Petrou? Is that it? And she was going to tell Brock? . . . Have a drink of water, Geoffrey, for God's sake . . . Oh *fuck,* get a fucking towel, Bill. He's dropped the water all over his *fucking* pants.

Brock grunted. 'Parsons sounds as if he's in bad shape.'

'Yes, that comes out all the way through, how tense he is, how they're afraid he's going to snap. They get a doctor in to look at him on three occasions as recorded here.'

'Does he say anything at all?'

'He responds a couple of times to references to Laura Beamish-Newell, who *is* his sister, incidentally. Here.'

DCI TANNER: Your sister's been charging up and down like a cat on hot bricks on your behalf, Geoffrey, but she isn't going to be able to do anything to help you until you start talking to us.

PARSONS: She knows . . .

DCI TANNER: She knows what?

PARSONS: She won't let you . . .

DCI TANNER: She can't begin to help you until you begin to help yourself.

PARSONS: She'll stop it. She won't let you do anything.

'It sounds as if he's reverting to childhood,' Brock said. '*My big sister won't let you hurt me.*'

'Or maybe, *She knows who really did it, and she'll stop this if it goes too far.*'

'Why not stop it straight away?'

'Because she's also trying to protect the person who did it – her husband.'

Brock scratched his beard. 'You said you knew Parsons didn't do it. How can you be sure from this stuff?'

'Read this.' Kathy pulled out another sheet and handed it to Brock. 'This is from the last interview from last Sunday.'

DCI TANNER: Well now, Geoffrey, you're really going to
    have to do better than that. We've found the rest of the
    rope you used to strangle Petrou with. We found it in a
    place that points only to you. Do you remember? Do you
    want to tell us about it?

(PARSONS mumbles)

DCI TANNER: Did I detect an answer there? Do you have
    something to tell us at last, Geoffrey? ... Well, let me
    remind you where you hid it. In your tool chest, in the
    stable block, under the work-bench. Remember? The
    locked tool chest, with your initials on it, with your old
    green sweater inside on top of the tools, and with a piece
    of the identical rope coiled up between the sweater and
    the tools, and bearing hair and skin particles that belong
    to you, and a cut end that matches the end of the rope
    that Petrou was hanging from. What do you say?

PARSONS: No . . . No.

'Very convenient of him to leave it in such an incriminating
place,' Brock murmured.

'Yes, except he didn't leave it there.'

'Presumably the search teams looked there when you were
investigating Petrou's death.'

'No, they didn't. I remember that Dowling came to ask me
about it. It was locked and had Parsons' initials on it. We
had no search warrant, and I told him to leave it until we
could ask Parsons' permission. We never got around to it.'

'So?'

'So I had a little private peek anyway. I was curious. There
might have been a blade that matched the serrations on the
end of the rope in the temple, or some duplicate keys to the
temple – who knows? At that stage we were desperate for
real clues. But there was nothing except his jumper and some
very old tools that didn't look as if they'd been out of the
box in years. So – the rope has been planted.'

'Very interesting. What do you suggest we do?'

'It means I have something to trade with Tanner,' Kathy

said. 'I can save his case for him if he'll drop any unpleasant plans he has for us.'

Brock thought, then shook his head. 'I don't think so. It's going to seem unbelievably convenient that you now happen to have remembered some uncorroborated evidence in order to save your bacon. And it's going to mean revealing Penny's role in supplying you with these documents.'

Kathy sighed. 'Yes, you're right. What, then?'

'We have to carry on. The only evidence that's going to count now is the confession of the real murderer.'

'Well, let's get on with it, then.'

'Now? They'll all be in their beds by the time we get there.'

'I put off going to see Beamish-Newell once before and found the next morning that I was too late. I think I'd like to go now.'

23

It was almost 10 p.m. when they came over the stone bridge and turned on to the gravel drive leading to Stanhope Clinic. It was a clear, cold night, and the lights of the house glimmered brightly across the black meadow. Kathy drove slowly past the car park and along the lane which curved beyond the staff cottages, thinking that the Director might be at home by that hour. His cottage was in darkness, however, its brick walls drained of colour under the faint moonlight. She turned at the end of the lane and returned to the car park. As she and Brock walked towards the house, she pointed to a window on the main floor. 'That's his study, isn't it? The one with the light?'

'Could be.'

The front door was still unlocked, the hall deserted. They both hesitated briefly as their noses picked up the familiar cloying smell, and then they walked down the corridor to the west wing. They stopped at Beamish-Newell's office and Kathy rapped on the panelled door.

He looked up from the desk and astonishment spread over his face. 'I didn't expect . . . What are *you* doing here?'

'I think it's time I took the statement from you that I never managed to get last November, doctor,' Kathy said. 'The one that takes us to the truth of the matter.'

Beamish-Newell stared at her and seemed confused. 'I didn't think it would be you.' He turned in consternation to Brock.

'Detective Chief Inspector Brock is not directly involved with this matter, sir. However, he has been helping with my inquiry and will be reporting to Scotland Yard on the outcome.'

'*Your* inquiry? I thought . . .' His voice trailed away. There was no aggression in it, only confusion, as if he had prepared himself for something else and now it was happening differently. Kathy felt like an actor who has blundered on stage at the wrong time, throwing the others off cue. She wondered what he had been expecting. She stared at his eyes, trying to read them. They seemed to have become even more piercing, their sockets, like his cheeks, more hollow and gaunt. There was a film of sweat on his forehead, and his voice seemed hoarser than before.

'You thought what, doctor?'

'I think . . .' Beamish-Newell seemed to rouse himself. 'I think I should confirm what you're doing here with the Deputy Chief Constable.' He reached for the phone.

'You might prefer to hear what we have to say before you do that, sir. It could affect the way in which we proceed.'

He hesitated, reluctant to refuse the offer of information. He withdrew his hand and waited.

Kathy extracted a notebook and pen from her shoulder bag, taking her time.

'You recall a patient here called Grace Carrington?'

He looked startled, as if it was the last thing he expected her to say. 'Of course. What of it?'

'You know that she died last Saturday?'

'I heard. I was sorry I wasn't able to go to the funeral.'

'Before she died she wrote to Chief Inspector Brock. A letter to be posted after her funeral.'

Beamish-Newell had become very still, his dark, hypnotic eyes staring at Kathy's.

'It was a suicide note.'

'My God,' he whispered, almost inaudibly. Then, 'No. She was very ill, terminally ill.' The protest was weak, his voice entirely lacking its previous forcefulness.

'In her note she confessed that she had been helped to die.'

Kathy paused. He said nothing and continued to look blankly at her. She went on, 'We're also interested in the death of another sick person that you were treating, the mother of Errol Bates.' She paused again and returned his stare.

He sat motionless, waiting for more. When Kathy remained silent he finally whispered, 'I have nothing to say.'

Brock now cleared his throat and began to speak, addressing himself to his hands on his lap until he had Beamish-Newell's full attention, then raising his head to speak to the man directly. 'We don't need to remind you of how the law stands at present, Stephen. I'm sure you're much more familiar with its ramifications than we are. A doctor may give drugs to relieve pain even if it shortens life, but may not shorten life even if it relieves pain. A frustrating distinction, no doubt, and perhaps one that will change. But that's how it stands at present. Nobody has the right, even with the patient's consent, to shorten life.

'I had a high regard for Mrs Carrington. While I was here she spoke to me about her condition and about the trust she put in you. Anyone who was of help to her when she needed it most has my respect. We have no real desire to pursue that matter. We are only interested in the Petrou and Duggan deaths. We know that Geoffrey Parsons was not responsible for them. We want to walk out of here tonight with your statement of what really happened. If we don't get it, then we shall pursue whatever other avenues we must.'

Beamish-Newell's face had become chalk-white, contrasting shockingly with the shiny black of his beard and hair. He opened his mouth in protest. 'You can't ... can't expect that!'

Again Kathy had the impression that he was following a different script.

Brock frowned at him and leaned forward, his voice intent.

'I *do* expect it. I think I can understand something of the position you were in – *are* in. There would have been intolerable stress.'

'My God!' Beamish-Newell groaned and leaned forward on the desk, cradling his brow. 'Stress!' he echoed. 'Unbelievable stress! But you can't ask that. You know that *I*, of all people, can't do that.'

Kathy's mind was racing, trying to understand.

Beamish-Newell gave a sudden grunt and sat up straight. 'Stress always has a long history. You know that, David – your shoulder. Stress is like memory, it ties the parts of our lives together. The unresolved, unhappy parts. You may think that you've come to terms with something when really you've only bottled up the poison, which secretly builds stress. Then something happens to break the bottle and the poison becomes a terrible weapon.'

The confusing homily on mental well-being caught them by surprise.

'One death leads to another,' he went on, 'and then another.'

Three deaths? Kathy thought, and, simultaneously with the thought came the words: 'Laura's dead baby.'

Beamish-Newell winced as if she had stabbed him.

He turned to her and said, 'She's told you?' and when Kathy nodded, it seemed as if a weight had been lifted from him. 'Then you do know.'

He took a sip of water from the glass on his desk to summon his strength, then began to speak. 'You must understand how difficult it was for her, at the end of a long pregnancy and after all the difficulties with my first wife, to lose the child.' He spoke as if he still couldn't quite believe that it had happened. 'But I knew that she was strong and that the pain would pass when she became pregnant again. Only she never has.'

Kathy interrupted softly. 'Doctor, you understand that I

am recording this conversation?' She placed the small recorder on the desk.

He nodded his head. 'I only want to explain the background. The stress was immense. How Petrou came to learn about the baby so long after the event, I have no idea. But it was typical of him. He had a way of wriggling his way into people's lives, discovering things about them, which was quite uncanny. And then he used the things he knew, played with them like a child with a machine-gun. But to use *that* against Laura was unforgivable.'

He shook his head, lapsing into silence again, still appalled by something which must have happened six months before.

'Yes, I see that,' Kathy said, trying to sustain the momentum of his confession. 'You must have felt obliged to do something.'

But he only spread his hands in a hopeless gesture. She found the change in him since their last encounter disconcerting. Despite the evaporation of his domineering manner, it was unexpectedly difficult to get to grips with him.

'Why don't you tell us what happened on that Sunday, 28 October last year?' she prompted gently, as if to an invalid.

'I don't see why. If you've spoken to her, surely –'

'We have to have *your* account, Stephen,' Brock broke in. 'You met with Petrou at what time?'

'Er . . .' For a moment it seemed he couldn't recall, then, 'I met him in the morning, when I came over here to interview incoming patients.'

'Tell us about that.'

'I walked over from our cottage at ten or soon after. I came through the basement, and passed Petrou going into the gym downstairs. It had become his sort of . . . den.' He gave an odd emphasis to the word.

'He asked to talk with me in private, and he closed the heavy door behind me. I felt uncomfortable about that and he recognized it immediately. I had noticed before how

298

attuned he was to people's sensitivities. It is a powerful talent, especially for a therapist, and one of the reasons I employed him in the first place. But it was the way he used it – he liked to give the impression that he could see your innermost thoughts.'

Kathy felt that, coming from Beamish-Newell, that was a remarkable acknowledgment.

'And found them amusing,' he added. 'What he had to say was bizarre. I could barely credit it. He said he intended to open a health club in London and wanted my endorsement and help in various ways. The more he went on, the more outrageous he became. His qualifications and experience were quite limited of course; but in any case, what he had in mind seemed more a social or entertainment club – at best. He wanted me to lend my name to it, become a nominal director, encourage our patients to go there, and even expected me to invest in it!

'I listened to this for a while and then told him to stop. I wouldn't have anything to do with that sort of place, I told him, and then I started to express my severe reservations about what he had been doing at Stanhope. I'd been getting quite uneasy about the cavalier way he was behaving. Laura had warned me about it, but I'd put off speaking to him. He was becoming a law unto himself, ignoring instructions and going his own way. The trouble was, he had quite a substantial following among the patients, and some of the staff as well. But I told him that I felt his attitudes were incompatible with the Stanhope way.

'He laughed! He said I shouldn't speak to him like that, because, underneath, we were closer than we seemed. He seemed to imply that there was some bond between us.' Beamish-Newell shook his head, 'He had an extraordinarily manipulative way about him.'

Again Kathy was struck by the irony of his description of Petrou.

'I took exception to the way he spoke to me – quite unapologetic, as if he was the employer and I was the one who needed to be brought into line. Then his manner changed. He told me he didn't need my help – he had plenty of powerful friends. But I *would* help him anyway, he said. He told me that some of my patients found the Stanhope way a bit tiresome, a bore. Their tastes ran to things somewhat stronger than carrot juice and hydrotherapy, and he had been able to cater to them. He told me, quite openly, that he had supplied narcotics to them.

'You can imagine how shocked I was. I lost my temper and then he told me he obtained some of the drugs from a friend of mine, Errol, who supplies greengroceries to the clinic. He began to tell me what Errol had told him about my help for his mother.'

Beamish-Newell stopped talking. He tried to refill his glass from the carafe, but his hand was trembling so much that Kathy had to get up and do it for him. He drank and gasped for air and drank some more. It was a while before he started talking again. 'That was all. I left him and came up here to my office. I spoke to Errol on the phone and arranged to meet him that afternoon. I wanted to find out what he had really told Petrou. It was all I could think to do.'

'And when you met Errol, he confirmed that Petrou did know what he claimed to know?'

Beamish-Newell nodded. 'Eventually, yes. It was a nightmare.'

'So you returned from seeing Errol at what time?'

'I'm not sure. It was dark, about five-thirty.'

'And you saw Petrou again? In the basement gym?'

He shook his head, 'No, no. I came back here to this room. Almost immediately Laura came in, and I could see from her expression that something was dreadfully wrong. She was pale, tense, seemed to be in a sort of controlled shock, the way nurses sometimes look when something terrible is happening in front of them and they can do nothing but stand still and watch. The odd thing that struck me was that she was clutching her cheque book.'

'Cheque book?'

'Yes. She was sort of cradling it to her breast.' He gulped more water. 'I asked her what was wrong and she said, "What did Petrou say to you?" and I was surprised, because I hadn't told her about seeing him or visiting Errol. I began to tell her about his threats if I didn't help him, and she cut me off. "Yes, yes," she said, "he threatened me too." I became angry, but again she stopped me and said that there was no need for me to do anything. There was nothing more to be done, she said. Her brother Geoffrey would help her, and they'd take care of everything.'

Beamish-Newell turned his face to Kathy in appeal. 'Then I understood about the cheque book, you see. I thought she had bought him off. She and Geoffrey inherited a little money from their parents, and I imagined that was what she meant. I began to protest, but she stopped me, said it was all arranged and I mustn't mention it again. It was only later, the next morning, when Geoffrey came to me to tell me about Petrou's body in the temple, that I began to think otherwise. I tried to remember her exact words, what she had been trying to say to me.

'That evening, after you and your colleagues had all left, Sergeant, she told me how Petrou had known about the baby, and how he had taunted her, said unspeakable things. Then I understood very well how she had been able to bring herself to kill him.'

Kathy and Brock stared at him, stunned.

'Your wife, Laura, killed Alex Petrou?' Kathy said the words slowly.

He nodded.

'That's an affirmation,' she said, for the tape.

'That's what she told you, isn't it?' he said. 'I knew she

would tell you in her own time. And I'm convinced that Geoffrey wasn't involved, not at first. Killing Petrou was an impulsive act, done under great stress and provocation. Geoffrey would have helped later to move the body to the temple.'

'Did you ever discuss it?'

'No. After she told me about his threats and . . . suggestions to her, she said it was all over and she didn't want us to talk about it ever again. I agreed.'

'And Rose?'

Beamish-Newell rubbed his forehead again, as if trying to keep his brain functioning. 'She buried it, you see. On the surface she'd buried it completely. Her behaviour, her manner, seemed completely normal, and I tried to do the same. Geoffrey was much less successful. It took a terrible toll on him, knowing what his sister had done and becoming an accomplice, and so in a way – in the eyes of the law – becoming as guilty himself. He fell ill – he was seized by vomiting fits. He couldn't sleep, couldn't even make love with his fiancée, Rose.

'She became very concerned. She spoke to me and Laura about it. It was very hard for us to deal with her. We both tried to help Geoffrey. I gave him a number of herbal treatments for his nerves, but they weren't very successful. Laura was quite hard with Rose, because of course it was so difficult for her to cope with her own memories, without having to continually reopen them in dealing with her brother. There was also the fact that Rose suspected Geoffrey's distress was linked to what had happened to Petrou, and she liked Petrou.

'Rose's persistence was driving Geoffrey mad – and I use that word advisedly. Eventually he felt compelled to tell her that Petrou's death had been an appalling accident in which someone close to him had been involved, and he had become involved too in order to protect them. She immediately guessed he was talking about his sister, and she decided to speak to the police about it, so that Geoffrey would be freed of the guilt he was carrying. Rose hinted to him that she would tell Mr Brock herself at his next acupuncture session, and Geoffrey in a panic told Laura.'

Beamish-Newell seemed to be losing control of his speech as he recounted this unravelling of their affairs. His tongue was having difficulty articulating words with the letter 'r', and longer words faded before their end.

'Take your time, Stephen,' Brock urged him softly.

'Laura came and told me. I said she should do nothing until I'd had time to reason with Rose. To give us more time, I gave you a sedative in your orange juice you had on your tray that lunch-time. I wanted to make sure you wouldn't be able to talk to her. When you fell asleep, I had to behave normally. A phone call came for me and I left the room, as if I weren't trying to prevent her from being left alone with you.

'When I returned ... All I can say is, that the ... the violence of what was done to Rose wasn't Laura. It was a measure of the awful stress that had built inside her. It must have been explosive when she finally let go. Since then she's been in the deepest torment. The fact that they accused her brother was the final obscenity. I knew that, eventually, she must come to you. But I couldn't help you. She is my wife.'

His head sagged and his eyes closed; his skin was a jaundiced grey, his breathing laboured. Kathy and Brock exchanged looks. Neither doubted the sincerity of Beamish-Newell's account. He seemed wrecked by what he had had to live with.

'Did your wife believe that Rose was pregnant when she died?' Kathy asked him quietly.

His eyes flicked open, startled. '*Pregnant*? I had no idea.'

'If she knew, is it possible she thought that you might be the father, that history was repeating itself?'

Beamish-Newell's mouth dropped. 'Oh my God,' he groaned.

'Where is your wife, Stephen?' Brock asked.

His head rocked slightly. 'Don't know . . . I thought you had seen her. We're avoiding each other. She's in the cottage, probably.'

'I'll go,' Kathy said quietly to Brock. 'You'd better stay with him.'

He nodded agreement. 'Be careful, Kathy. Shall I get help?'

'No,' she said. 'We're not there yet.'

24

Kathy began by going down to the basement to check Laura's office and the other therapy rooms along the central corridor. All were locked. She finally came to the external door at the end of the west wing and stepped out into the night. She paused and looked around. There were few lights remaining in the windows of the house, and no signs of light ahead through the trees towards the staff cottages. She was struck by how different the night always smelled compared to the day – cool, remote, secretive. An owl hooted from the area of densest darkness, the temple mound, and she turned her eyes towards it and saw a glimmer.

She started to walk without seeming to make a decision, as if her feet had received some external instruction. The sight of the looming grey skeleton of the temple front caused her heart to start thumping. A couple of times she stopped and blinked, trying to decide if the source of the faint glow was really there and not just a reflection of lights from the house in the glass doors of the temple. But when she mounted the steps and came right up to the doors, she saw there was no mistake: through the glass she could make out the far end of the nave and the dim light from the organ recess.

One of the doors was open a couple of inches, but not enough to squeeze through. Remembering the noise it made as it scraped the ground, she gripped the handle and took the weight, trying to ease it silently open. She was almost successful, but she couldn't prevent the sudden sharp squeak of the old hinges as she released the weight. She froze and held her breath, but could see and hear nothing. Perhaps after all the place was empty, the light and open door overlooked in Geoffrey Parsons' absence.

She walked silently down the nave, moving cautiously as she approached the brass rail overlooking the lower chamber. At first there was no sign of anyone, and then her attention was caught by the sight of a small bunch of spring flowers lying down below her at the foot of the side wall, on the unmarked marble panel set into the floor. She glanced down through the swastika grille, but not closely enough to see the face staring up at her from the shadows beneath.

She went to the spiral staircase and carefully descended to the foot. The lower chamber appeared deserted too, and it was only when she took a pace forward towards the flowers on the opposite side that her heart jolted. A figure stepped out from the dark recess beside the organ and she recognized Laura, her face haggard and pale.

Something metallic glittered in each hand. At first Kathy thought of a knife, but then she made out the hypodermic needle in one hand and its metal case in the other. It was a powerful-looking instrument, not a disposable plastic type but stainless steel and glass, and Laura was holding it as if she were ready to use it.

'What do you want?' she said, her voice barely carrying across the ten feet that separated them.

'I came to talk to you, Laura.'

'It's too late for that. You shouldn't have come here.'

Her voice was a monotone of despair and exhaustion. Kathy guessed from her red-rimmed eyes that she had had very little sleep since Rose died.

'I've been talking to Stephen. He's very worried about you.'

Laura sighed. 'I can't do anything. I just can't do any more.'

'I know. Please talk to me anyway. Just for a little while. Is

306

that where your child is?' Kathy pointed to the flowers and the little slab of marble.

Laura nodded, not taking her eyes from Kathy.

'Stephen told us that Alex Petrou taunted you about that. It was unforgivable.'

'Please don't come any closer.' Laura raised the needle. 'There's more than enough in this for both of us.'

'As you wish. I was just trying to understand how the mind of somebody like that works.'

Laura's mouth turned down in disgust. 'Don't try. It poisoned you to go near him. He had an appetite for people's weaknesses. He was filth.'

'You want to help your brother, don't you, Laura?'

Her eyelids fluttered closed in pain. 'Of course. He only tried to help me. I've written a note taking responsibility for everything.'

'Really? You didn't try to make him appear guilty, did you? Put the rope in his toolbox?'

Laura looked at her uncomprehendingly.

'Please,' Kathy said. 'Tell me what happened the afternoon that Petrou died.'

Laura shook her head. 'I just want to sleep,' she whispered. 'You shouldn't have come. I've made up my mind what to do.'

'You saw him that afternoon,' Kathy insisted. 'Was it in the gym?'

She nodded indifferently.

'Did you deliberately seek him out? Please take your mind back to that afternoon.'

'Stephen had told me that lunch-time that Petrou was going to make trouble for us,' she said wearily. 'I could see he was very worried about it, although he wouldn't give me details. After he left the cottage to go over to his office, I decided to speak to Petrou myself. I came down the corridor to the gym. The handle was locked, but I could hear sounds from inside.'

'What sort of sounds?'

'I don't know. Like someone grunting. I thought it must be Petrou working out on the equipment, so I decided to go to my office and wait. After a while I noticed someone through the rippled glass of my office door walk quickly past, and I thought they might have come from the gym.'

'You didn't see who it was?'

She shook her head. 'By the time I got to the door they had gone. I thought at first it was Petrou going upstairs to his room, but I decided to check the gym anyway. This time the handle turned. I went in and found Petrou there, alone. He was lying on the couch of this body-building apparatus he had us buy – Stephen didn't want it, but Petrou got Ben Bromley to persuade him, as usual. He said some of the patients had asked for it.

'Petrou was almost naked. What little he was wearing was so obscene that I turned to leave, but he sat up, as calm as anything, and said he had been expecting me. I was angry and told him to put his tracksuit on and come to my office at once.'

Kathy felt the cold seeping into her as she stood motionless listening to Laura. Her voice was becoming firmer and louder as she relived her anger.

'I was fuming as I waited for him. He sauntered in, so insolent. He just laughed when I asked what he had been doing earlier. He said he had been with a friend, a man, and he told me what they had been doing. He was very graphic. It made me feel sick. I didn't know how to respond at first. He seemed amused by this and made an obscene suggestion to me. I hit his face, but he only laughed more – it wasn't a laugh, really, more a sort of snigger. He held my wrists and said that what I needed was to have some babies. I was struggling and would have screamed for help except that then he said –' Laura's voice dropped to a whisper again '– he said he knew that I gave birth to dead babies.'

Laura came to a stop. The hand holding the syringe, which

had dropped to her side, rose to her face and she pressed it to her cheek. 'I didn't understand how he could know about that. And then I realized that only Stephen could have told him. I found the idea quite shattering that my husband had discussed me with this man, told him intimate things. Petrou made me sit down, and he sat on the edge of my desk, leaning over me, and I could smell him. He stank like an animal. He warned me that he knew a great deal. He said he had a bond with my husband because Stephen admired him and wanted to help him – he implied that it was more than that. He said I should be careful I didn't lose Stephen the way his first wife had.' She shook her head. 'He was repulsive. I felt violated by the way he had insinuated himself into our lives without my even knowing it.'

'Yes,' Kathy nodded, 'I can understand that. What did you do?'

'Do? Nothing. He just walked away, and for a long time I sat there in shock. Then I went upstairs to find Stephen, to talk to him. Only I couldn't find him. He wasn't in his office, and so I went back to the cottage to see if he was there. I felt I needed a shower to decontaminate myself, and while I was washing I calmed down a bit and tried to think more clearly.

'I decided that Petrou was probably really after money, and that the best thing would be to give it to him so he would go away. My mother left me some money, most of which I still had in the bank, and I decided to persuade him to leave us. It was probably a mistake.'

Kathy tended to agree. 'What did he say?'

Laura stared at her for a moment, then shrugged. 'Nothing. I went back to the basement with my cheque book and opened the door of the gym. He was lying on the couch again, only this time he didn't respond when I came in. I thought he was asleep until I saw the cord around his neck, and then I realized someone had done to him what I would have liked to do. I was glad, until it occurred to me who had most likely done it, and then I panicked.

'I shouldn't have. I'm trained not to panic in an emergency, but that's different. That's where it's somebody else's crisis, and you distance yourself and go into this professional mode. But this was *my* crisis, running out of control. I was terrified that Stephen had done it and that our lives would be destroyed . . . Well, they have, haven't they?'

'What made you believe Stephen was responsible?'

'I don't know, but I was so afraid. That morning I'd woken up not even realizing that Petrou meant anything to us, and suddenly it seemed he could ruin everything, alive or dead.'

'You say there was a cord around his neck?'

'Yes, like from a dressing gown. It was a silver-grey colour.'

'So what did you do?'

'I ran out of the gym and up to Stephen's office. He was there, and one look was enough. He was breathing hard and trembling, and I could see he was terribly upset. I asked him what Petrou had said to him, and he replied that he thought Petrou wanted to destroy us. That was when I got control of myself. Seeing him going to pieces in front of me, I knew I had to be strong. I told him he mustn't think about it again. I said I would take care of everything, that Geoffrey would help me.'

'Did he actually tell you, in so many words, that he had killed Petrou?'

'I don't know . . . I don't think so.' Laura shook her head. 'He didn't need to.'

'From what I remember of your husband when I came here the following day, I can't imagine him going to pieces.'

'You think he's so much in control – everyone does. You don't know how hard it is for him sometimes. He's put

310

everything into this clinic over the years. Alex Petrou was like a virus, threatening everything.'

A virus. It was the same image that Gabriele had used. Kathy said, 'Why Rose, Laura?'

With the thought of Rose, the pale figure stiffened. 'Oh,' she moaned gently as if a knife had been turned inside her.

'Did you believe she was pregnant?'

'Is it true, then? Please God, please tell me it isn't true. When Trudy, her friend, told me about Rose being sick sometimes before breakfast, I thought ... But then, all through February and March she didn't say a thing and I couldn't be sure. I said something indirect to Geoffrey about him becoming a father, and it was quite clear that he knew nothing, so I thought no, it wasn't true. I didn't want to believe it, you see. It was like seeing myself five years ago.'

Laura was becoming more and more agitated, as if this was the one thing she had been unable to come to terms with.

'A few days before she died, I spoke to her after I caught that man Brock questioning her. I wanted to know what he had been asking her. She became difficult, secretive, refused to discuss it with me. As we talked I suddenly noticed how her complexion had changed. She looked radiant and I thought, she *is* pregnant. It obsessed me, blotting everything else out, and I just had to know. If it wasn't Geoffrey's, whose was it? I asked her – she was in the middle of saying something about Brock, but I interrupted her and said, "Are you pregnant? Who's the father?"'

Laura paused, and Kathy could see that she was trembling.

'What did she answer?'

'She told me to mind my own business. I can see her now. Her face was flushed, her chin up – she was angry with me. She said something about me ...'

'What?'

Laura Beamish-Newell's eyes dropped to the floor. She

shuddered and forced the words out. 'That I must leave her and Geoffrey alone now, because I only destroyed things. She said she wouldn't be destroyed as Alex Petrou had been.'

'She accused you of killing him?'

'I wasn't sure if that was what she was saying. I didn't understand. I tried to tell her he had been an evil man, and that for Geoffrey's sake she must say no more about him. She burst into tears and ran out of my office.'

She stared wildly at Kathy. 'I never told Stephen! When he killed her, he had no idea that she might be carrying a child. You must believe that!'

'Laura,' Kathy spoke intently, 'listen to me. Stephen believes it was you who killed Petrou and Rose, and you believe it was him. You have each been trying to protect the other, just as Geoffrey has been trying to protect you both.'

Laura looked blankly at her. 'No,' she protested, 'that's not true. I don't want to hear any more. I'm so tired. You must leave now. I beg you, give me ten minutes before you come back.' She pulled back the sleeve of her cardigan and placed the needle against the inside of her forearm.

'It's true, Laura. Chief Inspector Brock and I interviewed Stephen just now. Brock is still with him. There's no doubt in our minds that he genuinely believes you were responsible for both deaths.'

Laura frowned, confused. 'That isn't possible ... Who . . .?'

Kathy hesitated. 'We need your help. Please, you must put that away and come back to the house with me.'

'I think you're just saying this,' Laura said, but she was either too tired or too stubborn to think it all through again. Her protest was half-hearted, and when she saw the look on Kathy's face her determination crumpled and her arms fell to her sides. Kathy stepped forward and took the syringe and its box from her fingers and packed them safely away.

'Come on,' she said. She reached out, took Laura's arm and

guided her towards the stairs. They made their way slowly back up through the temple.

As they reached the doors Laura stopped and said to Kathy, 'Was it Stephen who was with Petrou that afternoon when I first tried the door to the gym?'

'What's his blood group, Laura?' Kathy asked.

Laura looked puzzled. 'It's O.'

'You're sure?'

'Yes, of course.'

'Well, it wasn't him. Whoever it was, was AB.'

They didn't speak as they picked their way in the pitch darkness towards the house. Someone had switched off the basement corridor light and locked the entry door, so Laura used her master key. They reached the Director's office and opened the door. Beamish-Newell looked up and panic crossed his face as he saw his wife. 'Oh God!' he whispered, and tears welled up in his eyes. 'My dear, I'm so sorry . . . so sorry.'

'It's all right, Stephen. It really is,' she said, and went round the desk and put an arm round his shoulders. 'I think it's going to be all right.'

After composing herself, Laura told them all how she had found her brother the evening Petrou died and had persuaded him to help her. They had lifted Petrou from the exercise machine and hidden him temporarily in a corner of the gym under a pile of mats. Later, in the early hours of the morning, they had returned to the basement and carried him out to a wheelbarrow which Geoffrey used to move him to the temple. They took with them the hood and whip which they had found in the gym, as well as some rope which Geoffrey had brought. At the temple they took off Petrou's tracksuit and shoes before hanging his body as best they could.

'Why the temple, Laura?' Kathy asked.

She shrugged. 'I wanted to hide the time and the place where he died to confuse things. Also, I wanted to make it look like suicide or some kind of bizarre accident. Afterwards, when you wouldn't believe that, I wished we'd just driven his body miles away and dumped it somewhere.'

Kathy thought of the small white marble slab in the temple, and how odd Laura's choice had been, as if she had been gathering together her husband's sacrifices.

'Well, you certainly did confuse things. And again the next morning.'

'Yes, we hadn't anticipated Stephen wanting to change Petrou's clothing. Geoffrey put it down to his sense of guilt. So did I.'

'Didn't Geoffrey discuss it with you?' Kathy asked Beamish-Newell. 'Talk about what had happened?'

He shook his head. 'It was as if we were acting out parts, trying to do and say what an innocent person would do and say. After that, Geoffrey seemed to avoid any contact with me.'

'He was frightened of you,' Laura said. 'He was terrified by what he thought you had done.'

'What about the rope, Laura? Did Geoffrey have some left over after he'd strung Petrou up?'

'I don't know, I don't remember that. I carried the torch and tried to do what I could to help. It was dreadful, so cold, and the body was so awkward. Rigor had set in while it had been lying on the floor of the gym, and when we eventually got it into place it looked so twisted and wrong. I just hoped that its weight would straighten it by morning.'

She fell silent, head bowed.

Kathy looked across at Brock and murmured, 'I could do with some of Ben Bromley's strong black Italian coffee.'

Brock nodded. 'Good idea. In fact, I think we could do with Mr Bromley in person.'

25

Ben Bromley woke with a start, the telephone burbling in his ear. He had insisted that it go on his wife's side since, in a household with five women, he reckoned the chances of a call being for him were infinitesimal. He heard his wife mutter groggily that it was for him.

'What's the effing time, for God's sake?' he grumbled, but she had rolled over and fallen asleep again.

'Hello?' he said cautiously.

'Ben, it's Stephen here. Sorry to wake you at this hour.'

'Stephen? What time is it?'

'Just after two.'

'What! What on earth is the matter?'

'I'm sorry, but we have a bit of an emergency here.'

Bromley was waking up fast now. There was something odd about Stephen's voice, remote and expressionless. What the hell was going on?

'What sort of emergency?'

'I can't really talk about it over the phone, Ben. We need you here right away. Could you do that? Could you come to your office, please?'

'It's not another break-in, is it, Stephen? If that bastard's been into my bloody computer again –'

'Please, Ben. If you would just come over right away.'

Bromley put the light on and groped around for some clothes. The time-switch of the central heating was off, and it was damn cold. He swore and woke his wife.

'There's some stuffing crisis at the clinic,' he said. 'I have to go.'

'Oh Ben! Not another murder?'

'How the fuck would I know?' he muttered, leaving her to switch out the light.

It was a twenty-minute drive to the clinic, and he pulled up at the foot of the front steps. He could see a dim light in the entrance hall, and lights in the windows of both his own office and the Director's. He raced up the stairs, made his way along the corridor, and opened his office door.

He was startled to find Brock, alone, sitting behind his desk in his executive swivel chair, drinking a cup of his best coffee. Before he could sort through the expletives forming in his mind, Brock said, 'Ah, come in, Ben, come in. I hope you don't mind me taking advantage of your hospitality, but under the circumstances ... Sit down and have a cup of coffee.'

'What circumstances?' Bromley didn't move.

'Stephen and Laura are just tying up a few loose ends with Sergeant Kolla.'

'Sergeant Kolla?' Bromley repeated dumbly.

'You remember her from the first investigation of Alex Petrou's murder? I expect you know that I'm also with the police – the Metropolitan Police, Detective Chief Inspector.' Brock showed him his warrant card.

'What's happened? Why are you here?'

'We should probably wait until they can join us. Why don't you sit down and have a cup of coffee? Not much fun being woken up like that in the middle of the night.'

Looking slightly disoriented, Bromley took the visitor's seat Brock indicated, and accepted a cup of black coffee.

'I don't know where you keep the milk,' Brock smiled.

'Jay brings it for me fresh each day,' he replied dumbly.

Brock nodded, sat back and sipped appreciatively at his cup. 'Very nice, Ben. In fact the whole office is very nice. A centre of calm. I imagine you can really *think* in an office like this, unlike mine, which is always chaotic. I'd love to know how to get my desk as clean as this at the end of the day. I tell people that the only ones who can keep a clear desk are those who deal with simple problems, but I know I'm kidding myself. It requires discipline, I suppose. A tidy mind.'

'What exactly are we waiting for?' Bromley interjected.

'They shouldn't be too long. Please be patient.' Brock smiled sympathetically. He continued to look appraisingly around the room, as if filling in time, and his eyes fixed on Bromley's computer. 'And a systematic mind. Dealing with information in a systematic way.'

Bromley saw where he was looking and his face darkened with suspicion. 'Yes, well,' he said sarcastically, 'you'd know all about our computer system, wouldn't you?'

Brock beamed. 'That was embarrassing, Ben. I needed some information and I couldn't see how else to get it.'

'You could have tried asking.'

'True. That's probably what I should have done. But it concerned those special guests of yours – the Friends – what some of the patients call the "goats". I thought you might feel too protective towards them to want to help me.'

Bromley said nothing.

'Although I did get the impression that, even though you look after them, and bow and scrape when it's necessary, you don't really like them. Am I right?'

'Bow and scrape!' Bromley said indignantly.

'Well, it's a service industry, isn't it? But they're a toffee-nosed lot, aren't they, your Friends? Public schoolboys to a man. Privileged southerners who'd only willingly travel north of Watford Gap if there was some salmon or grouse in the offing.'

'Makes no difference to me, squire,' Bromley said coolly. 'I just get on with my job. You'd know more about that sort of thing, being a Cambridge man yourself. Dr Beamish-Newell tells me you're both *Cambridge men*.'

'Yes,' Brock nodded, ignoring the veiled contempt. 'I went

up from grammar school. I don't know what it's like now, but there were plenty of upper-class twits around then. I remember going into a pub one night, the Blue Boar it was, and two chinless wonders were ranting away at the bar. "I say," one said, "I knocked a chappie off his bike with my sports car just now. A black man. He put out his hand to turn right, but it was dark, so of course I didn't see it. Those chappies should be made to wear white gloves." I swear that's true, his exact words.'

But Bromley wasn't buying any of it. 'Is that a fact, David?' he said, unimpressed. 'It's hard to credit. But I suppose we didn't get too many viscounts at Burnley Tech, so I wouldn't really know. I'll leave that sort of thing to you and Dr Beamish-Newell.'

The sarcasm was like water off a duck's back to Brock. 'Now there's another thing,' he went on, 'a name like that. What kind of person would give themselves an absurd double-barrelled handle like that? Anyone with a pretentious name like that wouldn't survive five minutes at Burnley Tech, would they, Ben? And yet it seems to impress people down here.'

Bromley snorted and gave a crooked little grin. Before he could stop he found himself reciting the limerick he'd spent idle moments perfecting:

> 'Said a brilliant young doctor from Poole,
> Whose name was simply Steve Newell,
> To get where the cream is,
> I'd better add Beamish,
> And make them all eat Squeamish-Gruel.'

Brock smiled appreciatively. 'Still, despite the absence of viscounts in your formative years, you seem to have done very well. You've got a nice detached house near Redhill, I understand, and a charming family. Four daughters, is that right?'

Bromley looked suspiciously at Brock. He didn't remember telling him that.

'Are they at the pony stage? You'll be up to your armpits in manure with four of them. They'll be demanding a paddock and stables of their own. Your whole life will be spent mucking out. Or does your wife do that? She doesn't work, does she? Paid work, I mean – she'll have her hands full with the girls and the ponies.'

Bromley started to tell Brock to mind his own business, but the conversation took an abrupt turn.

'What I'd like to know, Ben, is what you really thought of Alex Petrou. I've been having difficulty understanding what he was like. To begin with, people seemed to be telling me that he was charming and attractive, but then, after a while, I got another, darker side. How did you see him?'

Bromley squinted closely at the figure across the desk – *his* side of the desk – to see if this was on the level. Then he said carefully, 'He was unusual. Not the type we usually get. Smoother, a bit of an operator. Good with the patients. He found it easy to establish a rapport with people. Interested in their gossip.'

'Like a woman? You implied to Sergeant Kolla that there was something odd about his sexuality – that he was bisexual.'

'I steer well clear of all that,' Bromley said stoutly.

'Do you, Ben? Well . . . And what about the dark side of his personality, were you aware of that?'

'Can't say I was, David. There was something . . . racy about him. Bit of a devil, I'd guess. Nothing sinister.'

'Really? A devil . . .' Brock was studying Bromley's face closely as he replied, his mood suddenly serious. 'So you saw him as an asset to the clinic?'

Bromley shrugged. 'Sure. He was popular with the punters. That was good enough for me.'

'No, there was more to it than that,' Brock said flatly.

'What do you mean?'

'Petrou could attract the punters all right, sniff out their predilections – he had a talent for it. He wasn't just an asset, he was a resource. On his own he was merely an opportunist, didn't really appreciate how things work, although he had a nice instinct. But to be really effective he needed a *manager*, someone to organize things for him, keep the Beamish-Newells off his back, line up the punters, give him advice, feed his ambition. He needed you, Ben. Together you created an alternative clinic within the alternative clinic – a neat idea. You had your own special patients and your own special programme, a bit more indulgent than Stanhope's, and almost invisible inside the respectable setting it provided.

'I'm not suggesting that you didn't steer well clear of his sexuality. You must have been about the only one around here who wasn't fascinated by it. Your interests were more practical. Where there's muck there's brass. The invisible clinic had its own fees and profit line and cash flow and investment portfolio too, didn't it?'

Bromley half rose out of his seat in protest, but Brock waved him down. 'I'm not much interested, really. I could turn it over to the Fraud Squad and they would get to the bottom of it. They know how to track down cash transactions. They don't look for records that are there so much as those that aren't, if you follow me – like looking for the invisible clinic. You know, you buy a pony for one of the girls, and there's no record in your cheque or credit-card accounts, so where did the cash come from? It's a tedious process looking for records that aren't there. Very expensive and very intrusive. The only satisfaction is that we get you twice – once when we discover how you made the money, and then again when we hand you over to the Inland Revenue for tax evasion.

'As I say, it's not the sort of thing I'm much interested in. If the members of your little club were daft enough to pay you good money for arranging some discreet hanky-panky with Mr Petrou, good luck to you. I'm only interested in who killed him. And if it was one of your club members and you try to obstruct me, then God help you, Mr Bromley.'

Ben Bromley had gone very pale. The coffee stood cold in the cup on the desk in front of him, and he found it difficult to break free of Brock's gaze.

'What do you want to know?' he asked.

'What I was trying to find in your computer was the record of who was actually here at Stanhope at the time of Petrou's death. I had discovered that Norman de Loynes was here, although his name never appeared in the records given to Sergeant Kolla. That was your doing, wasn't it, Ben?'

'Maybe ...' Bromley whispered speculatively, 'maybe I should get a solicitor or something.'

'Be my guest.' Brock indicated the phone. 'Perhaps Sir Peter Maples would organize one for you.'

At the mention of his boss's name, Bromley felt a flush of nausea rise up his throat. He fumbled his antacid tablets out of his pocket while he tried to think straight, but his head still felt fuzzy from being woken in the middle of the night. 'De Loynes went for a walk after breakfast that morning,' he said at last. 'He spotted the police car sitting out there at the end of the drive that goes past the cottages. He came back here in a tizz wanting to know what was going on. It took me a little while before I managed to get hold of Stephen Beamish-Newell, who told me that Petrou had been found hanged in the temple. I was stunned, as you'd imagine. I went up to the private lounge that the Friends use, and found two of them there.'

'Who?' Brock interrupted.

'Norman de Loynes and a bloke called Mortimer, Simon Mortimer. I told them what had happened, and how Beamish-Newell had told me that the police had asked that no one leave the clinic without their say-so. The two of them went into a blind panic at that. De Loynes had told his family he was somewhere else that weekend, and Mortimer had had a run-in with the police some time in the past, and neither wanted to get involved. They swore they had nothing useful to tell the police anyway. Apparently, they'd last seen Petrou on the Friday night, and neither had seen him on the Sunday. They more or less demanded that I keep them out of it.'

'What did you do?'

'I came back downstairs and found that Jay had started preparing a list of everyone who was there for Beamish-Newell to give to the police. I sent her off to make my coffee, and removed de Loynes's and Mortimer's names while she was away.'

'Were they the only ones you removed?'

'Yes. The only other Friend there was Mr Long, but I hadn't seen him. Anyway, I didn't think he'd need my help.'

'Go on.'

'I could see more police beginning to arrive, so I went upstairs again and told de Loynes and Mortimer that they'd just have to sit tight for the day until the police left. There was a good chance they'd get overlooked provided they never showed their faces, and that's exactly what happened. I called them a taxi about nine that night, after the last of the coppers had left.'

'Had you any way of knowing what the two of them had been doing on the Sunday?'

Bromley shook his head. 'I wasn't here on the Sunday at all.'

'So their claim that they hadn't seen Petrou on that day could have been false.'

'Yes, but they . . .' he hesitated.

'What?'

'Oh,' Bromley sighed. 'They just seemed convincing. They told me about this party that Petrou had organized for them in the gym on the Friday night, and they swore blind that they hadn't seen him since. In fact de Loynes said he'd arranged to see Petrou again on the Sunday evening and he'd been annoyed because he never showed up.'

'What kind of party was it on the Friday?'

'Don't ask, squire. *I* didn't.' He shook his head. 'Petrou got a couple of lads in from Edenham, or something.'

Brock sat back in the thickly padded chair and considered Bromley in silence. There was a kind of underlying swagger to the man's manner, an impudent gleam that he couldn't keep out of his eye, that tended to make you distrust him, even if he was only giving the time of day.

'Look,' Bromley said, feeling a need to fill the silence, 'the amounts were chicken shit, let's face it – I mean, compared to what you'd call real money these days. It was just a bit on the side, that's all, an appreciation for services rendered.'

Brock lowered his eyes and didn't respond, increasing the tension.

'It wasn't as if I invented him, for God's sake. One day, there he was. He already had it pretty well worked out. He made it clear that he had people looking after him. It was noticeable how Beamish-Newell let him have his way, and he more or less told me that he had you lot on side. I just lent a hand to make it all happen as unobtrusively as possible.'

'What do you mean, that he had us lot on side?' Brock asked.

'Well, Mr Long. He was Mr Long's favourite, right from the start.'

Brock nodded. 'This Mortimer, was he here when Rose was killed too?'

Bromley shook his head. 'No, he hasn't been back since Petrou copped it. Frightened him off, I shouldn't wonder.'

'But de Loynes was here on both occasions. And you're absolutely certain, Ben, that he is the only one of your Friends who was? I want you to think for a moment before you answer. I don't want there to be any mistake about this.'

Bromley nodded, then seemed to take in the implication of the question.

'Oh, but look, bloody hellfire. He didn't have anything to do with it!'

'How do you know?'

'Rose died sometime between two and three that afternoon, right?'

Brock nodded.

'Well, de Loynes was with me in this room throughout that time. I told that to your bloke who took my statement. De Loynes is investing in this time-share set-up in the south of Spain, and I was helping him with the paperwork that afternoon. You blokes should talk to each other, for God's sake!' There was an edge of panic in Bromley's voice.

Brock gave a little smile and got abruptly to his feet. 'All right, Ben. Now, I want you to stay here and make yourself a fresh cup of coffee and I'll be right back.'

Brock returned fifteen minutes later, accompanied by Kathy.

'Hello, Ben,' she said cheerfully. 'Got any new jokes for us?'

He regarded her sourly over the rim of his cup. 'Why does it take six premenstrual women to change one light bulb?' he said grumpily.

'Heard it,' Kathy smiled. 'Put your cup down now, Ben. We want you to come down to Division with us. We'd like you to make a new statement. OK?'

'You realize this is the middle of the effing night. Doesn't the United Nations have rules about this sort of thing?'

But he did as they said, going outside with them into the cold night and settling himself in the back seat of their car.

After a few miles he said to Kathy, who was driving, 'Where the hell are you going? This isn't the way to Crowbridge.'

Brock turned and spoke over his shoulder.

'We're just going to pick somebody else up on the way, Ben. Don't worry, we'll get there.'

It took another twenty minutes along empty country lanes before they reached a crossroads by a deserted village green. Brock consulted the map on his lap and pointed forward. Soon they came to a row of oaks, and behind them the dark outline of a large house. The headlights picked up two white gateposts marking the entrance, and Kathy turned the car up the drive.

26

It took Bernard Long an age to answer the doorbell. Eventually the porch light came on and the oak front door opened a crack.

'Who's there?' The voice was muffled and indistinct.

Kathy answered. 'It's DS Kolla, sir, with DCI Brock. We'd like a word.'

'Brock?' The door opened more fully and the Deputy Chief Constable stared out at them. He was wearing a scuffed pair of leather slippers, and the collar of his dressing gown was half turned in at the neck. It wasn't the white monogrammed outfit he'd had at Stanhope, but an old tartan item that was coming close to being recycled in the dog's basket.

'What the devil?' He coughed, his throat gummed up with sleep. He adjusted a pair of gold half-rimmed glasses on the beak of his nose and stared at them each in turn in the pool of light cast by the reproduction coach lantern hanging overhead, then past them to the car.

Kathy spoke. 'We'd like you to get dressed and come with us to Division, if you don't mind.'

'What time –?'

The question was interrupted by a woman calling from inside the house. 'Who is it, Bernard?' The voice managed to sound both imperious and frail.

He turned and called back. 'It's police officers, Dorothy. Go back to sleep, darling.'

'Don't be long.'

He turned back to them. 'You'd better come in.'

They followed him into a study off the panelled hall, distracted by the way he shuffled because his slippers were

326

too loose. It was only when they were seated in the light that Kathy noticed the tremor in his hand.

'Who was that in the car?' he asked, looking at Brock.

Kathy replied. 'Mr Bromley from Stanhope Clinic, sir. He's also accompanying us to Division to make a statement. We've just come from the clinic. Dr and Mrs Beamish-Newell have been helping us with our inquiries into the murders of Alex Petrou and Rose Duggan.' She watched the worry lines which had formed around the angles of his face stretch into a taut, pale mask.

Long stared across the room for a moment, then seemed to rally himself. He took a sharp breath and straightened his back. 'I see.' He turned to face Brock, and said, 'You're not saying anything, David?'

Brock shrugged, without taking his eyes off him. 'This is a County matter, Bernard. I shall be giving Sergeant Kolla a statement myself in due course.'

Long nodded. 'I'd better get dressed. Give me ten minutes.'

They sat in silence for a while until Kathy said, 'In the temple this evening, Laura asked the same thing – for me to give her ten minutes.'

Brock looked at her sharply, and then a muffled crash from upstairs brought them both to their feet.

The thick carpet pile absorbed the sound of their running feet. At the top landing Kathy hesitated, uncertain which door to try. The one in front of her opened abruptly and they were faced by a grey-haired woman, surprisingly large for the reedy tone of her voice. 'What on earth is going on?'

'Where did that noise come from?' Kathy demanded.

'The bathroom . . .' Her head turned towards a door at the far end of a short corridor.

Locked. It gave on the third heave of Brock's shoulder. He stood back, nursing his upper arm with an oath, and Kathy went in.

Long was sprawled absurdly across the edge of the large,

cast-iron bath, a collapsed scarecrow in pyjamas. From a knot around his neck, the cord of his old dressing gown looped up to the frame of a shower curtain, which his weight had brought down from the ceiling. The tiled floor of the bathroom was scattered with fragments of ceiling plaster and screws and plugs from the inadequate scaffold, and blood was smeared on his leg, where he had scraped his shin on the edge of the bath. There was a startled look on his face as he gazed up at Kathy.

'Are you all right, sir?'

'I . . .' he gulped. 'I don't think I can move.'

'Not the practical type, are you?' She went forward to help him, then paused as Mrs Long appeared in the doorway. She stared down at her husband for a moment, eyes wide, taking everything in. Then she said, in a voice brimming with contempt, 'Do you really think I didn't know?' She turned on her heel and they heard the bedroom door click shut behind her.

Brock advised that there be more than one witness for Long's interview at Division, so they got hold of Penny Elliot, because she was the only one Kathy trusted, and on Penny's recommendation Detective Sergeant McGregor from Serious Crime. They came into the building from the basement car park, using the stairs and avoiding the front entrance, and met in the conference room on the fifth floor, next to Long's secretary's office. It was 4.15 a.m. when Kathy began by formally cautioning the Deputy Chief Constable.

He ignored her. 'I'm not a people sort of person, David.' He seemed to feel a need to address himself to Brock, and Kathy let him go on. 'I'm a systems sort of person. I think you understand that, don't you? I have a record of achievement in that area of which I believe I can be justifiably proud.' His posture, like his speech, was stiff and formal. His eyes were bright, but his grey face was in need of a shave.

There had been a moment of farce at the house when it had seemed that Mrs Long might refuse to hand over anything for him to wear. Eventually, however, the bedroom door had opened briefly and a pile of his clothes had been dumped into the corridor.

'I have never seen it as my job to hunt criminals. I leave that to others. Frankly, I find that side of things utterly uninteresting. Some people don't understand my position on this. But those same people don't seem to expect the head of British Coal to wield a pick and shovel!' He gave a stiff little smile.

'My role has been to set in place the management systems of a modern police force. And that I have done. You really would have no idea, David, how derisory the procedures were here when I first arrived. Now they are leading-edge, I promise you. At the last review we scored more best-practice ratings than any other County force. The figures are in my office. I would like you to see them. I think *you* would appreciate their significance, something that cannot be conveniently swept aside by those few detractors – Neanderthals, that's my word for them. Yes.'

He paused, nonplussed for a moment by losing the thread. There was an embarrassed silence in the room, and then Kathy spoke.

'Mr Long, please tell us what happened on the afternoon of Sunday 28 October of last year.'

Her tone was not harsh or even unkind, but his face flinched as if she had struck him. His hand formed a fist, and he spoke through clenched teeth as he looked pointedly at Brock.

'David, I wish to continue this with you *alone*, please. I would consider it a personal favour. *Please*.'

Brock shook his head. 'No, Bernard.'

Long looked mildly shocked, sniffed and took in a deep breath, drawing together the remnants of his tattered dignity.

'The afternoon of Sunday 28 October of last year,' Kathy repeated, and this time they could see from his eyes that his mind had indeed gone back to that day. He gave a little shudder, and when he spoke there was no more protest in his voice.

'I had arranged to meet Alex in the gym at four that afternoon.'

'Not three, as you told me when I spoke to you the following day?'

'No.'

'So you met him at four. Was he alone?'

'Yes.'

'Why did you arrange to meet?'

'To talk. We often talked. We found it easy to talk.'

'What is your blood group, Mr Long?'

'Pardon?'

'Your blood group.'

'AB, I think. Why?'

'Do you know if you are a secretor?'

It was clear from his blank expression that he hadn't the faintest idea what she was talking about.

'Never mind. How would you describe your relationship with Mr Petrou at that time?'

'We were friends.'

'You were lovers.'

Long stared at the table in front of him. He said nothing.

'You were lovers.'

Nothing.

'You were lovers.'

'Yes!' he whispered hurriedly, anxious not to hear the words repeated yet again in front of this audience.

'And you had sexual intercourse with him that afternoon.'

'No ... yes ... not at first. At first we talked.'

'You could have talked in the drawing room upstairs or gone for a walk outside. You met him in the gym because you wanted to have sex with him there.'

'No!' Long's protest was almost a shriek. 'I needed to talk to him undisturbed. To discuss some matters – in confidence.'

'I ask you again. What was your relationship with Petrou at this time? What were your feelings for him?'

He sucked in a lungful of air, eyes staring, as if he were drowning. 'It was a madness,' he whispered at last. 'A madness. I couldn't help myself.'

'You couldn't control your feelings for him?'

Long nodded.

'And what about his feelings for you?'

'I knew that he was using me. That there were others he was using.'

'In what way was he using you?'

'At first, money. He needed money. I didn't mind helping him. Why should I mind? He repaid me fully.'

'He repaid you the money you gave him?'

'No, no. He repaid me in other ways.'

'With his body.'

Long said nothing.

'With his . . .'

'With his companionship, yes!'

'But he was greedy.'

'Yes. And cruel. He enjoyed making me suffer for him.'

'What else did he want besides money?'

'I told him there was a chance I would be going to London to a senior position in the Metropolitan Police. He seemed to think that this would be important for him. He had plans to set up some sort of club in London, and he seemed to think that he would need a . . . special arrangement with the police. I told him it was out of the question, of course, but he wasn't easily dissuaded. When he decided that he wanted something, he could be completely unreasonable.'

Long was breathing heavily as he spoke now, and sweat was gleaming on his forehead.

'You must have found that rather worrying.'

'Oh yes! It could have been absolutely disastrous, of course!'

'What did you do?'

'When I realized he was going to be so unreasonable, so demanding, I became very worried. I suppose I became frightened. One day I had a meeting here with a number of officers about some staffing matters, and at the end of it I was speaking to Chief Inspector Tanner – Inspector Tanner as he then was. On the spur of the moment I asked if he could make some unofficial inquiries for me about the immigration status of someone who was being a nuisance to some friends of mine. I wanted him to check if Alex's papers were in order, perhaps find out if something could be done to terminate his visa, have him sent back to Greece. That's what I wanted really, just for him to go away.'

'When did you have that conversation?'

'A week or two before that Sunday.'

'What happened?'

'Tanner came back quite quickly to say that Alex was an EU citizen, without a criminal record, that his papers were in order, and that nothing could be done unless he was found guilty of a criminal offence. Well, I knew that if he did get into trouble with the law he'd expect me to help him, so I didn't see any hope there. However, I thanked Tanner and left it at that. A couple of days later he spoke to me again about Alex. He seemed to know quite a lot about him, where he worked, and my connection with Stanhope. He asked if Alex was still being a problem to my friends. I said yes, and he asked me if I would like him to have a word with him, to persuade him, as he put it, to behave himself. I said I didn't think that a warning from the police would have any effect in this case, and he just laughed and said that, with respect, I didn't have much idea about what he called "practical policing".'

Long was sweating freely. The crisply ironed shirt that his wife had thrown out of the bedroom for him was now limp and stained around his armpits and in the small of his back.

'Did you take him up on his offer?' Kathy was speaking more gently to him now, coaxing rather than pushing him along as his explanation became fuller and freer.

'No, although I thought quite a lot about what he had said. Anyway, I had arranged to have a few days at Stanhope and decided I would bring things to a head with Alex while I was there. It was very difficult. He refused to take me seriously. When I told him I would have nothing more to do with him, he simply laughed. He also reminded me . . .' Long paused, swallowed, as if each awful memory had to be digested afresh each time he dredged it up. Kathy passed him a glass of water, which he gulped before continuing. 'He reminded me that he had a personal letter I had written him and some photographs he had taken.' Long hung his head. 'It was a nightmare, you see. An utter nightmare.'

'What did you do?'

'That was on the Friday. On the Saturday I saw him briefly and arranged to meet him the following afternoon. My idea was to make one final attempt to come to an arrangement with him, a financial arrangement to settle our . . .' He paused again.

'Affairs,' Kathy said.

'But I wasn't optimistic, so I phoned Chief Inspector Tanner. I explained that Alex was becoming more difficult and was threatening my friends with blackmail. They were going to make one final attempt to settle things, but if that wasn't successful, then it might be necessary to seek Tanner's help.'

'You were still saying it was friends who had the problem?'

'Yes, but I'm fairly sure that he suspected the truth by that stage.'

'Go on.'

'I gave him details of the meeting the next day, and he suggested that I ring him afterwards. If it wasn't successful, he would come over and speak to Alex.'

'Wasn't that risky?' Kathy asked. 'Weren't you worried about what Alex might tell your Inspector?'

'It was a last resort. I just wanted the problem solved. I saw no other way.'

'How did Alex react to your offer of a financial arrangement?'

'He was outrageous. I was prepared to be generous, very generous, but he simply laughed. He said that he would take my money *and* my help. He said I could refuse him nothing and that he would prove it to me. He did.'

The room was very silent.

'How?' Kathy said.

They waited, but Long said nothing.

'What happened?'

Long looked up suddenly at the ceiling, eyebrows raised as if trying to recall some prosaic event in the distant past. 'When it was over . . . as I was leaving, I said I had a friend I wanted him to meet. I asked him to wait there in the gym for him. Then I went out and phoned Tanner. I was upset. He could tell from my voice how upset I was. I mentioned the letter and photographs, and he asked me about Alex's room, whether he had a car or a flat outside the clinic, things of that kind. He said that I should go to my room and then ring him again later that evening.'

'Give me the times of all this. When did you leave Petrou?'

'I'm not exactly sure. Perhaps a quarter to five. I went upstairs to the public phone to ring Chief Inspector Tanner.'

'Did you see anyone?'

'No, it was very quiet. I went to my room and had a shower and came downstairs for the evening meal, then the recital. When it was over I rang Tanner. He asked if I'd heard anything concerning Alex, and when I said no, he said there was no need for me to worry any more, he had taken care of everything.'

'What were his exact words?'

'I'm not sure. Just that, I think. He had taken care of everything with Petrou. There was nothing more to worry about.'

'What did you understand by that?'

'I was amazed, frankly. I didn't dare believe it. I asked him what had happened, but he wouldn't say, only that I needn't worry any more. I asked about the letter and photographs, but he just repeated that everything was taken care of. He was very calm and matter-of-fact, and as I began to believe him I was quite overcome with gratitude. I told him I couldn't begin to express my thanks, and he said he would like to talk to me about a couple of matters in a day or two.

'I had absolutely no idea that anything had happened to Alex until you told me the following morning. I couldn't comprehend it at first. I thought what an extraordinary coincidence it was, and how, as things had turned out, I'd gone through all that worry for nothing and involved Tanner unnecessarily. In fact, as I came to realize that I need never have involved Tanner at all, I started to worry about what he must have thought of the whole thing, what Alex might have said to him about me and, above all, what had happened to the letter and photographs.'

So many worries.

'I tried to contact him during that Monday to find out what he knew. It took several calls to get hold of him, and eventually he said he would come to the clinic to meet me that evening in the car park.'

Kathy remembered her encounter with Tanner in the canteen at Division that first evening of the investigation. He must have gone to Stanhope after that.

'I began by telling him about the turmoil the day after Alex was discovered, and of course he knew – he said that Sergeant

Kolla was reporting to him. I said, in the light of Alex's suicide, I felt I had put him to a lot of unnecessary trouble on behalf of my friends. I said' – a flush spread upwards from Long's neck – 'my friends wanted to thank him for his trouble, confidentially, wanted him to have a drink on them.'

Long paused. 'Did you offer him something?' Kathy prompted. He nodded. 'An envelope with five ten-pound notes inside. He counted the money and laughed. I didn't really understand at first. I thought he was insulted by the idea of a gift. I didn't realize it was the amount that he found laughable.

'He called me "an old woman" and then explained that Alex hadn't committed suicide. He told me he had gone to speak with him after I telephoned on the Sunday afternoon. He had been in his car near Edenham when I rang, and it only took him ten or fifteen minutes to meet up with Alex in the gym. He said he soon realized that Alex wasn't going to be easily intimidated and also how indiscreet Alex was – apparently he told Tanner things, about me, and about other Friends . . . And finally, Alex said something to make Tanner angry. I don't know what it was, he wouldn't say, but I know how clever Alex was at picking up on things that provoke people. So Tanner killed him.'

There was total silence in the room.

'He told you that?'

'Oh yes, he was very clear about it. He said, "I choked the living shit out of that greasy faggot." Those were his exact words. I remember them very clearly.'

Kathy glanced at the others in the room. Penny was staring in blank horror at the bowed figure of the Deputy Chief Constable; McGregor was stony-faced; Brock was scowling and gripping the shoulder he'd hurt breaking through Long's bathroom door.

Long drew a deep breath. 'My head felt as if it were exploding and I found it very difficult to think. But Tanner was very calm. He explained there had really been no alternative and he would make sure there were no consequences. The investigation would find for suicide, and life for the rest of us would go on as before. He would like to think that if I went to London he would be accompanying me as part of my team there – with promotion, of course.'

Kathy frowned. 'Did he say what position Petrou was in when he strangled him?'

Long shook his head.

'You don't know if he was lying or standing?'

'No. He did say that he had intended to move the body, to make it look as if Alex had hanged himself. Only there was nowhere to hang him from in the gym.'

Kathy pictured the bare surface of the brick vaults.

'He went out to see if there was a suitable place in one of the adjoining offices, and then he heard someone coming along the corridor and opening the gym door. He waited till they went – I don't know who it was – and then he left quickly, thinking they would raise the alarm. He said he was as surprised as anyone when Alex turned up in the temple, but realized that someone else must have tried to cover the thing up just as he had been intending to do himself.'

'Wasn't he taking an extraordinary risk of being noticed, wearing outdoor clothes in the clinic?'

'He took a dressing gown – he said anyone wearing a dressing gown was immediately invisible at Stanhope.'

Kathy nodded. 'All right.' She suddenly felt tired, reluctant to move on. 'There are things that I'll ask you to expand on later concerning what happened last October, but now I'd like you to tell us about Rose Duggan.'

Long, too, seemed loath to continue. 'I don't feel well,' he complained hesitantly.

'In what way? Do you want us to get a doctor?'

The thought of confronting new faces brought the nausea back to his throat. 'No, no.'

'Would a cup of tea help?'

He nodded, and Penny got to her feet and made a phone call from the secretary's desk outside.

'Why don't we get this next bit over, then we can break for your tea?' Kathy suggested. 'How did it begin, with Rose?'

Long sighed. 'One day Stephen Beamish-Newell rang me here. It must have been January or February. He made some general remarks about the Petrou case and the coroner's verdict, which struck me as a bit odd. I asked if anything was wrong, and he said he was becoming concerned about one of his staff, Rose, who was still going on about the case. He said it was unsettling for everyone, and he wondered whether there was any possibility that Rose might be able to get the coroner to reopen the case. He was very worried about more bad publicity and so on. I explained that there was little chance of the case being reopened unless she had new evidence, and I asked him to try to find out if she did, and to keep me informed. I mentioned it to Tanner, of course.

'Then Tanner found out about Rose's letter to Sergeant Kolla and her meeting with you, David. You can imagine that this was the last thing we wanted. The nightmare was beginning all over again. I contacted Stephen and told him who you were, David, and about Rose's letter. He was as worried as I was, and only too willing to do as I suggested, to try to keep Rose away from Brock and to keep me abreast of any developments. I explained that Brock's visit was unofficial and that I might be able to dampen things down if Rose were able to get him interested in reopening the case. I must say that Stephen seemed absolutely terrified of that.

'The weekend of that first week you were there, David, Stephen contacted me again at home. Rose was becoming very difficult. Her fiancé had tried to talk to her, as had Laura, but she was becoming quite hysterical. Stephen had learned she intended to talk to Brock when they had an acupuncture session on the following Monday, because she had discovered something about Alex's death. I then phoned Tanner – I felt I had no choice. He told me to find out all about the arrangements for your acupuncture session, the time and place and what else would be going on in the basement at that time. He also suggested I propose to Stephen that he give you something at lunch-time, David, to make you sleepy.

'I went through all this with Stephen. He gave me the information and agreed that all we could do was to try to delay Rose's talking to Brock, and if possible persuade her against it. I gave Tanner the information he wanted, and he told me to get Brock's acupuncture session brought forward an hour, when the place would be quiet, and to make a call to the clinic at two-thirty – I was to insist on speaking to Stephen about an urgent, confidential matter.'

'Did he tell you what he planned to do?'

'No.'

'And you didn't ask?'

Long shook his head.

Someone came into the secretary's office with the tea, and Kathy stood up. Her skin felt grimy with perspiration and fatigue.

'We'll take a break there,' she said. 'I have some things to arrange with Sergeant McGregor, then we'll go downstairs.'

27

'It just feels like an anticlimax,' Kathy said. 'I would really have liked to march into the canteen and arrest the bastard there, eating his bacon and eggs in front of his mates.'

Brock smiled, manoeuvring the car along the winding road back towards London. 'Better that McGregor should pick him up, Kathy. In the long run you'll feel better about it all if you distance yourself and don't make it personal.'

'But it is personal.' She could see the glow of the orange street-lights of the built-up area in the night sky ahead, although here in the country the darkness was impenetrable. Soon the dawn would come, people would rise, taking up where they had left off. And Tanner, wherever he was, would rise too, and discover that his whole world had come to pieces while he slept.

'It was a beautiful example of what that American was talking about at the conference, come to think of it,' Brock said. 'Chaos theory. A malcontented butterfly flutters her wings somewhere in the north of Italy, and in the south of England all hell breaks loose.'

'Yes,' Kathy yawned. 'Bit ironic that the killer was the one person who wasn't personally threatened by Petrou.'

'The worst part of the whole thing,' Brock said, 'is that I've put my shoulder out again, breaking into Long's bathroom.' He glanced at Kathy's face, her eyelids beginning to droop. 'Are you sure you wouldn't rather I took you straight back to your flat?'

'Oh . . .' Kathy felt too tired to think. 'No, I might as well pick up my car from your place and get it home. Once my head hits the pillow I'm going to crash.'

Brock turned on the radio and a voice cheerfully predicted rain. It was followed by an old recording of 'Volare'.

A pale dawn was silhouetting the backs of the houses behind Warren Lane and picking out the young leaves on the horse-chestnut tree as Brock turned through the archway from Matcham High Street and swung to a stop in the courtyard behind Kathy's Renault.

'I'll ring you when you've had some sleep,' he said. 'Drive carefully.'

She nodded and trudged over to her car, feeling for her keys in her shoulder bag. She pulled them out, dropped them, groped around in the half-light on the cobble-stones, picked them up, opened the door and threw herself in behind the wheel. Thankful that the engine turned over first time, she strapped herself in, giving a little smile of pleasure at being alone again on her own territory. She put the car into gear, glanced up at the back of Brock's house as she rolled forward, and saw a light in his kitchen window snap off.

She pulled to a halt. There was no way that he could have got further than his front door in the time since he had left her. Whoever had turned off the kitchen light must have heard his key in the lock, the door pushed shut, his footsteps begin the weary climb up the stairs.

'Oh no.'

She switched off the engine and thought fast. She had no phone in the car. The nearest public phone would be in the High Street, but that would mean driving away. Which was what she should do. Except she still had the front door key Brock had given her.

She snatched it from her bag and hurled herself across the courtyard and round the corner to his front door. She bent down and opened the letter flap. A light was on in the stairway. She was just about to call out and warn him, when she heard the crash of breaking glass and splintering timber. Then total silence.

She thought again about leaving and getting help, or at least finding something to use as a weapon. What? The tyre lever? She slid the key into the lock as quietly as she could and carefully eased the door open. Still no sound. She closed the door and began to climb the stairs, the way she had learned as a teenager coming home late and not wanting to wake her aunt and uncle, by clinging to the wall, where the timber treads were less likely to creak. Half-way up, the light went off.

She froze.

In the silence she put her hand into her coat pocket and took hold of her bunch of keys, gripping a key between each of her knuckles. Not a lot of use, but still . . . She carefully slipped the long coat off her shoulders, laid it on the stairs and started to move forward again.

The darkness inside the house was relieved only by the faint glimmer of dawn which spread from the study across the landing and drew her into the room. It was light enough to see that there was no one standing waiting for her. Light enough, too, to see the chaos in the centre of the room, where Brock's body was a dark mound in the middle of a shattered coffee-table.

Kathy looked carefully around the room, then a second time, then over her shoulder at the landing. No sign of anyone else. Was there a back door the intruder could have left by? A window, perhaps?

She stepped forward cautiously and knelt beside Brock, reaching to feel the pulse in his throat, still making no sound, as if the slightest noise might start the furies. The smell of whisky was overpowering, and she guessed that the broken bottle that lay beside his head must have been close to full. There was a pulse, but no signs of consciousness. His laptop computer was lying beside him like a faithful dog, waiting for its master to wake up and give it instructions.

She picked it up and straightened, trying to remember

where the phone was, turned round and nearly jumped out of her skin when she saw Tanner's dark figure standing a few paces away in the doorway.

'Hello, Kathy.'

His voice was low and hoarse and probably the most frightening thing she'd ever heard.

'Hello, Ric,' she heard herself say, calm as anything. 'You didn't need to do that to Brock. You've hurt him. I think we should get an ambulance.'

He looked her over slowly before replying. 'Too late for that, Kathy. Thieves are getting more and more violent these days. I don't think he's going to make it, to be perfectly honest.'

'No, Ric. No one will buy that.'

'Oh, really? Why's that, now?'

She hesitated. 'Too much of a coincidence, don't you think?'

He was looking keenly at her. 'Come on, Kathy, what have you got up your sleeve?'

He took a step towards her.

'They know, Ric. Long has told them everything.'

'Ah.' He halted, a little smile frozen on his lips while his mind worked. 'Well, it was always on the cards. I've had time to make other arrangements. I do have some family business to attend to overseas, as it happens. It makes it easier to deal with you two, anyway. No need to pretend. In fact, I can positively show off. Enjoy myself. It would be poetic having you and Brock end up exactly the same way as the other two, wouldn't you say? Brock on the end of a rope like Petrou, and you with your throat sliced open like Rose. Couldn't have a plainer way of telling them all to get fucked than that, now, could you?'

He slipped his hand into his trouser pocket. When he withdrew it he was holding something, and Kathy watched as it clicked and sprung a long silver blade.

'I don't understand,' she said, her voice sounding implausibly relaxed to her own ears, 'why you killed Petrou at all. What did he say to you that made you so angry?'

Tanner stared at her balefully for a long, silent moment. 'It wasn't what he said, it's what he wouldn't say.'

'How do you mean?'

'I wanted the stuff he had on Long, didn't I. Photographs and a letter. Very indiscreet stuff. Stuff you'd spend a lifetime to keep hidden. Especially if you were Assistant Comissioner of the Metropolitan Police.'

Kathy was chilled by Tanner's voice, so detached, so quiet and unemphatic, as if he had already set aside all the feelings that modulate the way we speak.

'But eventually he told you where it was?'

'Eventually. I persuaded him.'

'How did you do that?'

'I sat on his chest and stuck a needle in his eyeball.' Tanner sniffed and rubbed the back of his hand across his nose, as if he was developing a cold. 'Then he told me. He kept them in a plastic wallet taped under the seat of his motor bike, together with his passport and a stack of money. His insurance – always ready for a fast getaway. That's probably the way you think if you've lived in Beirut. Well, then I had to kill him, didn't I?'

'What sort of needle was it?'

'What does it matter? It was on a trolley I passed on my way in. I was looking for something else to use – a scalpel or something. There were lots of needles sticking in a sponge and I reckoned that might do. My first thought was to stick it in his balls, but the eye was better. I could watch his face while I did it.'

He began to move towards her again, the blade poised. Instead of backing away she came at him, swinging the laptop towards his head. But it was just a little too heavy, the case a little too smooth to hold properly, and he raised his left hand and stopped her in mid-flight without any apparent effort. Then he brought up the blade in a graceful arc and sliced her right arm.

She recoiled, stumbling backwards over Brock's body, arterial blood spurting from her arm, and fell in a clatter against the gas fireplace, scattering the elements and almost knocking herself out with the impact of her head against the tiled surround. She could hear herself making some kind of noise, snuffling in panic, then her scalp was seized with pain. She opened her eyes and realized he was gripping her hair and forcing her head back She stared at his eyes, wide, excited, only inches away, studying her fear and then, as his head drew back, fixing on her throat.

'Goodbye, Kathy,' he whispered.

She had no way of calculating the blow, left-handed, as she tried to thrust the toasting fork up and into him somewhere, anywhere, before he could bring the knife down. Afterwards she would tell her friends – especially the men, who seemed very troubled by it – that she hadn't aimed there particularly: it just happened to be the spot that the long steel prongs met as she stabbed upwards. And at first she didn't think she'd done him any damage, for he just froze, kneeling over her, open-mouthed and wide-eyed. While he seemed to hesitate, she frantically pulled the fork away and tried to target his upper body in case he struck at her. And then his whole frame suddenly convulsed, and she thought in panic of that glittering razor-edged blade. She cried out and turned her head. She gripped the fork that Gordon Dowling had toasted crumpets with just a month before, and jammed it into his throat.

The ambulance men found her by the open front door, shaking like a motor on broken mountings, trying to control the bleeding in her arm with an improvised pressure pad.

'There's two upstairs,' she said through clenched teeth. 'Please be careful. There's a lot of blood and broken glass.'

One went upstairs, then reappeared in a hurry, calling down for help.

'One of them's alive,' he shouted.

'Which one?' Kathy called to him.

'Well, it's not the geezer with the fork in his bleedin' throat! Get the coppers here quick, Jimmy.'

'I've called them,' Kathy said. 'I can't understand why they're taking so long.'

Like her on that first visit, they had missed the archway into Warren Lane and had to circle the block before they spotted the blue ambulance lights in the courtyard. She didn't recognize the two young men. One came running and spoke to the ambulance man binding her arm.

'Domestic?' he asked.

'No,' Kathy replied, 'nothing like that. I've just killed someone.'

In the odd, jangled state of her mind, she thought it must sound as if she was boasting about it instead of asking for forgiveness, which in an absurd sort of way she was. He looked closely at her, then called his mate over. After a few words he went upstairs and returned a couple of minutes later, ashen-faced.

'Can you identify the man you killed, madam?'

'He's a police officer,' Kathy sighed. 'Detective Chief Inspector Richard Tanner.'

'I see . . .' They were both staring at her as if she was a freak. 'And you are . . .?'

'Kolla, Kathy Kolla. And I think you should step aside.'

'And why is that, madam?'

'Because I'm going to throw up.'

They waited till she had finished communing with the bushes on the other side of Brock's lane before they formally cautioned and arrested her for murder. She nodded, her eyelids heavy with fatigue and shock, and muttered. 'This is my first time.' It wasn't until they were sitting in Casualty, the bright morning sun dazzling through the tall windows, that it occurred to her to tell them to ring Penny Elliot at Crowbridge.

Three weeks later, on the evening of 3 May, Jerry and Errol threw a party to celebrate their twenty-fifth wedding anniversary. Organized by two women friends, one with pink, cropped hair and the other dressed entirely in black leather, it was held at the home of another friend outside Edenham, whose private lawn ran down to the river. Kathy and Patrick stood by the water's edge drinking champagne, watching the current swirl around the roots of the willow trees. On the far bank, hidden under the overhanging grasses, they could make out the dark hole of a river creature.

'Interesting friends you have,' Patrick said, looking back with fascination at the crowd. They formed every possible combination, it seemed, of age, gender, smoking habit and personal adornment.

'I think I'm only here as the token law-enforcement officer,' she smiled. 'But it was nice of them to ask me.'

'Jill tells me you're soon going to be doing your law-enforcing in the big smoke.'

'Yes. I'm going to work with someone I know in the Met.'

'Brock? Yes, I met him, remember? I thought you might have brought him here tonight.'

'He's in traction at the moment. Should be back on his feet in a week or two. But I wanted to ask you – you didn't mind coming, did you?'

'Of course not. I thought I got around a fair bit in this area, but I don't recognize a single face here. Want another drink?'

Kathy nodded. Her right arm was still bandaged under the sleeve of her blouse, but by now she was used to drinking with her left.

As they strolled up the slope of the lawn, Kathy caught

Patrick giving her an odd look. It was the second time she'd noticed it.

'What's the matter?' she said. 'Did I mess up my make-up?'

'Sorry,' he smiled, and shook his head. 'I just can't really believe that you . . .'

She stopped walking. 'That I what?'

'Well, that you actually . . . killed someone. Do you mind me saying that?'

She shrugged.

'It's not the sort of thing that happens in the real world, is it? I mean, I've never actually seen a dead body, let alone . . .'

'It seemed very real at the time, Patrick. Now . . . no, it isn't real. At least, not in daylight. What is real, anyway?'

There was an explosion of whistling and cheering from the house, and they turned to see the tight black trousers, red silk shirt and carefully groomed head of Jerry emerge triumphant through the french windows on to the terrace. Behind him Errol followed, a pair of cowboy boots conspicuous from his second honeymoon in the States, complete with spurs. He raised a glass to acknowledge a further burst of applause from the group standing around the drinks table.

Later, when the party had splintered into small groups chattering and dancing, Kathy and Patrick got the chance to talk to their hosts.

'Well,' Errol looked approvingly at Patrick, 'and how is your relationship working out?'

Patrick looked surprised, and Kathy replied, 'Oh fine. He does the cooking and I do the washing-up.'

'Lucky you!' Jerry said. 'I have to do both.'

'Never mind.' Errol put an arm around his shoulder and led him off towards a photographer, his cowboy boots jingling. 'There are worse things in life.'